A Harlequin

JANET DAILEY

Collector's Edition

D1533123

Harlequin

D JANET AILEY

Collector's Editions

A Harlequin
JANET DAILEY
Collector's Edition

Harlequin Books

TORONTO • NEW YORK • LOS ANGELES • LONDON
AMSTERDAM • PARIS • SYDNEY • HAMBURG
STOCKHOLM • ATHENS • TOKYO • MILAN

These books by Janet Dailey were originally published as follows:

ONE OF THE BOYS
Copyright © 1980 by Janet Dailey
First published by Mills & Boon Limited in 1980
Harlequin Presents edition (#399) published
December 1980

BEWARE OF THE STRANGER
Copyright © 1978 by Janet Dailey
First published by Mills & Boon Limited in 1978
Harlequin Presents edition (#256) published October 1978

ISBN 0-373-80605-1
First edition October 1982

CONTENTS

ONE OF THE BOYS

"YOU ARE ALWAYS MAKING ME ANGRY."

Dane moved closer. "The next time I do," he murmured, "why don't you try kissing me? I guarantee it will shut me up."

Bending his head, he moved his mouth powerfully against her own, parting her lips and invading them with a hot sweetness.

A whirl of confused sensation began taking over Pet's body. "Why did you make me think I was so incompetent?" she whispered breathlessly.

"I couldn't tolerate anything but the best from you because I knew you could give it to me. You could always give it to me."

There was the heady implication that he was referring to more than her work. As his hands glided slowly down her shoulders, Pet struggled for some semblance of control before it was too late . . . .

CHAPTER ONE

Two small round tables were shoved close together in the dimly lighted hotel lounge. There was hardly an inch of surface that wasn't covered with drinks, ashtrays, pretzel dishes and candle-burning globes. Almost a dozen chairs were crowded around the two tables, all of them occupied by men, except one.

Petra Wallis was the sole female in the group, but she was accustomed to that. At five foot nine she was as tall as most of them. Despite her khaki blouse and slacks of a mock-military fashion, there was nothing masculine about her. The very blandness of the unisex-designed clothes accented her slim willowy frame and served as a contrast to the long wheat-blond hair pulled away from her face and secured with a gold clasp at the back crown of her head. The length of it fell straight down her back in a shimmering silk curtain of gold.

Nature had blessed her with a flawless complexion and strong, classical features. Her jawline slanted cleanly to her pointed chin. Her mouth was wide with a sensually full lower lip, her nose straight with the faintest suggestion of an upward tilt at the tip. And her sea-green eyes possessed a naturally thick fringe of dark brown lashes.

Pet, as her co-workers affectionately called her, had often been told she was model material, but she wasn't interested in being in front of the camera. She preferred being behind it.

In the confusion of several conversations and jokes punctuated with laughter, Pet asserted herself with ease. "Have any of you seen the inside of Charlie's van?" Her teasing question was answered by a couple of chuckles while Charlie Sutton, who was sitting across from her, smiled like the Cheshire cat.

"You rode down here with Charlie, didn't you, Pet?" one of the men prompted.

"I did. Although after I climbed in that thing, I wondered whether I was asking for trouble or Charlie was asking for a slap in the face!" Her laughter was a rich, husky sound. "The van looks so innocent on the outside."

"Did you get it all fixed up the way you wanted to, Charlie?" one of the other men asked.

"Almost," he shrugged with a twinkling light in his brown eyes. "There are still a couple of things I want to add."

"I can't think what they'd be!" Pet retorted in an exaggerated reaction, and turned to the others. "He claims he uses it to go camping. It resembles a bachelor's playpen on wheels—silver shag carpeting on the floor, walls and ceiling; a single bed with a black fake-fur spread; a built-in bar," she began describing the inside of it. "The stereo speakers are hidden throughout. A flick of a switch and you have music to make love by. There's even a compact refrigerator to supply ice for the bar drinks!"

"You should have put those mirror tiles on the ceiling, Charlie," someone suggested. "What do the wife and kids think about it, Charlie?" another person teased.

"Sandy loves it," Charlie insisted. "We can slip away for a weekend and have all the comforts of a motel room without the cost."

"It's all prepaid in the money you spent fixing the van," Lon Baxter stated from his chair next to Pet's, and reached for one of the glasses of beer on the table.

"Whoops! That's mine, Lon." Pet rescued her drink and put another glass in his hand. "This is yours."

"How can you tell?" He looked skeptically at the half-empty glass of beer she had substituted for the fuller one.

"Unless you've started wearing lipstick, this has to be mine." She laughingly showed him the peach-colored imprint on the rim of the glass.

"In this light I don't see how you can see anything." He groped in mock blindness, pretending to discover the bareness of her forearm. "Ah, what's this?"

Setting his glass down, he took advantage of the fact that Pet was still holding hers. He turned in his chair to get closer to her while his other hand slid across her stomach, stopping on her rib cage just below the swelling curve of a breast.

"It may be dark, Lon," Pet smiled sweetly, "but I know exactly where your hands are. And if your left hand moves one more inch, you're going to get an elbow in the throat."

The warning was issued with deliberate casualness,

but it was no less sincere because of it. Conscious of the others observing this little byplay, she knew she had to put Lon firmly in his place without making an issue of it.

Lon Baxter was one of the few single men in the camera crew. Young and good-looking, he made passes at anything in skirts, certain he was irresistible to women. Admittedly, Pet found him attractive, but she had learned a long time ago that if she wanted the respect of her fellow workers, she had to stay clear of any romantic entanglements with them.

Lon she probably would have avoided under any circumstances, since she doubted he had a faithful bone in his body, but there had been a couple of men she wouldn't have minded dating. She had tried mixing her social life with work a couple of times, but the involvement invariably caused friction on the job, so since then she had made it a rule to date only men who were outside the television industry.

With an exaggerated sigh of regret Lon withdrew his hand and sat back in his chair, reaching for his beer. His retreat was noted by the others with a few taunting chuckles.

"Shot down again, huh, Lon?" somebody teased.

"Ah, but I'm alive to pursue her another day," he winked. Pet hadn't believed for one minute that he had given up.

"Why don't you put the poor guy out of his misery, Pet, and let him catch you once?" Charlie suggested, knowing exactly what her opinion of Lon Baxter was.

"I know what my competition is going to be in

12

these next couple of weeks," she replied, not taking offense at the ribbing. "I'm not in the class of Ruby Gale, singer turned sex goddess. Lon won't even notice me after he's spent a day looking at her through his camera."

"Ruby Gale, the new Jersey Lily." Andy Turner, the fourth cameraman in the production crew, lifted his glass in an acidly cynical toast to the star of the television special they had come to tape.

Pet, Charlie, Andy, and Lon made up the team of four cameramen. She loathed the tag "cameraperson." The term seemed unnatural and a needless attempt to differentiate her sex, but she usually had to endure the label.

"She is fantastic!" One of the sound technicians spoke up in the singing star's defense. "Do you suppose she'd mind if I asked for her autograph? My wife and I have every one of her albums."

"I wouldn't ask her for anything until the special is all done," Andy advised. "She can be a royal bitch."

"You've worked with her before, haven't you?" someone asked.

"On an awards special a couple years ago," he admitted. "All she had was one song and an award to present, maybe five minutes of the entire show, but her incessant demands created total chaos. I've seen my share of temperamental performers, but Ruby Gale is the worst! This isn't any picnic we're on."

"Dane can handle her," a lighting technician insisted.

A grimness pulled at the corners of Pet's mouth. "Dane Kingston, the big man himself, is going to be here. I understand this production is going to carry his personal stamp as both producer and director."

"I thought Sid Lawrence was the director," one of the gaffers questioned her statement.

"He's just the assistant director," Andy retorted. "When you're Ruby Gale, you can demand number one and get it."

"Dane is probably going to be on hand to protect his investment," Charlie suggested. "After all, this special is costing him a hefty chunk of dough. I'll bet he wants to be sure it stays within the budget."

"And I'll bet he makes a hefty chunk of dough out of it," someone remarked enviously from the adjoining table.

"I agree he's here to protect his interests," Pet inserted dryly. "Money as well as Ruby Gale."

"What do you mean?" Joe Wiles, one of the lighting technicians and the grandfather of the group, frowned at her comment.

"Dane Kingston and Ruby Gale are what the gossip columnists describe as a hot item. From all accounts, they're having a very torrid affair." A disdainful kind of sarcasm thinly coated the information Pet relayed. She tapped a cigarette out of the pack lying on the table.

Ever attentive to the female, Lon leaned over to light it for her. "Some say he wined and dined her just to get her to sign to do this special," he remarked.

"She's a highly talented performer, but if she's the bitch you say she is, Andy—" Pet blew out a thin stream of smoke while sliding a look at the sandy-

14

haired cameraman "—then it seems to me that she and Dane Kingston are perfectly mated."

"What do you have against Dane?" Andy laughed. "I wouldn't wish Ruby Gale on my mother-in-law, let alone someone like Dane. Besides, I always thought you women went for him. At least, my wife tells me he's quite a hunk of man. And I've always been convinced that she knows a good thing when she sees it—she did marry me."

The joking boast drew the expected round of guffaws and heckling from the group. The conversation could have easily been shifted to another topic, but the mere mention of Dane Kingston had set Pet's teeth on edge. She knew the tension wouldn't ease until she had talked out some of the animosity seething within, veiling it so the rest of the crew wouldn't guess how deeply it ran.

"I have no doubt Dane Kingston can be charming if he chooses." She tapped a long finger on her burning cigarette to knock off the ashes into the half-filled ashtray on the table.

"Let's hope he uses all his persuasive skills to charm our sexy star into performing without her usual temper tantrums," Andy suggested dryly. "Otherwise we'll be in for a long miserable time."

"Who says we won't with Dane Kingston?" Pet countered in a low, venom-filled voice.

"What did Dane Kingston ever do to you?" Charlie asked, subjecting her to his narrowed scrutiny. "I always heard he was an all-right guy."

"Dane Kingston?" She arched one pale brown eyebrow in mocking question, refusing to join the

15

male admiration society for a member of their own sex.

"Did you have a run-in with him or something?" Charlie frowned.

"Haven't you heard the story about Dane and Pet?" Lon Baxter leaned forward, smiling broadly.

Only a few members of the group made affirmative nods. The rest either shook their heads or admitted their lack of knowledge. Their expressions gleamed with curiosity. All of them who knew Pet were fully aware that she couldn't be pushed around, but she was also easygoing and easy to work with. Since she obviously had some kind of grudge against the producer, Dane Kingston, they were interested to know why.

"I don't remember you ever working on a production directly supervised by Dane," Andy commented.

"I haven't," Pet admitted stiffly.

"No, but you remember that variety series Dane produced last year?" Lon was eager to tell the story. "Pet worked on it. The very last show of the package ran into all sorts of problems, delays. You name it and it went wrong. It was way over budget. There was even some question as to whether it was going to be finished in time to make the air-date deadline. When the word finally filtered up through the ranks and reached Dane, he took action immediately and heads began to roll."

"I remember hearing about that," someone agreed. "He threw out the director and a half a dozen others in charge, and finished the last show himself."

"That's what happened," Lon agreed. "Of course, at the time there were a lot of rumors that he was coming to see what was wrong, but he didn't let anybody know when he would arrive. One minute we were talking about him, and the next minute he was there. It was hot that day, really hot. The air conditioner was broken, wasn't it?'' He glanced at Pet, a little vague on that point.

''It was making too much noise and they had to shut it off,'' she explained indifferently.

''That's right,'' he remembered. ''Anyway, he walks in and what's the first thing he sees? Our Pet in a pair of white shorts and a sexy red tank top. It was between takes and she was getting lined up for the next shot. Evidently nobody thought to tell Dane that we had a woman on the camera crew, because he immediately assumed she was somebody's girl friend. He lost his temper and began chewing her out—and everyone else around her—for messing around with an expensive piece of equipment. Did you know who he was, Pet?'' Lon paused in his story to ask.

''No. And I didn't particularly care,'' she retorted.

''That's for sure!'' he laughed. ''Nobody wanted to interrupt him to explain who she was, for fear he'd start yelling at them. So finally Pet just shouted at him to shut up. It got so quiet in that place you could have heard a flea scratch. Then Pet began reciting her résumé and wound up telling him that it was idiots like him who didn't know their rear end from a hole in the ground that were causing all the problems on the show, and suggested that he should take a long hike.''

There was laughter, but it was generally subdued. The glances that were directed at her, for the most part, held respect and admiration for the way she had stood up for herself. Yet she was fully aware that her defense had been dictated solely by the instinct of self-preservation. She had felt intimidated, over-powered and dominated by the raging giant who confronted her.

"What was Dane's reaction to that?" Joe Wiles was smiling.

"I thought he was going to knock her on her backside," Lon remembered with an amused shake of his head. "He gave her an ultimatum. Either she collected a week's pay and went down the road, or she changed out of the shorts and top into something more respectable and that reminded him less of a streetwalker."

"What did you do, Pet?" The question came from one of the younger men sitting in the shadows of the other table.

"I'm still working for Kingston Productions, so obviously I changed my clothes." Stiffly, she crushed the cigarette in the ashtray.

"It sounds like an honest mistake to me," Andy remarked after giving the story his thoughtful consideration. "You aren't still mad at Dane because of it?"

Pet had encountered prejudice before and usually dismissed it with a shrug of her shoulders. But Dane Kingston's treatment of her was not something she could forgive and forget.

"Dane Kingston is an autocratic, overbearing brute," she declared.

"Pet!" Charlie tried to shush her with a silencing frown.

"No, I'm going to say what I think. I don't like him, I've never liked him and I never will like him," she stated forcefully. "If he was here I'd say it to his face."

"Then maybe you should turn around," an icy voice suggested.

A cold chill ran down her spine. Pet turned her head slowly, her gaze stopping when it found the gold buckle of a belt around the trim waist of the man standing behind her chair. Traveling by inches, her gaze made the long climb up his muscled torso, past the set of huskily built shoulders, beyond the tanned column of his neck and the thinly drawn line of his mouth finally to reach the smoldering brown of his eyes.

Her pulse thundered in her ears, reacting to the male aggression of his presence. Pet's seated position intensified the impression that he was towering over her. Perhaps if she hadn't felt so threatened she would have acknowledged that he was a ruggedly attractive man. His dark hair was thick and full, inclined to curl while seeking its own style and order. The sheer force of his personality was enough to make her erect barriers of defense, rather than be absorbed by him.

"I believe there's an old saying that eavesdroppers never hear good about themselves, Mr. Kingston." Her voice was tight with the effort to oppose him.

The atmosphere around the two tables became so thick a knife could have sliced it. Someone coughed nervously while Lon shifted uneasily in the chair beside Pet. She continued to wage a silent battle of wills with Dane Kingston, refusing to be the first one to lower her gaze, but with each second it was becoming increasingly difficult to meet the iron steadiness of his eyes.

Andy cleared his throat. "Er—why don't you join us for a beer, Mr. Kingston? We can squeeze another chair in here."

"Miss Wallis can give me hers," Dane challenged, a mocking glint in his dark eyes. "I'm sure she's tired by now and ready to get some rest."

"Sorry to disappoint you, but I'm not tired—and I have no intention of giving you my chair," she defied him. "Besides, I haven't finished my beer." She turned to pick up her glass as an excuse to look away from him.

"Here, you can have my chair, Mr. Kingston." Someone down the way started to rise.

"Don't bother, I'm not staying," he refused the offer. "I only came by to remind you that we'll start setting up the equipment at six o'clock tomorrow morning. You'd better be thinking about breaking the party up and getting some sleep."

His statement was met with a few grumbles and self-pitying moans, but the advice was generally taken good-naturedly. By all but Pet, who felt she was capable of knowing how much sleep she needed without being told when she should go to bed.

"Good night." Dane included everyone in the group. "Don't forget, I expect you to be bright-eyed and bushy-tailed in the morning—or you'll wish you were."

"Right, boss."

"Sure."

"Good night."

The replies crowded on top of each other, drowning themselves out. Relief drifted through Pet now that Dane Kingston's unwelcome presence had been removed. She sipped at her beer, but it had grown flat and tepid.

"I feel as if I'm in a dormitory again, complete with curfew," she griped. "Do you suppose he's going to do a bed check and make sure we're all tucked in for the night?"

"Would you like me to tuck you in, Miss Wallis?" his voice came back to mock her.

She jerked around to find he was only a couple of steps away from the table, clearly close enough to have heard her ill-tempered complaint. She could have screamed in frustration, but managed to restrain her anger.

"No, thank you." She had to grit her teeth when she spoke.

"If you change your mind, let me know," Dane taunted deliberately, but his eyes were cold.

This time Pet watched him walk out of the lounge so she wouldn't put her foot in her mouth again. When she turned back to the table, the others eyed her askance, certain she had taken leave of her senses by being so antagonistic. There was a definite possibility that they were right.

"You're asking for trouble," Charlie mumured the warning.

"He rubs me the wrong way," Pet declared with a discouraged sigh.

"We noticed," was the dry response.

Dane's appearance had the desired effect of breaking up the gathering. After he had left, gradual stirring began. Drinks were finished and cigarettes snubbed out in the ashtrays. Chair legs scraped the floor as they were pushed back to allow their occupants to stand. Although she hated to think she was obeying Dane Kingston's instructions to have an early night, Pet followed along with the group as they left the lounge for their rooms.

"It must be nice to have a room all to yourself, Pet," Charlie remarked. "You don't know how lucky you are. I have to bunk with Andy and he snores like a freight train."

"Wait until you have to share a bathroom with Lon!" Joe laughed. "It takes him an hour to comb his hair in the morning."

At a fork in the hotel corridor, Pet turned to the left while the others started right. "This is where I leave you guys. Good night."

"Where are you going?" Lon stopped, although the others wished her good-night and continued on to their rooms.

"My room is down this way," she explained, dangling the room key she had taken from her shoulder bag.

"How come you're down that way when all the rest of us are down this way?" he frowned.

She lifted her shoulders in an indifferent shrug. "Maybe because I have a single room." The question had crossed her mind when she had arrived, but it hadn't seemed important. It didn't now.

"Good night, Lon." She turned to walk down her corridor, the silken straightness of her long blond hair swinging softly below her shoulder blades.

"Wait a minute, I'll walk with you." He hurried to catch up with her. Nearly the same height as Pet, Lon had the advantage of only an inch. As he curved an arm around her waist, his smile promised all sorts of pleasures.

"I can manage myself, Lon." She firmly removed his hand from her waist. "I don't need to be escorted. I won't get lost."

"I just wanted to be sure you got there safely." He looked affronted that she had taken his interest wrong.

"I'll tuck myself into bed. Good night, Lon," Pet repeated, and let her long legs carry her swiftly away from him.

He paused indecisively before he retreated to the fork in the corridor. Halfway down the hall, Pet reached her room. She had to wrestle with the doorknob before she could persuade the key to unlock the door.

The single room was small. The bed was a little wider than a single, covered with a quilted spread in a blue-flowered print. There was one blue green chair, the same color as the carpet, and a short built-in dresser with a mirror on the wall behind it. A proportionately small television was bolted to an extension of the dresser. The bathroom was about the only thing that was normal size.

Kicking off her flat shoes, Pet dropped her bag and the room key on the bed, and started to move away. On second thought she reached into her bag to take out the pack of cigarettes and her butane lighter, then walked to the single chair. She turned and sank into the seat in a single fluid motion.

Shaking out a cigarette, she snapped the lighter and held the flame to the tip. She glanced at the television, but didn't bother to turn it on. After exhaling the cigarette smoke, she leaned back in the chair to reflect on the lousy beginning of this production.

If she had kept her mouth shut and resisted the urge to vent her opinion of Dane Kingston, he would never have overheard it. Chances were that he had probably forgotten the hostility of their previous meeting. Now she had resurrected it all again when it had been better off buried.

She didn't like him. But just because she didn't like him, she didn't have to tell him that to his face. If you didn't like people you avoided them—or were civil if you had to be around them. But you didn't declare war, which was virtually what she had done.

A sigh broke from her throat. She was usually such an even-tempered person, patient and in control. So why was it that Dane Kingston had the ability to make her lose her cool—to use an outworn vernacular?

The ashes began to build up on the end of her cigarette. The nearest ashtray was on the dresser. Rising to her feet, Pet walked over to lay the cigarette in the glass container. She opened the dresser drawer where she had put her nightgown after unpacking, and laid it on top.

There wasn't much point in staying up since it was

after ten. It would be a long day tomorrow, even if Dane Kingston had reminded her of it. She began unbuttoning her khaki blouse and tugging the hem loose from the waistband of her matching slacks.

A knock at the door stopped her action with only two buttons left to unfasten. "Who is it?" Pet called.

"Dane Kingston," was the muffled reply.

She didn't for one minute believe that it was the producer. Some members of the crew had a weird sense of humor. It was more than likely somebody's idea of a really funny practical joke. Irritation surged through her in a quick rush.

"Oh, go away!" she grumbled.

But the person simply knocked again. She had started to tell him she wasn't in the mood for jokes when she decided it would be much more fun to turn the tables on the gagster.

"I'm coming." She deliberately put an inviting lilt in her voice and discreetly buttoned a couple of buttons, but left the top ones undone to permit a provocative glimpse of the shadowy cleft between her breasts.

She sauntered to the door, not bothering with the safety chain as she turned the knob and pulled the door open. "Have you come to tuck me in, Dane?" she murmured sexily.

But it *was* Dane Kingston standing in the hallway!

CHAPTER TWO

STUNNED, PET HELD the sultry pose she had unconsciously adopted, one hand on her hip and her forearm resting along the edge of the opened door. His dark gaze made a slow and insolent appraisal of her. It was only when he had finished that she recovered from the shock of finding him at her door. The blood rushed to her head, filling her senses with a hot awareness of the situation.

"I thought you were one of the boys—Lon or Charlie." She was instantly defensive.

"Coming to tuck you in?" He cocked his head to one side, a suggestive glint in the hard brown eyes, but the smile touching his mouth was anything but pleasant or amused.

Anger flared at the gibe. "If that's why you're here, Mr. Kingston, I'm neither amused nor interested!" Pet flashed, and stepped back to slam the door in his face.

But it was stopped short of the frame by a large hand moving swiftly to block it. For a fleeting second Pet leaned her weight against it, but she wasn't any match for his superior physical strength. As soon as she realized how undignified she must look, she straightened to simply block the opening.

"What do you want?" She let her exasperation show.

"I want to talk to you," he stated with a crispness that indicated the subject was not personal.

"You've talked to me. Now please leave. I want to get some sleep." She remembered the buttons and hurriedly began to fasten the strategic pair near her breasts. "As you pointed out, we have to be up early and work long hours tomorrow."

"This will only take a few minutes of your precious time, I promise you." Dane Kingston mocked her sudden show of concern for plenty of rest. "Are you going to invite me in? Or do we have this discussion in the hallway where anyone can overhear?"

The flat of his hand was still resting on the door. Pet guessed it would take only one push of that muscled arm to wrench it out of her hand. He could shove his way into her room if he wanted, and there was very little chance that she could prevent it.

"Aren't you worried that someone will see you come into my room at this hour of the night?" she taunted.

"No one that knows either of us. All the rooms for the crew are down the other corridor." There was a humorless curve to his mouth. "So you needn't worry that your reputation is going to be irretrievably damaged by this visit."

Damn! He made her look so foolish and unadult. "I was more concerned about yours," she retaliated, and spun away from the door, admitting him by moving away.

"What did you come to see me about?" She came

27

quickly back to the point of his visit since she hadn't been able to get rid of him.

"Tonight—" he began, then stopped. "Do you always leave cigarettes burning in the ashtray? Don't you know that's a dangerous habit?" he criticized.

"I only do it when someone knocks on the door. Maybe you would prefer that I answer with a cigarette dangling out of my mouth," she retorted, and walked over to crush it out. "My mother always told me that didn't look ladylike."

"Do you think it looks *ladylike* to be one woman sitting in a bar at a table with a dozen men?" He put biting emphasis on her term.

Pet turned to stare at him, seeing the disgust in his expression. Although she was tall, he still had the height advantage, being easily another six inches taller. It was rare that she had to look so far up to anyone, so it was equally disconcerting to have it be Dane Kingston.

"I don't see that it's any concern of yours." She had managed to recover from her initial amazement.

"It should be a concern to you," he countered.

"I work with those boys," Pet reminded him. "Most of them are married with families. Joe Wiles is a grandfather. Why is it a crime to sit around a table and have a drink with them?"

"Do I have to spell it out to you, Miss Wallis, how out of place you looked sitting among all those men?" His eyes had narrowed to dark brown slits. "Since you appear to have some interest in your reputation, may I suggest that you leave the drinking and the talking to the men?"

Pet was astounded by his suggestion—and angry. "What am I suppose to do on my off hours? Sit alone in my hotel room while the guys are in the bar having a good time? If that's your idea, you'd better think again," she informed him in no uncertain terms. "If I want to have a beer with the boys, I will."

"In case you haven't looked in a mirror lately—" he grabbed her by the elbow and turned her around to face the wall mirror "—you don't happen to be one of the boys!"

But it wasn't her own reflection that her turbulent sea-green eyes saw in the mirror. It was his, standing tall and dark beside her, overpoweringly masculine beside her willow-slim frame and wheat-tan hair. His innate virility aroused raw feelings of femininity in her. Pet tugged her elbow free of his hold and took a quick step away. She was used to feeling strong and independent no matter what man she was with, not weak at the knees.

"So what do you expect me to do—remain cloistered for the next couple of weeks or however long it takes to finish this special?" she demanded. "I'm not a nun! I like to laugh and socialize and—wait a minute!"

She turned on him roundly, a thought suddenly occurring to her. "Is there some significance to the fact that my room is in this corridor while the boys all have rooms in the other one? Was this your idea? Or is it just because this is a single?"

"When the hotel reservations were made, attention was paid to the fact that you are the only female

29

member of the crew outside of wardrobe and make-up," he admitted smoothly. "It didn't seem wise or proper to put an unattached female in a room next door to a couple dozen men."

"Then you're responsible for my being separated from the others," she said, feeling anger rather than appreciation for this thoughtfulness.

"Yes."

"Am I supposed to thank you for this?" Pet challenged. "Do you have any idea how hard I've worked to be accepted by them? To be treated as their equal? Now I'm in a different wing. You're saying I shouldn't socialize with them at all. What's next? Do I eat at a different table?"

"I suppose you wouldn't have objected to sharing a room with 'one of the boys,'" Dane jeered.

"I suppose next you're going to insinuate that I wouldn't be safe if I spent a night in the same room with Joe Wiles. For heaven's sake, he's a grand-father!" Pet went a step further. "He's old enough to be *my* grandfather." She went to brush past him and escape from the narrow path between the bed and the dresser to the wider space near the chair, where there was breathing room. "You certainly don't have a very high opinion of the members of your own sex!"

Dane stopped her, catching her by the arm and whipping her around to face him. Centrifugal force catapulted her against him, the solidness of his brawny frame bringing her to an abrupt halt. The air left her lungs in a rush at the unexpected contact with his body. As she was not a lightweight herself, the impact rocked him slightly. His large hands spanned her waist to steady both of them, the imprint of his fingers burning through the khaki material into her flesh.

Conscious of the masculine power of his thighs and the steel band of muscles flexing in his arms, Pet tried to collect her scattered wits and slip out of this accidental embrace, but her limbs wouldn't respond to the signals her brain sent out. She felt her heart skipping beats in sheer sexual attraction. Her mind reeled from the possibility that she could be physically attracted to the man.

"You're a stunning amazon." His low voice had a harsh edge to it. "Any normal, red-blooded American male—regardless of his age—would get ideas in his head if he spent a night alone in the same room with you. Don't tell me you aren't aware of that?"

The warmth of his breath fanned her face and hair like an intimate caress. Its potency was drugging. Fighting it, Pet abruptly turned her head to face him and make a retort. But in turning she discovered his head had been bent toward her, and in consequence her lips brushed the angle of his jaw. The resulting sensation was a shivery tingle that ran through her nerve ends, leaving them quivering for more. She twisted out of his arms as if she had been jolted by an electric prod.

"I'm quite aware of it. I didn't mean to imply that I wanted to share a room with one of—" That phrase "one of the boys" was becoming overused. "But I certainly don't think I have to be in an entirely different wing of the hotel from them."

The phone rang, and Pet nearly jumped out of her skin at the sound. Dane, in a purely reflex action, took the one stride necessary to reach the phone on the stand beside her bed and picked up the receiver. He had barely said hello before Pet realized he was answering her phone.

"Give that to me! Who do you think you are, taking my phone calls?" she demanded, and grabbed the phone out of his hand. "Hello?"

"Pet?" It was a very startled and confused Lon Baxter on the other end of the line. "What's Dane Kingston doing in your room?"

Oh, God, she thought. "He's lecturing me on the moral behavior proper for a young woman. Isn't that a laugh?" She vented her irritation toward the whole situation. "What did you want, Lon?"

"I...I wondered if...you wanted to join me for breakfast?" He sounded unsure whether he should even ask.

"Sure," Pet agreed with total disregard for everything Dane Kingston had said. "What time do you want to meet? Is five too early? We have to be at the Garden State Arts Center at six."

"Yeah, five o'clock is all right," he agreed with still a trace of uncertainty.

"Good night, Lon," she prompted him to hang up.

"Yeah, good night, Petra," he said absently.

She sighed as she hung up the phone. All the questions Lon hadn't found the nerve to ask tonight would be dumped on her in the morning. She did have an explanation—a true one. Whether Lon would prefer a meatier explanation of his own was another question. Men were such gossips.

Turning, she saw Dane standing at the foot of the bed, watching her, his hands in the side pockets of his pants.

"Problems?" It was a one-word question with no apology for causing them.

"Nothing that I can't handle," Pet replied shortly.

His dark gaze slid to the phone, then back to her. "So you've decided not to take my advice."

"About socializing with the boys? No, I'm not taking it." With space between them she could think more clearly. She realized the way she had been manipulated, always in reaction to his statements and accusations, and she was irritated that she had allowed it to happen.

"You and I have differing viewpoints. In the bar tonight you thought I looked like a tramp sitting with all those men. For me there's safety in numbers. Before you came to my room I wouldn't have dreamed of accepting Lon's invitation to have breakfast with him alone. But I just did because I knew you would disapprove."

"That's a stupid reason." The corners of his mouth were indented with grimness.

"You bet it's a stupid reason!" Pet agreed. "I can't be friendly to just two or three of the guys. If I do, the rest will assume that I go for them, and that destroys the camaraderie I've struggled so hard to achieve. Why did you have to interfere? Nobody asked you to!"

"I don't need permission to interfere. This is my

company, and my production. When I bring a crew on location I ultimately become responsible for a portion of the members' private lives—yours included, Miss Wallis," Dane snapped. "I doubted the wisdom of bringing your kind of temptation on location where the men are going to be away from their wives and girlfriends. The very first night I see you sitting in a bar, drinking with the whole lot of them. I have the feeling you're going to be a lot more trouble than you're worth!"

"Now maybe we've come to the heart of the matter." Her temper rose in direct proportion to his cold anger. "It's my job you want. What do you plan to do? Make my life on the set so miserable that I'll quit?"

"If you weren't good at your job, a highly skilled professional, you would have received your walking papers a long time ago," Dane informed her bluntly. "But if you—" he lifted a hand to point a finger at her and jab the air "—cause one ounce of dissension among the crew, if there's one quarrel among the men about you, I'll send you packing so fast you won't know what hit you."

"Then stay out of my personal life and there won't be!" she flared, and began stabbing the air with her finger. "You can dictate to me on the set, Dane Kingston, but don't you dare give me one order outside of work!"

"How many prolonged location shoots have you been on?" he challenged.

"I've been on quite a few two-day and three-day shoots." Which wasn't exactly a direct answer.

"How old are you?" he demanded next.

"Twenty-six." She would be in September, which was only two months away. The extra year implied more experience.

"I top that by eight years. And I've seen happily married men make complete fools of themselves when they've been separated from their wives for a week. Why do you think Miss Gale and her singers and dancers are staying in a different hotel?"

"I... presumed it was more luxurious than this one." Pet shrugged a shoulder uncertainly.

"It is. More importantly, it keeps my production crew separated from her cast so there won't be any socializing after hours. If it had been at all practical, you would have been staying in a different hotel, too. Unfortunately, it wasn't." His irritation with that was in his tight-lipped expression. "You just remember what I told you—any trouble and you're out!"

On that threatening note he turned on his heel and let his long, swinging strides carry him to the door. Pet's hands curled into fists.

"You just remember what *I* told *you,*" she called after him, trying to assert her own independence, but it was too late. Dane was pulling the door shut behind him as he stepped out into the hall.

Frustrated and dejected, Pet sank onto the squeaking mattress of her bed. She flopped backward to stare at the ceiling and rest the back of her hand on her forehead. This had not been her finest hour, she realized. Nor was the situation likely to improve unless she learned to control her temper around Dane Kingston. He was her boss, for heaven's sake! The

35

big boss! You couldn't go any higher in the company than Dane Kingston. Why hadn't she remembered that and behaved accordingly—regardless of the provocation?

Unable to answer that, Pet pushed herself off the bed and walked to the door. She flipped the security lock and the night latch and slipped the chain into place. Perhaps a shower and a good night's rest would put the whole thing in perspective.

THE NEXT MORNING Pet was deliberately late to meet Lon for breakfast. Wearing the same khaki blouse and slacks with their military creases, she had braided her flaxen hair into a single plait down the center of her back. Few women could get away with such a severe style, but Pet could, thanks to her strongly defined features and well-shaped head.

As she had hoped, two members of the crew had joined Lon at his table. She walked to the empty chair. "You saved a place for me. Thanks." The sentence was deliberately chosen to show Lon how casually she had accepted the invitation for breakfast.

"Good morning." She greeted them all as she sat down and felt the curiosity in each of their glances despite the normal chorus of replies. "Is there coffee in the pot?" Pet asked, and reached for the thermal container in the center of the table to pour herself a cup. "I need something to open my eyes this morning."

"Is there enough left for another cup?" Charlie Sutton inquired.

"About a half a cup," Pet answered after glancing inside the pot. The waitress stopped at the table to take her order, Lon and the others having already eaten. "I'm running late, so I'd better settle for toast and orange juice."

"Would you refill the coffeepot?" Joe Wiles handed the empty thermal container to the waitress.

When the girl had left, Pet leaned back in her chair, blowing on the hot coffee to cool it. Over the rim of her cup her gaze swept her three table companions in an encompassing arc around the table. It was early in the morning, but their unnatural silence wasn't caused by sleepiness.

"Come on, guys." She sipped at the hot coffee. "Isn't someone going to ask me what Dane Kingston was doing in my room last night? Or are you going to sit there eaten up with curiosity?" she teased. She had it all thought out, her explanation carefully rehearsed.

"That's our Pet!" Joe Wiles shook his head and smiled wryly. "Straightforward and open."

"You said he lectured you?" Lon looked skeptical.

"Yes. He went off on the same old tangent," she declared with a mock grimace. "Only this time it wasn't about the way I dressed, but what I was doing. He didn't think it was ladylike to have a beer with you guys and he suggested I behave with a little more decorum befitting my sex. Can you imagine?" she laughed, and took another sip of coffee.

"From now on, we'll make sure you order sherry—a proper drink for a proper girl," Joe teased.

"Dane suggested that I shouldn't associate with you at all." Pet blinked her deliberately rounded green eyes. "It seems you boys are a bad influence on an innocent young thing like me." She made it all appear to be a huge joke that everyone could laugh about.

"We *are* a wicked lot." Charlie twirled the end of an imaginary mustache in mock villainy.

"What did you tell Kingston?" Lon's eyes were gleaming with amusement; finally he was accepting her explanation without trying to turn it into something it was not.

"What do you think? I told him to mind his own business!" she declared with a twinkling look.

Her remark drew the expected chuckles and comments that suggested approval and encouragement for her stand. But Pet was careful not to mention Dane's threat about causing trouble or dissension among the crew. For the time being the men were on her side, and she didn't want to put ideas into their heads that might change their attitude.

Claude Rawlins, the floor director, stopped at their table when the waitress brought Pet's toast and orange juice, and the conversation was immediately shifted to a discussion of the day's schedule.

"When we're finished shooting here at the performing-arts center, where do we go?" Pet asked. "As I understand it, the idea is to show Ruby performing in different settings—the concert stage, a casino theater, and so on."

"That's right," Claude nodded. "From here we'll move to Batsto Village for some outdoor locations, then on to Atlantic City to tape her opening night at the casino.''

"We're really going to be plugging New Jersey, aren't we?'' Lon remarked on a less than enthusiastic note.

"This is her home state. She was born and raised here in New Jersey,'' Claude reminded them. "These backdrops will all be fresh and new to a viewing audience that's seen Las Vegas casinos and Madison Square Garden or the Kennedy Center hundreds of times.''

"I agree,'' Pet nodded. "I think it's a good idea.''

"Spoken like a homegrown Jerseyite,'' Charlie teased. Which she was.

"Your New York nose is in the air again,'' she countered.

Joe didn't take part in their playful feud, choosing to stick to the original subject. "It's fitting to tape the special in New Jersey. After all, Ruby Gale has been tagged as the new, American-born Jersey Lily.''

"Lillie Langtry was the original Jersey Lily, wasn't she?'' Pet remembered. "But she was from England, I thought.''

"She was,'' Claude admitted. "Now we have an American version—if you believe the publicity.'' He paused to glance at his wristwatch. "You'd better drink your coffee, boys. It's getting late.''

Pet quickly downed her last bite of toast and joined the others in line at the cash register. Everyone took it for granted that she would pay for her own meal, including Pet. The situation with the crew seemed to be back to normal.

Eight of them crowded into Charlie's van to make the ride to Telegraph Hill Park where the Garden State Arts Center was located. The early-morning sun cast a golden hue on the saucerlike white building with its supporting pillars. The summer-green setting of grass, trees and bright patches of flowers was serene and pleasing to the eye. Charlie drove around back where the semitrailer van filled with highly technical computers and control panels was parked. Several of the crew had already arrived, and others were driving in behind them.

Dane Kingston had just walked out the side door of the specially designed semitrailer rig and was coming down the set of metal steps shoved against the trailer door when Pet piled out of the van with the others. He noticed her immediately. His hard and narrowed look made her feel she was somehow responsible for their arriving late when in actual fact they were seven minutes early.

But there wasn't time to dwell on the injustice of his attitude. All the camera, lighting and sound equipment had to be set up and checked, which was an involved process. Everyone set to work at once. Pet, Lon, Charlie and Andy Turner entered the center to learn where the cameras would be positioned, and to what position each would be assigned.

In all there were four large studio cameras. One would be kept in reserve in the event of a technical failure of one of the others. Pet was assigned to camera two, covering center stage. Andy was manning camera one on her right and Charlie had camera three on her left. Lon was assigned to the hand-held camera, which allowed him the ability to move around with the lighter-weight camera and provide shots from in back of the stage, from the side, or below the footlights.

The first order of business was erecting the platforms to elevate the fixed studio cameras to a degree higher than stage level. Working as a team, they pitched in to help each other erect the scaffolding for the platforms one at a time. Pet worked right beside the men, not shirking any of the heavier work because she was female.

While they were busy with their work, other members of the production team were busy with theirs. It was a chaos of activity with two dozen people, sometimes more, hustling around, shouting orders amid general conversations. A web of cables was spun over the floor to relay power and feed into the main controls in the long trailer outside.

As soon as the platforms were finished they brought in the studio cameras, disassembled and packed in their metal traveling cases. It wasn't easy for Pet to handle the bulky and heavy pieces, but she had learned little tricks over the years that enabled her to compensate for the lack of muscles. It never occurred to her to ask for help. She would have refused it if it was offered.

"Wallis, what do you think you're doing?" a voice barked behind her.

The suddenness of the demand forced Pet to ease the camera onto the platform floor after she had finally levered it a couple of inches off it. Still kneeling, she turned to look behind her. Dane Kingston

41

was on the floor, glaring at her with his hands on his hips.

He wasn't dressed much differently from any of the other crew, except that his jeans were brushed denim and his shirt was a long-sleeved madras print with the cuffs rolled up to reveal his sun-bronzed and hair-roughened forearms. The modified work clothes emphasized his rugged male appeal, a factor that didn't make Pet feel any more at ease.

His gaze ripped from her to stab Charlie. "Get up there and get that camera mounted, Sutton," he ordered with an impatient wave of his hand.

"I can manage it!" she protested forcefully when Charlie started to vault onto the platform.

"I'm not interested in finding out whether you can or not," Dane retorted, and started to turn away.

"This doesn't happen to be the first camera I've ever assembled. I'm fully capable of doing it alone. I don't need any help," she insisted.

Dane swung back to face her with blazing dark eyes. "You can play superwoman another time. I'm not going to permit you to juggle an expensive piece of equipment like that camera. You'd probably drop it and break it; then I'd be without a spare. I can't afford this kind of idiotic display of sexual equality. You aren't strong enough to lift that camera, so let someone else do it. Do I make myself clear?"

Just in time she remembered to hold her temper, although it flashed in her green eyes. "Very clear, Mr. Kingston," she said, clenching her teeth.

"Good. Make sure I don't have to tell you again," he warned.

He waited at the base of the platform until Pet had moved stiffly out of Charlie's way so he could hoist the camera into place on the rotating head of its stand. As Pet went to help Charlie fasten it into place, Dane walked away. She glared after his set of broad shoulders.

"I've never considered myself superwoman," she muttered angrily. "And I've never asked for special treatment because I'm a woman. Damn him, anyway!"

Charlie's gaze flickered uncertainly over her. "You have to admit, Pet, the camera was a little heavier than you could handle."

"*Et tu, Brute,*" she retorted sarcastically, but Charlie didn't hear her as he turned to say something to Andy.

CHAPTER THREE

By MIDMORNING all three of the camera platforms were in place. One of the cameras was mounted and the crew was unpacking the second and getting it ready to assemble.

"Break time!" Claude shouted to make himself heard above the racket. "Coffee and sweet rolls down front!"

"Sweeter words were never said," Pet murmured, and hopped down from the middle platform. "Those two slices of toast I had for breakfast disappeared about an hour ago. I'm starved!"

"Just direct me to the coffee," Andy declared as he followed her down the aisle. "I must be eight cups behind my normal quota of caffeine for the morning, and I was on the verge of getting the shakes."

A long table had been set up near the fire exit along the wall to the right of the stage. A huge stainless-steel coffee urn was perched in the center of it with paper cups stacked on one side and boxes of Danish pastry on the other. Pet joined the others who had already lined up to help themselves.

With her coffee and pineapple pastry in hand, Pet wandered over to an empty area below center stage. Andy joined her there. Soon after Lon and Charlie came and a few of the other crew, to talk shop. Pet listened, but spent most of her time eating to quiet the hunger pains in her stomach. When it was gone, she licked the sticky frosting from her fingers.

Tired of standing, but intrigued by a technical explanation Andy was making, Pet set her cup of coffee on top of the stage. With her hands to lever her, she vaulted onto the stage, swinging around to sit on the edge, her long legs dangling. Between sips of her coffee she listened to Andy and asked questions when she wanted something clarified.

She reached for the pack of cigarettes that she usually carried man-fashion in the breast pocket of her blouse. Too late, she remembered they had fallen out when she was assembling the camera.

"Can I bum a cigarette from somebody?" she asked. "I left mine on the platform."

"Here." Lon lighted one of his and handed it to her, the filtered end first.

"Thanks. Coffee without a cigarette is as incomplete as a steak without salt," Pet declared.

"Or a bed without a woman in it!" someone suggested, and everyone laughed in agreement, although Pet just smiled.

"Pet doesn't think so." Lon noticed her silence and began to tease.

"Nope. I have a teddy bear to snuggle up to at night," she joked. "It doesn't complain if I have a headache."

"Do you have headaches often?" Charlie asked with a laughing smile.

"Working with you guys, I have them all the

45

time!'' she declared with mock seriousness, and drained the Styrofoam cup of its contents.

"Want another cup, Pet?" Andy offered.

"I'd love one," she admitted. "But I can get it."

"I was just going to refill mine. There's no sense in both of us walking over there," he reasoned, and reached for her cup, which she surrendered to him.

"If the queen is through holding court—" Dane appeared at the fringe of the small group, withering Pet with a dry look "—let's get back to work."

A few of the men murmured "Sure," and "You bet," as glances were darted at Pet sitting rigidly on the edge of the stage. Over the heads of her fellow workers her gaze was locked with Dane's. Holding court indeed, she thought angrily. Up until a few minutes ago she had been listening to an impromptu lecture by Andy. And Dane had made it sound as though all the guys had been dancing attendance on her! She was furious, but she held her tongue.

As the group around her began to disperse, it seemed a pathway was being cleared between her and Dane. When he moved to approach her, Pet stayed where she was. The stage gave her a height advantage. She would enjoy looking down on him for a change. No matter what he said to her, she was determined not to lose her temper.

Stopping in front of her, Dane peered at her through spiky male lashes as dark as his eyes. The powerful line of his jaw was hard and unyielding. An awesome mingling of danger and excitement danced along her nerves and she found that she couldn't maintain the silence.

"I wasn't 'holding court,'" she insisted stiffly.

In one smooth motion he came a step closer and spanned her slender waist with his large hands. Instinctively Pet clasped his bare forearms with the intention of repelling his hands, but he was already lifting her off the stage and setting her feet on the few inches of floor left in front of him.

His hands stayed on her waist, as if he knew that the minute he took them away she would move out of his reach. She was forced to stay where she was, their tall bodies almost, but not quite, touching. His nearness was suffocating.

"Don't deny you were the center of attention," Dane stated, a muscle working in his hard jaw.

"Maybe when you walked up, but not before." Her gaze moved restlessly over his shirtfront, looking anywhere but into his implacable male features.

She watched the steady rise and fall of his chest, noticed the curling, golden brown hairs peeping out through the V opening made by an unbuttoned collar, and saw the brawny muscles beneath the shirt sleeves over his upper arms. It was a disturbing observation of his utter masculinity.

"They were clustered around you like bees around honey." His voice was low, but that didn't lessen its cutting edge.

"That isn't true," Pet denied. "They'd gathered around the stage because it gave them something to lean against."

"They leaned against the stage rather than sit in those seats out there," Dane mocked. "In case you haven't noticed, there are several rows of them out there."

"Why don't you quit making mountains out of molehills?" she hissed. "Why do you keep looking for lusting motivations behind a perfectly innocent gathering?"

"Will you listen to me, you long-limbed Nordic witch?" His fingers dug into her waist, inflicting pain. If his intention had been to make Pet finally look at him, he succeeded. "I have a much clearer understanding of the fantasies a man could weave in his head when he looks at you."

"Such as?" Pet challenged, goaded by his superior attitude.

An eyebrow flicked upward in aloof amusement. "Such as wondering whether all your skin would be as marble-smooth and white as your neck if those clothes were taken off you." His downward glance seemed to strip away her blouse and heat her flesh before it finally returned to her whitened face and wide green eyes. "Such as wondering what you'd look like with all that long blond hair flowing freely over your naked breasts." Dane paused. "Do you want me to continue? Because I can, very easily."

"No." Her voice was all choked. She had to swallow to ease the strangling sensation. He had made it sound as if that really was what he thought when he looked at her. For a few seconds she had allowed herself to be carried away by the possibility that he was attracted to her. "Some men might fantasize like that, but not Andy, Charlie or the others. They know me."

48

"They work with you, but that doesn't mean it never crosses their mind to wonder what you'd be like as a lover. Men tend to think along those lines," he said. "Women probably do, too, but they're reluctant to admit it even to themselves."

"I don't think very many women think like that," she replied huskily.

"No? You've never wondered what it would be like if—for example—I made love to you?" Dane queried, tilting his head to one side.

"No." Pet rejected such a notion with a rushed answer and pushed at his forearms. "Now let me go. I have to get to work. I can't keep standing around here talking to you."

"Or the boys might start to think I was in your room last night for a reason other than the one you told them?" he suggested complacently.

"They wouldn't." But she turned to look toward the middle platform where Charlie and the others had gone to finish assembling the camera. As she watched them, Andy glanced over his shoulder toward the stage. The object of his attention was obviously her and Dane.

"They would enjoy thinking it," Dane insisted dryly.

"Well, I wouldn't!" Angered that he had placed her in another awkward situation, Pet wrenched out of his hands with a violent twist. "So just stay away from me from now on!" With a quick pivot she whirled away from him, her long braid flying out behind her and nearly slapping his face.

Anger gave her a surplus of energy. She burned a

49

portion of it walking up the aisle to the platform and hopping onto the planks. The rest she immediately put to use helping the others, aware of their speculative glances and telling silence.

Finally Andy teased, "Did you quarrel?"

She turned on him with a vengeance. "If you think for one minute that I'm interested in that muscle-bound know-it-all tyrant, then you aren't any friend of mine. If he'd been anyone other than Dane Kingston—my boss—I would have told him where to get off! He accused me of holding court. And all because you offered to get my coffee!"

"Are you saying it's my fault?" His look was incredulous. "Only a woman could reason like that."

"Yes, yours! And his—" she waved a hand toward the stage where Dane was talking with the lighting director "—overactive imagination!"

"Do you want us to help you find it?" Lon asked.

Pet turned to glare at him. "Find what?" she demanded.

"You've obviously lost your temper. I thought you might want us to help you look for it," he suggested. The other three were wise enough not to smile in front of her.

"No, thank you. I'll find it myself," she said tightly, realizing that she was unjustly venting her anger on them. "I just need to cool down a little bit."

"Let's speed up the process." Charlie picked up the piece of white cardboard and began fanning her with it.

"Very funny." But there wasn't any amusement in her expression.

She never fully recovered her sense of humor. By the time they broke for lunch, Pet had succeeded in pushing the disturbing incident to the back of her mind. The others had either forgotten or were careful not to bring it up.

In the afternoon, the impression of chaos was increased when the cast of entertainers arrived to practice their songs and dance routines. To an outsider, it had to look as though no one knew what was going on, but it was all very well organized.

Wearing her headset to communicate with the control booth in the semitrailer, Pet was checking out her camera to make certain it was functioning properly and transmitting a clear picture to the monitors in the control booth. Invariably when a sophisticated and sensitive piece of equipment such as this television camera was transported any distance, something needed adjustment. Although generally the adjustments were minor, they could be time-consuming, which was why a day was set aside more or less for the sole purpose of assembling and checking out the equipment, including the spare camera. Barnes was the name of the technician in the control booth with whom Pet and her co-cameramen were working.

"She's here. She just walked in the door." It was Lon's voice that came over Pet's headset. "Wow! She's sexier in person, if that's possible."

"You mean Ruby Gale? Where is she?" Charlie questioned.

Pet had the feeling she was listening in on a party line as the headset hummed with the intercommunication of the cameramen. The star of the television special had arrived and all thought of the technical checklist to be completed had been temporarily forgotten. Admittedly Pet was a little curious to see what Ruby Gale actually looked like in the flesh after having heard and seen her perform so often in the past.

"She's coming down the center aisle," Lon answered Charlie's question.

Turning her head, Pet saw the titian-haired woman skirting the camera platform. Her first thought was how small the star looked, then she realized she was guilty of carrying the larger-than-life screen image in her head. Instead of being as tall as she was, Ruby Gale was probably two inches shorter, but her long shapely legs provided that illusion of extra height.

Glimpses of those famous legs clad in tights were offered by the side splits in her skirt each time she took a step. She had a flaming mass of red hair that cascaded in thick glowing curls around her shoulders. Unfortunately, Pet's only view was of the star's backside as she walked down the aisle toward the stage, so she wasn't able to see if Ruby Gale was as naturally beautiful in the face as she appeared on screen and in photographs. Soon even that view was blocked by the two people who followed closely behind the star, no doubt part of her personal entourage.

Then Pet noticed Dane coming at right angles to intercept the star. A wide lazy smile added a potent charm to a man she regarded as being already too ruggedly appealing. Irritation pressed her lips into a thin line as she watched him greet the redhead with a kiss. In the entertainment business, kissing was as much a part of greeting as a handshake.

"Do you see the way she's cuddling up to Dane?" Charlie murmured. His voice coming over her earphones was an unneeded verification of the scene Pet was witnessing.

"I wish she'd press against me like that," said Lon, and imitated the sound of a growling tiger.

"Dane's certainly enjoying it," Andy observed dryly.

"There would have to be something drastically wrong with him if he didn't," Lon retorted. "Hey, you're awfully quiet, Pet. Isn't there any comment you want to make?"

It took her a second to find her voice. "About what?" With the pencil-thin microphone directly in front of her lips, it didn't take much above a whisper to make herself heard. "She's an absolutely gorgeous woman, but you can't expect me to be turned on about her the way you guys are."

Ruby Gale was very beautiful. Pet could see that now as the redhead half turned toward the audience seats. Her features were sultry and exotic. Her dark eyebrows were perfectly arched, winging to her temple. Full, sensuous lips appeared always silently inviting some forbidden pleasure. Although Pet was too far away actually to see the color of her eyes, she remembered from the photographs of Ruby Gale that they were a startling peacock-blue.

"A word of warning, fellas," Andy inserted. "She has a temper to match the color of her hair."

"I don't care," Lon declared. "All I know is that

these next few days it's going to be a treat having to look at her all the time. I'd be willing to pay for the privilege."

"Better not let the union hear you say that," Charlie suggested.

Barnes from the control booth spoke up. "Don't you think we'd better get back to the job at hand, fellas?"

"Joy killer!" Lon grumbled.

Fortunately Ruby Gale disappeared behind stage with Dane and the distraction was eliminated. Not for long, however. Fifteen minutes later she was on stage to rehearse some numbers with the dancers. The skirt and blouse had been discarded in favor of a dancer's leotard and a skintight body shirt that revealed every curve and contour of her breasts. Pet had to suffer through more profuse compliments on the redhead's beauty and well-endowed figure. She was heartily sick of the entire subject when a halt was finally called for the day.

Back at the hotel, Pet showered away her mild irritation and the day's tiredness. The khaki outfit was cast aside in favor of a pair of biscuit-colored slacks and a forest-green blazer over a tan sleeveless top.

She walked alone to the dining room, certain there would be somebody from the crew with whom she could share dinner. There were three tables' worth, with an empty place setting at each table. Pet avoided the one at which Lon and Charlie were sitting since they had been so vocal in their praise of Ruby Gale, and she had already had her fill of that subject.

She proved to be a minority of one. All through

dinner every other sentence contained some reference to the star of the television special. It seemed everyone had some anecdote to relate or gossip to add. At the conclusion of her meal, Pet stayed at the table to have coffee with the guys.

When the exodus began toward the lounge, she decided that she couldn't endure another minute of Ruby Gale and opted to return to her room. No one seemed to notice that she wasn't coming with them, which was rather bruising to her ego.

Perhaps that was why she didn't notice Dane Kingston standing near the exit of the restaurant until she was almost level with him. Her steps faltered for a brief instant.

"Good evening," she murmured, and would have walked on.

"Aren't you going into the lounge with the others?" His dark eyes moved over her with lazy knowledge.

"Not tonight. It's been a long day and I'm tired," she explained because she didn't want him to think her decision had been based on his admonition not to socialize with the men in the crew.

"It never crossed my mind that you were heeding my advice," Dane assured her. "But I can't say that you look tired, either."

Pet took a deep breath and released it in an exasperated sigh. "The truth is, Mr. Kingston, that I've become bored with the subject of Ruby Gale. It's all I've heard for the last several hours."

"You don't like playing second fiddle, is that it?" he mocked.

"Think what you like." She refused to argue about it. "You may find her to be a scintillating topic of conversation, but I don't. Good night."

"Good night," he returned. Before she had taken a step past him, he asked, "Is Pet a nickname?"

She was surprised by the personal question, or perhaps by the genuine interest in his voice. "In a way, it is. It's a shortened version of Petra, my given name." She tipped her head curiously to one side and frowned. "Why?"

"No special reason. I just wondered," he shrugged. "There's a meeting at seven o'clock in the morning."

"Yes, I know," Pet nodded, and glanced over her shoulder toward the restaurant. "Were you just going in for dinner?"

"No. As a matter of fact, I was just on my way out of the hotel." The glint in his eye seemed a little bit wicked, although his expression was impassively bland. "I'm dining with Miss Gale this evening."

His announcement seemed almost the last straw. First the crew, many of whom she had numbered as her friends, had talked of nothing but Ruby Gale. Now Dane Kingston was having dinner with her. The defection of a man Pet really didn't like was the hardest to take.

Her gaze swept over him, noting that he hadn't changed out of the brushed denims and plaid shirt. "You're going in that?" she questioned icily.

"It's informal." A smile tugged at the corners of his mouth without really showing itself. "We're just having some sandwiches in her suite."

"What? No champagne and caviar?" There was a certain acidity to her murmured taunt.

"That's being saved to celebrate the completion of the special," Dane responded easily.

"How nice. Enjoy your evening," she said, and hurried on her way before he could stop her again.

It was too early to go to bed. After twenty minutes in the small hotel room the walls began to close in on her. Jamming her writing pad and paperback book in her large shoulder bag, Pet left the room and went out of the hotel through a side door leading to the pool area.

There were two families with children swimming in the pool, but few of the deck chairs were occupied. Pet chose one with a small wrought-iron table beside it. It was nearly a full hour before sundown on this warm summer evening—not that it mattered, since the pool area was lighted.

Shedding her blazer, Pet settled into the deck chair and got out her writing pad. She had barely written "Dear Rudy" when a shadow was cast across the paper. She looked up to find Joe Wiles's wide bulk standing beside her chair.

"Writing love letters?" he smiled.

"It's to my brother. He's in the coast guard. Right now he's stationed in Texas, along the Gulf Coast," she explained. "Are you taking an evening stroll?"

"Yeah, I'm taking my nightly constitutional before turning in," he grinned, and pulled up a chair to sit beside her. "Do you have any other brothers or sisters?"

"An older brother, Hugh. He lives in Connecticut,

married with three kids—all boys. His wife, Marjorie, is a fantastic girl. We all love her. Do you want to see some pictures of my nephews?'' she asked.

At his nod, she reached in her bag and took out the small photo album to show him the trio of boys with the Wallis blond hair and green eyes. Then Joe took his billfold out of his hip pocket and showed her pictures of his grandchildren, all seven of them.

"How come you aren't married, Pet? You should have pictures of your own kids to show off, instead of your brother's. I hope you aren't one of those modern females who don't want to get married,'' Joe stated with a disapproving frown.

"You sound like my dad! I hear this lecture every weekend about the blissful state of matrimony.'' There was a laughing twinkle in her eyes. "I can't seem to convince him or mom that I'd get married in a minute if the right man asked.''

"Somebody must have asked you before now,'' he insisted. "You're a lovely creature.''

"Thanks. I have been asked,'' Pet admitted. "I was even engaged for a year, but it didn't work out.''

"It must have been very painful.''

"Strangely, it wasn't,'' she remembered. "I really liked Bob. As a matter of fact we're still very good friends. When we mutually decided to call off the engagement, I was sorry—disappointed that it hadn't worked for us—but my heart wasn't broken. It wasn't even cracked or bruised. Which proves it would have been a mistake to marry him.''

"I guess so,'' he agreed with regret.

"I think I'll have a Coke. Would you like one,

Joe?'' she offered, and reached in her purse to get change for the drink machine standing against the exterior wall of the hotel.

"No, thanks," he refused, and pressed a hand against his rotund stomach. "Those carbonated beverages give me heartburn."

There was a definite golden cast to the western sky. Pet noticed it when she walked back to her chair after getting the cold can of soda. For a fleeting second she allowed herself to wonder whether Dane and Ruby were admiring the sunset together in her suite.

"Why do you suppose Dane Kingston has never married, Joe?" she asked with absent curiosity. "Or has he been?"

"Not that I know about," he answered her last question first. "Could be his reason is the same as yours—never met the right girl. He's certainly had more than his share of beautiful women hanging on his arm over the years."

"And probably hopping into his bed, too," Pet added on a note of disgust. "I'll bet no one has ever said yes to him, because he's too bossy and pushy. A woman can't tolerate that for long."

Joe shook his head in disagreement. "In this life you have to go after what you want. Nobody is going to hand it to you. I admire the way Dane never lets anything stand in the way of what he wants. He knows what it is and goes for it. I like that. There are very few men like him in this world."

"That's heartening," Pet murmured dryly.

"I'm not going to argue with you about him," Joe declared, and pushed to his feet. "I'd better finish my stroll and let you finish that letter to your brother. Good night, Pet."

"Good night." But it was several minutes before she reached for her ·pen and resumed the letter to Rudy.

CHAPTER FOUR

THE ORCHESTRA WAS POSITIONED to the rear of the stage, the pianist testing a few quick chords to loosen his tension. The dancers in their practice leotards were posed around Ruby Gale, standing at front center stage. Beyond them the backup vocal group was fanned out.

This was a practice session, a dry run before tomorrow's dress rehearsal and the following night's concert. Each one of the songs and dance routines would be performed so camera angles could be corrected and the lighting adjusted.

The cameras were warmed up. Everyone on stage was waiting for the cue from Claude, the floor director. Dane Kingston was in the control booth in the van parked outside. It was his instructions and directions that were coming over Pet's headset.

"Camera two, we'll be opening with you," he informed Pet. "I want a close-up shot of Miss Gale, widening on my order. We'll be coming to you next, camera three. All right, we've been through this number twice already. I want the tape rolling on this one."

Pet nibbled at her lower lip, tension building as she rechecked her focus. She knew the procedure. The practice tape would be made and reviewed later that night for any final changes in angle or lighting. All of tomorrow's dress rehearsal would be taped, since the concert show was a one-time performance. There were a dozen things that could ruin a song at a live show. In that event, the dress-rehearsal tapes would be a back-up that could be edited into the final product.

"Tape is rolling," Dane stated.

"Let's have it quiet!" Claude instructed the cast, and absolute silence descended on the center.

From this point on, the only voice would be Dane's as he communicated with the cameras, Claude, the sound man and the lights. Mentally Pet blocked out everything else. Someone else would be responsible for the quality of the sound, the tempo of the music and the volume of the singer on stage.

"All right, two." Dane's voice was calm, and Pet relaxed, too, now that the taping had begun. She didn't notice the signal Claude gave, nor hear the heavy beat of the base drum begin the song. The titian-haired Ruby Gale filled her camera lens, inviting and beguiling blue eyes staring straight at the camera.

As she began to sing the first lyric, Dane ordered, "Widen the shot, two! *Slowly,*" he emphasized, then a little sternly as she began to reverse the zoom, "Don't lose focus, Wallis! Camera three, get ready. We're coming to you. *Now!*"

Pet didn't need to consult the paper clipped to her camera, listing the various angles of her coverage in this song. The next one was to be an overall shot of the entire stage, including the orchestra and performers, then narrowing in to isolate the star singing within the circle of male dancers.

"Hold the shot, two. We're on you," Dane advised. "When she moves stage left, go with her, Wallis." Pet tried, not very successfully, as Dane's angry voice informed her, "You're letting her get behind a dancer. Three, take it on the turn—quick! You blew that shot, Wallis."

She gritted her teeth, not convinced the fault had been entirely hers. She suspected the dancer had been out of position, although no one was ever precisely where he was supposed to be. Either way, there wasn't time to dwell on who had been in error. She had to be in position for her next shot.

Meanwhile, she listened to Dane heaping praise on Andy. "Great shot, one." The even pitch of his voice didn't change, although a level of amusement entered it. "I didn't know you had it in you, Turner. You'd better make certain you can do that again." Then, crisply, "You're off center, Wallis. I can't come to you until you have Ruby in the middle. You've got it!"

Concentrating, Pet followed the star through her next sequence of steps and its accompanying song lyrics. Her coverage was flawless. But she didn't receive the deserved praise from the control booth; Dane's attention was occupied elsewhere.

"Baxter, you're in three's picture. Duck behind the reed section," he ordered the cameraman on stage with the handheld camera. "Okay, three, it's yours."

As the song drew to an end, Pet's was the last shot. It was to be a close-up on the star while she belted out the last line, then opening to full length and finally widening to full stage. The first Pet executed perfectly but she faltered on the second.

On the third, Dane was barking in her ear, "Loosen it up, two! I said, loosen it up," he complained. "Hold it!" The song was finished. There was a mental countdown ticking in everyone's head. Then Dane gave the order, "Stop tape."

"Good job!" Claude called to the performers on stage.

His voice unfroze them from their positions. There was an instant gabble of voices and movement everywhere. Pet released an unconscious sigh and turned off her camera. The tension of needing to be as soundless as possible had been lifted.

A public-address system had been connected between the stage and the control van to extend Dane's communication link to the performers. It was switched on now and his voice filled the theater.

"That was a great number. You were sensational, Ruby," he praised her.

The compliment brought a radiant smile to the star. She blew a kiss in the direction of the loudspeaker over which his voice had been projected, and glided into the wings. Just as quickly, the PA system was switched off and Dane's voice was again restricted to the headsets of the crew.

"Claude, get the group set up for the next number," he advised the floor director.

But it was Lon Baxter's voice that dominated the earphones. "Hot damn! Did you guys watch her strutting through that number? She sent my blood pressure soaring!" His compliments became punctuated with swearwords, as if vulgarity somehow emphasized his enthusiasm.

"Let's clean up the language!" Dane snapped. "You're forgetting, Baxter, that there's a lady listening."

"A lady?" Lon questioned, then hooted, "You mean Pet?"

"That's exactly who I mean!" was Dane's angry and silencing retort.

In the past, Pet had always turned a deaf ear to that kind of language rather than inhibit her male co-workers. If they weren't able to talk freely, she had always felt she would be driving a wedge between herself and them. So she didn't welcome this interference from Dane Kingston.

"Don't worry about it, fellas," she said into her microphone. "I have special earphones that automatically censor any words that might shock my virgin ears. All I hear is a confusing set of bleeps."

"Miss Wallis—" Dane's voice came low and threatening over the headset "—I give the orders around here. It's of little interest to me whether you would be offended or not. As long as I'm running this show, there isn't going to be any more of that kind of language around a woman. Is that clear?"

"Perfectly." She ground the response through her teeth, crimsoning at his sharp reproof.

"Now that we all understand one another, let's get ready for the next number. Ruby is doing a solo on stage. You shouldn't have any trouble this time, Wallis, in making sure no one else blocks the star out of your shot," he suggested sarcastically.

Pet seethed at that totally unjustified slur on her ability, and clamped her teeth down hard to hold back a sassing reply. She had already been the recipient of several rebukes from him and she didn't intend to invite another.

But it seemed nothing went right after that. One major production number went continuously wrong. Either a dancer missed a cue, or Ruby Gale muffed the lyrics, or the assigned camera lost the shot—usually Pet, it seemed. Finally Claude murmured to Dane that maybe it was time for a midafternoon break since their star was showing signs of screaming.

The minute Dane voiced a reluctant agreement, Pet tugged her headset off and hopped down from the platform. Her long blond ponytail was swinging back and forth like a cat's tail lashing in anger as she walked swiftly down the aisle for a tall cup of iced tea.

Without saying a word or waiting to see if anyone wanted to join her, she pushed out of an exit door and walked outside. Frustrated by her own apparent inability to do her job right and angered by the way Dane kept pointing it out to her, she needed to escape the tense and stifling atmosphere inside the building.

It was a hot July afternoon, but the air was fresh, circulated by a gentle breeze. She found a shady place to sit where the breeze reached her, and lighted a cigarette, hoping the nicotine would calm her jangled nerves. Some of the others wandered outside, as well. When Charlie walked over to enjoy the shade she had found, Lon and two others followed him.

"It may be hotter out here, but it's a lot more peaceful," Charlie sighed.

"It's a good thing Claude suggested a fifteen-minute break," Lon remarked. "We came very close to seeing that temper Andy has been telling us our star has. You should have heard some of the things she said to that poor dancer who forgot the routine! If Dane thought my language was out of line, he should have heard some of the words Ruby Gale used."

Pet wished he hadn't brought that earlier matter up. As if he realized what he had said, Lon glanced at her, noting her strained and downcast expression. A rueful grimace twisted his mouth.

"I guess I do owe you an apology, Pet. Some of the things I said were really off color. I forget sometimes that you're not one of the boys. I'm sorry," he offered.

"Forget it. I have." She crushed out the tasteless cigarette.

"I agree with you, Lon," Charlie inserted. "Dane was right to remind us that Pet's a woman. A lot of times we don't show her the respect that we should."

"Listen, I've never asked for any special treatment from you guys," she reminded them.

"If you think I'm going to open a door for you, you're crazy," Lon joked, trying to make Pet see the situation with a little humor.

"Sorry, I'm a little touchy. It's been a rotten day what with Kingston constantly harping on me," Pet explained with a genuine effort to contain her irritation. "I can't seem to do anything right."

"Maybe you're trying too hard," Charlie suggested.

"It sure sounded like Dane was singling Pet out for more than her share of criticism. Of course, that's just my opinion," Lon shrugged. "I don't know how it looked on the monitors. Maybe you had it coming."

"I just wish he'd quit picking on me—in general," Pet sighed. "I can take criticism, but I'd like a pat on the head every now and then."

"Don't let him get to you," Charlie urged, and rubbed a comforting hand on her shoulder. "You're good at what you do. Just remember that."

"Hey!" Claude stuck his head out of the exit door. "Everybody back inside. Let's get to work!"

Pet followed the crew inside and took one last drink of her iced tea before throwing the cup in the wastebasket. Then it was back on the platform to warm the camera up and try the same number that proverbial "one more time."

The short break didn't seem to improve anything. By the end of the day she was a ball of nerves, stretched thin and coiled tight. As always, the ride back to the hotel was noisy, which didn't help. The crew tended to make up for so many hours of enforced silence by laughing and joking at a fever pitch of excitement. Usually such gaiety was the ideal means of relieving their stress, but it didn't work for Pet this time.

At the hotel she didn't dawdle in the lobby or corridor with the boys, but went straight to her room and almost directly into the shower. She didn't take the time to dry her long hair. Instead she wound it into a golden brown bun on top of her head, crisscrossing a pair of jade pokes through it for an

Oriental look. Her jade silk blouse buttoned up the front with a mandarin collar and a hand-embroidered water lily on the left side. The top was complemented by a pair of mother-of-pearl slacks. It was usually a morale-boosting outfit that enhanced her proud carriage, but she didn't feel any better when she studied her reflection in the mirror.

Sighing, Pet left her hotel room. Too on edge to have dinner yet, she decided to stop in the lounge and have a relaxing before-dinner cocktail with the boys. Her plans went awry when she walked into the dimly lighted bar and didn't see Charlie, Andy or any of the regular group. At a table near the bar she noticed Claude, Joe Wiles, Dane Kingston and the audio man, Greg Coopster, all seated together.

She started to leave, then decided to have a quiet drink by herself; after all, that was the reason she had come into the lounge. When Joe spoke and the others glanced around, Pet just nodded. She didn't approach their table as she made her way to a secluded booth in the corner. The barmaid came to take her order.

"A glass of sherry, please." Why on earth had she ordered that, Pet wondered when the miniskirted girl had walked away. Was she trying to prove what a "proper" lady she was?

Reaching for the pack of cigarettes in her purse, she shook one out. The lighter flamed with a quick snap. As she lifted the light to the cigarette, a shadow blocked what little light reached the corner booth. Her hand began to shake even before she looked to see who was there.

Because she had already guessed it was Dane

Kingston. Lowering the hand holding the cigarette to the table to hide its trembling, she slowly turned her head to meet his gaze. The forbidding thinness of his mouth didn't make her feel any more comfortable. He bent forward to lean a hand on the table. It was an action that struck her as threatening despite his cold attempt at a smile.

"Would you care to join us, Miss Wallis?" he invited.

"No." She didn't temper the flat refusal and looked away to take another puff from her cigarette, pretending to ignore him. Which was an impossibility.

"I insist," Dane commanded firmly. "You shouldn't sit alone in a strange bar."

"You're impossible, do you know that?" Pet flared, unleashing the anger she had kept bottled up inside her all day. "First you criticize me for being the sole female drinking with a group of men I happen to work with, saying that it didn't look ladylike. Now you're upset because I'm here alone. Why don't you make up your mind?"

She didn't like the sudden flash of amusement that glittered in his dark eyes. Agitated, she looked away again. "Nothing I do ever pleases you," she complained bitterly.

The barmaid came back with her glass of sherry. Dane had to move to one side so she could serve it. After the girl had left, instead of resuming his former position, he slid onto the booth seat beside Pet. Initially she was too startled to offer a protest. Once she felt the contact of his hard thigh alongside hers, she couldn't seem to breathe, let alone speak.

Aware that his head was turned so he could watch

70

her, Pet stared at the glass of sherry sitting on the cocktail napkin. She didn't even notice the ashes building up on the end of her cigarette or the gray blue smoke curling from its tip. His gaze was making a slow inspection of her profile; she could feel it as certainly as if he were touching her.

"Do you want to please me?" The drawled question suggested intimacy lightly spiced with a vague curiosity.

His implication sent her imagination off on a forbidden tangent. If he could affect her this deeply just by sitting next to her and hinting at familiarity, how would she feel if he made love to her? Her heart knocked against her ribs.

"I couldn't care less," she lied, impatient with herself for being physically disturbed by him. It gave false credence to her statement. She reached for the sherry glass. "Why don't you go away and leave me alone? I was doing fine before you came along."

"A woman alone in a bar is a target for any man who walks in. You can't sit here by yourself," Dane insisted, gently this time.

But it only increased his attraction and made her all the more determined to resist it. "Did it ever occur to you that maybe I wanted to be picked up by some—traveling salesman?" she challenged angrily.

His gaze narrowed to bore relentlessly all the way to her soul. "Is that what you want?"

Bravado failed her, but she managed to hold on to her poise. "All I wanted was a quiet drink before dinner and a chance to relax. If you're finally satisfied, will you please leave?"

"I'm not going to let you sit here by yourself.

71

Bring your sherry over to my table. We're going over tomorrow's schedule," Dane told her.

Sighing, Pet could see that she had about as much chance of persuading him to leave as she did of moving a mountain. If she couldn't move the mountain, the only alternative was to remove herself.

"You obviously didn't hear me. I said I wanted a quiet drink and a chance to relax. Neither would be possible in the middle of a technical discussion," she retorted, and opened her purse to take out the money for her drink and leave it on the table. "Would you please get out of my way so I can leave?"

"But you haven't had your drink." His gaze roamed over her face, stubbornly not moving until he found out her intentions.

"I'm taking it into the restaurant with me. Surely it can't be a crime if a woman has a glass of sherry in the restaurant before dining alone?" Pet challenged.

"It might be a shame, but I don't think it's a crime," he agreed, the corners of his mouth twitching slightly in amusement.

"Then would you mind getting up so I can leave?" she demanded in a voice that was growing steadily thinner with the strain of his nearness.

With the suggestion of a smile still playing at his mouth, Dane slid his brawny frame out of the booth and rolled effortlessly to his feet. The touch of his hand was pleasantly firm as he helped her out.

"We'll be playing today's tapes about an hour from now in one of the meeting rooms to make any last-minute changes. If you're through with dinner by then, you can join us." He didn't release his hold of her elbow even though she was standing and didn't require his assistance anymore.

His fingers transmitted the natural warmth generated by his body and sent it spreading up her arm. It made her flesh tingle quite pleasurably. Briefly, she was tempted by the prospect of spending more time in his company until she remembered the tapes they would be viewing. She had endured enough of his criticism for one day.

"Is that an order?" she questioned, turning to pick up her drink and thus forcing him to release her arm.

"No, you aren't required to attend." Something flickered in his look—displeasure, perhaps.

"Then I respectfully decline," Pet replied with faint mockery. "Excuse me."

Pausing long enough to inform the barmaid that she was taking her drink into the restaurant, she entered the dining room through the connecting door to the lounge. She did eat alone. It wasn't until the waiter brought her coffee that any of the crew arrived. Pet could have joined them, but there wasn't any point.

Too restless to return to her room, she wasn't in the mood for the kind of shoptalk the group would be having in the lounge, so she wandered outside to stroll around the pool area and watch the sunset from a lounge chair. Reentering the hotel, she stopped by the small gift shop and newsstand to look around.

Ruby Gale's face stared at her from the cover of a movie magazine. Curious, Pet leafed through the pages to find the article about the star. Several photographs of Ruby accompanied the write-up. One of them was a picture of the redhead and Dane Kingston lying side by side on a beach mat. Ruby Gale was wearing the scantiest bikini Pet had ever seen, but it wasn't the woman that riveted her attention.

It was Dane in his dark swimming trunks. Lean and powerful muscles rippled across his chest and shoulders and held his stomach flat. The implied strength in the sinewed columns of his legs reminded Pet of nude sculptures she had seen of Greek gods. The tight-fitting material of his swimming trunks molded his narrow hips, sending her blood pounding with its emphasis of his virile, male shape.

She quickly studied his expression. He wasn't smiling, but there was a self-satisfied look about him that indicated just as plainly that he was enjoying himself. And the lazy way his eyes were lingering on the woman beside him indicated that she was the cause of his pleasure.

Irritated at herself for becoming so absorbed in the photograph of him, Pet abruptly closed the magazine and set it back on the shelf. She was adult, no longer given to crushes on men who were unattainable. But was he unattainable, a little voice argued. She ignored the question. That kind of thinking would ultimately bring her grief. Before leaving, she bought a pack of cigarettes and promised herself she'd stop smoking soon.

Crossing the lobby, she turned down the main corridor of the hotel. Joe Wiles walked out of a meeting room, leaving the door ajar, and started down the hall ahead of her. Pet glanced in the room as she went by, but there was only a member of the hotel

74

staff inside, emptying ashtrays and carrying away the coffee cups. She quickened her steps to catch up with the heavyset man.

"How did the meeting go?" she asked.

The carpeted hallway had muffled her footsteps. Joe's balding head turned with a jerk at her question.

"You startled me," he accused without anger.

"Sorry. Did you make many changes after you saw the tapes?" She walked with him. For the time being, they were both going in the same direction.

"Surprisingly, very few, and most of those were minor," he replied. "Audio has some problems that they have to correct, but Dane was satisfied with the video. He's going to experiment with the switcher tomorrow, try for some different effects on the solo numbers."

"But it looked good?" Pet persisted. It didn't seem possible that Dane was as satisfied with the results as Joe implied.

"Of course. Did you think it wouldn't?" His smile was a little confused. "It will be even better tomorrow. Having everyone in costume will really make a difference in the finished product."

"Yes, I know it will," she agreed absently.

"What time does the dining room close?" Joe glanced at his watch. "I haven't eaten yet and I'm starved."

"I think they stop serving at eleven."

"I'd better hurry." He raised an eyebrow. "I'd like at least to wash and change my shirt before I eat."

They reached the point where the corridor

branched into two separate halls. Pet turned left. "I'll see you in the morning, Joe."

"Good night." He waved.

Arriving at the door to her room, she searched through the bottom of her bag for the key. Just as she found it, the door opened in the room directly opposite the hall from hers, and Dane stepped out.

"Is that your room?" Pet blurted in surprise.

"Yes, conveniently located to keep an eye on you." The corners of his eyes crinkled with a smile.

She hadn't expected him to admit such a thing. His frankness irritated her. She turned to unlock her door.

"As you can see, I'm retiring for the night—all alone—without any of the boys tagging after me. You don't have to worry about checking on me tonight."

"I'm not checking on you," Dane chuckled. "It's purely coincidence that my room is across the hall."

Instead of feeling better, she felt worse. She had been foolish to believe he was so concerned about her that he was virtually standing guard over her. To add to her difficulties, the lock was being its usual stubborn self and resisting her attempts to turn the key. Dane was watching her struggle with it, which made Pet even more uncomfortable.

She tried to urge him on his way. "If you're going to the dining room to eat, you'd better hurry. I think they stop serving at eleven."

"I'm not on my way to the restaurant." He crossed the hall. "Give me the key. There's a trick to unlocking hotel doors."

It was simpler to hand him the key than to argue, so she did. "Have you had dinner already?" she frowned. "I thought the meeting finished only a little while ago. I just met Joe in the hall."

"It just broke up," he agreed, and inserted the key in the lock again. "And no, I haven't had dinner."

She studied his bent head and the curling thickness of his dark brown hair, and her hands itched to run their fingers through his hair and feel those vigorous strands beneath her palms. She was shaken by the force of that unbidden desire. She clenched her hands tightly around her bag in case she unconsciously gave in to it.

"You have to eat." She tried to concentrate on the subject. "It isn't healthy to skip meals."

With a deft twist of his wrist he turned the key in the lock and pushed her door open. "Don't worry. I'll have room service send a sandwich or something up to the suite," he promised smoothly as he turned to face her.

"The suite?" she repeated. Separated from him by only a few feet, she noticed the shadows along his cheeks. The lights overhead were bright, clearly illuminating his rugged features. The darkness was obviously caused by a fast-growing beard.

Her thoughts returned to the implication of his statement. "Then you're on your way to Miss Gale's hotel."

"Yes," he nodded, and moved out of her doorway.

"At this hour?" She said exactly what was on her mind and instantly regretted it. "I'm sorry, it's really none of my business."

"It isn't," Dane agreed, but he regarded her with lazy indulgence rather than anger. "After viewing the tapes tonight, I have a couple of things I want to suggest to her before tomorrow's dress rehearsal and taping.''

''You don't have to explain to me.'' Pet didn't want him lying and making up excuses. Surely he realized that she had heard the gossip about the torrid affair he was having with Ruby Gale!

She had taken one step across the threshold into her room when his finger touched her chin and turned her head to look at him.

''Don't I?'' he queried softly.

He was suddenly very close. His rough male features seemed to fill her vision, leaving room for nothing else. Alarm fluttered her pulse, sending danger signals through her veins. She didn't dare believe what her senses were saying. Dane was on his way to see Ruby Gale. She mustn't forget that, or that photograph of the two of them in the magazine.

''Don't you think you should shave first?'' she suggested with an admirable degree of calm.

His hand was removed from her chin to rub his cheek. The action produced a faint rasping sound of beard stubble scraping across his skin. He seemed to have been unaware of the growth until she called his attention to it.

''Does it bother you if a man shows up to see you with a five o'clock shadow?'' he asked.

''It doesn't bother me,'' she shrugged. ''But I'm not Miss Gale.''

''No, you aren't.'' When he took a step forward, Pet took one backwards and bumped against the door. ''Your key.''

She felt foolish for retreating like a timid schoolgirl before her first kiss when she saw the room key in his hand. Her fingers loosened their death grip on her handbag to reach for it but they weren't given the chance to take it from him, because the key was forgotten entirely as he lowered his mouth onto hers, blotting out everything.

A splintering shock held her motionless until the warm taste of his mouth melted her stiffness. She responded easily to the persuasive ardor of his kiss, a glow spreading through her veins. There was even pleasure in the light scrape of his beard against her soft skin. Desire grew within her to deepen the kiss, to realize the potential delirium that it promised.

Something cold and flat slipped inside her blouse where the top set of buttons was unfastened. Her skin shrank from the contact, but couldn't elude it. It took her a dazed second to identify the object as a metal key. The discovery was followed close on the heels by the realization that Dane's fingers were guiding it inside the left undercup of her bra.

Before she could protest his flagrantly intimate action, Dane was lifting his head and withdrawing his hand from inside her blouse. She tried to look indignant, but she wasn't very successful—the smoldering gleam in his dark eyes told her so.

As if to prove how completely within his spell she was, he circled her left breast with his large hand. The possession was light, in no way forcing her to endure his caress, while claiming his right to do so.

"Now you've finally pleased me, Pet," he murmured in a voice that nearly melted her knees. "Get a good night's sleep, hmm?"

While she was still trying to surface, he was moving away from her and striding down the hall. In a wonderful kind of daze she stepped the rest of the way into her room and closed the door, trying to figure out how it had all happened and what it meant.

The first was easy because she recalled vividly the comment she had made in the bar that she couldn't please him. She remembered that Dane had asked if she wanted to. If that kiss was a sample, she definitely wanted to please him.

But why had he kissed her? Because she was an attractive woman and willing to be kissed? There was nothing wrong with that: it was a normal, healthy reaction. Except that Pet hoped it was more than that. She didn't like to consider the possibility that it might never happen again.

Sighing, she turned to bolt and latch the door. The action caused the room key to jab its point into the soft curve of her breast. She reached inside her blouse to take it out and return it to its rightful place in her handbag.

CHAPTER FIVE

THE NEXT MORNING it was work as usual, with a meeting scheduled first thing to go over the few changes. Other than a vague smile and nod in her direction, Dane paid no more attention to Pet than to any other member of the crew. She tried to tell herself that she wasn't disappointed, that she hadn't really expected anything different.

In an effort to show she was heart-whole and carefree, Pet threw herself into her job and worked to establish the old camaraderie with the boys. She had kissed men before without it meaning anything and forgotten it the next day. She could do so again.

It was later in the morning before they were ready to actually begin taping the dress rehearsal. The production crew had plenty to do to keep busy while the cast spent their time in Makeup and Wardrobe.

All the performers were finally on stage for the opening number except for the star, Ruby Gale. When she walked out to take her position, Pet gave an audible gasp at the gown the redhead was wearing. At first glance it didn't appear to have any sides. She stared to see why it didn't flap open and that was when she noticed the flesh-colored netting at the sides.

An assortment of reactions came over her headset from the male members of the production crew. They ranged from a breathless "Wow!" to "Sweet momma!" Amusement deepened the corners of her mouth and sent a sparkle of laughter into her green eyes.

"If I didn't know better, gang," Pet murmured teasingly into the small microphone, "I'd swear I was receiving an obscene phone call, with all this heavy breathing that's going on!"

"What's keeping that dress on?" Lon groaned.

"It must be glued." Charlie made a choked guess.

"It's sheer willpower, fellas," Pet teased, not explaining that the three-inch-wide strip of skin they saw on either side was not bare flesh but covered with netting.

Dane's voice briskly inserted itself. "Cut the chatter," he ordered. "Get the white boards up. I want color checks on these cameras again. Joe, I'm getting a hot spot on the vocal group. What's wrong?"

His briskness snapped them into action. But it didn't end the speculation or the avid interest in the daring gown and the stunning creature wearing it. Absent comments continued to find their way into the otherwise technical communication over the headset.

"If it's glued on, what do you suppose is going to happen if she starts perspiring?" Charlie wondered. "Do you think it will stay on? Will the glue hold?"

"Oh, Joe, turn up the lights and bake this stage," Lon pleaded. "Turn this into a sweat bath."

"Then bring in the fans," Andy inserted.

"All this panting is going to melt my earphones, guys," Pet warned on an impish note.

"I said cut the chatter, Wallis!" Dane barked in her ear.

It didn't matter that he was out in the large van where she couldn't see him. A mental image of him sprang into her mind—his mouth hard and tight-lipped and his dark eyes blazing. Pet was stung by the injustice of being singled out by his barbed tongue.

"Why pick on me?" she griped to herself, but forgot to push the highly sensitive microphone away from her lips. "I'm just about the only one whose eyes haven't popped out of his head."

Since she hadn't intended her comment to be heard by anyone, she visibly jerked when Dane answered her question. "That is exactly the reason. The others can't help themselves, but you can, Wallis. So straighten up!"

"Yes, sir! Anything you say, *sir!*" She masked her angry defiance with exaggerated obedience that left no one in doubt of her temper.

Any question about what last night's kiss might have meant no longer existed. As far as Pet was concerned, the meaning was clear: it had been nothing more than a passing whim. Dane was going to be hard and rough on her today to make sure she understood that and didn't get any ideas. The message was loud and clear. Pet was neither deaf nor stupid. After all, she hadn't really thought she could successfully compete with that red-haired sex goddess on stage. And she hadn't forgotten that Dane had been with Ruby Gale after he had left her.

It was another ten minutes before the floor director told the performers to take their positions on stage for the opening number. When Dane informed the crew that the tape was rolling, Claude asked for quiet and began the countdown: "Ten, nine, eight, seven, six...." He stopped there and continued it with his fingers, so his voice wouldn't be picked up on tape.

All that was mainly for the performers' benefit. Dane was issuing his own instructions prior to that. "Do you remember the sequence of the opening number, Wallis? A close-up frame of Ruby. Open it *when* I tell you and the *way* I tell you or I'll strangle you with my bare hands," he warned, and began counting. "Ten, nine, eight...." It was his countdown that the floor director repeated.

So it began. If Pet thought he had been demanding the day before, it was mild compared to the relentless way he drove the crew today. The slightest flaw or imperfection in a shot drew sharp and immediate criticism. Although everyone felt the razor edge of his tongue at some point, the majority of his censure seemed to go to Pet.

Take after take, number after number, Dane pushed them. Even when the fault belonged to the star, Ruby Gale, for missing her spot on stage or going beyond it out of camera range, it was the crew he blamed over the loudspeaker system. A couple of times Ruby flubbed the song lyrics.

Over the PA speaker Dane's voice was benevolent and forgiving as it filled the theater. "Don't worry about it, Ruby. After all the mistakes we've made, you're entitled to blow one now and then. You're perfect. You're doing great."

Silently Pet seethed at this preferential treatment for the star. Nothing remotely resembling a critical word was ever directed at Ruby Gale. Why couldn't Dane snap at her the way he did everyone else, she thought angrily. In his eyes Ruby Gale could do no wrong, while Pet couldn't seem to do anything right. She felt raw, suffering from a thousand needling remarks, oversensitized by a barrage of pinpricks.

She had the closing shot on another production number. "Hold that frame, camera two," Dane's voice advised sternly in her ear. "Hold it. Hold it!" Impatience inched into his tone and scraped at her nerves. "Okay, stop tape."

At the statement, Pet immediately closed her eyes and lowered her chin in wary relief. Her long blond ponytail swung forward to brush the top of her left shoulder. Releasing her grip on the control handles of the camera, she wiped her sweaty palms on the legs of her faded denims. She straightened to glance across the rows of seats to Andy's camera position and he gave her a crooked smile and a thumbs-up signal.

"We made it through that one," his voice murmured through her earphones.

Before she could reply, Dane's voice came over the public-address system. "Good job, gang. I think we've earned a twenty-minute break."

The richly resonant pitch of his voice vibrated over Pet. "Ah, a voice from above," Charlie joked, and lifted his hands in mock awe.

"Regardless of what he thinks, he isn't related to God Almighty," Pet muttered, assuming that Dane had already removed his headset after announcing the break.

Her mistake was quickly pointed out to her by Dane himself. "If I was related to him, Wallis, I would use my influence with him to do something about you," he said curtly. "And the next time I tell you to hold a shot, that doesn't mean you should move."

She wanted to scream at him to stop criticizing everything she did and to tell him that she had read between the lines and knew he wasn't romantically interested in her. Some perverse streak made her do just the opposite.

"Darling, it isn't any good," she cooed over the headset mike. "Everyone has guessed that you're madly in love with me. Trying to hide it by yelling at me all the time isn't fooling anybody. We can't keep it a secret anymore."

There was an incredulous laugh from someone, but it wasn't Dane. Pet knew she had invited his wrath upon her and grimly tugged off her headset. With her mouth clamped tightly shut, she hopped off the platform into the aisle.

Charlie called to her, still wearing his headset. "Hey, Pet! Dane wants to talk to you!"

Holding her head at a proudly defiant angle, she didn't slow her strides as she yelled back, "Tell him that's tough! I'm on my break!"

At the refreshment table set up for the crew, Pet skipped the insulated container of iced tea in favor of the coffee urn. It was left over from the morning break, which made it strong and inky black. Pet felt in need of its strength.

"What got into you, Pet?" Charlie came up to stand beside her. The smile on his face seemed to be there in spite of his better judgment. It was as if he admired her for talking back while he thought she was crazy for doing so.

Lon was there, shaking his head. "You really believe in flying in the face of danger, don't you?"

"I just want him off my back," she grumbled, and swore under her breath when she tried to take a drink of the scalding black coffee and burned her tongue.

The explosion of a door being forcefully slammed shut thundered through the cavernous theater and echoed in shock waves. A quick glance over her shoulder saw Dane striding toward them. Squaring around, Pet kept her back to him and hooked a thumb through the belt loop of her jeans, trying to adopt an attitude of nonchalance while studying the black liquid in her cup.

"I'm afraid you're in for it, Pet," Andy murmured, glancing at her over the rim of his drink.

With an exaggerated blink of her eyes, she pretended she didn't care. The skin along the back of her neck prickled a warning. Out of her side vision she saw Dane stop on her right, but she wouldn't look at him.

"You didn't really think you were going to get by with that, did you?" Dane sounded remarkably calm as he made the low challenge.

There wasn't an adequate reply she could make to that, so she didn't try. To cover her silence, she started to raise the cup of coffee to her mouth, but Dane reached out to take it from her.

"Hey! That's my coffee." When she tried to hold onto it, the hot coffee sloshed over the side and burned her hand, forcing her to let go. "Ouch!"

"Hold this." Dane handed the cup to Andy, then turned back to her. She was wary of the glint in his eye and the hint of a smile on his mouth. "How wonderful that everyone knows and I don't have to hide it," he taunted softly.

In the next second his hand had clamped itself on her arm to pull her toward him. Her protesting outcry was choked off by shock at the form his retaliation was taking. She tried to ward off his chest with her hands, but she was no match for his sheer brute force. His palm cupped the back of her head to hold it still, his fingers tangling in the length of her hair, while his mouth made an unerring descent onto hers.

The encircling steel band of his arm held her fast, arching her waist to bring her more fully against him. Pet had expected his kiss to be a bruising and punishing assault. There was driving force, but no brutality. He dominated her lips, moving over them as if satisfying a burning need to consume their softness. Her senses were filled with the sensation of his hard length bent protectively over hers, the thrust of his hips, and the solid muscles of his torso flattening her small breasts.

Aware of the interested spectators watching the embrace, Pet pushed at him, but the only surface available to her hands was the sides of his waist. It was an ineffectual attempt that gained nothing at all. Not that she really minded; the things his kiss was doing to her rivaled her imagination. The wild singing in her veins was hotly sweet, searing her with a buoyancy that convinced her she was floating on a cloud. She stopped resisting and began kissing him back, her hunger matching his appetite.

Before her hands could begin their final, submissive curve around his middle, Dane was drawing away. There was a disturbed roughness to his breathing and the smoldering darkness of passion in his eyes. Yet the clearest impression Pet had was the scattered cheers and applause of those around them.

The crew regarded the kiss as a huge joke, thinking that Dane had deftly turned the tables on her. And it was true. The heat of embarrassment rushed into her face, staining her cheeks scarlet. Pet couldn't remember ever blushing in her life, but she had never made such a fool of herself. For a few seconds she had forgotten all that had gone before the kiss.

She lowered her gaze to the tanned hollow of his throat, his arms still containing her within their circle.

"Why did you do that?" she asked huskily. Had she really deserved this kind of humiliation?

Dane crooked a finger under her chin and forced her to look at him before he would answer her question. "It seemed the most effective way of shutting up a smart mouth." The lazy glint in his dark eyes seemed to hold only amusement at her discomfort. "And if you do it again, the next time I'll bite off your nasty tongue." He tipped his head back and to one side, as if to get a better angle of her face. "Truce?"

Before she could answer, someone called to him

from the stage. "Miss Gale would like to see you in her dressing room, Dane."

With a sigh he loosened his hold and let Pet stand free. "I'll be right there," he replied. Reaching around, he took the cup of coffee from Andy and gave it back to Pet. As he walked past the refreshment table on his way backstage, he stopped to take two sugar cubes out of their box and tossed them to her. "Put some sugar in your coffee—it might sweeten your disposition."

Sheer reflex enabled her to catch them. "I haven't been the one snapping at everybody all day." She tossed them back, surprised she could move or speak.

"Women!" Dane turned away with a wry shake of his head.

Pet had the feeling she had just been lumped into a category labeled "Impossible." Warily, her gaze flashed around the semicircle of men, almost daring them to make a comment.

Joe Wiles was the only brave one. "If you're going to dish it out, Pet, you'd better learn to take it," he advised.

"I can take it," she insisted, and gulped down a swallow of tepid coffee.

But the crew was careful not to tease her about the kiss. Ten minutes later Claude was summoning them back to work.

THE NEXT DAY was Friday. Ruby Gale's concert was scheduled for that evening at nine o'clock. Since they were taping it before the live audience, the production crew had the morning and the bulk of the afternoon off.

Dressing for the taping that evening, Pet chose the dressier biscuit-colored slacks and a peach crepe-de-chine blouse and wrapped a brown braided rope belt around her waist. Her everyday work garb was too casual to wear in front of the public, and a dress or skirt was out of the question since she still had to climb off and on the platform.

The audience began arriving at the Garden State Arts Center half an hour before the performance was scheduled to begin. Perched on her platform in the center aisle, Pet became the cynosure of many eyes that had nothing better to do than look around while waiting for the show to start. It was amusing to listen to some of the comments.

A young brunette about her own age pointed Pet out to her date. "Look, there's a woman operating that camera."

Her date had a typical chauvinistic reply. "She's probably only a helper."

A few stopped to ask questions, most of them concerned about when the show would be seen on television. "I don't know the air date," was Pet's stock answer. "Probably in the fall or winter."

Sometimes they asked where she had learned to operate the camera. "I went to college and took courses in it."

In a way, the most difficult question to answer was why she wanted to be a cameraman. "It's what I always wanted to do," rarely satisfied them.

As the time drew closer to nine o'clock, Dane's voice came over her headset. She had barely seen him at all since yesterday's episode. The few times she had, he had been in conversation with someone else and she didn't receive any more than a preoccupied glance. In the interim, Pet thought she had got things back in their proper perspective—until she heard his voice and her pulse went skittering all over the place.

His initial comments were instructions to the crew in general, then he was directing a remark solely to her. "What about you, camera two? Do you think you have the sequence of the opening number down pat?" There was a certain drollness to his tone that implied inoffensive mockery.

"If I don't, I'm sure you'll tell me about it," she replied with surprising ease.

"You can bet on it," he chuckled softly.

"I would, but nobody will give me odds," Pet returned, joking with him.

"Watch your mouth, girl, unless you want another lesson in keeping it shut." It was a mock threat, issued with a smile in his voice that made light of yesterday's incident as if it had been all in good fun.

"Promises, promises," she faked a sigh. "That's all you men ever do—promise and forget to follow through."

"I'll remember that," he warned. Then it was back to business. "Claude, how are things moving backstage?"

"We'll be on time," the floor director promised.

"Baxter, I want you to get me plenty of audience shots," Dane instructed Lon, who had the hand-held camera. "You shouldn't have any trouble when the houselights are up. The rest of the time there should be enough light falling back on the first two or three rows to give me reaction shots, not just applause."

"Gotcha, boss."

Precisely at nine the curtain went up. Right from the opening number the first half of the show went without a hitch. The mistakes by both crew and performers were so few and minor they were practically nonexistent. It seemed that all the rehearsing, the countless takes, the endless criticisms had all paid off to achieve near perfection.

Ruby Gale's performance had been electric, charged by the applauding audience. She was sexy, stunning, scintillating, alive as Pet had never seen her before. Everything flowed with such magic that when intermission arrived Pet couldn't help wondering what would happen when the clock struck twelve and the coach became a pumpkin again. Would the spell wear off?

"Excuse me, miss." An elderly man was standing beside her platform. Pet had noticed him before since he was sitting in one of the aisle seats near her position.

She shifted the mike wand of her headset away from her lips. "Yes?" She thought he probably wanted direction to the men's room. She supposed she could always ask Andy or Charlie.

"I've been watching you and I just wanted to say that you're a very beautiful woman," he said, smiling quite benignly. "You belong in front of the camera instead of behind it."

"Thank you." Her smile was wide and wholly natural.

"I know you're busy, but I just wanted to tell you that." He nodded in a gesture of apology and turned to go back to his seat.

"What did that man want?" Charlie asked, having seen the man stop to talk to her from his camera position. "Did he want you to go out with him?"

"He was very sweet," she insisted. "He told me I was beautiful and belonged in *front* of the camera."

Dane joined the conversation to state unequivocally, "Well, you don't. You belong *behind* the camera."

"That's a pleasant switch," she drawled.

"Why?" he demanded.

"Most men think women belong in a kitchen either in *front* of a stove or *behind* a sink full of dirty dishes," Pet explained in wry amusement.

"Better you than me," Dane returned in a mocking underbreath, then crisply, "Okay, gang, we have five minutes. Five minutes!"

As Pet had feared, the second half of the show didn't run as smoothly as the first. Midway through the second number, camera three went out. They had to do some fast improvisations of camera angles to cover the shots assigned to Charlie. When the problem defied immediate rectifying, the spare camera was hurriedly carted in and mounted.

In all, camera three was out for three songs, an amazingly short period. Yet that frantic race for time had thrown everyone off tempo and they were never able to regain that effortless coordination that had made the first half of the show so flawless.

It was a relief when the concert was over and the tape stopped rolling. While the audience filed out, the crew began shutting down the equipment. It was twenty minutes after the last curtain call before Pet had finished.

"Are you driving back to the hotel with me?" Charlie called to her from across the seats.

"Yeah! But I left my bag in the van," she explained. "I'll run out and get it now. Wait for me!"

The seventy-foot-long semitrailer had seemed the safest place to leave her bag during the taping. She couldn't have kept it with her on the platform since it could have been stolen too easily. Nor had it seemed wise to leave it backstage with so many people coming and going all the time.

As she walked in front of the stage, a woman stepped out from behind the curtains. Pet had seen her before. She was usually a part of Ruby Gale's personal entourage. Pet suspected she was a secretary or something.

"Excuse me," the woman requested Pet's attention with an uplifted finger. "Could you tell me where I could find Mr. Kingston?"

"I—" Pet glanced around the theater "—haven't seen him. He might still be in the trailer outside. I'm on my way out there. Shall I send him in?"

The woman considered that, then said, "Could you give him a message?"

"Sure," Pet nodded.

"Miss Gale is leaving now for her hotel. She wanted to remind him about the party she's having in her suite tonight. Would you mention it to him? Miss Gale is most anxious that he should come," the woman added.

"I'll remind him," Pet promised.

"Hurry up, Pet!" Charlie shouted.

With a quick wave to acknowledge that she had heard him, she hurried out through a side exit to where the van was parked. Its long white-painted sides gleamed in the moonlight, emblazoned with the Kingston crest and the letters spelling out Kingston Productions. A bare light bulb illuminated the metal steps leading to the side door.

As Pet reached for the railing to climb them, the door opened and Dane stepped out. He frowned in surprise when he saw her, his gaze narrowing at her haste.

"Is something wrong?" He was down the steps and grabbing her shoulders almost before she could catch her breath. "Has something happened?"

"No, I. . . ." She was momentarily flustered by his touch. "I left my handbag in the van and Charlie's waiting to give me a lift to the hotel."

"Oh." He seemed to smile at his overreaction, and let his hands fall from her shoulders. "You'd better hurry, then. If he's ready to leave, he's probably getting impatient."

"He is." She started up the steps, brushing past him, before she remembered the message she had promised to deliver. "Oh, Dane, I forgot." She stopped and half turned, unconsciously using his given name.

"What did you forget?" He moved back within the circle of light cast by the bare bulb. There was something warm and velvety in his look that tugged at her heart.

"I think it was Miss Gale's secretary. She asked me to remind you about the party Miss Gale is having in her suite tonight," Pet explained.

"Damn!" He released a long, tired breath and

rubbed his forehead. Both his sound and his action made it plain he wasn't overjoyed by the message.

Pet watched him, feeling a little glad that he didn't look happy about going. "She also said Miss Gale was most anxious for you to come," she added.

"I don't have any choice," Dane said wryly. "It's more or less obligatory on both sides. Ruby has invited some of the local dignitaries and the press over for drinks. It's good public relations—and good publicity. It's good for her, and for this television special of mine," he explained. "It's one of those business affairs masquerading as a social event."

Pet wasn't exactly sure why he was telling her this. It wasn't really any of her business what this party was for or why he felt obligated to attend. But the fact that he had made her feel . . . well, a little important.

"That's often the case in the entertainment business, I've heard," she offered in sympathy.

"Have you ever been to one of these parties?" Dane asked, tipping his head to one side and smiling faintly.

"Heavens, no!" she laughed.

"Why don't you come with me tonight?" he suggested. "Then you'll always know what you're not missing."

For a minute she thought he was serious, then she wasn't sure. "You don't want me along." She shook her head, her long blond hair swinging loose about her shoulders, and started to climb the last steps to the van door.

"I wouldn't have asked if I didn't want you come

with me, Pet." His voice was low and almost deadly serious.

Startled, she looked back. There wasn't a hint of mockery or amusement in his roughly hewn features. His look was silently questioning as he patiently waited for her answer.

"But I'm not dressed for a party...." Pet managed a faint protest to give him a chance to back out of the invitation if he wanted to.

"As you can see, neither am I." He lifted his hands in a gesture to indicate the casualness of his beige silk shirt and brown slacks. "But I'm going like this. And they can hardly turn you away when you're with me. Are you coming? It will be a new experience for you. I can't say it will be one you'll want to repeat, but—"

"I'll never know, though—" she began.

"That's right," he agreed.

"Okay," Pet accepted, and shrugged, trying to be as offhand about the invitation as he was. "Why not?"

But she knew precisely why she was accepting. She wasn't at all curious about what the party might be like, nor the experience of it. It was the chance to spend a couple of hours with him that she was accepting. It was crazy, and probably foolish, but that was the truth.

"Go get your bag, I'll wait here for you," Dane said, and rested an arm on the railing at the bottom step.

The word "wait" reminded her. "Charlie's waiting for me. He thinks I'm going back to the hotel."

"I'll tell him to leave without you, that you'll be with me. The gang will really be confused then," he grinned. "I'll meet you here."

"Okay," she agreed.

When she opened the trailer door, Dane had disappeared into the semidarkness. Pet didn't understand this spell he had cast over her. One minute she was infuriated with him, and in the next he could have her melting in his arms. It didn't make sense, but she wasn't sure if it had to.

Her bag was right where she had left it, tucked under the bench seat inside the door. She glanced once at the multitude of television monitors across the control panel, the screens glassy and gray, all the little lights out. Behind the panel, out of sight behind the partition, was the sophisticated computer that controlled everything and turned the semitrailer van into a portable television studio, complete with all the latest electronic gear. Pet shuddered to think how much it cost, or how wealthy that made Dane, since he owned it.

CHAPTER SIX

A POWERFUL SPORTS-MODEL JAGUAR made short work of the drive to the star's hotel. Pet was surprised at how easy it had been to talk shop with Dane, as easy as it was to chat with the boys in the crew. Of course, his knowledge was far more encompassing than hers. Perhaps that was what had made his comments all the more interesting and thought-provoking.

Things she had previously regarded only from the production side, she now began to consider from the management and executive side. She had learned a great deal. She was almost sorry when Dane guided her out of the elevator and down the hallway to Ruby Gale's suite, because it meant their private conversation was coming to an end.

Gradually she realized the reason for her regret was more subtle than that. Discussing television kept her from thinking about Dane as a male escort. She had been using the talk as a defense mechanism to keep that sense of physical attraction at bay.

She realized it while they were standing in the hallway at the door to the suite, waiting for Dane's knock to be answered. His hand had found the curve of her waist, his palm covering her hipbone. The warmth of his touch was melting through her clothes to her skin, heating her flesh with an awareness of him.

Under the sweep of her lashes she slid him a look out of the corner of her eye. His roughly sculpted profile caught at her breath, disrupting its evenness. She was struck again by his height, something she didn't notice about most men since they generally weren't so much taller than she was.

As if he felt her eyes upon him, Dane's gaze swept down on her in a lazy caress that upset her heartbeat. She quivered all over inside with the desire to have him make love to her. It was faintly shocking to be so completely aroused by just a look. In delightful agitation she averted her gaze to the door, her ivory-smooth features hinting at this inner disturbance through the fluttering of her lashes and the tilting of her chin.

Dane's hand applied slight pressure on her hipbone as if he wanted to pull her closer. "You look very lovely," he murmured, and she guessed the reassurance was intended to eradicate any nervousness about her appearance. But how could she explain that a Dior gown wouldn't change the physical reaction erupting from his nearness?

"Thank you." It was a breathy answer, barely audible.

With excellent timing, the door was opened to the suite by the same woman who had given Pet the message for Dane. The polite smile she gave Dane faltered when she saw Pet with him. "Good evening, Mr. Kingston. Miss Gale will be so glad you could come."

"Hello, Clancy." There was a ghost of mockery in the look he gave the officious brunette. "You remember Miss Wallis, don't you?" he prompted as he swept Pet along with him inside the suite.

"Of course." Behind the polite nod, it was obvious the woman was trying to figure out what Pet was doing with Dane. "Miss Gale is—" The woman took a step, obviously intending to take them to their hostess.

"I see her, Clancy," Dane interrupted, glancing across the room.

Ruby Gale's red hair was a beacon, standing out in the crowd of people, mostly men. Pet had spied her almost instantly, too, but mostly she was staring at the decor of the suite. It boggled the imagination.

Pink. Everywhere there were shades of pink from the thick, powder-puff carpet to the rose velvet sofas and chairs. On nearly every other antiqued-white tabletop there were vases of flowers, mainly dark pink roses. White woodwork outlined the pastel print silk covering the walls. Even the caterers were wearing dark rose red jackets over black trousers. Pet felt as if she was gawking as Dane guided her into the main room of the suite.

Removing two glasses of champagne from a proffered tray, he pressed one into her hand, and her gaze flickered to his face in faint surprise. Amusement glittered openly in his velvet brown eyes at her stunned reaction to the room. She let her gaze sweep around it again before lifting the glass to sip the bubbling wine.

"I thought hotel suites like this existed only in Hollywood movies," she commented.

"It's horrendous, isn't it?" he agreed, keeping his voice low, too. "You should see the main bedroom. It has a round bed with a red velvet canopy draped into a rose design. I think I prefer mirrors to staring at giant red roses above my head."

A sick feeling weighted Pet's stomach. Was he speaking from experience? Of course he was. She was angry with herself for even questioning it. How else would he have known about the bed unless he'd lain in it? Only a completely naive fool would believe he had only been testing the mattress for firmness. And she wasn't naive. She had always suspected— known—that he and Ruby were lovers, so why had she accepted his invitation to this party? The answer was so plainly simple. She had a fatal fascination for this sexy, exciting man who could enrage or arouse her by turns.

This inability to resist him made her feel spineless. She took another sip of champagne, wildly hoping the effervescent spirits would temporarily stiffen her backbone. The constricting muscles in her throat rejected it with a tiny choking cough.

"I'm surprised the champagne isn't pink," she managed at last, her long fingers delicately covering her lips.

"Ruby probably didn't think of it." A smile twitched the corners of Dane's mouth as his gaze ran interestedly over her face, a little aloof. "I told you this would be an experience. You find it distasteful, don't you?"

103

There were many things she found distasteful, mainly the discovery that she was envious of Ruby Gale for the time she had spent with Dane in that round bed with the rose canopy. Although her features were schooled not to reveal her feelings, her expressive sea-green eyes obviously reflected them for Dane to see. Since he had misguessed the cause, she didn't choose to enlighten him.

"This suite, it's all so phony." Pet shrugged to show her dislike of it, lowering her gaze to the sparkling liquid in the crystal wineglass.

Dane's fingers touched her cheek to turn her face to him, then moved away. "And you aren't, are you?" He studied her more closely as if discovering something he hadn't noticed before.

Pet became uneasy under his scrutiny and immediately Dane ended it, shifting his gaze to the room of people, buzzing with hearty conversations that rang false.

"This is all part of the image," he said, a sweeping glance encompassing everything. "All of these people would have been disappointed and disillusioned if this suite had turned out to be no different from any they could have rented for one night. Ruby Gale is a star. Nothing ordinary would suit her—in their eyes. A star deserves to be surrounded by a spectacle. Ruby is smart. She gives them what they want. It keeps them coming back for more."

His narrowed gaze drifted back to Pet. She wondered if that explanation was true for him, as well. "It's fake, a fantasy world of red-hots and candy canes—sugar and spice wrapped up in glitter and sequins. It's called packaging the product.''

"I suppose that's true,'' Pet conceded with a trace of his cynicism.

"You haven't been formally introduced to the 'product,' have you?'' Dane remembered, and closed a hand on her elbow. "We'd better correct that omission before Ruby starts throwing real poisonous darts instead of invisible ones.''

Following the direction of his callously amused glance, Pet saw their hostess through a gap in the cluster of guests. Her long hair was about her white shoulders in a mass of titian curls. The daringly cut spangled gown was the same peacock-blue shade as her eyes—eyes that glittered with impatience and irritation whenever they rested on Dane, which was often.

When Dane and Pet had weaved their way through the crowd to the star's side, Ruby Gale gave Dane one of her radiantly provocative smiles. "I wondered when you were going to show up, darling,'' she chided him playfully for his tardiness, and curved a scarlet-nailed hand along the back of his neck when he bent to greet her with a kiss.

Their lips clung together a few seconds longer than the length of a merely casual kiss. Pet was prepared for the violent surge of rage that shook her. She stood motionless, her face frozen into blankness, while the three men Ruby had been speaking to exchanged knowing glances and raised eyebrows.

When Dane lifted his head, the star wiped the traces of lipstick from his mouth with her fingers.

The gesture, more than the kiss, implied a long-standing familiarity and intimacy between them. It was also possessive. Pet was rigidly aware that Dane didn't protest against any of it.

Then the redhead was linking both her arms though the crook of his elbow, further staking her claim to him while turning to the trio she was with. "You all know Dane Kingston—my producer, my director, my—" Ruby paused deliberately, sweeping him a look through her long lashes as if exchanging a secret "—dear friend."

The phrase drew a faint smile from Dane, which made a total mockery of it. Pet would have slipped away, but he chose that moment to remember she was with him and turned to take her hand, drawing her within the circle. She half expected to be murdered by Ruby's blue eyes, but they seemed blank of expression when they regarded her. Her burgundy-glossed lips were parted in a welcoming smile of interest.

"I don't believe I know this young woman, do I, Dane?" she asked, and extended an open hand to Pet.

Pet let her hand be clasped warmly by the star and even managed a stiff smile. Pride kept her head high while a defensiveness masked her gaze with a wary coolness.

"How do you do, Miss Gale," she greeted the redhead with exaggerated politeness.

"You haven't actually met her before, Ruby," Dane explained. "But you have spent the last few days looking at her without knowing it. This is Petra

Wallis. She's been operating the number-two camera."

"The center one?" Now the star's gaze became sharp, slicing Pet into unimportant pieces. "You actually have a woman in sole charge of a camera? I didn't realize you were so liberated in your views, Dane. You've never exhibited that tendency before."

"Haven't I? Maybe you just never noticed," he suggested, turning aside the comment.

"Are you his token female, Miss Wallis?" the star inquired archly. In explanation to the other men, Ruby Gale defended her question. "With all these new laws nowadays about hiring women for traditionally male jobs, it's almost mandatory for an employer to hire a woman if she applies for a position. Me, I'm not in favor at all of this new equality for women. I love being the weaker sex, and dominated by a big, strong man." Her glance at Dane made it obvious who that "big, strong man" was.

Pet seethed with jealousy and the sensation of betrayal by one of her own kind. What Ruby Gale was insinuating was insulting and demeaning to her. Worse, the three men with their glasses of champagne and lascivious looks were nodding agreement with Ruby Gale's remarks.

"I can assure you that I wasn't forced to hire Miss Wallis," Dane inserted lazily. "Her sex had nothing to do with her employment. I doubt if it was even taken into consideration by anyone in the company."

His support didn't bring the reassurance that it should have. Instead, one of the younger men—a reporter by the cynical look of him—gave Pet an assessing look that stripped her quite naked. Anger flashed in her eyes, the turbulent green of storm-tossed seas.

"I certainly could never interview you, Miss Wallis, without being conscious of your sex," he remarked suggestively, and everyone chuckled in total agreement.

Pet struggled to contain her anger. Usually she could ignore such biased and prejudiced remarks from men, dismissing them as small remarks from small minds. Yet she was bristling from them.

"It's a shame that employers are forced by law to hire incompetent help. It's so expensive in the long run," Ruby Gale was saying, and turned to Dane. "Just look at all the delays and technical problems we encountered taping this concert simply because of one or two unskilled members of the crew."

"As a professional, Ruby, you know there are always problems of one kind or another," Dane stated with a hard glint in his eyes. "But you certainly can't blame Miss Wallis. She's the best technician in the company—that's why I put her on camera two. When you're on center stage you deserve to have the best covering you, so I made certain you had it. You'll see for yourself when we review the tapes of tonight's performance."

"My, my!" The redhead blinked her startling blue eyes and teased him with a smile. "Such praise coming from you, Dane!" Her gaze shifted to Pet, who had been stunned and skeptical of his assertive defense. "You must be very flattered."

108

"I am," she admitted, since flattery also implied exaggeration.

"Is that why you brought Miss Wallis to the party? As a reward for all her work?" Ruby questioned, and rose on tiptoe to kiss his cheek. "How sweet of you, darling! You really are very thoughtful."

The conclusion Ruby had reached sent Pet's mind racing. Was that the explanation for this unexpected invitation? Was she to regard her attendance at this party as a bonus for a job well done? She had liked it better when she believed it was just a friendly invitation.

"I'm not certain if Pet would agree with you, Ruby." Dane commented, and sent a roguish glance in her direction. "I think she's convinced I'm a cross between an ogre and a tyrant."

"You neglected to mention an interfering busybody," Pet reminded him smoothly.

"So I did," he agreed, and lifted his champagne glass in wry acknowledgement of the omission.

"What's this all about?" Ruby glanced from one to the other, suspicion shimmering in her hard blue eyes.

"A minor rebellion in the ranks against authority." Dane dismissed their previous skirmishes with an indifferent shrug of a shoulder and sipped at his wine. "I neglected to tell you how sensational you were this evening, Ruby. You had the audience in the palm of your beautiful hand all the time."

Diverted by his compliment, the redhead beamed, "Thank you, darling."

"Hear, hear," one of the men murmured in agreement, and lifted his glass in a silent toast to her successful performance.

"Yes, to a very triumphant performance by our own Jersey Lily." A second man made it a verbal salute.

"In case you men haven't noticed it, your star is a tiger lily—a wild, exotic flower," Dane remarked with an admiring glance running warmly over the titian-haired entertainer.

Pet could almost see the reporter making a mental note of the phrase. She was certain it would show up somewhere in the postperfomance publicity.

"You know all the right things to say to make a woman feel special, Dane," Ruby purred, and let her hand glide along his arm to curl her fingers through his. "I should be upset with you for bringing a blond to my private party, but here I am—putty in your hands."

"Never putty," he denied, and lifted her fingers to his mouth with continental ease. "Rare blue clay, maybe."

Her faint laugh was a low, throaty sound. "I never know whether to believe you. I guess that's part of your dangerous charm," the star suggested. For once, Pet was in total agreement with the red-haired performer, regarding her assessment of Dane Kingston.

Ruby slipped her hand out of the loose clasp of his fingers. "But I really must circulate, darling. You're making me neglect my guests. Be sure to introduce. . . Miss Wallis around."

"I will," he replied smoothly.

Pet had the distinct impression that Ruby Gale had given him permission to escort her. It would have proved more bolstering to her self-esteem if the star had resented Dane's accompanying her. This way the woman obviously didn't regard her as representing a serious threat.

The three men introduced themselves, but Pet didn't make an effort to remember their names. Dane chatted with them a few minutes, then took Pet by the arm to wander to another group. The procedure was repeated several times, and Pet realized that Dane was doing his own brand of circulating, advertising his product and making himself known to those who were important. A necessary part of any business was socializing.

But she had a great deal of difficulty relaxing in his company. She could talk quite naturally with others, yet could manage only a stiff nod or some stilted reply when Dane addressed a remark to her. Tension began drumming at her temples, demanding a respite from the constant strain of his presence.

A particularly garrulous guest had trapped Dane into a conversation about the merits of the present television programming, and Pet took the opportunity to touch his arm lightly to briefly claim his attention.

"Excuse me, I'm going to freshen my lipstick. I'll only be a few moments," she murmured as his gaze wandered over her mouth to assess the need.

Without waiting for his permission, Pet moved away. The brunette secretary whom Dane had addressed as Clancy showed her where the ladies' powder room was located in the suite, and Pet sank onto the strawberry velvet stool in front of the lighted mirror and gazed at her reflection.

A pair of plain gold studs gleamed on the lobes of her ears. The sides of her long hair were pulled high on the crown of her head and secured with a wide gold barrette. Strong, mat-smooth features were sculpted in clean, pure lines of classical symmetry rather than prettiness. With its jade eyes, it was an arresting face that would wear well.

Pet saw the absence of raw sensuality and animation. Noting the pallor of her lips, she removed the tube of gloss from her bag and outlined her mouth with the burgundy stick. She ran a comb through the ends of her hair and flipped it down the center of her back. With a sigh she accepted the fact that her cool blond sophistication was no competition for the earthy appeal of the auburn temptress.

Entering the spacious main room of the suite, she spied Dane with a state politician, and the independent streak in her asserted itself. Instead of making her way to his side, she wandered over to the hors d'oeuvres table, sampled some caviar, which she loved, and stuffed mushroom buttons, then accepted another glass of champagne.

"It's quite an affair, isn't it?" a cynical male voice remarked to the right of her elbow.

Turning her head, Pet glanced down at the man easily three inches shorter than she was. She resisted the age-old impulse to hunch her shoulders, an impossibility with the thin shoulder pads under her peach silk blouse. The man was familiar, but it was a

112

second before she remembered he was one of the three who had been talking to Ruby Gale when she and Dane had joined them. At the time she had decided he was a reporter.

"Yes, it is." She continued to stand straight and tall.

"Petra Wallis, isn't it?" he remembered her name.

"Either you have an excellent memory or else you know everyone else here," Pet replied with a wry look over the rim of her champagne glass.

"It's a combination," he admitted. "I know most of the people who are here, remembering names is part of my trade, and a man would he a fool to forget yours."

He smiled for the first time without some inner cynicism. In his late thirties, he wasn't really an unattractive man without that expression of bored superiority. Plain brown hair and shrewd brown eyes went with his unassuming features. As his gaze made a thorough study of her, it didn't contain the suggestive stripping quality that he had subjected her to before. Pet didn't feel any of the initial hostility he had generated in their earlier meeting.

"I know you've probably forgotten. The name is Nick Brewster." He wasn't offended that she had.

"You're with the newspaper, right?" She wasn't sure if she had been told or if it was only a guess.

"Yeah, I'm doing a feature article on the 'Tiger Lily' for the entertainment section. I'll probably send it around—syndicate it to a few other papers." He shrugged to hide the boasting tone, then studied her again. "You might have given me an idea on a different angle."

"Me?" Pet was startled.

"Yeah. The star through the eyes of a television camera." He made an imaginary frame with his hands.

"I'm not sure that I understand what you mean." She shook her head, vaguely confused.

"I'd be writing it from your viewpoint," the journalist explained. "What Ruby Gale is like to work with, that kind of thing. You've seen her in rehearsal and in concert. How is she different?"

"That's easy. Before an audience she's electric. When she's rehearsing, she's concentrating on technique, delivery, the routine." Pet didn't see how that was particularly interesting or new.

"But what about her temperament? Is she congenial to work with? Demanding?"

She began to see where his questions were leading. "Naturally she's demanding—of herself and everyone else."

"Come on, Miss Wallis, you can tell me." The reporter eyed her with a mocking yet confiding look. "It's common knowledge that she can be a temperamental bitch, throwing tantrums, walking off the stage. From some of the things I've overheard, this last session hasn't been without its problems."

"Of course we've had some problems," Pet admitted. "But I haven't seen any evidence of this temper you're describing."

He raised a skeptical eyebrow. "Dane must have her eating out of his hand!" When Pet showed signs of becoming aloof, he chided her, "Everyone knows that the two of them are having an affair. They aren't trying to hide it, even if he did drag you here."

"I wouldn't presume to discuss Mr. Kingston's private life with you, even if I were privy to any of that kind of information—which I'm not," she retorted. "I'm an employee, nothing more."

"Such loyalty!" he mocked her, his gaze sliding sideways. "It should be rewarded, Mr. Kingston. But I forgot," he pretended as Pet turned to find Dane standing near her elbow, "this invitation to the party was by way of a reward."

"You should ask who's being rewarded, Mr. Brewster." Dane smiled pleasantly and laced his fingers through hers. "Maybe the pleasure of Miss Wallis's company is my compensation for a week of hard work and long hours."

"I wouldn't be surprised," the reporter laughed. "Some people can have their cake and eat it, too."

"Then you won't mind if I don't share. Excuse us."

Dane led Pet away. The smile faded from his expression, if it had ever really been there at all, and his dark gaze was sharp as it examined her. "I'm sorry. I hope Brewster didn't subject you to too much of his dirty digging."

"He didn't." She was curt as she pulled her hand free from him. She disliked being used as a red herring. "Not that it matters. I'm not in the habit of airing other people's dirty linen, even if I had possession of it—which I don't."

"What's that supposed to mean?" Impatience clipped his voice.

"It means that I didn't have any 'dirt' to give him," Pet shrugged with feigned indifference and refused to meet his gaze.

"He did upset you," he concluded grimly.

"He didn't," she insisted. If she was upset, it was because of the round bed with the rose canopy, Dane's insincere praise of her skill, the nonthreat she was to Ruby Gale and the farcical invitation to this party. "I have been around television and news reporters before. I didn't need to be rescued."

"I can't win with you, can I?" Dane sighed with thinly disguised anger. "I try to do a good deed and I'm accused of meddling again."

"Is that my fault?" Pet countered defensively.

"I had hoped for a pleasant evening, not another one of our verbal matches of word slinging." The reply was underlined with tautness.

On that, Pet agreed. "Perhaps we're both tired. It's been a long, tension-filled evening in many respects." She was thinking of more than the taping.

"Yes." But there was a grim reluctance in his acceptance of her explanation. "We'd better make our apologies to Ruby and leave."

Without waiting for her reply, he cupped a hand under her elbow and guided her to the corner of the room where the flame-haired woman was flirting with one of the several politicians in attendance.

"Darling!" When Ruby Gale saw Dane, she must have read his intention in his face. "You're not leaving so soon?"

"We must," he said firmly, and sent an aloofly apologetic glance to the others for having interrupted them. Smoothly, he bent forward to kiss an artfully rouged cheek.

"I suppose you must," Ruby sighed, and let her glittering blue eyes wander to Pet. "After all, Miss Wallis is a working girl." The tone seemed to relegate Pet to an inferior class. "Call me tomorrow, darling. But not too early."

"It probably won't be until the afternoon. I'll be busy in the morning," Dane replied.

"Good evening, Miss Gale," Pet inserted so she wouldn't be ignored or treated as if she weren't there.

"Good evening, Miss Wallis." The phrase was returned, but most indifferently.

Then Dane's hand was on her waist, guiding her away toward the door. When the stocky secretary appeared Dane dismissed her with a brisk, "We can find our own way out. Good night, Clancy."

"Good night, Mr. Kingston."

CHAPTER SEVEN

THE SILENCE BETWEEN THEM was almost tangible, charging the air with crackling undercurrents. Not a word had been spoken since they had left Ruby Gale's hotel. Pet sat motionless in the bucket seat, an arm resting on the padded upholstery covering the door, a hand covering her mouth while she stared out of the side window of the car.

She ached inside—ached for the pleasure that could have been. If things had been different! But they hadn't. The evening had been a disastrous experience. She would rather have not discovered how deeply attracted she was to Dane Kingston, how jealous she could be and how easily hurt. The one consolation was that such intensity couldn't last; it would burn itself out. She had only to wait. In the meantime it was sweet agony to be sitting beside this vitally male member of the opposite sex, and forcing herself to ignore him.

In an empty parking stall next to the side entrance of the motel, Dane braked the car to a stop and switched off the powerful engine. Feeling his gaze burrowing into her, Pet collected the leather handbag from her lap and reached for the door handle, but Dane was quicker, leaning over to seize her wrist and prevent her escape. His arm was an iron band running diagonally across her, the sensitive nerve ends in her breast aware of every rippling outline of his muscles beneath the silken material of his shirt sleeve.

"What's bothering you, Pet?" His voice was low and taut with command.

Her head turned away from the door to bring him into her side vision, but she didn't look at him. She was conscious of the hard cast of his features, the determined grimness in the set of his jaw, and the harshness of his thin mouth.

"Nothing's bothering me," she insisted in cool dismissal.

"Something is," Dane persisted, not relaxing his hold so she could open the door. "And I don't believe it had anything to do with that reporter Brewster anymore. You were acting like this before he cornered you."

"I don't know what you're talking about," Pet lied in a weary breath. "I'm tired, so will you please let go of my hand? I'd like to go to my room and get some rest."

For a long second she didn't think Dane was going to release her. A barrage of suffocating sensations closed in on her. The air was warmly thick with the male scent unique to him, spiced with a whiff of his after-shave lotion. Under his muscled arm her heart was drumming its panic, while her flesh quivered ecstatically beneath his touch.

Then the talon-hard grip of her wrist was loosened and the restricting band of his arm was removed, setting her free. She sensed the impatience and irritation in his action, just as if he knew he could have obtained a truthful answer if he had pursued it. She was grateful he hadn't as she climbed out of the sports car. Simultaneously the door was slammed on the driver's side.

The summer night air was refreshingly cool against her heated face. Dane was waiting on the sidewalk to walk with her to the side entrance of the hotel, his eyes never relaxing their inspection of her until she was at his side. Pet held her head unnaturally high, keeping her face empty of expression.

Dane made no attempt to touch her, no guiding hand touched her arm or waist as they walked. There was something aloofly mocking in the way he held the door open for her to enter the building first, a tinge of smoldering anger in his brown eyes.

When they reached her room door, Pet already had the key out of her bag but, before she could make a move to unlock the door, Dane was taking the key from her hand and turning coldly to insert it in the lock. Her pulse was racing with the memory of the last time he'd done it, and the result.

At the click of the lock, Dane pushed the door open and stepped aside. The key was in his hand, yet he seemed hesitant to return it to her, as if he, too, was remembering the last time. She held her breath for those few seconds. When he started to hand it to her, she knew she had to say something to him before going inside.

"Thank you for a lovely evening," she coolly recited the meaningless phrase that was intended to dismiss him.

A savage anger darkened his expression. "Don't pawn that polite garbage off on me!" he rejected it with a low snarl. "It was a lousy evening and we both know it."

"All right, it was!" Pet agreed sharply, reacting to his anger out of self-defense. She forgot about the key in her need to get inside the room and shut the door on him.

Before she could succeed, his outstretched arm had stiffened to keep the door jammed open. "I want to know why," he demanded.

The hollow wood door seemed an inadequate shield against the man filling its frame and bracing it open with an arm. Yet Pet stood partially behind it, taking advantage of whatever protection it offered. The silken material of his beige shirt was stretched across his male physique, outlining his muscled torso and intimidating her with the contained strength that lay beneath it.

"Maybe I don't like being patronized!" she flared. "Did that ever occur to you?"

He shoved the door all the way open, pushing her backward as if her weight against it were no more of a deterrent than a feather. His long stride carried him past the door.

"You're going to explain that remark!" he snapped, stopping before she felt threatened enough to retreat in the face of his advance.

With a backward push of his hand he sent the door swinging shut, although it didn't latch, only fell closed in its frame. His hands were on his hips, his stance challenging. Pet found the strength to confront him with all the many wounds to her pride she had endured that night.

"For starters, I didn't appreciate those absurdly

flattering things you told Ruby Gale about me," she retorted.

"What things?" He looked taken aback, startled confusion entering his harsh frown.

"You know very well what things!" Pet stormed. "Those ridiculous lies that I was the best cameraman in the group! If you felt you had to defend me and rationalize my presence for her benefit, you could have simply said I was good. You didn't have to insult me with all that false praise!"

Her voice was choking on the last. Conscious of the sting of bitter tears pricking her eyes, she pivoted before he noticed, intending to put distance between them, but Dane grabbed her arm and spun her back.

"False praise!" he exploded.

"Yes!" She twisted her arm, trying to pull it out of his hold, but his fingers tightened to dig into her flesh.

"You little fool, that happened to be the truth," he muttered through clenched teeth.

"Oh, come on now!" Pet derisively mocked him. "I should have made a tape recording of the cross talk." That was the term for the communication over the headsets. "Some of your rebukes were positively scathing!"

When she tried to walk away, Dane turned her back and pinned her shoulders to the wall. "You're not going anywhere," he informed her roughly. "You're going to stay right here and listen to me!"

"I'm not interested in hearing any more of your lies!" But she didn't have any choice. His arms were the bars trapping her between the wall and his towering frame.

"Then listen to reason," he demanded, and brought his face close to hers, his tanned features etched with fierce determination and suppressed anger. "You must have some small idea of how much money I have wrapped up in this special. Do you think that I chose this production crew at random? Every member I personally handpicked, because I wanted the best! And that includes you! I've reviewed everything you've done. I knew I was borrowing trouble by bringing a single woman on location—a *beautiful* single woman, I might add. But trouble or not, I'd have the best. That's why you're here, so what I told Ruby wasn't a lie."

His explanation made sense, but Pet couldn't relate it to the way he'd treated her these past few days. She eyed him warily, distrusting her ability to sort fact from fiction where he was concerned. He simply had too much influence over her ability to reason.

"Is that what made you angry, Pet?" he questioned in a gentler tone as his gaze roamed over her face, then paused to linger on her mouth and watch it form an answer.

"You're always making me angry." That was easy to admit. "You're always saying something to irritate me."

"The next time I do," he murmured, moving closer, "why don't you try kissing me? I guarantee it will shut me up."

Bending his head, he took her lips. Pet stood very still, inwardly shaking with the desire to put her arms around him, but she permitted her hands to go no farther than his chest, resting lightly on his shirt and feeling the heat of his body warm her palms. His mouth moved powerfully against her own, parting her lips and invading them with a hot sweetness.

A whirl of confused sensation began taking over her body, spinning a fine web of dazzling brilliance. His hands pulled her from the wall and into the support of his arms. When his mouth grazed a path across her cheek to the lobe of her ear, Pet dipped her head against his shoulder in mute surrender, clinging to him.

"Why did you say those things?" she murmured, still not understanding that part. "Why did you make me think you believed I was incompetent?"

"I never intended you to think that." His voice was soft against her ear, his mouth brushing the cool metal of the gold stud earring. "I couldn't tolerate anything but the best from you because I knew you could give it to me. You could always give it to me."

There was the heady implication that he was referring to more than her work. His hands glided slowly over her spine to press her against his hard, lithe body. Her head was spinning as he kissed her throat and followed the wildly pulsing vein in her neck to the sensitive hollow below her ear. Then he was seeking her lips again, consuming her with his hunger. Pet struggled for some semblance of control before he undermined it completely.

"That party—" her lips were against his cheek, their moist softness scraped by the rough stubble of his beard, increasing their sensitivity "—was it a reward for doing a good job?" With each breath she inhaled the intoxicating smell of him and weaved at its potency. "Is that why you invited me?"

"That damned party was the last place I wanted to go tonight," he muttered, lifting his head to satisfy himself that she did look kissed and aroused. "But I had to go. It was as compulsory for me to attend as it was for Ruby to give it. And I knew the crew would be having a celebration of their own. If you weren't with me, you'd be with them."

"So you were just keeping me out of trouble again." Hurt, she flattened her hands against his chest, resisting, yet aware of the heavy beat of his heart.

"I wasn't looking after you." Dane shook his head wryly. "I was looking after me. You get into a man's blood, Pet. I thought I had a chance of enduring that insufferable chatter if you were with me, but it all went sour within minutes after we arrived, and I couldn't understand why. I thought you wanted to be with me as much as I wanted to be with you."

"Did you really?" She wanted to believe him, but she was afraid to. The doubt glistened in her green eyes.

"Can you doubt it?" he demanded, and crushed her lips beneath his mouth, devouring them in a rapacious assault of passion that left her breathless and dazed.

The pressure of the hand at the small of her back was fiercely possessive. She was hardly conscious of his other hand moving to stroke her hair. His fingers found the gold barrette that secured the top and sides in a single clasp at the crown. With a deft snap he unfastened it to let the silken length tumble free, and a half-muffled groan rippled from his throat as he tunneled his hand beneath the golden mass.

"I've wanted to do that for so long." His mouth formed the words against hers, roughly moving over her lips with uncontained urgency.

Desire flooded her mind and body, sweeping her high on a tide of emotion that was dizzying. In Dane's arms, held close to his hard shape, Pet forgot about the round bed and the rose canopy, and his ongoing affair with Ruby Gale. His dominating kiss could make her forget everything but this aching need for his possession, to be a part of his hard male vitality.

His shirt became an irritating barrier, keeping her from the closeness she sought. Her eager fingers found the row of buttons and began unfastening them one by one until the metal buckle of his belt stopped them. Unable to resist any longer, she slid her hands inside his shirt and over his hard, flat stomach to caress the taut skin covering his rib cage. His hand took the same license, slipping off the rope belt to glide under her blouse onto the bare skin of her back. When it moved to the front to enclose a firm breast in its palm, a searing joy quivered through her.

The loud voice singing in the hallway made little impact on her passion-charged senses, which blocked out the intrusion of noise. The crew's merrymaking had no part in her sensual revelry.

"Hey, Pet!" A loud, slurring voice remarkably resembling Lon Baxter's called her name. "Wake up! You've got to come to the party!"

The first hand to pound on the unlatched door swung it open while the combination of noise and movement cleaved their lips apart, but there wasn't any way they could untangle their hands from inside each other's clothes. In cold shock, Pet stared at Lon and the handful of other crew members clustered around her door.

Dane recovered a shade quicker than she did, withdrawing his hand from under her blouse to let it rest reassuringly on her arm. His action drew her glance, and she shuddered at the grimness in his features and the accusing silence from her co-workers.

"The door was open," someone mumbled in an attempt at an apology.

"Yeah," Lon agreed, swaying belligerently in the opening. "We wanted to invite you to our party, but you were having a little private one of your own, weren't you, Pet?"

The color that had receded from her cheeks came flooding back. She looked away from the door, pushing at the rumpled length of hair near her ear. Vaguely she was conscious of someone urging Lon to come away from the door, then Dane was letting her go to button his shirt.

"*All* the parties are over, boys," he stressed in a tired voice. "It's time we all called it a night. We have to tear down and pack the equipment first thing in the morning."

A few embarrassed mumbles of agreement followed his statement. The quiet shuffling of feet was a vast contrast to their exuberant, revel-rousing arrival as the men retreated down the hallway.

"Pet?" His quiet use of her name lifted her head. Dane was near the open door, half-turned to study her.

"You'd better leave," she said stiffly. "They'll hang around to see if you go."

"I'm aware of that," he replied dryly.

Staying close to the wall, she moved to the door and wrapped her fingers on the knob to close it while keeping a distance from him. Aftershock had started her thinking about the round bed with its giant rose canopy and a red-haired woman in his arms.

"Good night." It was a tight sound, but she accompanied it with a proud toss of her head.

Dane took a half step toward her, his mouth thinning, then stopped. "Good night."

As soon as he was in the hall, Pet closed the door and locked it. She leaned against it, her knees shaking in reaction. Across the hall she heard his door open and close, then silence.

She managed to keep her mind blank as she undressed and slipped on her nightdress. Switching off the light, she crawled under the covers of her empty bed. A few minutes earlier she wouldn't have been lying there alone, she realized, and tightly closed her eyes. The thought started a war between regret and gratitude. There wasn't a clear-cut victor by the time she fell asleep.

FIRM AND WARM, a mouth eased itself onto her lips, gently moving over them to explore their curves. It coaxed them into a sensual pliancy, masterfully persuading a response. A sharp, masculine fragrance tingled her nose, clean, fresh and divinely heady.

What a delicious way to wake up, Pet thought as that warm mouth drifted kisses over her cheek and jaw. She arched her neck to allow access to the sensitive skin along its curve, and the mouth nibbled a slow path to the base of her throat and returned up the other side.

A soft, sensuously contented sound came from her throat, inviting that pair of masculine lips back to hers to urge a further response. Arms that had been flung above her head in sleep were lifted to find the one who was causing all these wonderful sensations. Her languorous hands encountered a muscled set of wide shoulders encased in some smooth material that allowed her to feel the contoured outline of his hard flesh.

A forearm rested on the mattress alongside her to position him above her while his other hand caressed the bare skin near the curve of her opposite shoulder. It was all so beautiful, so enchanted—like a dream that had come to life. Dane felt so solid and real, his thick springing hair curling around her fingers as she curved them to the back of his neck.

Gradually it dawned on her that the dream was real. It was all the better when she slowly lifted her lashes and saw that rugged face poised an inch above her own. Finding him sitting on her bed and kissing her awake was much too pleasant a surprise for Pet to be shocked. Her initial reaction was curiosity. She shifted her head on the pillow to get a better look at him, her gaze wandering to the lazy half curve of his mouth and her hands sliding from his back to his arms.

"How did you get in here?" she murmured with a flicker of a curious frown.

"I forgot to return your key last night. Evidently I

slipped it in my pocket," he explained absently while his fingers stroked the delicate curve of her neck. "This morning I found it when I was transferring my keys and change from my brown pants to these."

"What time is it?" she wondered, rousing a bit from her delicious lethargy.

"Seven-thirty," Dane admitted, and bent his head to let his tongue trace the hollow of her throat.

For an instant Pet surrendered to the provocative sensation. Then his answer awakened alarm bells in her head. She shrank against the mattress to end the distraction of his caress.

"Is it that late?" Pet protested. "I have to be at the center by eight to help pack up the equipment."

"I know," he sighed, and lifted his head. "I stopped at the desk to leave your key. That's when I realized you'd probably forgotten to leave a wake-up call. I checked with the clerk and he verified it, so I used the key to do it personally."

"You could have used the house phone," she pointed out impishly.

"This is much more rewarding." He was so close, his mouth brushed her lips when he spoke. "I fully intended to wake up with you this morning until we were so rudely interrupted. This is the next best thing."

Pet wished he hadn't brought that up. It reminded her of the stunned and accusing expressions that had been on the faces of the boys when they had accidentally barged in on her and Dane. She knew it wasn't because they had caught her in the arms of a man. No, it was worse than that. She had been in the arms of their boss.

"You'd better let me up." She nudged him with her hands in a gentle reproof to move. "I still have to get dressed."

"I have a better idea," Dane murmured, settling more firmly into place. "Instead of you getting up, why don't I climb into bed?"

"No!" Her refusal was too quick and too weak, because she had never been exposed to a sweeter temptation in her life.

"Why not?" It wasn't a question to which he expected an answer as his mouth traveled onto her lips as soft as a wind song, and the probing point of his tongue traced their outline.

His fingers slid the strap of her nightdress off her shoulders. It immediately loosened the dark lace of the gown's bodice, allowing his hand to slide inside and cup her breast. Pet breathed in sharply in an unconscious and searing response. With masterful ease Dane explored and caressed its sensitive point into pebble hardness.

It took a concerted effort to turn her mouth away from his tantalizing kiss. "Dane, I have to go to work," she insisted tremulously.

"Have you forgotten?" He laughed softly against her throat, confident and male. "I'm the boss. I'm giving you the morning off."

"A special assignment?" She resented the use of his authority.

"If you want to call it that." He missed the hint of bitterness in her tone. "I want you, Pet. I want to make love to you." An element of urgency entered the rough pressure of his mouth against her cheek, rubbing closer to the edge of her lips. "I'll see that you're satisfied, too—I've been told I'm a good lover. But with you, Pet, I'll be even better."

He should have known it was the wrong thing to say. With a muffled cry Pet twisted from beneath him and rolled to the opposite side of the bed from where he was seated. She came quickly to her feet, grabbing the thin cotton robe draped over the end of the bed. A dark frown of confusion clouded his face.

"Who told you you were good?" Pet stormed. "Ruby Gale? While you were lying in her round bed with the giant rose overhead?"

"What the hell are you talking about?" he demanded, coming to his feet to glare at her across the width of the bed.

She hurriedly tugged the robe on. "This hotel room doesn't come equipped with mirrors on the ceiling. You'd better find yourself another room!"

"Will you make sense?" Dane exploded.

"I am making sense!" Pet retorted. "That's what makes it so...awful!" She choked on the last and pivoted away, blinking at the tears filling her eyes.

"We aren't going to start this again," he warned.

The knock on the door was a welcome interruption. "Yes? Who is it?" Her voice was strained. She quickly wiped at the trickle of tears on her cheek.

"It's me, Lon. Aren't you awake yet?" There was a taut frown in the answer he called.

"Damn!" she cursed softly. Of all people, why did it have to be him? Or was he checking up on her because of last night? Behind her there was a faint sound from Dane that suggested similar irritation, but Pet wouldn't turn around to look.

132

"Yes, I'm awake," she answered back, her voice growing steadier in its volume.

"When you didn't show up for breakfast, I thought I'd better check," Lon replied in explanation of his presence. "What did you do? Oversleep?"

"Yes," Pet admitted. "Thanks for checking."

"I've brought you some coffee."

Which meant she had to open the door. She threw an anxious glance over her shoulder at Dane. His mouth was compressed in a tight, hard line, a grimly resigned expression on his features. She pushed her tousled hair away from her ear and walked reluctantly to the door, holding the front of her robe shut.

Behind her, Dane made no attempt to conceal himself from view. Lon saw him standing at the end of the bed the instant she opened the door and his gaze flashed over Pet in silent condemnation.

"I should have known why you overslept," he jeered.

"It isn't like that at all," Pet denied his conclusion in a weary voice.

"Like you, I also noticed she wasn't around," Dane inserted. "I brought her coffee, too. One cup." He lifted a Styrofoam cup to show the camerman. "So you can lift your imagination out of the gutter."

"Listen, you may be Dane Kingston, the big man around here—" Lon stabbed an angry finger in the air adopting a belligerent stance "—but you want to crawl in bed with her the same as I do!"

Pet shivered at the cold rage that flashed across Dane's face. "I'm going to forget you said that, Baxter. Now get out!" he snapped.

"Like hell!" Lon took a step forward.

"No, please." Pet half lifted a hand to stop him. "Both of you leave. Mr. Kingston was just going anyway...weren't you?" She cast a challenging look at Dane, her heart hammering at her ribs. The last thing she wanted was an ugly scene.

He held her gaze for a fraction of a second, then strode forward. His hard glance flicked over her as he brushed past her into the hallway occupied by Lon Baxter. There had been a promise in his look that their discussion wasn't over, merely postponed.

"I'll wait for you in the lobby, Pet," Lon stated.

She simply nodded and closed the door. Her gaze strayed to the bed and the rumpled covers. A weakness attacked her legs, but she made them support her. What had begun as a blissful awakening had ended in such turmoil that she felt torn apart.

Pet released her tense frustration in a flurry of activity, going to the closet and dragging out her faded jeans. She grabbed a soft chamois blouse, as well, and tossed them both on the bed.

CHAPTER EIGHT

PET DRESSED in a hurry, taking time only to put some lipstick on and tie a green scarf into a knot that gathered the hair at the nape of her neck. Leaving the room, she mentally braced herself for Lon's inquisition, but he wasn't in the lobby when she reached it.

Dane was, however, looking out a window in a relaxed stance. But when he turned to meet her, she realized he wasn't relaxed at all. He was a coiled spring, all poised to unleash that contained energy.

"Where's Lon?" Pet glanced around, knowing she wouldn't find him, but the action provided her with a few seconds to readjust her defenses.

The dark impatience of his eyes swept her. "I imagine he's at the center by now."

"He said he'd wait for me," she reminded him.

"I changed his mind." Dane stated what she had already guessed.

"I fully hope that you intend to give me a ride, otherwise I'll be without transportation to work." There was the right inflection of challenging humor in her cool voice to make it a casual remark. Her raw nerves hadn't betrayed her.

"I don't need to be reminded that you prefer work to a morning in bed with me. You've already made that clear." His smoothness was like the flat edge of a blade stroked threateningly across tender skin, and she paled a little at its silken quality of steel. "My car is out front."

"Shall we go?" Pet walked to the door without waiting for him.

Outside, she had to wait beside the sporty Jaguar while he unlocked it. Anger was in every controlled move he made, from the severely polite way he opened the car door for her to the deadly quiet way he shut it. Pet felt she was sitting on the edge of a volcano with an eruption minutes away, unsure whether the first blast would kill her or if she would be swept down the slopes on a river of molten lava. In any case, she doubted that she would come away unscathed.

An unearthly silence reigned until Dane turned the car onto the main road. "What was that idiotic remark about roses and mirrored ceilings all about?" He stabbed her with a glance, his features hard and uncompromising.

Pet continued to look straight ahead. "It should be self-explanatory," she shrugged.

"Then I must be incredibly dense, because I can't make head or tail of it," Dane replied in a tautly edged voice.

"I've heard that's a problem when you sleep in a round bed. It's impossible to tell the head of the bed from the foot." Pet forced the casual response.

A muscle played along the edge of his strong jaw. "I should have known this was all tied up with Ruby." He released a heavy breath that held anger and impatience. "You're jealous of her."

"You're mistaken," she denied calmly while a hot pain twisted her stomach. "I'm not interested in anything she has."

"And you think she has me?" he mocked, the corners of his mouth deepening in derision.

"Haven't you heard?" Pet cast him a false look of surprise. "It's common knowledge."

"And you believe it." Dane challenged with a hard glance.

"Do you deny it?" she countered.

"I didn't think I had to." On that half-savage note, he pressed his foot on the accelerator to send the Jaguar shooting past the slower car in front of them. It was an awesome display of power and agility that Pet found somehow characteristic of him.

"I'm sure you didn't. There are probably plenty of women who would be glad to go to bed with you without caring who else you might be sleeping with, but I'm not one of them," Pet stated when the burst of speed was over.

"And what was last night? A momentary lapse of moral principles?" Dane mocked derisively.

"I didn't go to bed with you." It was a moot point but the only defense she had.

"No, but you were damned well willing!" he reminded her brutally. "Or are you forgetting that you were undressing me!"

Her cheeks flamed with the memory of it. "I'm trying very hard to forget that."

But Dane didn't pay attention to her tightly worded reply. "In another fifteen minutes the boys would have walked in on something much more intimate than a simple embrace."

"That's something we'll never know, because they didn't walk in fifteen minutes later," she retorted, her hands clenched tightly in her lap.

"Are you going to deny—" he began angrily.

"Physically...sexually, you excite me, so I'm not going to deny your ability to make me feel aroused," she interrupted, since he wouldn't believe her if she tried. "But I don't wish to pursue an involvement with you. Their arrival was a mixed blessing. It saved me from making a stupid mistake."

There were two long beats of tense silence, then Dane prompted, "And? If it was a mixed blessing, there must be something you regret."

"There are two things. One, that it happened in the first place, and second, that they had to see me with you at all." She stared out the window, sitting rigidly in the seat. "I've worked so hard to get them to accept me as an equal. Now," she laughed bitterly, "I can just imagine what some of them are thinking. That I thought they weren't good enough, so I went after the boss."

Just as quickly as the bitter anger had surfaced, it vanished on a sigh. Pet brushed a limp hand over her face. "I should have had my head examined for going to that party with you last night. I was crazy to let myself in for all this grief."

"If you're so concerned about their opinion, you should have yelled 'Rape!' last night," he taunted.

"I wish I'd thought of it," she lied. "I would have."

138

When they reached the turn to the center, Dane took the corner fast, the low-slung sports car hugging the curb as it whipped around it with a squeal of tires. He braked abruptly near a side entrance where men were entering and exiting to get all the gear loaded.

As Pet reached for the door handle, Dane said, "You can tell the boys I'm docking your pay for being late this morning. I know you won't want them to think I'm showing you any favoritism." There was a sarcastic curve to his cruelly thin mouth.

"Thanks." She matched his tone as she climbed out of the car and slammed the door.

She had one foot on the curb when he leaned across the seat to add, "By the way, I haven't slept with Ruby since a green-eyed blonde invited me into her room to tuck her in. So you might give me credit for some degree of constancy," he accused harshly, and gunned the motor before accelerating away.

Momentarily stunned, Pet couldn't persuade her legs to move. She stared after the fast-moving car and its driver. What exactly had he said? She knew the words, but what did they mean? *No, no,* she admonished herself, *don't get your hopes up. Don't be a fool. You were right—it's just a physical thing, and the last complication you need in your life is an involvement with your boss.*

Heads turned when she entered the building. Self-conscious, she paused, aware of the hushing of voices. Squaring her shoulders, she walked briskly forward to the partially dismantled studio camera at the number-two position.

"We wondered if you were going to show up for

work this morning." Charlie said what was on everyone's mind, but with a teasing gentleness.

"Why not?" Pet shrugged, and hopped onto the platform. "I'm a working girl."

"But what are you working at?" Lon taunted.

She guessed that his sarcasm came from bitter resentment and jealousy that Dane had succeeded where he had failed. She understood the fragility of his male ego, but that didn't prevent her from defending herself.

"I know how it looked last night." There was a hint of pink in her cheeks, but she didn't hang her head. "I don't blame any of you for what you thought. I'm just as susceptible to a good line as the next person. You're going to believe what you want to regardless of what I say, so let's just drop the subject."

"Pet's right," Andy agreed. "We've got a lot of work to do."

By the middle of the afternoon all the equipment had been packed and loaded up, and after a stop at the hotel to pick up their luggage, the production crew went out for the next location. The majority of the technicians and equipment would head for Atlantic City. Pet was among the group destined for Batsto; the outdoor segments were to be taped there.

Riding in the passenger seat of Charlie's snubnosed van, Pet incuriously watched the Sunday traffic on the Garden State Parkway. Rick Benton, one of the sound men, and Ted, a lighting technician, were sitting on the black fur cot at the back, part of the skeleton crew that would be needed.

"Don't forget to watch for my exit," Charlie reminded her, not for the first time. "We'll probably get lost before we get there."

"I doubt it," Pet offered dryly.

"I'd like to know whose harebrained idea this was," he muttered. "Location shots in New Jersey of all places!"

"New Jersey is more than a corridor you have to pass through between New York and Pennsylvania." Her state pride insisted that she couldn't let that remark go unchallenged. "I know that's all most people see as they zoom through on their way someplace else. No one wants to believe we have swamp, marshes, miles of beach, farms, forests and lakes. If they can't see it from the highway, it isn't there."

"This must have been your idea, then," Charlie declared with a laughing glance.

"Why do you think it's called the Garden State?" she retorted, ignoring his remark.

"Because it has 'gardens' of concrete," he joked. "That's all I've ever seen. Hey!" He smiled broadly. "I just thought of something. Ruby Gale is the lily of the Garden State. That's a pretty good slogan, isn't it? Why don't you mention that to Dane?"

"Why me?" Pet stiffened because she knew precisely why. Charlie believed she was on very friendly terms with Dane. She could have been, but she wasn't going to go into a long, detailed explanation of why she wasn't anymore. "It was your idea. You tell him."

"He'd be more apt to listen to you, wouldn't he?" Charlie probed for information.

"I seriously doubt it," she replied with assumed indifference.

At that moment a midnight-blue Jaguar swept past them. Her heart did a somersault at the sight of the familiar car. It was highly unlikely that there would be two identical cars on the road. When she saw Ruby Gale's red head in the passenger seat, she knew she hadn't made a mistake about the car's owner.

"That was Ruby Gale, wasn't it?" Charlie frowned.

"Yes, with Dane," she added briskly, and sent him a cool look. "Do you still think he would listen to me?"

Charlie took one look at her strained face and let the conversation die a natural death. Confusion tore at Pet. Dane had indicated that his interest in Ruby Gale had waned since meeting her. But Ruby had been riding with him. Was it because of the television special—purely business? Or, because Pet herself had turned him down, had Dane turned to Ruby again?

Why were the answers so important? Her heart was becoming involved, that was why, a little voice warned. Pet sighed dejectedly and gazed out the window. The Jaguar was far out of sight.

Located on the fringes of Wharton State Forest, Batsto Village was a restored Revolutionary War town. Growing up around an early bog-iron furnace, it was a major supplier of munitions to the colonists. There were tours of old houses, coach rides and demonstrations of an operating water-powered saw-mill. Weekend fare also included craft displays and flea markets. The picturesque colonial town sat on the bank of the Batsto River with shaded streets and the verdant backdrop of the forest.

There was no work to be done on their arrival. All the location shots would be set up the following morning, which left Pet and the small crew free to wander through the village on the late and lazy summer afternoon.

Pet would have been content to stroll along the streets and browse through the curio tables, but typically the men were soon bored with such passive entertainment. Someone produced a Frisbee, and before Pet knew what was happening she was engaged in a lively game of catch in a park square. It was boisterous fun, leaping high to catch the soaring disk and trying difficult catches behind the back or under the leg. It was exactly the kind of distraction her tense nerves needed.

The Frisbee came sailing in her direction, but just as she got set to catch it, the wind caught it to change its trajectory. The disk drifted backward, and Pet realized at the last minute that it was going to be high and to her right. She turned to make a diving leap for it and rammed right into a solid object.

Her not inconsiderable height and weight staggered Dane backward, but she managed to keep them both upright. Pet wasn't sure if it was the impact or the shock of finding herself in his arms that stole the breath from her lungs. She stayed there, unable to breathe for several seconds while her fingers were spread across his chest and her head was thrown back as she stared into his vitally male face.

Her hair had long ago escaped the confining knot of the scarf and was a windblown mass of wheat gold. Dane's hands were on her waist, holding her hips against the disturbing support of his thighs. Desire flamed rawly through her when his gaze drifted down to linger on her mouth.

Her lips parted, wanting his kiss, inviting it, and there was an answering tightness in the grip of his hands to let her know the message had been received and understood. There was even a faint movement of his dark head in her direction.

"You really should watch where you're going," a musically female voice chided.

Pet's startled green eyes clashed with a pair of vivid blue ones that studied her with a calculating coldness. The sight of Ruby Gale standing near Dane brought her quickly to her senses. She pushed out of his hold, nervously brushing her palms over the terry-cloth material of her shorts, the blue jeans abandoned earlier in the day in favor of something cooler.

"Excuse me," she apologized to Dane on a breathless note.

"No harm done," he assured her as a mocking grimness tautened his expression.

"Hey, Pet! Are you going to get the Frisbee or not?" Charlie shouted from across the way.

Glancing around, Pet saw that it had landed a few feet behind Dane. Before she could retrieve it, Dane was there bending over to pick it up. His gaze raked her as he straightened. She was conscious of the perspiration shining wetly on the skin of her neck, beads gathering in the hollows of her collar bone to start a trickle running down between her breasts. The thin cotton knit of her tank top was clinging to her damp skin. Dane made her aware of just how revealing it was before he returned the Frisbee.

144

"Thank you," she murmured awkwardly, and turned away. He couldn't know how much he had contributed to the color in her hotly flushed cheeks.

Taking a few quick steps, she sailed the Frisbee back to Charlie with a flick of her wrist. But it took a nose dive short of its target, and a shirtless Charlie came trotting forward to retrieve it.

"You're welcome to join us if you like, Miss Gale," Charlie invited, puffing slightly behind his wide grin.

"No, thank you." The redhead refused with a laughing recoil at the thought. She sent a coy glance at Dane and slipped a hand under his arm. "Dane would hate it if I looked as hot and disheveled as she does," she declared with a pointed glance at Pet.

Pet had been conscious of her appearance before, but that remark made her doubly uncomfortable. Which was just what the star wanted. Ruby looked as if she had just stepped out of an advertisement for sports clothes in her snow-white skirt and candy-pink blouse.

Rather than stay where the contrast in their appearance was so marked, Pet decided to switch with one of the others. "Let me have the shady side for a while, Rick." If she looked hot and disheveled, there wasn't any point in quitting. Besides, she didn't want to give Ruby Gale the satisfaction of knowing she made her feel self-conscious and unattractive.

After she had traded places with the sound man, she saw Dane and Ruby strolling away arm in arm. It hurt, because she wanted to be the one walking with Dane. If she had stayed in bed, it was entirely possible she could have been. She shook her head to rid it of that tantalizing thought.

Monday morning meant a return to the work schedule, rising early to get the equipment ready and the outdoor shots set up. The weather cooperated with a clear sunny day, a warm temperature and little breeze to mess the star's coiffure.

There was no need for headsets or lights. The smaller and lighter-weight hand-held camera took the place of the fixed studio models, although it meant a helper was needed to carry the recorder. Someone was walking through Ruby's positions so it could be decided where the shiny reflectors would be needed to alleviate facial shadows.

Dane had already explained the setup to Pet in crisp, strictly businesslike tones. She was strapping on the battery packs that powered the camera and the shoulder pad to cushion its weight. The equipment had all been tested to make sure it was working properly. Now they were waiting for Ruby Gale to emerge from her private motor home/dressing room. Pet cast another glance in its direction, acutely aware that Dane was with the red-haired entertainer.

When they came out together, she quickly veiled her glance. But she noticed his arm affectionately around the woman's shoulders, the warmth and charm in his look, and the easy way he responded to Ruby's provocative glances. He was going over the particular sequence of this taping and reiterating the effect he planned to achieve.

Pet hoisted the camera onto her shoulder and adjusted it to a relatively comfortable position. While Dane walked Ruby to her starting point, Pet began lining up her opening frame. Her long hair was swept on top of her head, secured on the sides with combs and on top with a leather hair poke. With it loose there was too much risk of catching a strand on a part of the camera or between the pad and her shoulder, which often resulted in a sudden and painful yank on her scalp when she moved or altered position.

Dane's gaze made an absent inspection of her hairstyle as he approached her, but it was the only recognition of her sex that he made. His rugged features were impassive, all his attention focused on the business at hand. The fluttering of her pulse revealed that she had not achieved his objectivity.

"Ready, Wallis?" His gaze centered on her for a piercing second, long enough to see her positive nod. When he turned away, virile charm leaped from the smile he gave Ruby. "We can begin whenever you say, Ruby."

If he had wanted to make clear the difference in his attitude toward the two women, he had succeeded. Pet felt almost chilled by his callous lack of interest. Instead of being enchanted by the warmth Dane had shown the star, Ruby Gale appeared anything but pleased.

"What's *she* doing here?" she demanded, and pointed a scarlet fingernail at Pet.

"She's operating the camera, of course," Dane smiled.

"How can I possibly flirt with the camera the way you want when I'm looking at her?" Ruby protested with an angry gesture of her hands.

"Flirt with the lens, my love, and think of the male

147

audience that will ultimately be watching you," he replied easily, using that smile again.

But Ruby wasn't to be persuaded. "That's impossible! I want a man on that camera. Get rid of her!" She flung an impatient hand in Pet's direction. "I want her off the set."

"Darling, you aren't being reasonable." Dane moved toward the star.

"Do you want to know how unreasonable I can be?" the redhead flashed, exhibiting the temper Pet had heard so much about. "Either she goes or I do. Take your pick, Dane. You can't have us both."

There was silence all around. The ultimatum seemed to have a dual meaning. Pet was well aware which one would go even before she heard the low chuckle from Dane.

"Darling, I'm not arguing with you," he insisted calmly, amused by her outburst. "There isn't any need to make an issue of it. If you're more comfortable with someone else operating the camera, then I'll simply replace Miss Wallis. As lovely as you are when you're angry, I would rather you conserved all that volatile energy for your performance."

Ruby Gale was instantly and provocatively contrite. "Darling, I'm sorry for making a horrible scene. Will you forgive me?"

"Naturally I forgive you." He bent to brush a kiss across her cheek and turned to dismiss Pet. "Sutton will handle the camera today, Miss Wallis. We won't need you."

"Certainly." Her voice was barely above a whisper as she acknowledged his order.

As she shifted the camera off her shoulder to set it on the ground, Charlie moved over to help her. His eyebrows were raised in a sympathetic look. She managed a grim smile and a supposedly uncaring shrug, then began unstrapping the bulky packs from around her waist.

"It will take us a few minutes, I'm afraid, to switch the equipment," Dane explained to Ruby. "Why don't you relax and have another cup of coffee while you're waiting? There's no need for you to stand around."

"Are you sure you don't mind, Dane, about using a camera*man*?" the redhead persisted. "I'd hate to think I was interfering in your job."

"If I thought she was irreplacable, I would argue with you. So you needn't be concerned that you've upset me," he assured her.

As soon as Pet had removed all the gear and given it to Charlie, she slipped self-consciously away from the location set. She was aware that Dane had observed her departure without comment. By getting rid of her, he had averted a scene and a possible delay. It had been the sensible thing to do, she knew that, but it did sting to be rejected so readily.

CHAPTER NINE

SITTING BENEATH THE SHADE of a tree with the trunk for a backrest, Pet laid the paperback book aside. It couldn't hold her interest, or else she wasn't concentrating. She sighed and plucked a long blade of grass to twirl it between her fingers. Eyeing the sun, she wondered if its lengthening shadows had called a halt to the day's shooting yet. In a little while she would wander over to Charlie's van and wait, but it was cooler here and more peaceful, although her surroundings didn't seem to soothe her.

A bird flitted in the branches overhead. Drawing her knees up, she pulled the blade of grass apart and discarded the pieces. It was worse having nothing to do. Finally she pushed to her feet and absently dusted the seat of her pants. The soft rustle of footsteps on the grass turned her head toward the sound.

A breath stopped in her throat. Dane was walking toward her, lithe and supple. His gaze never ceased its study of her while he approached, gauging her reaction to his arrival. Pet knew her eyes could be much too expressive, so she made a casual half turn, bending to pick up her book.

"Are you finished for the day?" She was able to ask the question without having to look at him.

"We wrapped it up about twenty minutes ago. Too many shadows." He leaned a hand on the rough bark of the tree trunk and let his gaze roam the surroundings. "It's peaceful here."

"Yes," she agreed. Her glance slid away before it actually met his. "Charlie will be waiting for me, then."

"He was packing the equipment up when I left. I told him I'd find you and send you along to his van." Dane continued to study her with disconcerting directness.

"He'd probably like some help. I'd better go." But she didn't want to leave.

"Pet, about this morning, it wasn't by choice that I ordered you off the set." His dark eyes were grave as they searched her face, waiting for her response.

"I know." She looked across the green grass to the village center, liking its quaintness. "You did it because you had to keep Ruby happy for the sake of the production."

"Yes." He reached out to take hold of her forearm and force her to look at him. "But who's going to keep *me* happy? Will you?"

Unable to answer, Pet could only gaze into the masculine face with its tanned skin drawn tight over angular features. But the longing to be the one who could keep him happy was written in her jade eyes. She heard his sharply indrawn breath, then his mouth was coming down to crush hers.

His arm hooked her waist to haul her against his length. The contact with the taut columns of his thighs and hard flatness of his stomach made her weak. Her hands clutched his waist, hanging on while the world spinned at a dizzying speed. Nothing seemed to exist as her mouth opened under his passionately to return the hungry kiss. Then his hand moved onto her breast, circling it, cupping it, flattening it, and fighting the restriction of her blouse. When she felt his fingers tugging at the buttons, she partially returned to her senses and pulled breathlessly away, half pivoting out of his arms while she had the strength.

"Don't!" There was a catch in her voice, a deep, tearing desire interfering with the protest.

"Don't what?" Dane yanked her around, punishing her with his hard grip while his angry gaze burned her already heated flesh. "Don't touch you! Don't hold you! Don't kiss you! Don't what? Don't want you? That's impossible!" he raged in a savagely low voice. "I've tried. I've tried it all—working till all hours of the night, cold showers, and endless recriminations for getting mixed up with someone who works for me! It hasn't changed a damned thing."

Pet was shaken by the ferocity of his emotional response. This intensity was more than she had bargained for. She didn't know how to cope with it, any more than she knew how to handle her own abandonment of common sense.

When he slackened his hold, she didn't try to escape him. There was no resistance as his hands moved to her hair to release it from the confinement of the combs and leather poke. His fingers slipped through its length and gathered it into silken handfuls.

"You have beautiful hair, Pet," he groaned, and rubbed his mouth across her cheekbone, drawing closer to her lips. His breath was warm and moist, caressing on its own. "I keep seeing it this way—the way it was yesterday morning, a tawny, rumpled cloud on your pillow. I never should have used that key, or else I should have thrown Baxter out."

"Why didn't you tell me you weren't...involved with Ruby anymore?" Her voice throbbed as her arms curved around his middle.

"Why didn't you ask me?" Dane countered. "God, I thought I'd made it obvious. Do you actually believe I would invite another woman to a party given by my mistress if she and I were still lovers?"

"You...you could have been having your cake and eating it, too." Pet recalled the phrase the reporter had used. It had sounded so plausible at the time.

"I could have." He tugged at a handful of hair to force her head back. His gaze seemed to stab deeply into her. "But I'm not the type. What are you doubting now? I can see it in your eyes. Very expressive eyes they are, too."

"I was just wondering how you knew about the rose canopy above her bed," Pet admitted, because the question would plague her until she knew. "You said you hadn't slept with her lately, but—"

"I haven't." Irritation put a harsh edge on his voice. "All entertainers seem to have little eccentricities; hers happens to be going over new arrangements while sitting in bed. In order to have a discussion of them, it seems logical to join her on the bed. I suppose I could have pulled a chair up, but I don't happen to be bashful or easily embarrassed."

"But you and she were lovers."

"Yes, we were lovers, for the lack of a better term." The flaring of his nostrils revealed his dislike of Pet's continued pursuit of the subject. "Do you expect me to be a virgin?"

Pet attempted a negative shake of her head, and succeeded as much as his grip on her hair would allow. "I just wondered if you were always so quick to discard a woman once you grew tired of her." Because she wasn't certain how well she would take it if he dropped her as quickly as he had seemed to abandon Ruby Gale. "Everyone still believes the two of you are having an affair," she reminded him when she saw the darkening anger in his eyes. "You act like it when you're together."

"As you pointed out earlier, I have to keep her happy. Dammit, Pet," he muttered in exasperation, "you know how costly delays can be. No other producer would touch Ruby with a ten-foot pole. Her reputation for walking off a production or causing endless changes has thrown a hundred budgets out the window. A television special with her can be a gold mine if it doesn't cost you two gold mines to get it. I'm walking a tightrope with her. Why do you think I'm personally handling this project?"

"How far would you go to keep her happy, Dane?" Pet hated herself for asking, because it wasn't fair. She had no right to ask that kind of question.

"You have to ask!" He stared at her, an incredulous frown narrowing his gaze.

"Dane, I'm not sure about anything," Pet whispered on a tiny sob. "I'm unsure of how I feel, what I think, what I do. Every ounce of sense I have tells me I shouldn't want you, but I do."

With a muffled groan he pulled her forward against the hard warmth of his mouth. The hand at the nape of her neck began stroking it softly and sensuously, sending shivers tingling down her spine. A faint hungry sound rolled from her throat as she arched against him, surrendering to this wild joy that flamed from his kiss.

When she wound her arms around his neck, his mouth parted in an irresistible invitation to deepen the kiss, and Pet accepted it eagerly. In direct response, his hand flattened convulsively on her hips, shaping her more firmly to him to give her potent evidence of his need, and she trembled uncontrollably.

Abruptly Dane dragged his mouth from hers, the hand at the back of her head applying pressure to bury her face against his neck while shudders racked his torso. She could feel the hard, uneven thud of his heart. The rate of her own pulse would have rivaled the speed of his car. Happiness was such a fragile thing. Its beauty filled her eyes with tears and swelled her heart to the point of bursting. How could she ever contemplate denying this ecstasy that she was a kiss away from discovering?

Her hands spread across the broad muscularity of his back to hold him closer while her lips began exploring his throat, savoring the taste of his skin and absorbing the heat of his flesh. In a slow, roundabout way she reached his ear, her tongue delighting in the shape of it. A raw sound of desire came from his throat before he turned his head to stop the arousing caress, his mouth rough against her cheek and his breathing heavy.

"Don't," he ordered in a low, thickened voice.

"Don't what?" she whispered, and teased him with his words while her fingertips sensuously traced the strong column of his neck. "Don't want you. Don't kiss you. Don't—"

Angrily he silenced her with a hard, bruising kiss that was brief in its fury. Then he growled against her skin, "Half the time I never know whether to kill you or kiss you!"

"I prefer the latter," Pet murmured, careless of the provocation in her reply. The world had stopped its frenzied spinning, but she wasn't ready to get off.

His hands firmly created a space between them, the support of his hard length denied her as he held her a few inches away. Her gaze ran warmly over the rough planes of his essentially male features, aware of the sobered slash of his mouth.

"We've got to come to an understanding," he insisted. "These next few days aren't going to be easy." In a trembling underbreath he reluctantly issued, "God, that's an understatement!" Then he turned his hard gaze away from her for an instant.

"I think you could be right," Pet sighed, because it was hard staying out of his arms. It was always like that when she was near him.

"I know I am. Pet—" he used her name so he could have her complete attention, which had become distracted by the opened neckline of his shirt and the springy chest hairs it revealed "—I have to

156

leave now for Atlantic City. There are a few details I have to iron out with the management at the casino. Then I have to be back here for the taping tomorrow. We aren't going to have any time to be together."

"I see." She didn't ask if she could go with him. If Dane had wanted her along, he would have invited her. He had to know she would accept.

"I still have a company to run, so my schedule is going to be like this until this damned special is done," he said, revealing his impatience and irritation at the circumstances, which offered some consolation. "I want you to understand that isn't the way I want it. I don't want you getting any crazy notions in your head that because I'm not with you, I don't want to be. No more of that imagination of yours working overtime about rose canopies and being patronized or whatever ridiculous molehill you can make into a mountain."

"No more." Pet shook her head in promise.

"There's another thing you'd better know. I don't give a damn what the crew thinks about us. You can keep on trying to be one of the boys if you want. But if I get a chance to touch you or kiss you, don't you dare shy away from me because one of them might be watching," Dane warned. "I'll be discreet. There won't be any passionate clinches in front of them, but I'm not going to guard my every look and action. If they want to accuse you of receiving special treatment, you can tell them for me that you damned well *are* special! Any objections?"

"None. Half of them think we've already slept together anyway," she admitted, a little thrilled by his possessiveness.

"I wish we had. Maybe I wouldn't be twisted into so many hard knots inside." His gaze raked her, smoldering with the frustration of unsatisfied desire. Pet saw the effort he made to get a grip on himself, to bank the fires that burned in his eyes. "There's still the matter of Ruby to be settled," he added.

"Dane, I—" Pet began.

"Listen to me," he insisted. "She has to be the center of attention all the time. She won't share the spotlight with anyone. So when I'm around her, it will appear that I'm totally indifferent to you. You saw what happened this morning the second she suspected my interests weren't wholly devoted to her. She immediately made a scene. It doesn't matter to Ruby whether the attention she receives is genuine or not, just so long as she can command it. Until this taping is wrapped up, she will *appear* to have my undivided attention. Do you accept that?"

"Yes," she nodded, beginning to understand the spoiled and self-centered temperament of the talented performer. It also explained why Dane had been so very attentive to the star.

"You know she isn't going to let you work on the taping tomorrow." Dane eyed her with grim resignation. "She's going to keep you off the studio cameras at the casino, too, which means you'll be working the hand-held, providing she doesn't demand that you leave the production altogether."

"Maybe it would be best if I did. I don't want to cause problems. You can get someone to replace me," she suggested. "I can go back—"

"No." He rejected that idea out of hand. "You

158

aren't going back, not even if I have to replace you. You're going to stay with the crew. You aren't going back until we all go home. I know I'll be working all the time and maybe I'll only get to see you five—ten minutes, half an hour at a time. But I'll know you're there and if I get the chance to be with you, I will.''

Keeping her at a distance, he kissed her, his mouth clinging to her lips for an enchanting instant before he lifted his head. The sweet torment of longing made his expression bleak and grim. Pet wanted to smooth away the hardness in his face with her hand, but he wouldn't let her touch him, as if not trusting his reaction.

"You said before that you were unsure," Dane said tightly. "Maybe you can appreciate the way I feel. The times I've been with you haven't been among my more rational moments. It's like being trapped between two battling weather fronts—one hot and the other cold. I never know which it's going to be with you.''

"You pick a lot of the fights yourself." Pet wasn't that submissive that she would accept full responsibility for their arguments. He had been at fault, too. "You shouldn't say things you know will irritate me.''

"Maybe I have." He granted that it was possible without admitting it. "From now on, understand the pressure I'm under. If I'm sharp with you, be tolerant...at least until this taping is done. I'd sell my soul to have it finished right now." Then Dane laughed, a wry sound. "Some say I made a pact with the devil when I signed the contract with Ruby.''

"Don't laugh!" A sudden pain brought a quick frown to her forehead. "It isn't funny."

Dane stared at her, his eyes narrowing in anger. "I don't want to know what you're thinking right now. I haven't got time to correct whatever erroneous impression is forming in that mind of yours." He raised an arm to glance at his watch. "I'm already five minutes late. Ruby will be wondering where I am."

"Ruby?" Pet stiffened. "I thought you said you were driving to Atlantic City?"

"I am," he said tightly, and released her.

"She's going with you." Her voice sounded remarkably flat.

"Yes, she's going with me. She wants to check on the dressing rooms backstage. God help us if they aren't up to her standards," Dane grumbled, and irritatedly ran a hand over his hair.

"I'm sure you'll make it right, Dane." Pet managed a smile, an attempt at reassurance, yet strangely the words had an ominous ring to them.

"I have to go," he said as if needing to impress her with the inevitability of it.

"I know. Go ahead." This time she really worked at the smile and it felt more natural. "Tell Charlie I'll be along in a minute. I just have to gather up my things." Such as the combs and the hair poke he had scattered on the ground, as well as her handbag and the book she'd been trying to read.

Dane took a step away. "I probably won't see you until tomorrow."

"Drive carefully." A sarcastic little voice wanted to add, *the star of the show will be riding with you*

and nothing must happen to her. But Pet didn't let
that voice speak.

ALTHOUGH PET WASN'T PRESENT during the next
morning's taping, she gathered from what Charlie
had intimated at lunch that it wasn't going well.
Ruby Gale was being difficult and demanding, and
Dane wasn't satisfied with the results they were getting. Only the crew knew of his displeasure, from
what Pet could tell. Not a shadow of blame was ever
cast on the star.

Professional curiosity got the better of her. Bored,
with nothing else to do, she wandered over to the
mobile television unit parked some distance from the
shooting site. The snub-nosed van was no bigger than
Charlie's. She tried the door and found it was
unlocked. Even though the van was parked in the
shade, it was stuffy and hot inside. She left the
sliding door open to let the fresh air in.

The interior was equipped with a monitor and a
videotape player among other things. Those were the
two items that interested Pet, along with the three-
quarter-inch cassettes she found on top of the player.
Charlie's handwriting on the labels identified the
contents as part of this location's taping. She
punched them into the player and adjusted the monitor screen, sitting back on the little stool to see what
had been taped and what might be wrong with it.

Twice she played them through, nagged by something she knew wasn't right yet unable to fault the
performer or the cameraman. The lighting was perfect and so was the background. Punching the cas-

settes in for the third time, she kept asking herself how they could be improved.

Halfway through it the third time, Pet had the germ of an idea. She stopped the tape, rewound it and punched it through again. In her mind she made the changes, the additions, and checked them mentally to see if they would work. The elation grew with each passing second.

"No one's allowed in there!" Dane snapped the order before he saw it was Pet inside the van. "What are you doing?"

"I know what's wrong!" She stopped the tape and pushed the rewind button.

"You know what's wrong, do you?" he mocked. "What's wrong is you haven't kissed me hello."

"I was talking about the tape." But she quickly brushed her lips across his mouth and grabbed hold of the hand that reached out for her. She pulled him inside, too excited by her discovery to be put off by his impatient look.

"What about the taping? There aren't any problems," he denied as he crouched to keep from bumping his head on the van's ceiling.

"Charlie mentioned at lunch that you weren't pleased with what you had, but you couldn't find anything wrong with it. I got curious and since I didn't have anything to do anyway—"

"You decided to snoop," he concluded.

"It isn't snooping," she protested. "I work on the production, too. There's nothing wrong with wanting to see the results." She was kneeling in front of the tape player, anxiously waiting for it to finish rewinding.

162

"I've looked at those tapes fifty times. I'm taking what we've got, Pet. Let's not waste time looking at them again." Dane slid his hand across her stomach to hook her waist and attempt to draw her back to where he was sitting on the stool.

She pushed his hand away. "But I know how you can improve it." The tape had finally stopped re-winding and she could punch it up on the monitor.

"I happen to be an experienced director. Are you trying to tell me how to do my job?" There was a thin thread of anger in his incredulous question.

"Be quiet and throw your manly pride away." Pet flashed him an irritated glance. "You could listen and give me a chance to explain my idea."

"I'll listen." He sat back on the stool, folding his arms in front of him and looking anything but open-minded.

"You could give me credit for knowing a little about what I'm talking about, instead of acting so damned superior," she retorted.

His mouth twitched. "Didn't I tell you once how to shut me up if I was making you angry?"

"The problem is that you've made me too angry to do it. If I kissed you, you'd like it, then it wouldn't be a punishment," Pet reasoned in a thinly impatient tone.

Pivoting on her knees, she turned to watch the screen, which put her back to Dane. His hands closed firmly on her shoulders to draw her back to rest against his legs. Lifting the weight of her hair, he gently draped it over her shoulder.

"Then sit next to me, because that will definitely be a torment," he gently mocked. When she turned her head to look up at him, regret for her sharpness flashing in her green eyes, his finger pushed her chin toward the screen. "Show me what you found."

"You were experimenting with camera angles," she began as the first take was being played, minus the sound since it wasn't a problem. "But it's the elevation that's wrong."

"The elevation?" By his tone she could tell that this hadn't occurred to him and his mind was racing in examination of the tape the same way hers had.

"Yes. Charlie should be up high and shooting down; up about five feet, I would say. Maybe smear some Vaseline around the circumference of the lens so the outer edges of the picture will be in a kind of dreamy focus. And here—" she drew attention to the particular sequence "—where Ruby does that half turn to the right, Charlie should make a half turn to the left—sort of a sweeping arc with the camera to give that illusion," she explained with growing enthusiasm. "It will be tricky. Some sort of ladder or scaffolding."

"I wonder where I can get a crane," Dane mused.

"It's obvious that would be best, but there's the time factor, and the delay it means. I think you can rig something up—Charlie's good at that kind of thing. And here—" another part came up that she had an idea for "—the camera could swing a little bit in tempo with the music."

Turning, she found Dane was leaning forward to watch another take, visualizing her ideas in place of the ones that had been used. His expression was a study of concentration and inward reflection. She

164

nibbled at her lip, anxious for his reaction and certain it had to be positive.

But there was only silence that lasted through two more takes. Unable to wait any longer, Pet unconsciously swayed against him and laid a hand on his thigh, her fingers curling into the hard flesh. She was immediately the recipient of his glance.

"What do you think?" she asked.

"I think you pick the damnedest times to touch me." His eyes glinted with a wicked, dancing light before directing a glance out the open door to a crew member approaching the van. "And I think you do it deliberately." His hand closed warmly over hers and moved it to a more discreet location near his knee.

A hot wave of color flooded her cheeks, but he wouldn't let her look away from him, holding her gaze with some invisible thread. Pet was jolted by the intimacy of the moment—an intimacy that didn't rely on a kiss or a caress, but could be accomplished with a look.

"In answer to your question, you've come up with the solution," Dane admitted. "I doubt if we can achieve that pirouette shot unless Charlie is directly above her."

"We're all set up for the next number, Mr. Kingston," Rick announced, pausing at the open door of the van. "Are you coming? I'll bring the new tape Charlie wanted."

"I'll be there in a minute." He opened the storage cabinet to take out a clean cassette tape. "Here." He tossed it to the man, then began uncoiling his length to maneuver himself out of the cramped quarters of the van.

Pet followed him out, hopping the last foot to the ground, a hand on the door frame for balance. "Do you admit that I did know what I was talking about?" she asked in half challenge, her green eyes sparkling at his previous arrogant skepticism.

Dane paused, running his eyes over her in dry amusement. "I admit it. Now why don't you suggest how I'm going to convince Miss Gale to do that number again without arousing her temper?"

"Keeping her happy is strictly your department," she retorted, conscious that Rick was dawdling on his way back to the location, remaining within sight of them.

Dane was aware of him, too. His hand stroked her hair, then traced the clean line of her jaw to her chin, where his fingers outlined her lips. The sensual caress started her trembling.

"Aren't you sorry you didn't kiss me when you had the chance?" He tapped the end of her nose with a finger, an affectionate reprimand for her stubbornness. Without waiting for a reply, he walked after Rick.

Pet sighed.

CHAPTER TEN

ATLANTIC CITY is famous for its beach and the magic of its street names—Boardwalk, Ventnor Avenue, Baltic and Oriental Avenue—familiar to every child who has played the game of Monopoly, its creator having taken the names from this city's streets. The Miss America Beauty Pageant is held at Convention Hall on the Boardwalk, which now boasts gambling casinos.

The whirring reels and clanging bells of the slot machines dominated everything. At the tables, the voices of the gamblers and dealers seemed almost muted in comparison to the din of the machines. Pet followed Charlie as he elbowed his way through the crowd of guests eager to part with their money. Coins clattered into a metal tray and a woman shouted excitedly to her husband.

"It's really something, isn't it?" Charlie shook his head.

Pet laughed at his seeming disdain. "Five minutes after you put your things in your room, you'll be down here and you know it!"

He grinned suddenly and let his hand find her elbow where the crowd thinned, enabling them to walk together. "Don't tell Sandy. She'll have my hide," he said, referring to his wife.

"I won't," she promised.

"I'm hoping she'll be so glad to see me that she won't even know I'm a few dollars broker than when I left." He pushed the "up" arrow on the elevator. "I need some relaxation after these last three days. I thought Ruby was going to bring down the whole town with that screaming fit she threw when Dane told her we were going to reshoot that first segment. It was a great idea you had, Pet. It worked like a charm once Kingston talked her into it."

"I saw the tapes. It did look great," she agreed, but didn't comment on the star's outrage over being asked to do the number again. Nor did she want to know too much about Dane's role in changing Ruby's mind.

"What are you going to do after you get your things in your room?" Charlie stepped aside when the elevator doors opened, and let Pet walk in ahead of him.

"Shower, then probably grab a sandwich." She supposed Dane would be busy that evening. She had seen practically nothing of him the past two days.

"I'm hungry, too. We could eat together, if you want. It would keep my money in my pockets a little while longer," he grinned, and pushed the floor number for his room. "What floor for you?"

"The next one." One floor above him—Dane's travel arrangements again separated her from the male members of the crew.

"The place was probably too crowded for all of us to be together," Charlie offered his own explanation. "I'm surprised we're even booked into the same hotel as the casino."

"Dane probably didn't want to provide us with any excuses for being late," she shrugged.

"About the sandwich?"

"Sure, we can eat together." It was better than eating alone. "Where do you want to meet?"

The elevator stopped at his floor. "Why don't I just stop by your room in half an hour?" he suggested. "It will be easier than trying to find each other in that madhouse downstairs."

"Okay, but make it forty-five minutes. I want to wash my hair," Pet explained hurriedly, and he waved an acknowledgement before the elevator doors closed.

At the next floor Pet got off the elevator and found her room. She heard a phone ringing as she set her weekender bag down to unlock the door. Hurriedly Pet opened it, certain that the caller was Dane but the phone was silent when she stepped into the room. She wasn't even sure if it had been her phone that was ringing.

Opening her suitcase, she shook out the uncrushable dress she had brought with her, the only one, and laid it on the bed. The taupe and beige dress was simple almost to the point of plainness, with button-tab roll-up sleeves, deep side pockets and a tie belt. After more than a week of slacks and jeans, it would be a pleasant change to wear a dress, Pet decided.

She unpacked her makeup and shampoo from her

cosmetic case and carried them into the bathroom. Forty-five minutes wasn't much time to shower, dry her hair and dress, so she left the rest of her things to unpack later, stripped and stepped into the shower.

Her hair was lathered with shampoo when she realized the phone was ringing, the sound muffled by the running water of the shower. Grabbing a towel, she made a quick dash for the phone in the bedroom, leaving a trail of water and shampoo bubbles on the carpet. It stopped ringing as she reached it. She waited a few dripping seconds before returning to the shower to rinse her hair.

It happened again when she was drying her hair with the blow dryer, the hum of the dryer blocking out the ring of the phone. Again the caller hung up before Pet reached the phone. If it was Dane, she was becoming thoroughly frustrated. She returned to the bathroom and finished drying her hair, shutting the motor off every few minutes to listen for the phone. Only it didn't ring.

Not until she was brushing her teeth. With a mouthful of toothpaste she ran into the bedroom and stubbed her toe on the end of the bed. An involuntary cry came from her throat at the shafts of pain that stabbed her injured toe. She hopped the last six steps to the phone. This time she heard the line click dead before she could get the receiver to her ear.

"Damn you, Dane Kingston," she cursed tearfully, then noticed the clock. It could have been Charlie, checking to see if she was ready early, she realized.

The thought lent impetus to her haste to dress. Five minutes before she was supposed to be ready, she buckled the strap of her beige sandals and reached for the tie belt to knot it around her waist. At the knock on her door, she glanced at the phone. She would positively scream if Dane called her after she had gone. But how would she know if she wasn't there?

The knock sounded more impatient. Sighing, she walked to the door while making the first loop in the knot of her belt. She was adjusting the trailing ends to hang smoothly down her side as she opened the door.

"Where the hell have you been?" Dane demanded, striding inside the room and slamming the door shut. "I've been trying to reach you for the last forty-five minutes!" Pet's surprise turned to indignant shock at his raging demands that didn't permit her a reply. "I've called three times without an answer. The desk verified that you checked in more than a half hour ago. I finally called Charlie to find out where the hell you were and he told me you were on your way up here when he left you. I've been half out of my mind! Why didn't you answer the phone?"

"Why didn't you let the damned thing ring long enough to give me a chance?" she hurled back at him with equal anger. "The first time I was just walking into the room. Then I was in the shower. And then I stubbed my toe trying to get in here because I knew it was you! How dare you yell at me, you arrogant, pig-headed—"

"No." The one low word cut across her angry retort, his hard features unrelenting in their severity. "We aren't going to have another shouting match, not this time! I've waited too long."

Seizing her shoulders. he jerked her against his lean, hard length. Pet struggled, resisting the appeasement of his bruising mouth, but she couldn't escape it. Twisting angrily within the steel circle of his arms, she beat at him with tight fists.

The sheer absurdity of her actions finally struck her, holding her motionless for an instant. This was what she wanted, where she wanted to be. Her arms went around his neck, her body becoming pliant to his hands.

The kiss that had been subjugating became deeply sensuous, and Pet returned it with equal passion, arching closer to him under the guidance of his shaping hands. His roaming caress excited her flesh, swamping her with the totality of her love, the sheer, sweet impossiblity of it.

When breathing was permitted again, she whispered achingly, "I've missed you so, Dane." The licking of his moist, hard tongue along her throat drew a shudder of desire.

"I can't believe the way you can destroy me." He lifted his head to frame her face in his hands, fingers curled into the just-washed fullness of her hair. "When I walked through that door I could have strangled you for the hell I'd been through." Weary lines were etched in his tanned skin, the strain of long hours leaving their mark. A gentleness glinted in his dark eyes as a half smile touched the corners of his mouth. "Do you know this is the first time I've seen you in a dress?"

"Is it?" she murmured absently because it didn't seem all that important to her.

"Of course, I've always been fully aware that you were all woman." He slid a hand down to cover her breast, letting its round contour fill his palm. "But it's an attractive sight to see you in a skirt just the same. Were you going somewhere?"

"Didn't Charlie tell you?" Pet couldn't seem to drag her eyes away from his mouth with its traces of her lipstick. Those strong male lips could create such an upheaval in her senses. "We were going to have a sandwich together."

"He's married," Dane stated.

"Yes. He's just a friend," she explained in case he wondered. "I didn't want to eat alone." Hope leaped with an eternal flame. "Are you free? I can tell Charlie—" But Dane was already shaking his head.

"No, I'm tied up this evening." He didn't volunteer any specific information as to whom he would be with or why he was wearing an evening suit and tie. "I wanted to be certain you'd arrived safely. I expected you an hour ago."

"Charlie doesn't drive as fast as you do," Pet smiled, and tried not to wonder about his plans for the evening.

His light kiss seemed to be a reward for not asking. "I want you to have dinner with me tomorrow evening, after the taping is finished. No one else. Just the two of us," he invited.

"I accept." She let her lips tease his. "On condition that you don't take me where I need to dress. This is all I brought."

"On the contrary." Dane returned the torment, rubbing his lips against hers while his fingers found

173

her nipple beneath the bodice of her dress and teased it into erectness. "I'll take you somewhere that you have to *un*dress."

"You would!" Pet accused.

"You bet." His mouth closed on hers, parting her lips to drink in her sweetness.

A knock at the door brought the kiss to a lingering end. "It's probably Charlie," she whispered against his mouth.

Reluctantly Dane let her go. "You'd better answer it. I have to leave anyway."

Pet moved unwillingly out of his arms to walk to the door. Remembering, she half turned to warn him, "You have lipstick on your mouth."

When she opened the door, Charlie had brought Lon Baxter with him. "I bumped into Lon in the elevator, so I invited him to join us if that's all right," he explained, and glanced past her to see Dane. "Hello."

Pet glanced over her shoulder to see Dane returning his handkerchief to the inside pocket of his suit jacket. She supposed the two men would reach the obvious conclusion as to why he had needed to wipe his mouth. She would have been less than honest if she didn't admit she was a little self-conscious.

"Hello, Charlie, Lon." Dane nodded to both men, but his gaze narrowed dangerously on the latter. Then he was moving alongside her, touching her shoulder lightly in farewell and smiling. "I'll see you tomorrow." An oblique reference to their dinner engagement.

"Tomorrow," she promised, saying more with her eyes.

The two men stepped to one side to let Dane pass, then Charlie raised a questioning eyebrow. "Ready?"

"Just let me get my bag," Pet nodded, and went to retrieve it from the dresser.

Nothing was said initially about Dane's being in her room, although Lon's gaze was often half-angry when it met hers. The conversation during their meal centered on the production, with Lon filling them in on what had gone on here while they were in Batsto. After the waitress had cleared their plates and served coffee, Pet took a cigarette from her pack and bent her head to the match flame Lon offered.

"Dane sounded worried when you didn't answer your phone." Charlie finally brought up the subject that had occupied both men's minds. "Where were you?"

"Taking a shower." She didn't go into the circumstances of the other times.

"You're making a fool of yourself, Pet," Lon said irritably. "All he wants is to take you to bed."

"That's the pot calling the kettle black, isn't it?" Pet challenged, releasing a thin stream of smoke and tapping the end of the cigarette in the ashtray.

"Maybe it is." Lon reddened, but he wasn't deterred. "But it doesn't change the facts."

"And those facts are?" Her voice was as cool as her glance.

"The only way there's a future in having an affair with him is if you're sleeping with him to get some promotion in the company. Even then, I wouldn't be too sure that you wouldn't be out of a job when the affair ends. Why would somebody like Dane Kingston want an old lover working for him?" He leaned forward to stress his arguments.

"I haven't slept with him, and I'm not becoming involved with him because I want a promotion, a raise or anything like that," Pet denied, and sipped at her hot coffee, trying to appear indifferent even though Lon's blunt appraisal of her motive had stung.

"Then the only thing you're going to get out of this affair is a lot of painful memories and regret, because it isn't going to last," he insisted.

"Why won't it?" she challenged.

"Leave it alone, Lon," Charlie urged. "It's none of our business."

But Lon ignored him. "He's Dane Kingston and you're Petra Wallis, that's why it won't last. You may be a beautiful woman, but his world is one long string of beautiful women. You can't compete with the glamour and excitement of the likes of Ruby Gale. Maybe he's through with her now, but there'll be someone else like her down the line. What are you—little Pet Wallis—going to do then?"

He shook his head as if despairing that he could get through to her. But he was. Everything he was saying was being driven into her like a nail in a coffin. "If you want an affair, have it with an average guy like me. If not with me, then with someone like me. At least you'd stand a chance to have something that might last."

"I appreciate the advice," she said stiffly.

He sighed. "I know you aren't going to believe this, coming from me, but I like you, Pet. I don't want to see you get hurt."

"I like you, too, Lon," was the only reply she could make.

It was hectic getting ready for the last taping. Because another performer had given his show the night before they weren't able to set up the bulk of their equipment until the day of the taping. An hour before show time, Pet was helping Andy secure a cable that had worked loose from the adhesive strip taping it to the floor.

"Hey, Pet!" Rick called to her from the stage and motioned. "Dane wants to talk to you."

"Tell him I'll have a headset on in a few minutes."

"No. He's backstage," Rick explained.

Andy glanced at her. "Go see what he wants. I'll finish up here."

Wiping her moist palms on the hips of her brown slacks, Pet left him—but none too eagerly. Yesterday she would have raced for the chance to speak to Dane. But Lon's warning had forced her to take a long, hard look at where she was going. She didn't question anything Dane had told her or his desire for her. It was the things there hadn't been time to say—things she wasn't even sure he would have said if there had been the time. She was getting nervous about having dinner with him after the show because she knew where it would lead, and she wasn't sure anymore if that was where she wanted to go.

Backstage it was becoming a confusion of singers, dancers and stagehands arriving and mixing with the production crew. Pet hesitated, glancing around for the familiar sight of Dane's tall muscular frame. But she didn't see him. Instinct guided her in the direction of Ruby Gale's private dressing room.

He was standing outside the door, half-turned away from her. Pet stopped when she glimpsed the red-haired woman with him. She didn't want to approach him while he was with Ruby and possibly arouse the star's temper by her presence. Since neither of them had noticed her in the midst of all the people, Pet stayed where she was until he was finished.

In a punishing kind of fascination, she noticed the way Dane's hands rested on Ruby's hips with such familiar ease. Her fingers were playing with his shirt-front and running through the curling collection of exposed chest hairs. Something plummeted to the pit of Pet's stomach when she realized her hearing had become attuned to their voices.

"Darling, I feel so badly about tonight," Ruby was saying. "We've planned for so long to celebrate with champagne and caviar, and now I can't make it."

She couldn't make it? Pet had thought the date was off because Dane had canceled to have dinner with her. No, she wasn't going to think of herself as a substitute. Dane had said he and Ruby were finished, so what did it matter?

"Naturally I'm disappointed," Dane replied, and didn't mention anything about having another engagement. It wasn't necessary that he should. "I shouldn't be celebrating now anyway. My work is just beginning, editing it all together into a smooth, fast-paced show. It's just as well that we have to postpone it."

"You're always so understanding, Dane." Ruby beamed and stretched on her toes to kiss him.

"I understand that the star has a show to get ready for and she's letting me detain her." The kiss he gave back was little more than a peck. He turned her around and gave her a gentle push toward her door. "Go and make yourself beautiful."

With a husky laugh, Ruby Gale slipped into her dressing room. As Dane turned to leave, his gaze immediately fell on Pet. She started forward quickly, so he wouldn't guess she had been standing there watching and waiting, a bright smile fixed on her expression. His features gentled at her approach.

"Rick said you wanted to talk to me," she explained.

"All the time...about the silken texture of your hair, the softness of your lips, the heady warmth of your body against mine," he murmured, caressing her with his voice and his velvet dark eyes. Then he seemed to catch himself and took a deep, regretful breath. It was strange, because Pet couldn't breathe at all. "But on this occasion it was business. I want you to get some behind-the-scenes action before the show starts—dressing rooms, makeup, wardrobe, musicians, stagehands. You know the kind of color I want. And concentrate on what goes on in the wings during a performance. You should be able to pick up some audience shots in the background."

"Sure." Pet continued to stand there, looking at him, loving him, and struggling to display the professionalism of her craft.

"Then you'd better get a move on," Dane urged with a dancing look, "before I take you behind that curtain and make love to you."

Her pulse went to pieces, losing any semblance of normality. Behind that glint of amusement in his dark eyes a desirous light burned.

"Yes, sir." Breathless, she mocked a formal salute and turned to hurry away.

By the time she had got the hand-held camera, strapped on all its paraphernalia and commandeered a helper named Tom to carry the recorder and keep the attached wires and cords out of the way, it was half an hour before show time and preparations for the performance were in full swing backstage. She noticed Dane standing on center stage in consultation with her three co-workers who would be manning the cameras out front. They were going over his detailed notes on each number.

Her gaze lingered on his lithely brawny build for an aching second, but her task had already been assigned, so she set to work to begin fulfilling it with Tom tagging along after her like a faithful dog carrying its master's newspaper; only in this case he carried the recorder.

As she was setting up to get a shot of the general hubbub around the dressing rooms, a florist arrived with a huge standing bouquet of bloodred roses. Pet quickly seized on this piece of glamorous backstage color and followed him to the star's dressing room, the tape rolling.

Pet was standing some ten feet away when the door opened at the florist's knock. Luck gave her the perfect angle over the shoulder of the florist into the dressing room.

Clancy, the secretary and girl Friday to Ruby Gale, answered the door. Beyond her, Ruby Gale was sitting in front of a mirror with her back to the camera and the door, dressed in a lavender robe. The mirror's reflection gave Pet a view of the star's face. If it had all been rehearsed, it couldn't have been more perfect.

Evidently the florist had added some flattering comment of his own to the delivery of the roses, because the red-haired entertainer half turned to give him one of her sexy smiles. Her blue gaze flickered past him to the camera and Pet. She was instantly livid, coming to her feet and storming out of her room in a volcanic fury as flaming as her hair.

"You snooping little bitch!" she screamed at Pet. "What are you doing sneaking about out here?"

"I'm sorry." Pet tried to apologize and explain about the flowers, but her voice was drowned by the vicious abuse and accusations Ruby Gale hurled at her. She attempted to retreat, backing away, but she was relentlessly pursued. Too stunned by the vitriolic attack, Pet understood only half of the insults.

"What were you hoping—that I'd be half-naked so you could sell the tapes to some gutter magazine? I know how you got your job! How many men did you have to sleep with to get it? I know your kind! You're nothing but a tramp!" Ruby raged.

Pet's face was scarlet, aware that everyone backstage was witnessing this vile scene. "You aren't on this production because of your skill with the camera!" Ruby went on. "It's your skill in bed, keeping the rest of the crew happy while they're away from home! You're a—"

"What's going on here?" Dane's angry voice was the most wonderful sound Pet had ever heard. She turned as he came striding foward, relief cooling her hot cheeks.

"This blond slut was snooping outside my door!" His arrival did not abate the redhead's abusive tongue. "She—"

Pet interrupted quickly, "The florist delivered some roses and I was—"

"You were sneaking about trying to—"

"No more." Dane intervened to lay soothing hands on Ruby's shoulders, which trembled with the fury of her wrath. "I don't want you getting upset. I'll take care of it. You can leave it to me now."

Pet stared at him incredulously, shock giving way to indignation. She was aware of the calming effect he was having on the star, but she wasn't the least bit interested in whether Ruby was pacified.

"I won't have her sneaking around out here," the redhead insisted. Some of the venom had been removed from her tone although it remained imperious.

"I promise you she won't bother you anymore." He curved an arm around the lavender-covered shoulders and turned Ruby toward her dressing room. "Don't worry about it."

Tears scalded Pet's green eyes. She furiously blinked them away, turning to see Tom staring at her, wordless in profound sympathy. Stiff with righteous anger and raw pain, she couldn't respond to his look. She didn't need to communicate her desire to move away from the star's dressing room as Tom picked up the recorder to walk with her. Pride kept her shoulders squared and her head high, but she was trembling inside from Dane's abandonment of her. She was determined not to let it show how deeply she was hurt.

That resolve flew out of the window when Dane came in search of her a short few minutes later. A wall of stormy tears kept her from seeing him too clearly, but she had a blurred image of his tight-lipped countenance, which was all her temper needed.

"How could you let her talk to me like that?" Her angry voice scraped her throat to make the accusation hoarse. "How could you let her get away with it?"

"It's only twenty minutes before the show starts!" Dane flared. "What did you expect me to do? Try to defend you and have her do one of her exit scenes? Then where the hell would I be with all this equipment and crew and a half-finished special?"

"I don't care who she is or how important she is, nobody has a right to talk to anybody like that—not to me! Not to Tom! Not to anybody!" Pet retorted in a husky protest.

"And what about the show?" he challenged.

"Oh, God, yes. The show!" Her voice was breaking, cracking under the strain. "You said you'd sold your soul for it—and you were right. You'll get your show, Mr. Kingston. And I hope it keeps you happy, because I won't!"

"Of all the damned time and places to pick—" he began in exasperation.

"You'd better leave. You've got work to do before the show starts." She turned away from him, pretending to adjust something with the equipment while she choked on a sob. It was an eternity of seconds before she heard him walk away. She closed her eyes at the shattering pain in her chest.

"Are you all right?" Tom murmured anxiously.

"I'm fine," she sniffed, and wiped at her nose before lifting her chin. "We'll do his damned show."

The decision created a strange detachment that permitted her to get through the taping of the performance, functioning mechanically, completely emotionless. From the wings she got a shot of Ruby Gale accepting the final ovation from the crowd, a heartily applauding audience in the background, and exiting to the opposite side of the stage to receive the congratulations of her personal entourage.

The minute it was over Pet set the camera down and began unstrapping all the gear. "Take care of this stuff for me, Tom," she said tightly, and started to walk away. "I'm leaving."

"But if Mr. Kingston—"

"Tell him he has his show. . .and he can't fire me, because I quit."

CHAPTER ELEVEN

MOONLIGHT SILVERED the foamy caps of the waves rushing onto the sandy shore. Pet lifted her face to the ocean breeze, closing her eyes to the pain that hadn't found a release. Her hair had long ago been freed from its confining pins as if loose and falling free it would somehow allow the hurt to tumble from her. But it hadn't.

Turning parallel to the ocean, Pet began to walk again along the stretch of beach. To her left was the Boardwalk and its towering buildings and hotels etched in lights against the night sky. She didn't know how far she had walked since she had bolted from the casino theater to wander aimlessly up and down the quiet beach, avoiding the piers with their noisy rides and bright lights. She wasn't the only one walking along the oceanfront. A few others were strolling its expanses, mostly couples.

A wave came rushing in to lap the firmly packed sand near her feet, but she ignored its mild threat. Her gaze wandered ahead, studying the strip of glistening wet sand that marked the extent of the tide's encroachment onto the beach. The dark figure of a man was standing ten yards in front of her by the water's edge, but facing her and not the sea. Her heart gave a painful thump in her chest as she recognized Dane and paused.

Refusing to run or walk up to him, Pet took a few steps into the soft sand beyond the reach of the waves and sat down. Her hand shook as she lighted a cigarette and stared out to sea. Drawing her knees up, she rested her forearms on them. The sand crunched under Dane's approaching footsteps, but she didn't look up when he stopped beside her.

"I'd just about given up hope that I would find you." His voice was low and husky. "I looked everywhere—the hotel, the casino, up and down the Boardwalk. If it hadn't been for all that golden hair shining in the moonlight, I would probably have gone on looking all night for you."

Pet made no reply, not even acknowledging his presence with a look. She took another puff of the cigarette and watched the breeze blow the curling smoke away from the burning red tip. Inside she was dying.

"Don't you know you shouldn't be walking alone at night?" But when his question was met by her continued silence, Dane sighed heavily. "I can't even make you angry, can I?"

There was an agonizing tightness in her throat. The paralyzing numbness that had kept everything dammed up inside was wearing off. She started shaking and had to bury the cigarette in the sand to keep from dropping it.

"You were right, Pet," he said with a throbbing hoarseness. "I sold my soul for that show."

A tiny, agonized sound slipped through the constricted muscles of her throat.

He continued to tower motionless above her. "Pet, you're the only one who can buy it back for me."

The husky appeal in his voice finally pulled her head up. She searched his shadowed face. The pride and strength remained forever carved into his features, but his dark eyes were haunted.

"When the show was over and I found out you'd walked out, I didn't try to find you right away. I went back to the control van and sat there, going over in my mind what had happened and what you'd said." Turning, Dane sat down on the sand beside her, adopting her position and letting handfuls of sand run through his fingers. "I thought I had the thing that was most important to me right there in front of me—the show tapes. Not in so many words, but you told me what an arrogant, selfish bastard I was. I've been called that before, but coming from you...." He sighed heavily and clasped his hands between his spread knees, studying his linked fingers. "What I'm trying to say, Pet, is that what's important to me is your love and respect. Nothing else means anything."

"You don't really mean that, Dane," she whispered sadly. "You just want me to forgive you so you'll feel better. You don't care whether or not I love you. We haven't even known each other long enough to fall in love."

"Maybe you haven't, but I've been waiting for you all my life." His gaze locked onto hers and refused to let it go. "I love you, Pet. I realized it the morning that I came into your room to wake you up, and I knew that I wanted to wake you up every morning for the rest of my life. It was too soon. I couldn't tell you then. You would have thought I was handing you some line to persuade you to sleep with me. So I waited, knowing you were attracted to me and hoping that after this show was finished I'd have the time to make you fall in love with me, too."

"You don't even know me." She shook her head for a moment, breaking the spell he was casting.

"I know you. After our run-in a year ago, I made it my business to know about you. At the time I told myself my interest was purely professional," he said with a humorless laugh. "I personally reviewed everything you did, every project you were on, your past employment, your education, your family, everything. If you weren't any good, I was going to get rid of you—this green-eyed blond who told me to shut up."

"You've finally got rid of me. I quit." She wouldn't let herself be swayed by his revelations. He had hurt her too deeply tonight. It wasn't something that could be easily forgiven or forgotten.

"Pet, I erased the show tapes—all of them."

"What?" She jerked around to stare at him, wary and frowning.

"It wasn't an impulse. I thought it over very hard before I did it. You can call it a noble gesture if you want, but it was the only way I could prove that you were more important to me than the special."

"You shouldn't have done that!" She was stunned, incredulous.

188

"Why not?" Now he was watching her, his gaze searching through every nuance of her expressions.

"Because...all that work...all that time...." It was impossible to think of all the reasons when there were so many. "You've spent a lot of money."

"A lot of money," Dane agreed. "But it's worth every dime if you finally believe me."

"I believe you." After that kind of sacrifice, how could she doubt him?

"Do you forgive me?"

"Of course," Pet breathed, just beginning to realize the fulfillment this meant. "Dane, I fell in love with you, too. I was the most wretched person in the world when I thought the man I loved could care so little about me that—"

But she was never allowed to complete the sentence as his hand reached to pull her off balance and into his arms. He was kissing her and murmuring love words that she would cherish in her heart forever.

When Dane finally allowed her to surface from his loving assault, she was lying on the sand, her head pillowed on his sinewy forearm while he leaned partially over her. She drank in the sight of his compelling face above hers, passionately ardent in its expression.

"When will you marry me?" he demanded.

An old fear returned. "Do you really think I can keep you happy?" she whispered with a catch in her voice.

"No one else can. Haven't you accepted that yet?" he mocked. "No one else can irritate me and goad me into an argument quicker than you can. No one else

189

can touch me and make my senses swim with desire. From no one else do I demand such perfection as I do from you. You make me happy with a smile.''

"Ruby Gale—'' Pet began.

His mouth thinned in grimness. "Once and for all, let me exorcise that devil from us. It was always business between Ruby and me. The physical side of our relationship developed out of it because we were members of the opposite sex. She had sexual needs and so did I. Emotions were never involved on either side. I can't say that I'm particularly proud of it, but she's a stunning and sexual creature, and I am just a man.''

"That's just it, Dane,'' she tried to explain again. "In your business there will always be women like Ruby Gale.''

"God forbid!'' he muttered.

"Please, I'm serious,'' Pet insisted.

"But none of them will be you. Can't I get it through your head that I love you? It isn't just desire or physical gratification. It's love.''

His mouth closed onto hers to convince her of the difference. Pet became quite enchanted with his efforts as his weight pressed her onto the soft bed of sand. She was breathless and starstruck when he finally transferred his attention to the hollow of her throat. She splayed her fingers through his dark hair, quivering as his hands worked deftly at the buttons on her blouse.

"Do you think this is a proper behavior for a lady?'' she whispered with a trace of teasing amusement. "Letting a man make love to her on a public beach? After all your lectures, Dane Kingston, what will people think if they see me?"

"Dammit, Pet!" He started to get angry, then laughed. "I have champagne chilling in my room." He kissed her hard. "And if you dare say a lady wouldn't go to a man's hotel room, I'll strangle you!"

She linked her fingers around his neck and gazed at him impishly. "Who ever said I was a lady?"

BEWARE OF THE STRANGER

"THIS IS NOT A GAME. I DON'T PLAY GAMES."

His warning was quiet but his hand grasped her wrist, forcing her to drop the telephone receiver.

"Don't you?" Samantha's brown eyes shimmered with defiance. Temper threw caution to the winds. "You've been playing games with me all along—first letting me believe you were Owen Bradley, then lying— " She bit her lip, realizing she had virtually admitted that she knew he wasn't who he pretended to be.

The narrowing of his gaze indicated he had guessed what she'd been about to say. Her heart skipped several beats, but she had gone too far to turn back now.

"I don't know who you are," she said flatly, "but you aren't Chris Andrews!"

CHAPTER ONE

SAMANTHA'S FINGERS punched relentlessly at the typewriter keys. A furrow of concentration formed between her dark eyebrows and the line of her mouth was grim with determination. Regardless of her efforts, she couldn't achieve any speed with the manual typewriter. She might as well have been pecking the keys with one finger. Her little finger missed the "a" in "Yale" and the typed word became "Yle."

Sighing impatiently, Samantha reached for the eraser, nearly worn out from frequent use. The image of the sleek electric typewriter at home flitted wistfully through her mind. If only she could bring it to work, she thought, and immediately shelved the idea. An expensive model like that would raise too many eyebrows and too many questions.

The eraser gouged a hole in the paper, completely obliterating the error. "Damn!" Samantha muttered in exasperation, and ripped the sheet from the carriage.

"Problems?" The question was loaded with good-natured ribbing.

Samantha shot the dark-haired girl a quelling look. "None that a little manual dexterity wouldn't cure.

Why don't you lend me some of yours, Beth? You can afford it."

The snappish reply carried a trace of envy. There wasn't a machine in the place that Beth couldn't operate with lightning speed and efficiency. It didn't matter whether it was a manual or an electric typewriter, a copy machine or the teletype in the adjoining news wire room.

"Poor Sammi," Beth laughed. "Why don't you try the one-finger, hunt and peck method? Mr. Lindsey has used it for years." Referring to their mutual boss and the owner-editor of the newspaper.

"This is one reporter who's going to be a speedy typist—even if I have a mental breakdown first," Samantha grimaced, but her sense of humor had returned, however wryly.

"What are you working on?" Beth ignored the comment except for a faintly sympathetic smile that touched her lips. "I'm not busy. Maybe I can type it for you?"

"No, thanks." Samantha shook her head firmly, thick, luxurious seal-brown hair rippling about her shoulders. "It's the Around and About column. It's so dull you'd fall asleep before you were half-done. I wish Har—Mr. Lindsey would let me spice it up a bit." She quickly corrected her near reference to their boss by his first name.

Beth wrinkled her nose. "How could you ever spice up that boring column? 'Mrs. Carmichael's daughter Susan was home for the weekend.' 'Mr. and Mrs. Donald Bradshaw entertained guests from out of state.'" She irreverently mimicked the type of copy that appeared in the column.

"It would be easy," Samantha asserted, "if I were allowed to do a little snooping. Take this item about Frank Howard, our esteemed attorney and Yale graduate, who had one of his former classmates spend the weekend. It just happens that this former classmate applied for the position of District School Superintendent and Frank Howard just happens to be chairman of the school board. Now if that doesn't smack of political maneuvering and collusion, nothing does."

"Really?" Beth breathed, her eyes widening at that piece of gossip. "But no one's been offered the position yet?"

"Not yet," Samantha agreed dryly. "But I doubt if anyone else will get it other than our chairman's friend and fellow alumnus."

"Does the boss know?"

"Yes." She inserted a new sheet of paper into the typewriter and turned her disgruntled expression to her notes. "And he reminded me that he doesn't print that type of column."

Harry Lindsey had said a bit more than that. Samantha had listened to his twenty-minute lecture concerning the diplomacy needed to operate a small-town newspaper. He had pointed out that any of the innocent items in the column could be turned, through conjecture and supposition, into juicy gossip, a fact Samantha was well aware of.

He had also forcefully pointed out that these same

people who liked to see their names in print in the innocent column were generally business people in the community. The same business people he relied on to run advertisements in his newspapers and provide him with an income to keep the newspaper going. And a good editor didn't offend his clients just to sell copies unless there was ample justification. A little political back-scratching did not fall into that category unless there was fraud or criminal intention involved.

It was a statement Samantha couldn't throw stones at for fear one of them would boomerang. Her father did plenty of back-scratching. It was his considerable influence that had obtained her this job with Harry Lindsey for the summer. She had wanted to learn the basics of newspaper reporting, and what better place to do it than on the staff of a small-town newspaper? With this experience and a diploma in journalism that would be in her hands at the end of her next college year, Samantha was confident that she could get a job with a big publication. Her ambition was to become one of the best investigative reporters around.

But realistically, Samantha sighed, she had to concede the wisdom of Harry's attitude. For the time being, she would simply have to stem the instinctive urge to delve below the surface of a given situation. Her natural curiosity could run free later when she had achieved her ambition.

It wasn't a goal she talked about too much. Few people she knew would understand her desire. Most of her female classmates and even her co-workers on the paper, such as Beth, still considered work of secondary importance. Their first ambition was to find a man, with luck, to marry. There were one or two who were as dedicated as Samantha was to the pursuit of their careers, but each one also planned to have a man to share in her future.

At twenty-two, Samantha had few illusions left about men, at least as far as she was concerned. She didn't hate them or even dislike them. Samantha had simply faced the fact that there never could be "one" man in her life.

It wasn't that she was repulsive to look at—quite the contrary. Her freshly scrubbed, wholesome features were quite pleasing to the eye. There was even a suggestion of sensuality to the curve of her lips. The brown of her eyes, the same richly dark shade as her hair, sparkled often with animation and a zest for life. There was a frankness to their expression that was decidedly fresh and appealing. Her eyes didn't know how to be coy and flirt. Occasionally there was a glimmer of shrewdness in the warm brown depths, an inheritance from her father and a trait that Samantha intended to put to use in her chosen career.

The truth was that she was every man's ideal of a perfect sister. It was a backhanded compliment received so often that it had lost its sting. That could have been overcome with the right man. But Samantha doubted that there was a man alive who could overcome her biggest obstacle.

This summer's charade had pointed that out to her.

Being a new female face in a small town had attracted a lot of male attention to Samantha. Most of it was dissolved by her sisterly looks. At a local dance, she had overheard her date being teased that it must be like kissing his sister when he took her home. It was the last time the man had asked her out.

The few, very few, who had remained attentive would run to the hills the minute they found out she was Reuben Gentry's daughter, Samantha knew. She had discovered very early in life that the male ego was too fragile. Men weren't willing to marry a woman whose father would overshadow them their entire lives. Unless they wanted to share in the wealth and power he commanded, and Samantha wanted no part of that kind of man. Thanks to the shrewd perception she had inherited from her father, she usually spotted that kind the instant she met them and steered clear.

For a while Samantha had thought if she could find a man as powerful and wealthy as her father, she wouldn't have to worry about the problem of being Reuben Gentry's daughter. She had even been engaged to such a man when she was eighteen, but it had lasted only a month. She had found out two things. One was that money always wants more money and her fiancé considered their engagement more of a business alliance with her father. And secondly, she didn't love the man.

The broken engagement had also brought an end to any plans for a man in her life—at least in the singular. In time she would probably have affairs with men. She was a red-blooded woman with physical needs, too. It was even possible that she would fall in love with someone, but it wouldn't last—Samantha knew that. She loathed the terms "spinster" and "old maid." She preferred to think of herself as a confirmed "bachelorette." In these liberated times there was nothing to be ashamed of in not being married.

Reuben Gentry had always silently understood the burden she carried as his daughter. Only once had he said anything about it, and that had been after her engagement was broken and Samantha had explained why she had done it. He had suggested that she might prefer some anonymity, hinting that he wouldn't object if she changed her name.

Samantha had refused outright, declaring, "I'm not ashamed of who I am!"

Her cheeks dimpled slightly as Samantha concealed a smile. Only for this summer had she concealed her identity, wanting to work for the small newspaper without the usual notioriety that followed her. The smile continued to play about the corners of her mouth. Only minutes ago she had been wanting to spice up the column with a bit of gossip. And she was the biggest story in the entire town. Imagine how everyone would be set back on their heels if they found out that the innocuous Samantha Jones was really *the* Samantha Gentry!

"What are you smiling about?" Beth wanted to know.

Samantha let her mouth curve into a full smile. "Just imagining the readers' reactions if I actually printed the truth," she replied, without explaining further her exact meaning.

Beth shrugged, not finding the idea nearly as humorous as Samantha did. She continued flipping through the magazine lying on her desk and stopped turning pages when a particular article caught her interest.

"Here's my horoscope for the month," Beth said aloud and began reading it. "'June will be a calm month with plenty of warmth and laughter. Weekends will mean pleasant jaunts but not too far from home. Your closest friends will be a source of joy.' Nothing about weddings," she sighed. She glanced over the rest of the page. "Here's yours, Sammi. Do you want to hear it?"

"I dont' care," Samantha shrugged. She didn't put any stock in horoscopes. To her they always seemed to be couched in words that could be interpreted any way the reader wanted.

Her lack of enthusiasm didn't deter Beth. "'June will be an uncertain month. Beware of strangers entering your life. They may not be what they represent. Check the facts before trusting your intuition. Travel is not recommended.'"

"Wait until I tell the boss that," Samantha laughed. "I've finally got him to agree to let me do a feature article on that lady celebrating her hundredth birthday in the next town, and now I'll have to tell him I can't do it because my horoscope says travel isn't recommended."

"He'll be furious," Beth agreed seriously.

"Oh, honestly, you don't really believe all that hog-wash, do you?" Samantha declared with an incredulous shake of her head. She had been kidding, but Beth seemed to have taken her joke literally.

There was a defensive tilt of Beth's chin. "These forecasts are quite accurate."

"It depends on how you read between the lines," Samantha muttered, a little surprised that someone as efficient and practical as Beth could be superstitious about astrology forecasts. Most of them were turned out as haphazardly as pieces of paper in a fortune cookie.

But she wasn't about to become embroiled in any discussion about the facts or fantasies of astrology. With a dismissive shake of her head, Samantha turned back to the paper in her typewriter and began punching away at the keys. Beth said no more, slightly offended by Samantha's openly skeptical attitude toward something she half, if not completely, believed to be gospel.

When the column was typed, Samantha removed it from the carriage and began double-checking the spelling of the names with her notes. The street door opened and Samantha glanced up automatically. The tall, dark-haired stranger who walked in caught and held her attention.

Although Samantha had been living in the small town less than a month, intuition told her positively that the man was not a local resident. He was dressed casually in a forest green blazer and plaid slacks, nothing flashy nor overly affluent. His easygoing air wouldn't attract attention, yet Samantha couldn't shake the feeling that word would have reached her if there was such a man around. He wasn't the kind anyone ignored.

He walked directly to Beth's desk, which, besides being a reception desk, doubled as the classified advertisement section. Behind his relaxed attitude, Samantha sensed an uncanny alertness. The smooth suppleness of his stride suggested superb physical condition. Beneath the jacket, she guessed that the breadth of his shoulders tapering to a lean waist would confirm it.

The stranger stopped at the desk. "I'm looking for Samantha—"

A warning bell rang in her mind. "I'm Samantha Jones," she interrupted swiftly.

The man turned toward her at the sound of her clear voice. Instinct insisted that he had been aware of her watching him from the instant he walked through the door. She rose from her chair, the frankness of her gaze not wavering under the steady regard of his. Again with deceptive laziness, he smiled and walked toward her desk.

"The photograph on your father's desk doesn't do you justice, Miss Jones." There was the slightest inflection on her assumed name. The man spoke quietly yet firmly, as if he was unaccustomed to raising his voice. The iron thread of command was there without the need to shout.

Perhaps that was what had first tipped Samantha off to the fact that he had come to see Samantha Gentry and not Samantha Jones, the reporter. It was a trait her father looked for in his executives and associates. The reference to her picture on Reuben Gentry's desk seemed to confirm the stranger's connection with her father.

Samantha didn't recognize him, but that wasn't so strange. She knew very few of the people who worked with and for Reuben Gentry. Mostly they were faceless names.

"Your father?" Beth's voice echoed blankly from her desk. "I thought you said your father died two years ago, Sammi?"

For a fraction of a second, Samantha felt trapped by her own charade. "Yes, he did," she continued the white lie, calmly meeting the faint narrowing of the stranger's gaze. "But this man evidently knew my father."

"Yes, that's correct." The well-shaped masculine mouth, an underlying hardness in its line, twisted briefly as the man went along with her story.

Obviously he was bringing a message from her father, one he couldn't deliver in front of Beth, who believed Samantha's father was dead. Samantha reached for her handbag sitting beside her chair.

"Beth, we're going to the back room for some coffee," Samantha stated without satisfying the curiosity gleaming in the girl's eyes.

A table and folding chairs occupied the corner of a back room. A large coffee urn sat at one end of the table cluttered with clean and dirty paper cups and plastic spoons. It hardly resembled the plush boardrooms where Reuben Gentry held his meetings, but Samantha didn't even attempt to apologize for the ink- and coffee-stained tabletop. She walked to the urn and began filling one of the clean paper cups.

"I'm sorry, but I don't know you." Her gaze flicked briefly to the stranger. His veiled alertness was almost a tangible thing. "I assume Reuben sent you." It had been years since she had referred to her father as such.

"Owen Bradley, your fa—"

Samantha straightened. "You are Owen Bradley!" The statement came out smothered in an incredulous laugh. A dark eyebrow flicked upward in silent inquiry. Immediately she pressed her lips together and tried to stop smiling. "I'm sorry, I didn't mean to laugh. It's just that, well, you're not at all like I pictured Reuben's Man Friday to be."

Her frank brown eyes traveled over the man again, now identified as Owen Bradley, her father's secretary and general everything. Her image of Owen Bradley had been somewhat effeminate—a short, thin man perhaps with pale skin and thick glasses, highly efficient and a walking computer.

But this Owen Bradley, the real Owen Bradley, seemed to belong to the outdoors. His features were roughly hewn out of teak wood. There was nothing effeminate about him. Male virility was chiseled from the solid angle of his jaw through the faint broken bend of his nose to the smooth slant of his forehead.

At closer quarters, Samantha realized that his eyes were not dark brown as she had first thought. They were deep charcoal gray, like thick smoke, with the same obscuring ability to conceal his thoughts. There was nothing handsome about him, yet she felt some invisible force stealing her breath away.

Turning back to the coffee urn, she set another white cup beneath its spout. "Do you take cream or sugar?" The husky quality always present in her voice was more pronounced.

"Black."

"It's liable to be very black," Samantha warned. She handed the cup to him, noticing his large hands and the roughness of his fingers that suggested hard physical labor. "That's the way Harry likes it. Since he's the first one here in the mornings, that's the way he makes it, regardless of anyone else's preference." She added two spoonfuls of powdered cream to her own cup of the almost syrupy black liquid.

"I don't mind." And he sipped the potent liquid without the slightest grimace.

Samantha suppressed a shudder at the undiluted strength of the coffee he had just swallowed. Normally she preferred black coffee, too, but this wasn't really her idea of coffee.

"Have a seat." She gestured toward the dilapidated folding chairs.

The man named Owen Bradley chose one that put his back to the wall. His gaze scanned the room and corridor with lazy interest. Samantha doubted if he had missed any detail in that brief look.

"I was informed you had changed your name, Miss Jones, but I hadn't realized you'd killed your father off in the process." On the surface it sounded like an apology for his inadvertent reference to her father in front of Beth, but Samantha didn't think it really was.

"Only for the summer." Sitting in a chair opposite him, she absently smoothed the fold of her denim wraparound skirt. "It seemed easier than coming up with a fictitious background and activities for him as well as myself." Samantha wasn't entirely sure why she was explaining except that she didn't want her father's secretary thinking she had permanently disposed of her father even in her mind. "Why did Reuben send you instead of relaying a message through Harry?" Harry Lindsey, the editor, had been Samantha's communication link with her father.

"He tried, but Harry went out of town yesterday, so your father sent me up from New York."

"I'd forgotten about that." Belatedly Samantha remembered Harry's sudden departure from the office yesterday and his expected return at any moment. Then she tipped her head to one side, curiosity gleaming in her candid brown eyes. She wasn't surprised that her father hadn't attempted to contact her directly, but she did wonder why he had thought it necessary to send Owen Bradley to see her. "Is there something urgent?"

"Your father has arranged to have a couple of weeks free. He wants you to spend them with him," the quietly spoken voice informed her, not a flicker of expression chasing across his raw-boned features. "As Reuben put it, he wants you to spend one last vacation with him before you spread your wings and permanently leave the nest.''

That sounded like Reuben, Samantha thought with a sigh. Her fingers raked the thickness of the hair near her ears as she hesitated before responding.

Owen Bradley must have sensed the reason for her hesitation, because he said, ''A leave of absence can be arranged for your job. Harry never needed another full-time reporter on his staff anyway.''

Her temper flared for an indignant second. Initially Samantha had thought he was accusing her of being a spoiled and indulged rich girl whose daddy had created a job for her. But the dark smoke of his gaze was without censure. She checked her rising anger, giving Owen Bradley the benefit of the doubt. Possibly he was only reassuring her that she wouldn't be leaving Harry in the lurch.

''I could spend a week,'' she conceded, wanting to be with her father yet knowing the summer was short and wanting to gain all the experience working on the newspaper she could. ''Where's he going to be? Bermuda? St. Croix? Hawaii?'' she asked, naming his favorite vacation haunts.

''Thousand Islands,'' was the calm reply.

''Thousand Islands?'' Samantha repeated.

''Yes, near Clayton in upstate New York, the chain of islands in the St. Lawrence Seaway. He's rented a summer place on one of the islands,'' he explained patiently.

''I've heard of it.'' It would have been nearly impossible not to, because she had lived the majority of her twenty-two years in the state of New York.

The area had once been known as the millionaires' playground. Samantha suspected that her father had avoided it for that reason. Reuben Gentry rarely hobnobbed with the so-called élite. He preferred being included in a gathering because of his merits as an individual and not the size of his bank balance. Now that it had become a simple vacation spot, she supposed he had decided to investigate it.

"Is there anything wrong?" Owen Bradley had been watching her turn over the information in her mind and now questioned the result.

"With his choice?" Samantha returned, then immediately made a negative movement of her head. "None. It just surprised me, but I should have learned to expect that from Reuben by now. When am I supposed to leave to meet him?"

"Today."

"What?" Her mouth opened.

"It's short notice," he agreed with a faint smile. "A couple of important meetings were postponed and Reuben took advantage of it to arrange some time off. I'm to drive you there today."

Samantha sighed. Once her father made a decision, he never wasted any time carrying it out, and this spur-of-the-moment vacation was no exception. She thought of the clothes she had to pack and the washing she had been putting off until the weekend and all of her sportswear hanging in her bedroom closet at her father's apartment.

"You don't have to bother about packing any

clothes," Owen Bradley said, reading her thoughts. "Your father doubted if you would have the kind of clothes along that you would need, so he sent some clothes up this morning. Any personal items that were overlooked you can buy when we get there."

"He's thought of everything," Samantha mused, lifting her shoulders in a helpless shrug of compliance. "I suppose he's already there waiting for me."

"He'll meet us there the day after tomorrow, Saturday."

She had just lifted the paper cup to her lips when he answered. "Us?" she questioned, taking a quick sip. The cream hadn't improved the bitter flavor. "Is this going to be one of those half-business half-pleasure vacations?"

"Something like that," he agreed and finished his coffee.

Samantha did the same, but she couldn't contain a grimace of distaste. His charcoal gray eyes crinkled at the corners in smiling sympathy, but he didn't comment. As he straightened from the chair, she couldn't help noticing the bulky fit of his dark green blazer across his chest. It seemed a pity that a man with his muscular physique couldn't afford her father's tailor, but Samantha would have been the first to admit that there were more important things in life than clothes.

"It's about a six-hour drive to Clayton. If we leave now, we can make it before dark," Owen Bradley stated.

"Can't we wait until Harry comes back?" She frowned. "I'd like to explain...."

"I have a letter here for him." He removed a plain white envelope from the inner pocket of his jacket. "I'll leave it in his office while you freshen up before we go."

There were no more objections left to make. With a quiescent nod, Samantha rose. As they entered the corridor leading to the front offices she pointed out Harry Lindsey's private office and continued to her own desk as Owen Bradley stopped to leave the letter. Beth was instantly at her side.

"Who is he?" she whispered eagerly.

"A friend of the family." Samantha covered her typewriter and quickly began straightening her desk.

"Did you know him?"

"Not exactly. I knew *of* him." She handed the other girl the column she had completed just before Owen Bradley arrived. "Give this to Mr. Lindsey when he comes. There's been a family emergency and I have to leave."

"With him?" Beth's eyes rounded. "Are you sure it's safe? He looks kind of dangerous to me."

"He looks like a man to me," Samantha smiled. In her mind she put "man" in capital letters.

"Are you positive you know who he is?" Beth persisted in a low whisper. "Did you ask for any identification? Remember what your horoscope said: BEWARE OF STRANGERS."

"Oh, honestly!" Samantha laughed aloud this time. How could Beth take that nonsense seriously?

"It's just coincidence, I suppose, that your horoscope warned you about strangers this month and now a stranger that you think you've heard of walks in today," Beth declared in a wounded voice.

"That's all it is." Shaking her head at the disbelieving look in her co-worker's face, Samantha turned and gazed squarely at Owen Bradley standing silently in the hall opening.

There was a flash of white as he smiled. "Ready?"

"Yes," Samantha nodded, deciding that the only thing dangerous about him was the havoc he could wreak with her senses. That smile had increased her pulse rate and its charm had been directed at her only for a few seconds. It was a shame he worked for her father. Nothing would ever come of the attraction she could feel growing.

Enjoy it while it lasts, Samantha told herself. A series of pleasant interludes would probably be the only love life she would know. There was no sense shying away from the first potentially exciting male to come her way simply because the attraction was doomed to die.

Why not take advantage of the fact that it would be difficult for him to say no to the boss's daughter, especially when the boss was Reuben Gentry? But Samantha smiled at herself, knowing she would never take advantage of that fact, no matter how attractive she found a man.

CHAPTER TWO

THE TELEPHONE POLES were whizzing by so fast that they looked as close together as fence posts. Samantha's hand tightened instinctively on the car door's armrest as they approached a curve in the highway. Centrifugal force pressed her against the door, but the car hugged the road all the way around the curve into another stretch of straight highway.

"Is someone chasing us, or do you just always drive this fast?" she murmured, half-jesting and half-serious.

"Sorry." Owen Bradley's gaze flicked to her absently, almost as if he had forgotten she was sitting in the passenger seat. For the past two hours, Samantha was nearly positive he had. His foot eased its pressure on the accelerator and the powerful car slowed to a speed closer to the posted limit.

"I didn't mean to frighten you by driving so fast," he apologized.

"Normally it doesn't bother me when it's on the divided highway of an interstate, but on these secondary highways with their curves and intersecions ...." Samantha left the rest unfinished.

It wasn't that she questioned his driving skill. It was

superb. She was certain he was probably in control of the sports car every minute. But it was some of the other idiots with licenses that she worried about meeting.

"True, but the secondary highways offer a much more scenic route," he replied.

Staring out the window at the rolling hills dotted with groves of trees and pastoral farms, Samantha silently agreed it was beautiful, especially now that it wasn't so much of a blur. She shifted to a more comfortable position in the seat and the dark gray eyes slid briefly to her again.

"Getting tired?" he inquired.

"Stiff from sitting," she acknowledged with a smile that said it was to be expected after more than four hours on the road. They had stopped once to refuel and she had stretched her legs then, but that had been two hours ago.

"There's a good restaurant in this next town. We'll stop there to eat," he told her.

More silence followed; but it wasn't really so bad, Samantha conceded. In fact, it was rather nice. Not that she wouldn't have liked to find out more about the real Owen Bradley now that she had met him. He had answered her general question readily enough at the start of their journey, but he hadn't volunteered any information she hadn't already heard from her father.

He had been disinclined to talk about himself and the conversation had drifted into generalities and finally into silence. Although she knew a lot of facts about Owen Bradley, the man remained an enigma in many ways.

His latent animal grace suggested a man with physical pursuits as well as mental. It was hard for Samantha to visualize him spending as many hours in boardrooms and offices as his position with her father demanded. He was in his middle to late thirties and unmarried—that fact had been relayed by her father because he had wanted someone at his beck and call and not tied down with family.

But had he never been married? His blatant masculinity would attract a lot of women; Samantha could feel its pull on her. Was he divorced or widowed? Or a confirmed bachelor like herself? She would find out the answers eventually. She wasn't training to be a reporter for nothing. As a matter of fact, she could find out the details from her father when she saw him on Saturday.

Three-quarters of an hour later, they were sitting in the restaurant, their meal eaten, and lingering over their coffee. Owen had asked her a couple of questions about her job with the newspaper, which she had answered.

"This coffee is a definite improvement on Harry's," she added after answering his questions.

With a smile, she glanced from her cup to his face. He wasn't looking at her but watching the activities of the various people in the restaurant. Their corner table gave him an unlimited view and he had been taking advantage of it ever since they had sat down, only occasionally glancing at Samantha.

His lack of attention irritated her. She was the boss's daughter and he could at least pretend to be interested in entertaining her. Samantha tipped her head to one side, seal brown hair falling around her shoulders.

"Am I boring you?" she asked with frank candor.

The unreadable dark smoke screen of his gaze turned to her, dark brown nearly black hair growing thickly away from his wide forehead. The well-molded mouth was slightly curved, a suggestion of hardness in the otherwise sensual line of his masculine lips.

"Not at all," Owen Bradley assured her in his low voice that never seemed to vary in volume.

Now that Samantha had begun, she wasn't going to turn back. "I wasn't sure you were paying attention to what I said," she commented honestly.

"That's not true. You were telling me about a feature article you were going to do on an elderly lady named Jane Bates who's celebrating her hundredth birthday, and your unique idea about having her discuss how women's attitudes have changed over the years and how it's affected her, if at all." Very concisely he condensed what she had told him.

"I stand rebuked," Samantha apologized wryly. "I thought you were thinking about something else."

"I never forgot for a minute that you were sitting beside me." He regarded her steadily for several disturbing seconds.

Samantha wasn't certain how she should take that—whether he meant that he wished he could have forgotten about her or that she had made too much of an impression for him to do so. She had the uncomfortable feeling he was indulging her.

"Do you have a sister?" she asked finally, bracing herself for the words that would sting. She had lost her immunity with him.

"No." Amusement gleamed briefly in his eyes. "But if I did, she'd probably look like me and not like you." Samantha blinked. He pushed his chair away from the table and rose. "The sun's going down. We'd better get back on the road."

Inside the car once more, Samantha didn't attempt to check her curiosity. Half turning in her seat, she studied the roughly carved profile for a thoughtful second.

"Why did you say that?" she asked.

"What?" The headlight beams were slicing through semidarkness of twilight. His gaze didn't flicker from the road.

"That I wouldn't look like your sister if you had one," Samantha answered evenly.

"It's true. But that isn't what you're really asking, is it?" He glanced into his rearview mirror before pulling into the other lane to pass the car ahead. "No one who has worked very closely with Reuben could fail to hear the comments made about him and his daughter."

"So you've heard me described as attractive in a sisterly kind of way," she concluded.

"I've met a lot of men and none of them had a sister that looked like you." The mocking glitter of his charcoal eyes held her gaze for an instant. The quiet voice was teasing her and Samantha laughed softly. A pleasant warmth invaded her limbs. The contentment she felt had nothing to do with a full stomach or the refreshing draft of outside air from the vent. She relaxed in the bucket seat and gazed out the window at the first evening star twinkling in the purpling sky.

The stars were out in force when they finally drove through the quiet streets of Clayton, New York. Unerringly Owen Bradley drove through the town, not stopping until he reached a docking area on the river front.

No boats were moored there, so Samantha assumed it was a place where boats simply took on or let off passengers. When Owen reached behind the seat for his briefcase and stepped out of the car, she followed suit.

The night's darkness had colored the river black, and the rippling current reflected the silvery beams of a crescent moon, creating an effect of silvery lace against black satin. The horizon was an indistinguishable mound of lumpy shapes.

A strange voice broke the gentle silence, causing Samantha to nearly jump out of her skin. "The boat will be here shortly."

Spinning to face it, she saw a man, as tall as Owen Bradley, standing beside him. The shadows of a building concealed his features from her gaze.

"Thanks, Bert," said Owen Bradley, who then handed the man something.

Evidently it was the car keys, since the man opened the driver's door and slid behind the wheel. He reversed the car and started back the way they had come. Almost instantly the sound of the car's motor was joined by that of a boat, its navigational lights approaching the dock.

Samantha's elbow was taken and Owen led her to the side of the street within the shadows of a building. "Wait here," he ordered firmly, and walked in long easy strides towards the river's edge.

A sailboat came into view, its canvas furled, an empty mast jutting into the darkness. At almost the same instant that the boat cut its power to come into the dock, Samantha heard the car stop at the corner. She glanced at it, seeing a woman step from the sidewalk and climb into the passenger side before it drove off. Bert whoever-he-was obviously had a girl friend, she thought, smiling to herself, and turned back to the dock.

A line was being tossed to Owen from the boat. With quick expert twists, he had it looped around a mooring pin and was signaling to Samantha to join him. An older, burly-looking man was on deck to offer her a steadying hand aboard. He was built like a football player, muscle-necked and barrel-chested.

"Thanks," she murmured, but the man was already disappearing to another part of the boat.

The line was freed and Owen stepped on deck. "You'd better go below while we get under way."

The night air was cool on the water. If Samantha had had a sweater to cover the bareness of her arms below the short sleeves of her blouse, she might have argued that she would rather stay on deck. Instead she went below without protest.

The boat's engines throbbed with power as they moved away from the dock. The lights of the town began to recede. Samantha doubted if two minutes had elapsed between the time the car had stopped at the dock and the boat had left.

There was a brief shake of her head as a bemused smile touched her mouth. Only Reuben Gentry could have organized an operation as efficient as this, with someone waiting to take the car and the boat probably waiting just beyond the dock.

Settling onto a cushioned seat in the cabin, Samantha rubbed her shivering skin to erase the chilling goosebumps. On deck, footsteps approached the stairwell to the cabin. A few seconds later Owen Bradley's tall frame appeared above.

"Comfortable?" he inquired with that lazy movement of his mouth into a smile. His briefcase was set on a nearby cushion.

"Fine," Samantha nodded, "although I wish I'd brought a sweater."

He glanced sharply at her crossed arms that gave her a faintly huddled pose. "I think there's a spare windbreaker around here that you can wear."

He walked past the galley area and disappeared from her view. She could hear him opening and closing doors in what was probably the sleeping quarters. For an instant, Samantha had thought he might offer her the use of his jacket. She smiled wryly. Such gestures of chivalry were usually confined to the motion picture screens. He certainly was familiar with the boat and its contents, though.

"Here you go." He reappeared, offering her a light blue windbreaker. Samantha quickly slipped it on, losing her hands in the long sleeves. It was several sizes too large, but it offered protection, and that was what mattered. "Sorry, but there wasn't anything smaller."

"That's all right." She rolled the sleeves back to her wrists and spared a glance out through the narrowed windows. But the glass reflected a dark picture of the interior of the cabin. "How much longer before we arrive at the island?"

"An hour, more or less," he shrugged blandly and moved toward the steps leading to the deck. He paused. "There's some coffee in the thermos. Help yourself." He gestured toward the galley to indicate its location. Warmth was briefly visible in his smoky gaze. "I can't guarantee it's better than Harry's, but it is hot."

"Thanks," Samantha smiled, and he disappeared up the steps.

The coffee turned out to be delicious. She curled both hands around the cup to let her cold fingers take advantage of its heat. Relaxing against the cushion, she leaned her head back and listened to the throb of the boat's engines. It seemed to be the only sound in the entire world, except for the occasional murmur of voices between Owen and the burly boatman above.

Almost inevitably it seemed, her thoughts became focused on Owen Bradley. In so many ways, he was a contradiction—for instance, his muscular physique and keenly intelligent mind. Not that the two couldn't go together, but Samantha had difficulty visualizing him as her father's secretary.

The position involved limited, nearly nonexistent physical activity. And there was that air of indolence he adopted to disguise his ever constant alertness. The air of idle distraction bordered on aloofness, yet he was aware every second of what was happening around him.

The quiet, low-pitched voice was always firm with purpose and authority. Something in its tone suggested that whoever decided to cross him should beware of the consequences. Behind the bland expressions and slow smiles lay an unrelenting hardness, a hint of ruthlessness stamped in the rough features.

It would be interesting and a challenge to find out what made him tick, Samantha decided. Swallowing the last of the coffee, she leaned back again and closed her eyes. His subtle compliment that Samantha didn't look like the sister of anyone he had known returned. She realized Owen Bradley was very adept at handling women, too.

One minute she had been irritated because he didn't seem to be paying any attention to her, and within the space of a few words, he had made her feel important and beautiful without uttering any extravagant compliments she would have doubted. He had to be aware of the impact his virility had on the opposite sex.

Yet it wasn't the direct assault that a strikingly

handsome man would make. It was a slow undermining that removed the ground from under a girl's feet and sent her toppling before she realized what was happening. That was the danger Beth had instinctively sensed, Samantha decided. Admittedly, he was a devastatingly potent combination.

The long drive had tired Samantha more than she had realized. She drifted into a state of half sleep, aided by the hypnotic throb of the engines. Her head bobbed to one side, waking her. She sat up straight, rubbing the side of her neck and chiding herself for dropping off like an old woman.

The steady rhythm of the engines altered its tempo. Stifling a yawn, Samantha glanced at her watch, but she couldn't remember what time they had arrived at the boat. She had the feeling that she had been dozing for much longer than it seemed. As she started to peer out of the narrow windows, footsteps again approached the stairs to the cabin.

"We're coming into the island now," announced Owen, coming halfway down the stairs.

"I'll be right there," Samantha answered.

Picking up her cup, she carried it to the galley sink and rinsed it out. As she started toward the steps, she noticed the briefcase sitting in the cushion and picked it up, glancing briefly at the initials. Her ascent to the deck was in time to catch a shadowy glimpse of rocks, trees and shrubs before the island was obscured by a solid wall of black that suddenly surrounded three sides of the boat and blocked out the night sky. It took her a full second to realize that they had glided silently into a boathouse. The engines were cut. In the dimness, Samantha could just barely make out the shapes of the two men making the boat fast as it rubbed against the side of the inner dock. A solitary light bulb was switched on when the boathouse doors to the river were shut. It cast more shadows than the darkness it illuminated.

After the incessant hum of the engines, the silence seemed eerie. Water lapped against the hull and the men's footsteps echoed hollowly on the boards of the dock. The boathouse seemed like an enormous cavern with its high walls and roof to allow the tall-masted sailboat within.

"Ready?" Owen Bradley's voice prompted from the dock.

Samantha moved toward him, accepting the steadying hand on her arm as she stepped from the boat deck onto the dock. The boat rocked slightly as she pushed off and she stumbled against him, the briefcase making her balance awkward. Immediately, his large hands spanned her waist to hold her upright. The hard length of him was imprinted on her hips and thighs.

Tipping her head back, Samantha started to make a self-deriding comment about her clumsiness, but the words never left her parted lips. The mesmerizing quality in his gaze stole her voice and breath. Her pulse tripped over itself in rapid succession. When his attention slid to her mouth, she was certain he was going to kiss her, and she held her breath in anticipation.

225

The grip on her waist lingered for several more seconds, then he firmly held her steady as he stepped back. Disappointment surged through Samantha. She tried to hide it with a shaky laugh and a change of subject.

"You should ask Reuben for a raise when he gets here on Saturday," she jested as if that moment of intimacy had never been about to happen.

His expression was immediately shuttered, yet there was considering alertness behind the lazy smile. "Why do you say that?"

"Because it doesn't suit his corporate image to have his secretary running around carrying a briefcase with someone else's initials," she answered as she offered the briefcase to him.

The expensive briefcase carried telltale marks of much use. Near the handle were two gold letters: C.S. Samantha had noticed them briefly when she had picked the case up from the cabin seat.

"I think Reuben can afford to buy you a briefcase with your own initials, Owen," she declared.

She hadn't placed any significance on the incorrectly initialed briefcase. If she had thought anything about it at all, it had been only an idle assumption that he had purchased it used because it was sturdy and durable, capable of taking the beating of travel and use that his position would demand.

He took the suitcase, glancing at the initials thoughtfully before meeting her smiling and unwary look. "I'd forgotten that as a reporter it's your job to notice things," he mused aloud. The smoke screen of his gaze made his thoughts unreadable as he paused. "I'm not Owen Bradley."

Samantha's brown eyes widened. "You said—"

"No, you said I was Owen Bradley," he corrected lazily. "I simply didn't bother to deny it. Actually what I had been going to say was that Owen Bradley had told me where I could find you."

"Then who are you?" she demanded with an accusing frown.

"Chris Andrews. The 'S' is for Steven, my middle name." His finger tapped the initials on the briefcase. "The 'A' was knocked off sometime or another."

"Chris Andrews?" Samantha repeated in disbelief. "*The* Chris Andrews?"

"I don't know how many you know." A mocking smile played with the corners of his well-shaped and firm mouth.

As far as Samantha was concerned, there was only one Chris Andrews. He wasn't exactly a rival of her father's, but they held competitive interests that often clashed. But Reuben Gentry admired his business and financial skills even when he cursed him. And like her father, he shunned publicity. Samantha couldn't ever remember seeing a picture of him.

"Does Reuben know you've brought me here?" she demanded, still trying to sort through the astounding revelation and find its true significance.

"Of course," Owen Bradley, who now turned out to be Chris Andrews, replied, nodding without hesitation. "I told you, he'll be here Saturday."

"Why?" She tipped her head to the side.

"Because I invited him," he returned blandly.

"This is your home?" confronted Samantha. "Your boat?"

"Yes."

"Why am I here? And why is Reuben coming?" All of her reporter instincts rushed to the fore, and she sharply questioned his motives as she drew herself up to her full height of five feet six inches and still had to look up to see his face, raw-boned and unreadable.

"Reuben owns stock in some companies I have been trying to buy and he has been unwilling to sell. It's an amicable disagreement. I invited him here for two weeks in hopes of negotiating a compromise. He accepted, but I wouldn't attempt to guess at his reasons," the man who had identified himself as Chris Andrews replied.

"That still doesn't answer why I'm here," Samantha reminded him smoothly.

"You're here for the same reason I gave you at the newspaper. Reuben wants to spend some time with you before you fly away into the world. He asked if you could come and I agreed."

"Why would you agree? Wouldn't I be disrupting you from your purpose and distracting my father?" she accused.

"Possibly, but I'm willing to take the risk," he shrugged diffidently. "Besides, if having you here will put your father in a good mood, it might make the negotiations easier."

"What you mean is that my presence might make

228

him less resistant to your persuasions. I'm here to soften his stand, is that it?''

"And with luck to have a peaceful and relaxing week with your father," Chris Andrews added.

His logic was convincing her of the truth in his answers, however selfish the motivation was. But there was one point that Samantha still wanted to have clarified.

"Why am I here now? Before Reuben comes on Saturday?" she wanted to know, boldly meeting his veiled look.

"Obviously we've never met," he acknowledged the fact. "I thought it would be prudent to get to know you a bit beforehand to see which way the wind blew."

"In case I turned out to be an obstacle." She completed what he had left unsaid. "You'll find out, Mr. Andrews, that I don't even attempt to influence my father one way or the other when it comes to business matters."

"Then we all should have a very pleasant vacation. Especially if you started calling me Chris." The suntanned corners of his eyes crinkled as he smiled. "Shall we go to the house?"

His hand was raised in a gesture that indicated she should precede him to the door leading out of the boathouse. Samantha took an agreeing step and stopped, a question suddenly occurring to her.

"Why didn't you tell me who you were in the beginning? Why all this secrecy until now?" she demanded with another faintly defiant tilt of her head.

"If I told you at the newspaper office, I'm not certain you would have agreed to come with me. You might not have agreed to the vacation at all. When you mistook me for Reuben's secretary, I took advantage of it to get you here. Once you were here, I thought I would be able to persuade you to stay. Have I?" The dark head was tipped to one side, the glittering light in his eye mockingly asking to be forgiven for the harmless deception.

"If I said no, would you take me back?" Her eyes were bright. They had lost their accusing darkness as his explanations satisfied her without eliminating the trace of irritation she felt at being deceived.

"At this hour? I'm afraid not." His eyebrows slid upward. Chris Andrews knew she wasn't seriously expecting him to agree and his response was in the same light vein as her question.

"In that case, since you've succeeded in tricking me here, you might as well show me where I'm going to sleep tonight," Samantha declared in a sighing agreement that was only partially reluctant.

"This way." Again Chris indicated the door, standing to the side for Samantha to lead the way.

As she opened it and stepped into the night, the interior light from the boathouse revealed a path of dirt and bedrock worn smooth from frequent use. The light was switched off when Chris walked through the door.

Samantha stopped. "The man who was on the boat is still in there," she reminded him, knowing the boathouse would be pitch black without the one light.

"Tom? No, he left within minutes after we docked. He's at the house drinking coffee by now," he assured her, tucking a hand beneath Samantha's elbow to guide her over the path that was unfamiliar to her.

A light gleamed distantly through the thick stand of trees lining the path.

It appeared to be their destination as they wound along the trail through the trees. Samantha couldn't help reflecting on the day's events and the man whose hands so firmly guided her along. She was unaware of the soft laugh that escaped her curved lips until Chris Andrews asked in a tone of amused curiosity, "What's so funny?"

Samantha darted him a sideways glance, but little of the light from the stars and the sliver of the moon penetrated the dense tree limbs overhead. His craggy features were shadowed.

"Beth, the girl at the newspaper office, read my horoscope today for the month of June." Her smile deepened as she paused, considering her skeptical reaction to the forecast. It had been more like outright disbelief.

"Are you a follower of astrology?" His voice echoed her own previously held opinion that it was a great deal of nonsense.

"I haven't been, but after today, I might reconsider," Samantha conceded, the curve remaining on her mouth.

"Why after today?"

"Because my horoscope said to beware of strangers,

that they wouldn't be what they seemed," she explained with a short laugh. "It certainly turned out to be prophetic in this case. I was just becoming accustomed to the fact that you were Owen Bradley, a man I'd long pictured as being pale, short and thin, wearing glasses. Now I learn that you're really Chris Andrews and not Owen Bradley at all."

"I see what you mean." But the inflection of his voice didn't seem to find it as genuinely amusing as Samantha did, and she let the subject drop.

The house of native stone and wood was a rambling, one-story structure nestled in the trees. The spacious interior was designed with traditional simplicity. Although all the furniture was finely crafted, the casual atmosphere gave the impression that feet could be put up anywhere.

A tray of coffee and an assortment of cookies had been set near the sofa in front of the massive stone fireplace in the living room. A yawn rose in Samantha's throat as she tried to take another drink of her coffee. She covered the action quickly with the back of her hand, but not before Chris Andrews noticed it and suggested she would prefer her bedroom to more coffee.

"Maggie!" he called, and a tall blond woman appeared in the living room archway. "Would you show Miss Gentry her room?" he asked before introducing Samantha to Maggie Carlton, identified as Tom's sister.

The woman, in her mid-thirties, had inherited some of her brother's looks. She was pleasantly attractive, although some of her features were forcefully strong, almost intimidatingly so. There was keen intelligence in the blue eyes that met Samantha's smile with reserved friendliness.

Yet there was something that didn't seem quite right, and Samantha couldn't decide what it was. Maybe it was the look that Maggie Carlton had given Chris Andrews before she had shown Samantha to her bedroom. It wasn't exactly the type of look that would be exchanged between employer and employee. There was something more familiar in it that indicated a relationship more like the one Samantha had with Harry Lindsey, a friend of her father's and known to her long before she went to work for him this summer.

There was nothing wrong with a suggestion of friendship between the two, except that the age difference of Chris Andrews and Maggie Carlton was not as vast as the one between Samantha and Harry. Samantha didn't want to dwell on why that bothered her.

CHAPTER THREE

IT WAS NEARLY MIDDAY before Samantha wakened, a discovery that hurried her movements to dress. The bedroom closet was filled with sports clothes of every description, although the majority of them were decidedly casual and made for physical abuse.

Wearing a pair of wheat-colored denim pants and a matching tan and brown plaid blouse, Samantha hurried from her room into the hallway. A complementing gold scarf had been in a dresser drawer. She had folded it and used it as a hairband, the shimmering tails of the scarf partially lost in the rich seal brown shade of her dark hair.

Relying on her memory of the house's layout from the previous night, she retraced her way to the living room, then let instinct guide her to where the dining room should be located. Voices were coming from the room she had chosen as her destination. Samantha paused in the doorway to listen without being conscious that she was virtually eavesdropping.

Chris Andrews—she had readjusted her thinking to call him by his right name—was standing in front of a large picture window. Cream-colored slacks of a roughly corded material molded the muscular length of his legs. A windbreaker of navy blue covered most of a knit shirt in a lighter shade of blue.

But it was the expression on the roughly chiseled features that claimed Samantha's attention. It was hard and unrelenting as his gaze narrowed on the blond woman facing him.

"There won't be any discussion." The tone of his ominously low-pitched voice was clipped with command. "I don't like it any more than you do, but that's the way it stays."

Samantha must have made some involuntary movement at the chilling sound of his voice, because as Maggie Carlton started to protest with a grim voice, "But..." his narrowed gaze swung to the dining-room entrance and Samantha. A bland mask immediately covered his tanned features.

"Good morning. So you've finally decided to rejoin the living." The fine thread of mockery in his greeting held amusement. If Samantha hadn't witnessed the incident a second ago, she would never have guessed a controlled anger broiled beneath the easygoing surface Chris Andrews now displayed.

She considered excusing herself, but that would have meant silently admitting that she had overheard what had been a private and personal exchange. She decided to pretend that nothing was amiss as far as she was concerned.

"Good morning," she returned cheerfully and advanced into the room. "I can't remember the last time I slept so late. It must be the fresh air."

"Undoubtedly," Chris Andrews agreed, darting a

pointed glance at his so-called housekeeper.

Maggie Carlton turned to face Samantha and smiled. There was a tightness in the movement that suggested the other girl wasn't as adept at concealing her emotions as Chris Andrews was. "I'll bring you some coffee, Miss Gentry. Do you have any preference for breakfast?"

"No breakfast for me," Samantha refused. "Coffee will be fine for now, since lunch is barely an hour away."

"Are you sure there isn't something you would like? Toast? Or a sweet roll to tide you over to lunch?" he inquired with a lifted brow.

"Quite sure," Samantha said, nodding decisively.

Slipping her fingers into the front pockets of her denims, she walked nonchalantly to the large picture window, but her side vision caught the look exchanged between the two. It was more than a signal of dismissal for Maggie to leave. Somehow Samantha had the sensation that Chris Andrews was transmitting a message that everything was all right.

As Maggie left the room, Samantha concentrated on the scenery outside the window. Considering the spectacular view offered, it wasn't hard to do. Some time during her life she had probably seen pictures or brochures of the Thousand Islands area, but nothing had prepared her for the breathtaking beauty that unfolded beyond the window.

The unending expanse of the majestic St. Lawrence River reflected the electric blue color of the sky. Its stunning breadth resembled a lake, rather than a river. The vivid green of tree-studded islands dotted its length. On the island closest to view, still some distance away, Samantha could see the white boards of a building shining through partially cleared trees.

"It's quite a view, isn't it?" Chris was standing beside her, gazing out the window.

"I never dreamed it was like this," she murmured in agreement. "It's all so—" she searched for the words "—so unspoiled. Are there really a thousand islands?" From the window's view on this rocky knoll of their island she could see possibly five, varying in size from fairly large to very small.

"There are over seventeen hundred islands in the St. Lawrence, most of them privately owned." He pointed toward the north. "That far island is in Canadian waters."

"Over one thousand seven hundred." Samantha was still caught by the number. "That's unbelievable!"

"The largest island has more than a hundred square miles and the smallest is a rock and two trees. By government definition, an island is land surrounded by water with at least one tree. Without trees, it's considered a shoal." A lazy smile was directed at her. "Do you think there's a chance now that you'll enjoy your stay here?"

"I might even write up a travel article to put in the paper when I get back," Samantha laughed. Her enthusiasm for the time she would spend here was growing. It was no longer based mainly on being with her father.

"Do you swim?"

"Yes, why?" Samantha glanced up at him, an impish light dancing in her brown eyes. "Are you trying to tell me that if I want to leave this island before my father comes, I'll have to swim?"

"I had something else in mind when I asked." There was silent laughter in his expression. "But I'll go along with that thought, too."

"Why did you ask, then?"

"It's supposed to be warm this afternoon. This island is crescent-shaped, forming a sheltered cove that's perfect for swimming. I was going to suggest we make use of it this afternoon," Chris replied.

"Sounds wonderful," she agreed as Maggie reentered the informal dining room with the coffee.

IT WAS more than wonderful. It was perfect, Samantha concluded, as she rested a cheek on the back of her hand. The sunbaked boards of the raft anchored in the cove were warm beneath her. Her black swimsuit was backless, exposing her skin to the burning rays of the sun.

A tiny sigh of regret slipped out. An hour of swimming and diving in the cove, plus another hour sunning on the raft—soon she would have to retreat to the shade or risk turning into a boiled lobster.

Through the slit between her lashes, she could see Chris sitting on the other side of the raft, muscles bronzed and rippling in the sun. His gaze was slowly sweeping the river, betraying an alertness in her otherwise relaxed pose. Only a few boats had ventured anywhere near the island. Chris had explained that the pleasure craft mainly stayed near the ship channel unless they were operated by people who knew the river and shoals well.

The ship channel could be seen from the island. Samantha had glimpsed several large freight ships gliding, silently it seemed from her distance, up the river toward their ports of call on the Great Lakes. It was an impressive sight to see them moving majestically in such a contrified setting along the international seaway.

As if feeling her gaze, Chris turned. Samantha didn't pretend she hadn't been studying his decidedly masculine physique. Instead she let her lashes rise more and smiled leisurely.

"Ready for another swim?" he asked.

"No," she sighed ruefully and levered herself onto her elbows, "but if I don't get in the water or the shade pretty soon, I'll be burned to a crisp."

Fluidly, he was on his feet, offering a hand as she started to rise. It was an impersonal grip that pulled her upright, firm and releasing her without lingering for any suggestive moments, although Samantha wished it had.

At close quarters, the sight of him clad in brown swimming trunks with a gold stripe at the side was disturbing her senses. He was so vibrantly male that the primitive urges had awakened within her. If Samantha hadn't already been aware of their existence, she would have been shocked. As it was, she tried to ignore the sensations.

His attitude this afternoon had been friendly, but it hadn't invited any gestures that might put their relationship on a more familiar level. Samantha wondered if it was because of Maggie Carlton or because he wasn't interested in her as a woman. Regardless of his comment that she didn't look like a sister, she hoped that wasn't what he had in mind.

With an over-the-shoulder, downward look, his glance told her to follow an instant before he dived cleanly into the water. Her shallow dive paralleled his course. She surfaced a few feet from him, treading water as she pushed the wet hair away from her face with one hand. The coolness of the water against her sun-warmed skin sent an uncontrollable shudder through her that clattered her teeth.

"It feels like an ice cube now," she said with a shiver.

"Want to call it a day?" he asked, raking fingers through the wet thickness of his own hair.

Samantha's answer was to strike out for the cove's shoreline. Within a few strokes, he was pacing beside her, powerful arms slicing effortlessly to draw him through the water. Samantha didn't attempt to race him; she knew she would soon be outdistanced. Even though she was a good swimmer, she was no match for him.

The physical exertion helped to ease the chill of the water, but the shivers returned the minute her feet touched bottom to wade ashore. The beach towels were lying on a large boulder near the shore. Chris was closer and he reached them first.

"I think you need this," he smiled indulgently, and unfolded a towel to wrap it around her shoulders.

The sun had warmed the thick terry-cloth material. As it encircled her shoulders, Samantha closed her eyes in silent enjoyment of the warmth. She clutched the front of the towel around her, as Chris began rubbing the material against her shoulders and upper arms.

Opening her eyes, she murmured in appreciation, "Mmm, thanks... that feels good!"

Without realizing it, she swayed toward him, partially the result of the massaging pressure of his large hands. Her head was tipped back to gaze at him, water glistening on her lips. His hands stopped their motion, but they didn't release her.

A magnetic current flowed between them, stopping time. There was an imperceptible tightening of the strong fingers on her shoulders as his head made a slight downward movement toward her lips, and Samantha's heart thudded in anticipation of his kiss.

A motorboat swept close to the island, throttling down to a low drone as it passed the cove. The charcoal gaze flickered to the sound, wavering for tantalizing seconds, then focused on the boat. He lifted his head, his hands resting impersonally on her shoulders again. The withdrawal was complete. When his gaze returned to her, there was nothing in it to suggest that for a few seconds he had intended to kiss her.

"Let's go up to the house so you can change into some dry clothes," he suggested.

One hand fell away as he stepped to the side. The

other slid between her shoulder blades to direct her toward the well-worn path. Disappointment was bitter on Samantha's tongue. She wasn't about to pretend that he hadn't been about to kiss her—not this time.

"You were going to kiss me, then stopped. Why?" she demanded, her innate candor demanding the same from him.

The pressure of his hand propelled her forward despite her stiff resistance. She thought he was going to ignore her question and would have repeated it if his gaze hadn't slid to her. The mocking light in the dark gray depths didn't completely mask the hard glint.

"Maybe I didn't like the idea of being observed." His gaze swerved pointedly to the boathouse.

Samantha followed it, spying the burly figure of Tom Carlton messing around with the canvas from a sail. He had been in the vicinity of the boathouse all the while they were swimming. But she didn't believe for a minute that his presence had anything to do with Chris's changing his mind and said so.

"Don't give me that line!" Her temper was igniting. "It was the motorboat going by that distracted you. And I don't believe you would care whether Tom or a bunch of strangers saw us. It was something else that made you change your mind. You're using them as an excuse."

They had reached a section of the path that wound through a thick stand of trees, concealing them from the view of anyone from the house or the cove. His hand stopped pushing her forward as he stopped. Samantha did, too, bristling with wounded pride. His fingers slid through the tangle of wet hair to the back of her neck.

"Don't be ridiculous." The smile he gave her was lazy and warm.

The magic of it momentarily held her captive. Samantha remained motionless as his head dipped toward her. The touch of his mouth on her lips was light and cool and broke the spell. She didn't want gentleness. Violently she twisted away, her eyes flashing fire.

"And don't you be patronizing!" she snapped, spinning to storm up the path toward the house.

"Wait a minute."

His hand grabbed her arm to force her to obey, his fingers digging through the towel into the tender flesh of her arms. She stopped, not trying to wrench free. She slid a freezing look of distaste to his hand, despising his touch with force equalling the one that had a moment ago desired his kiss.

"Let go of me!" she demanded coldly.

"Sam, I—" A fine thread of steel ran through his voice, a grim warning that Samantha interrupted.

"Reuben is the only one who calls me Sam. To everyone else I am Samantha or Miss Gentry—and that includes you, Mr. Andrews," she informed him with icy disdain.

Something she had said struck a sensitive chord. A muscle jerked in his lean cheek as he clenched his jaw to check a retort. The habit of observing people's reactions and pursuing their cause had already become

243

too deeply ingrained for Samantha to ignore it.

"It's Reuben, isn't it?" she demanded grimly. "You're afraid of my father."

"I am not afraid of Reuben Gentry." She could hear the hardness of his low voice as he enunciated each word.

"Probably not in the usual sense that most people are," Samantha conceded, shaking her head. "No, you don't want to indulge in any dalliance with his daughter for fear of offending him." Sarcasm laced her voice. "Are you afraid I'll run to him and accuse you of—what's that delightful old phrase—trifling with my affections? If I did that, he just might get angry at you and never agree to sell you that precious stock you're so anxious to buy. What a story this would make!"

Her laugh was short and contemptuous. His other hand took a matching grip of her opposite shoulder. The bright fire of her gaze unflinchingly met the dangerous storm clouds gathering in his eyes, but she felt insulated from his fury, despite the punishing grip of his hands that threatened to shake her to pieces.

"Maybe I should spread the word of how you cower at the thought of my father," she continued caustically. "I bet it would amuse a lot of people to discover that you tremble at the prospect of his displeasure. You pretend to call the tune, but you're the one doing the dancing. If it wasn't so pitiful, it would be—"

She was jerked to his chest, his mouth smothering the rest of her sentence. With brutal force, his kiss ravaged her lips, inflicting pain. Neither resistance nor response occurred to her. Her only thought was to survive the cruel assault of her senses.

She was caught in the thunderous storm of his male dominance. The reverberating roll of her heartbeat was loud in her ears. Lightning flashed through her veins, carrying a searing exhilaration of fear and excitement. But the punishing kiss had been obtained by arousing his anger, so there was no satisfaction in the crush of his hard embrace.

The iron bands of his fingers kept her trapped against his muscular length as he lifted his head. Feeling beaten and bruised, the sigh that escaped her throbbing lips was one of defeat rather than relief.

"That was what you wanted, wasn't it?" The cold steel of his eyes was impossible to hold.

"No." Samantha shivered uncontrollably, and this time it wasn't from the chilling swim. Her gaze slid away from his face. "No, it wasn't what I wanted."

He didn't try to stop her when she pushed herself out of his arms. The towel slipped and Samantha pulled it tightly around her, wanting to huddle into the rough material. She couldn't explain, not without admitting how much he had hurt her, first with his chaste attempt at a kiss and then with the latent degradation of the second kiss. She had the family pride, if not her own, to uphold. Squaring her shoulders, she lifted her chin.

"No, it wasn't," he said.

It took her a second to realize Chris was agreeing with her earlier assertion. The harshness had left his voice, causing her to glance at him warily. He seemed vaguely bemused.

"Aren't you afraid I'll run to Reuben and tell him the way you treated me just now?" she accused.

"You aren't the type to run to your father. You're as independent and self-sufficient as he is," he said with absolute certainty. "I guessed that all along."

Mystified, Samantha stared at him. "If you weren't afraid I would cause trouble for you with Reuben, then why didn't you kiss me?" She challenged him to prove his statement.

"But I did kiss you," he answered complacently, admitting with a slight shrug, "more roughly than I originally intended, but you have only yourself to blame for that. Your tongue has barbs."

"I don't understand." Samantha shook her head, not quite believing him. "That doesn't explain what stopped you before."

"I told you—I wanted more privacy. Come on." His hand slipped under her elbow, turning her toward the house. His attitude indicated that he had no intention of discussing it any further. "Let's go to the house."

Samantha bit her lip, more questions arising from his answer, but she sensed this time he would ignore them. He had said all he was going to say. Instinct told her that she wouldn't be able to rile him a second time regardless of her persistence. He was firmly in control and she doubted her ability to shake his hold.

Instead, she silently let him direct her toward the house, mulling over the answer he had given her to see if she could find any credence in it. Privacy, he had told her, supposedly because of Tom's watching. Yet Samantha knew that it had been the motorboat that had distracted him. Perhaps the distraction had reminded him that Tom was in the vicinity.

But why should that matter? Chris Andrews didn't seem the kind of man who would care what others saw or thought of his actions. Unless—a possibility glimmered—unless Tom would have related what he saw to his sister Maggie. Perhaps that was what concerned Chris and made him withdraw.

Was Maggie his mistress, his lover? It was certainly plausible even if she wasn't startlingly attractive. And there had already been one disagreement between them—Samantha had overheard part of it that morning. Had it been over her? Was Maggie jealous because he had a young female guest in the house, someone who would be entitled to his attention?

It was very likely. What was it Chris had said—that he didn't like it any more than Maggie did, but that was the way it had to be. Yes, because that was the way Reuben wanted it. He had specifically asked for Samantha to be invited. Chris could hardly refuse.

There was a dejected curve to her mouth as she reached the conclusion. She regretted the instinct and training that had refused to let the incident rest until she had discovered the reasons behind it. He had kissed her, yes, because she had expected it, invited it. Being the perfect host, he had obliged. Ruthlessly he would use anyone and anything to get what he wanted.

"Damn!" Samantha swore silently in bitterness. Why was it she was always attracted to the men who ended up only wanting something from Reuben Gentry? Her identity as an individual always seemed to get overshadowed by her position as his daughter. She had thought she had accepted that, but now she realized she hadn't.

Chris Andrews had made her resentment of her situation rise even higher than before. Whatever had made her think that he was any different than the other men she had known?

He wanted to use her to accomplish his own ends just as all the others did.

The knowledge erected a barrier. Behind it, Samantha remained outwardly friendly and congenial, going along with suggestions he made to entertain her the rest of the afternoon and evening, but making sure there was never any opening for intimacy. If he had noticed the difference in her behavior, he didn't indicate it. And Samantha went to bed that evening confident that she had restored her pride and self-respect.

When she entered the living room the following morning en route to the dining room for breakfast, she saw Chris seated at a desk located in a far corner with walls lined with shelves, a mock study area in the large room. A black telephone receiver was in his hand. He glanced up as she entered, recognition replacing the look of total concentration in his expression.

"I'll let you talk to her yourself," he said into the

mouthpiece before covering it with his hand. "It's your father," he told Samantha. "Something unexpected has come up and he won't be able to come until the first of the week. He wants to be sure you're all right and won't mind waiting until then for him to come. I told him you wouldn't mind, but I think he'd rather hear it from you." There was something faintly mocking in his tone.

Did Chris think she would welcome more days spent alone with him, Samantha wondered as she walked to the phone. He was probably so conceited that he thought she hadn't guessed the falseness of his attention. In his arrogance, he probably thought he was playing her along very expertly. But she wasn't a toy to be used and discarded.

Putting those thoughts aside, Samantha took the phone from his hand and said with determined brightness, "Hello, Reuben."

"How are you doing, Sam?" came the response.

She smiled a bit wryly. "I'm surviving." Chris Andrews leaned negligently backward in his chair. Yet every fiber sensed the intensity with which he listened and watched.

"Sam, I'm sorry about this delay. Believe me, if I—"

"You don't have to explain," Samantha interrupted. She read through his concern and heard the faint preoccupied air in his voice, a telltale sign that he was engrossed in some weighty and no doubt serious problem. She had long ago learned that her father rarely postponed anything unless there was a crisis looming. "I know you're doing everything you can," she assured him. "And don't worry about me. It's lovely here and I know Chris will keep me entertained until you come."

"Chris?" Reuben Gentry echoed blankly.

"Yes, Chris," Samantha laughed. He had sounded miles away, thinking of other things.

"Oh, yes, Chris, of course," he said as if it had suddenly dawned on him whom she was talking about. "Everything will be fine. You just mind what he tells you," he added absently.

An incredulous smile curved her mouth. It must have been some problem he had on his mind. He sounded as if he had forgotten she was twenty-two and able to take care of herself. But it was at times like these that she found him the most lovable. He aroused the maternal instinct in her.

"Of course, Reuben," she agreed in the same tone of voice she had used when she was nine. "Did you want to speak to Chris again?"

"No, it won't be necessary. Take care, Sam."

"Yes. I'll be seeing you, Reuben." They never said goodbye to each other. It was a habit they had begun when Samantha was a small child and had cried unceasingly whenever he got ready to leave on a business trip. He had made a pact with her not to say goodbye because he would always be back. It had struck some childish logic in her that enabled Samantha to let him leave without tears.

A smile lingered, faintly dimpling the corners of her mouth. She was aware of Chris's speculating look as she replaced the receiver back onto its cradle.

"Everything all right?" Chris asked, rising as Samantha turned toward the dining room.

"Fine," she answered smoothly without glancing around. "It's just as you said. Something rather important has come up to delay him."

There wasn't any need to mention that Reuben's preoccupied manner indicated that it was a very serious problem. It wasn't any of Chris's business, especially since she didn't know the nature of it. It might concern something that would be of benefit to her father's rival company.

"You and your father are very close, aren't you?" He pulled a chair away from the table in the dining room as he made the comment.

"It's always been just the two of us since I can remember," agreed Samantha. "I enjoy being with him. Lately, with college and work, I haven't been able to be with him as much as I'd like." Which was the truth, but she was adult enough to realize it was part of growing up.

"You admire your father a lot, don't you?" Chris sat in a chair on the opposite side of the table.

"Of course." Samantha sensed it wasn't an idle remark. "Why?"

"I was just thinking it would be difficult for a man to compete with your father."

A pitcher of orange juice sat on the table. Samantha filled two glasses before glancing up to meet his hooded look. It was on the tip of her tongue to say that she didn't expect a man to compete with her father. "Yes," she agreed out of obstinacy, "few men can compare with Reuben Gentry."

A grimness entered his features and satisfaction ebbed slowly through her. She hoped somewhere in his personality there lingered a bit of inferiority. Maybe he wouldn't be so sure of his ability to attract her.

CHAPTER FOUR

PUNCHING THE FLUFFY PILLOW, Samantha snuggled her head into the hollow made by her hand and closed her eyes. For several seconds she lay motionless in the bed. Then she opened her eyes with an impatient sigh. It was no use; she simply wasn't sleepy.

Her hand fumbled over the bedside table until she found the light and switched it on. Her watch was beside the light. Samantha picked it up, sighing again when she saw it was a few minutes before midnight. She had been tossing and turning for the past hour and a half and she wasn't any nearer falling asleep than when she had first laid down.

The covers were thrown back as she slipped out of bed. A book was lying on the dresser, but she felt too restless to read. A walk seemed the better answer. Stripping, she changed into dark blue denims and a dark green and blue plaid blouse. The light blue windbreaker Chris had loaned her during the boat trip to the island was hanging beside the hooded sweatshirt she took from the hanger, and she made a mental note to remember to return it to him as she slipped on the sweatshirt and zipped the front.

Her canvas shoes with their rubber soles made no

sound on the carpeted floor. She moved stealthily down the corridor, through the living room and into the dining room, not wanting to awaken anyone in the silent house. She carefully slid the patio doors open and stepped into the cool of the night.

The silvery light from a crescent moon softly illuminated the rocky clearing that provided the house with its view of the river. She started forward, a destination in mind. A flashlight would have been useful, but Samantha didn't have any difficulty finding the path through the growth of evergreens, sprinkled with oak and maple.

It was not as well worn as the one leading to the boathouse but still easy to follow even in the night's shadow. Samantha had discovered it that morning when she had explored the island. The path led to the convex side of the crescent-shaped island where a gazebo had been built near a rocky promontory overlooking the river. The gazebo was Samantha's destination.

The island, she had discovered, was much larger than she had suspected, being several hundred yards wide and two or three times that long. It could have easily accommodated two homes without either of them aware of the other, but there was only one with its private boathouse and gazebo.

The small circular structure was ahead of her, gleaming whitely in the moonlight. The scrolling wood trim of the overhang and around the wooden railing gave it a dainty look. In the starshine, with the shimmering silk of the silent river flowing by, it looked enchanted. Samantha's restlessness vanished under its spell.

Sitting crosswise on the wooden seat inside the railing, she leaned a shoulder against a supporting post and hooked her arms around one knee, stretching the other leg out on the bench seat. Her wristwatch was still on the table beside the bed and she had no idea how long she sat there, drinking in the serenity, thinking about a multitude of things, none of them very important.

She could have stayed there all night, but the breeze off the river became more cool than refreshing. Flipping the hood of her sweatshirt over her head, she lingered for several more minutes before the invading chill drove her to her feet. A yawn claimed her as she reluctantly turned to retrace her path. It brought a lazy smile to her lips. At least that was a good sign that she might sleep when she got back.

With the hood covering the seal brown of her hair and her hands tucked in the slanted pockets of the sweatshirt, she strolled unhurriedly toward the house. A night bird cried in the stillness, the only sound to herald her return.

Carefully Samantha slid the patio door open and stepped inside, freezing when a low voice snarled behind her, "I wouldn't make a move if I were you!"

Instantly the room was flooded with light from an overhead fixture, momentarily blinding her. Her hand went up instinctively to shield her eyes from the unexpected brilliance.

"What's going on?" Alarm and astonishment mingled in the breathed question, the hood of her sweatshirt sliding a few inches back as she jerked her head away from the light.

"Sam!" The identification was made in a mixture of anger, exasperation and relief. "What are you doing wandering about at this hour?"

The recognition of Chris Andrews's voice turned her around. "I couldn't sleep." Her eyes were just beginning to focus properly. She was certain she had seen dark metal in the hand that was just sliding out from the inside of his jacket. A gun?

He was shaking his head in wry amusement, his gray eyes running over her. She could almost see the tautness leave him as he adopted an indolent stance.

"Tom!" His voice was directed to the open patio door that Samantha hadn't a chance to close. His hands were on his hips and his gaze never left her although his head turned slightly. "It's all right. It's Miss Gentry."

"Miss Gentry?" came the muffled reply of astonishment before the burly man stepped into the light shining on the patio. "How did she ...?"

The question wasn't finished as Tom Carlson saw the way Samantha was staring at the revolver in his hand. He quickly tucked it inside his jacket, breaking her trancelike stare.

"I swear I didn't steal a thing!" she laughed, raising her hands in a mock gesture of fear and surrender as she turned to Chris once more. "I only went for a walk."

A throaty chuckle joined her laughter. "Well, you can't blame us for being cautious," Chris pointed out. "Isolated homes are ideal for burglars, although they generally prefer them to be unoccupied. We've only been here a few days, so they might not have known that. I hope we didn't frighten you too badly."

"Just for a few seconds," she admitted, able to smile now at the way her heart had stopped beating.

"I'm sorry, but we—" Chris began.

He was interrupted by Maggie Carlton calling something. Samantha understood the rest of what she said as her voice drew nearer.

"She isn't in her—" A harried-looking Maggie stopped in the archway between the living room and dining room, staring in disbelief at Samantha.

"—in her room?" Chris finished the sentence. "No, Miss Gentry couldn't sleep, so she went for a walk. She's the one Tom heard prowling around outside."

The blonde's gaze skittered almost guiltily away from his face to Samantha. Smiling tightly, she walked into the room where they were, her hands nervously reknotting the belt of her quilted robe.

"You gave us quite a scare, Miss Gentry," she declared with a hollow laugh.

"And vice versa," Samantha returned.

"After all this excitement, I don't think any of us can go back to sleep right away," Chris said. There was nothing rumpled about his appearance to indicate that he had ever been in bed.

257

"Maggie, why don't you fix us all some chocolate?"

"Of course," the woman agreed after a slight hesitation.

"Want some help?" Samantha offered.

"I can manage," Maggie assured her, and walked toward the kitchen.

Shaking the hood from her head, Samantha unzipped her sweat jacket against the prevailing warmth of the house and took it off. Tom closed the patio doors and moved toward the table to sit in one of the chairs. Samantha followed suit.

"Where did you go?" Chris straddled a chair, leisurely resting his hands on the straight back.

Samantha told him and they spent a few minutes idly discussing the benefits of a late-night walk. Then Maggie reappeared with the mugs of hot chocolate. By the time Samantha finished hers, she had already begun to feel its calming effect. That and the discovery that it was already nearly two in the morning made her drowsy.

With a tired "good night" to the trio seated at the table Samantha started for her room. Halfway there, she remembered she had left her sweatshirt on the chair.

A few steps into the living room she heard Chris say, "I'd like to know how she got out of the house with none of us hearing her."

Samantha hesitated. She was tired and didn't want to become involved with any more rehashing of the incident. With a shrug, she turned back toward her room. The sweatshirt could stay there until morning.

A knock on the door awakened her the next morning. Frowning her resentment at the intrusion of her sleep, she peered through her lashes at the sunlight peeking through the closed curtains.

"Who is it?" Samantha grumbled without stirring from her exceedingly comfortable position.

"Rise and shine." The door opened and Chris Andrews stood in its frame, tall and vital, looking as if he had had eight hours' sleep, which Samantha was sure was impossible.

"What time is it?" she mumbled, running a tired hand through her tousled hair and rolling onto her back, pulling the covers with her.

"Nearly ten," he answered.

Eight hours was almost possible, she conceded, although he looked as if he had been up for hours. Her sleepy eyes focused on his leanly muscled shape. Snug-fitting denims of faded blue covered the length of his legs. A yellow windbreaker, the zipper hooked at the bottom, covered most of the blue chambray shirt opened at the throat.

"I feel as if I've just gone to sleep." Her mouth was all cottony, adding to the naturally husky pitch of her voice.

"No worse for last night's adventure?" he inquired with a mocking lilt.

"I don't think so." Samantha's head made a negative movement on the pillow. Her sleepy brain suddenly realized he must have had a purpose in wakening her. "What do you want?"

"I thought we'd go sailing today. Since you've

259

never been here in the Thousand Island area of New York before, I decided it would be a good idea to show you around. There isn't any better way to see it than by boat. Are you game?" He tipped his head to one side in mocking challenge.

The suggestion sounded good even in her half-awake state. "Of course," she agreed. "Just give me half an hour to wash the sleep away and dress."

"You've got half an hour. Coffee's waiting in the dining room and Maggie is packing us lunch. The boat's ready as soon as you are," he concluded, reaching out to close the door.

Three-quarters of an hour later, the boat had left the shelter of the cove. The sails were raised and the motor turned off. Tom Carlton had come along to crew, a fact that momentarily surprised Samantha. It must have shown on her face, because Chris had explained almost immediately that sailing around the many islands through various small channels could be tricky with the changing currents.

Samantha decided it was probably best he was along as she covertly studied Chris Andrews at the helm. A breeze was ruffling the thickness of his dark hair. The ruggedness of his sun-bronzed features was disturbingly compelling in this setting of earth and sky and water. Lusty and virile, he was in his element. The sharpness of his gray eyes was far-seeing, like the eagle's.

All of it combined to heighten the physical attraction Samantha felt, despite a common sense that told her it was futile and possibly dangerous. She was here as Reuben Gentry's daughter and not simply as a female named Samantha. Maybe Tom Carlton's presence would help to remind her of that. The tour was to keep Reuben's daughter from being bored.

The charcoal gaze swung to her and Samantha pretended to be looking at a landmass beyond him. She felt the sweep of his gaze run over her from head to toe and knew she looked fresh and nautical in her white slacks, navy top and white scarf for a headband. Dark curling wings escaped the scarf to wave across her forehead.

"Are you awake now?" There was chiding amusement in his tone.

"Very much so. This is beautiful." Her enthusiasm was entirely false. "Is that Canada there?" she asked, waving a hand toward the landmass she had supposedly been studying.

"It's a Canadian island, yes, but not the mainland."

"Aren't we going to follow the ship channel?" she asked. They were steering an easterly course, but they were a considerable distance from the large ocean liner moving upriver.

"The Seaway Channel is mainly on the American side. I thought I'd show you the Canadian side first, the Admiralty and Navy groups of islands, so you could get an idea of the natural beauty to be found before we take in some of the man-made splendor of the American Islands," Chris explained, the line of his mouth twisting wryly.

Samantha spent a few minutes studying the sapphire water and the emerald islands. "It certainly is beautiful," she absently repeated.

"The Indians referred to this area as the 'Garden of the Great Spirit.' The early French explorers gave it the name we know it by—'Les Mille Iles' or the Thousand Islands. The St. Lawrence River was an Indian highway. They called it the 'River Without End,' which wasn't exactly true as far as boats were concerned because the rapids kept it from being navigable."

"What's the difference between the St. Lawrence River and the St. Lawrence Seaway?" Her reporter's instincts to discover all the facts went to work.

"The river has always been here, but the seaway is an inland water route, about 2,300 miles long, stretching from the Gulf of St. Lawrence to Lake Superior, connected by a series of locks and canals, including the seven-lock system needed to lift ships up the Niagara escarpment."

"Fantastic!" Samantha murmured.

"Ships from all parts of the world travel the waterway system," he added. "It was accomplished by the combined efforts of the U.S. and Canadian governments. Have you ever stopped to think that the border between Canada and the United States is the longest undefended border in the world?" There was a quick flash of a white smile being directed her way.

Her head bobbed negatively. "No, I don't think I have thought about it quite that way."

As the boat glided silently through the waters, with the loudest noise coming from the billowing of the sails, Chris gave her a brief sketch of some of the area's history during the early wars, mentioning the War of 1812 and the Patriot War of 1837 when the steamer *Sir Robert Peel* was sunk in the American channel. All the while, they cruised slowly by islands of varying size, some without signs of habitation and others with cozy bungalows amid the trees.

"This area was a natural during the rum-running days of Prohibition. It was easy enough for smugglers to dodge customs boats with all these islands to disappear between. One island became so infamous as a place to stash bootleg whiskey that it's known as Whiskey Island." The Admiralty group was behind them now, and Chris pointed to the left, indicating the buildings on a jutting point of land. "That's Gananoque, Ontario, on the mainland of Canada. It's a very picturesque town."

"Are we stopping there?" Samantha asked, warming to the idea of wandering through the streets.

"We won't have time."

He did swing the boat close enough to allow her a tantalizing glimpse of the village. A tour boat was docked at the harbor, making her wish she was one of the passengers, but Chris was already turning the sailboat toward an open expanse of water, and she didn't have time to dwell on the town.

He was talking again, explaining that while most of the island homes she saw were strictly summer residences there were permanent inhabitants, such as the one on the island they were approaching—Grindstone Island, en route through the Navy group of Canadian islands. They were mainly farming communities, he said, adding that they had once been dairy centers. Grindstone Island used to make its own cheese, called, appropriately, Grindstone cheese, but now they had switched mostly to cattle.

"They have their own elementary-school system, which the children attend until the seventh or eighth grade. Then they have to go to the mainland for the rest of their education, usually staying with friends or relatives during the school year."

"Talk about leaving the nest early!" Samantha smiled.

"How about going below and breaking out that picnic lunch Maggie packed?" Chris suggested. "I don't know about you, but I'm getting hungry."

"You?" she laughed. "I haven't even had breakfast, only coffee."

"Don't be too long or you'll miss the scenery," he called after her.

When Samantha returned with the sandwiches and cold beer, Tom took his to the forward part of the boat and ate alone. Samantha wondered if he was just naturally antisocial or simply a well-trained employee. She rarely noticed him watching her and Chris. He seemed more interested in the other boaters on the river than the fresh, unspoiled scenery. Of course, he was probably quite used to it. For her, it was an all new experience. She had never seen anything quite like it before. Munching contentedly on the halved roll layered with slices of ham and cheese, she pitied the person who looked on this with jaded eyes.

A sideways glance at the man at the helm tried to judge his reaction, but the carved bronze features only revealed intense concentration as he negotiated a narrow channel between two islands. Considering his knowledge of the area, it was something he had seen many times.

Dressed as he was, it was difficult to remember he was Chris Andrews, entrepreneur, financier, tycoon. He certainly didn't look like any ordinary working person, but neither did he fit the image her mind associated with the name Chris Andrews. Before she had met him, Samantha would have visualized Chris Andrews going sailing in snappy white ducks and a blazer with a captain's hat instead of going bare-headed with the wind ruffling his hair and wearing faded denims and a windbreaker.

Samantha much preferred this Chris Andrews to the one of her imagination. Then she pulled herself up quickly at the thought.

Careful, she warned herself. *Remember you're only here because he wants something from Reuben.* The sandwich lost much of its flavor.

Through the Navy group, their course took them to the Canadian channel. A tall white tower off the starboard bow beckoned to them. Samantha was told it was the Skydeck complex on Hill Island and it offered a lofty and panoramic view of the area. A section of the Thousand Island bridge system came into view with the islands used as stepping stones to span the river.

Chris pointed out the maze of islands, the area

known as Lost Channel. During the early wars, the pirate days and the Prohibition era, it had been often used by men knowledgeable about the area to lose their pursuers.

After they had sailed beneath the bridge, Chris instructed Tom to lessen the amount of canvas offered to the wind and their pace was slowed. Samantha glanced at him curiously.

He met her look and announced simply, "The Palisades."

Glancing ahead, Samantha saw the rocky cliffs they were approaching. Craggy and steep, they rose from the placid river to loom above the boat gliding by. The slashed, sharp stone of their faces was tinged with pink. The silence of the sail made their intimidation more profound and their harsh beauty more awesome.

As they passed the town of Rockport on the Canadian side, Chris began an arcing course to take them to the opposite side of the river. His smile to her was brief and slightly cynical.

"Now for that man-made splendor I told you about—the millionaires' playground," he said.

It wasn't along before Samantha knew what he was talking about. The islands she had seen up to now had been raw wilderness with rustic bungalows, but now as they approached the American channel, the islands and their homes began to change. The heavy brush and thick foliage of the trees that filtered the summer sun's rays to the virgin soil began to give way to expensive, manicured lawns, green and lush. The summer homes were now nearly palatial vacation villas for the rich. Not satisfied with the ornamentation of nature, the owners had statues and flower gardens adorning the lawns. The architecture of some of the homes took Samantha's breath away. There was beauty here, too, but a direct contrast to what she had seen before.

When they had passed through the Summerland group, Chris said, "The granddaddy of them all is coming up. Or it would have been," he qualified cryptically. "You've heard of Boldt Castle, haven't you?"

"Yes," Samantha answered hesitantly, trying to remember what she had heard about it and finding her recollection hazy. "Something about a castle a man built for his wife."

"Yes, George Boldt was his name," he said. "His was one of those Horatio Alger, rags-to-riches stories. He immigrated to this country around the time of the Civil War, eventually made his fortune sevral times over. He came here with his wife in the 1890s when this was an élite resort area for the very wealthy. As a boy in Europe, he had seen the castles along the Rhine and it was always his dream to own one. When he and his wife saw Hart Island, which at the time was shaped roughly like a heart, he decided to buy it and make his dream come true. Evidently he was quite a romantic, because he went to considerable expense to complete the shape of the heart and renamed it Heart Island. Then he began building his castle. He envisioned a whole colony with several buildings and the capability of entertaining a hundred guests and their

267

servants. Marble, tapestry, silks, rugs, all were imported to furnish his castle. He had spent over two million dollars on it when his wife died. All work was stopped at her death and it was never completed.''

Towers, medieval and grand, jutted above the treed island ahead. As the boat drew nearer, the castle itself began to take form. Tourists wandered about the island and tour boats were tied up at its dock.

"Has it been restored?'' asked Samantha.

"No. When the work was stopped, thieves and vandals stole or destroyed most of the valuable goods. For years, it was abandoned to the bats and birds and insects. It's virtually a ruin now, with only a few of its four hundred rooms that can be viewed by the public. At today's inflated prices, it would probably take twenty fortunes to make Boldt's dream a reality.'' Chris paused, frowning slightly. His narrowed gray eyes focused on the turrets rising above the trees. "Now it's a romantic symbol of a dream that became empty without the love of a man's wife.''

Crazily there was a lump in her throat as Samantha felt herself gripped by the tragic and poignant story. It was silly to be moved by it and she tried to shake away the sensation and view the place objectively. A family of tourists was wandering along the dock.

"Let's stop,'' she suggested eagerly.

His gaze swept over the island and the strolling clusters of people. Then with an abrupt, resolute shake of his head, he said, "No. We don't have time.''

Samantha glanced at her watch. "Granted, it's after two, but surely we can stop for a half an hour," she argued.

His gaze sliced to Tom standing near the middle of the port-side deck. The burly man had clearly been able to hear her request and the negative answers she had received. His expression was grim as he met Chris's look, then he scanned the other boats slowing to view the castle. Only a few seconds had passed.

"I'm afraid not," Chris refused again. His mouth curved into a smile, but it didn't ease the unrelenting and forbidding set of his features. "Maybe another time."

Shrugging an acceptance, Samantha glanced away, focusing her puzzled brown gaze on the tall boat-house buildings opposite Heart Island. She was consumed by the strangest feeling that even if the whole afternoon was before them, Chris would still have refused to put ashore.

It didn't make any sense. He was making a special effort to take her on a tour of the Thousand Island area, yet he seemed to be restricting the tour to the boat deck.

With half an ear, she listened to the commentary he began as the sailboat swept gracefully by the castle. Her eyes noted the stately buildings of the Thousand Island Club, more elegant summer homes of note-worthy people, the island known as Devil's Oven that had once been the hiding place of a notorious pirate, the towering American span of the international bridge, the Rock Island Lighthouse, which was no longer in use, and the Thousand Island Park, but none of it claimed her interest.

The town buildings of Clayton prompted her to make one last test of her theory, especially when Chris mentioned the museum there.

"I don't suppose we'll have time to stop there, either."

The faint challenge in her tone drew the swift appraisal of his charcoal eyes, the speculation in their narrowed look not quite hidden.

"Not this time," he answered without elaboration.

Not ever. The premonition was so strong it nearly was spoken. The force of her certainty startled her, more so because she couldn't think why he didn't want to let her go ashore. During the last hour of their sail back to the island, she thought and thought, but she couldn't come up with a logical reason to explain his action.

CHAPTER FIVE

SAMANTHA FINGERED the stem of her wine glass. A few drops of red wine colored the bottom. The scarlet spectacular of sunset made no impression on her as it faded into a purpling twilight. Nothing had since she had become preoccupied with the question that remained unanswered. Why hadn't Chris wanted her to leave the boat?

Her gaze slid to him and found him studying her. She smiled quickly and took her hand away from the empty glass, realizing that neither of them had spoken for the past several minutes. The tip of her tongue nervously moistened her lower lip as she searched for an innocuous comment.

"It's peaceful, isn't it?" she said.

"Yes."

Both had changed for dinner that evening. He was wearing a white turtleneck shirt with a dark blue blazer and light blue slacks. This was another thing that confused Samantha. With all his money, she wondered why he didn't have jackets tailored to fit his broad shoulders and muscular chest. What he was wearing was attractive, but it would have been more so if it wasn't so tight around the shoulders.

Sighing, she rose from the table, smoothing her palms over the soft material covering her hips. The crimson two-piece suit had a floor-length culotte skirt and a long-sleeved top with the complementing draping folds of a tunic neckline. The vivid color accented the silky brown of her hair.

"Restless again?" Chris questioned, rising from the table, too.

"Again?" Her head jerked toward him, his question disconcerting her.

"Last night you couldn't sleep," he reminded her.

"Oh, yes," Samantha nodded her understanding. She supposed she hadn't done a very good job of concealing her abstraction. This was one time when she wasn't prepared to be candid, not until she had some hints of what was going on. Since he was prepared to blame her distraction on a restlessness, she was ready to go along with it. "I suppose I am a bit restless," she admitted.

"Rather than risk a repeat of last night, I think I should suggest a walk before midnight."

Samantha flipped the hair away from her cheek. "Not a bad idea." But her voice was hollow.

As they stepped through the patio door into the dusk, Chris glanced around. "Did you want to just walk or do you have a particular destination in mind?"

After an indecisive movement, she answered, "The gazebo."

His hand lightly rested on the back of her waist, and she let the slight pressure guide her toward the path she had taken the previous night. A scattering of pine needles littered the path, rustling under the soles of her sandals. Samantha couldn't ignore her awareness of the footsteps accompanying her, nor the invading warmth of his hand on her lower spine.

It had been a mistake to come out here, she decided, but it was too late to turn back now. The lengthening shadows of the trees seemed to shut out the rest of the world. It was a relief when they thinned and the gazebo was before her. She breathed easier as Chris's hand fell away, her pulse reverting to a less erratic beat.

Walking onto the octagonal platform, she paused on the side closest to the river. The smooth surface of the water was shimmering with the approaching darkness, reflecting the dying light of the sunset. Chris stood next to her, a shoulder leaning against a post, a leg bent to rest his foot on the wooden seat, but his attention wasn't fixed on the river. He was watching her with alertness veiled by aloof indolence.

"Is something troubling you, Sam?" he asked quietly after several minutes of silence had passed.

"What makes you ask that?" she returned lightly as if the question was really quite ridiculous.

But her gaze could only make a pretense of meeting the penetration of his. Mostly it skittered over the rugged masculinity of his features.

"You look as if you have something on your mind." The thread of seriousness didn't leave his tone despite her attempt to jest.

"Doesn't everybody?" Samantha shrugged, trying

273

to indicate to him that it really wasn't important.

She found it difficult to think with him so nearby. It became worse when he straightened as if he wanted a closer look at her expression.

Pretending an indifference that her thudding heart was far from endorsing, Samantha tipped back her head to gaze at the sky shading into a midnight blue. The first evening star winked at her and the silver crescent of the moon occupied another corner of the sky. The setting was too disturbingly romantic for her peace of mind. The musky scent of his after-shave cologne drifted in the air, and a sigh broke unwillingly from her lips.

"Did you enjoy yourself today?"

"Oh, yes." Her head turned jerkily to face him, an artificial smile of enthusiasm curving her lips. "The islands are lovely."

A breeze from the river teased at her hair, blowing a few strands across her cheek to be caught in the moist corner of her mouth. She lifted her hand to brush them away, but his fingers were already there pushing the silky strands behind her ear, then tangling his fingers in the thickness of the hair at the back of her neck.

At almost the same moment, he slid his other hand under her arm and around her back, drawing her to the right side of his chest. Startled, she gripped the flexing muscles of his right arm, pressing the heel of her other hand against his left shoulder to arch away from him.

But the enigmatic darkness of his compelling gaze

held her captive. She should protest, but she didn't really want to. He had to be aware of that fact. He was too experienced not to know when a woman wanted to be kissed. He let several more seconds stretch tautly to heighten her anticipation.

Then his mouth settled warmly over hers, caressing and arousing and melting the stiffness of her lips. Samantha had neither the will nor the desire to withstand his persuasive expertise. Her limbs weakened under the sensual assault until she was leaning against his hard length for support.

This response brought an insistent demand to his kiss, parting her lips, the invasion and possession more vividly exhilarating than any sensation she had ever known. The taste of his mouth was an aphrodisiac, heady and addictive. Her hips were molded against the solid muscles of his thighs.

In the sweetness of surrender, her fingers clung to his arm, the half fist of her right hand spreading open to caress the bulge of his shoulder. He caught her right wrist, lifting his head to gaze into the dazed shimmer of her eyes. The smoldering darkness of his charcoal eyes revealed the physical disturbance her response had made on him, although he was more in control of his emotions than she was.

For several seconds the iron band of his muscular arm continued to press her against his length while he held her wrist in his hands. A thumb rubbed the sensitive inside of her wrist while her pulse was drumming.

The line of his jaw tightened in decision. Samantha

was set away from him as he turned, moving into the shadows. Light flared and a match flame was cupped to a cigarette. In the next instant, a lit cigarette was thrust into her hand.

She accepted it shakily, inhaling on the filtered tip and hoping the nicotine would have the desired calming effect. But the silence was unnerving. She had certainly made it obvious that she had enjoyed his kiss and hadn't indicated any desire for it to end. So why had he ended the embrace?

There was a possible explanation, one that filled her with waves of self-disgust for reacting so naturally to his caresses. And the possible explanation made it necessary that she attempt to restore some of her pride.

"You weren't obliged to kiss me, Chris." Her voice was treacherously husky. She felt the thrust of his sharp gaze, but continued looking over the river. "When I agreed to your suggestion of a night walk, that was all I expected. It never occurred to me that the moonlight might make you think I was anticipating a flirtation."

"Is that why you think I kissed you?" There was a grim hardness in his voice. His fingers caught her chin, turning her face to the moonlight so he could view its expression. Her eyes had lost their dazed look and were wide and frank. "Out of a sense of duty because of the moonlight?"

"Isn't it?" Samantha countered, faintly accusing. "After all, I am your guest and Reuben Gentry's daughter."

"Therefore," he followed her train of thought aloud, "I'm entertaining you even to the point of indulging any romantic fantasies you might have about the magic of moonlight." The freezing scorn in his voice hinted at a savage fury. "You couldn't be farther from the truth, Miss Gentry, in nearly every respect."

"I don't understand." A confused frown partially arched an eyebrow as she searched the shadows to see his face.

"It isn't necessary you do." Clipped and harsh. "Nothing is necessary except—" Abruptly he checked the rest of the sentence, staring at her for taut seconds.

An expletive was muttered beneath his breath. Her chin was released and the cigarette torn from her grasp to be thrown into the night. An iron trap closed around her, pinning her arms tightly. A fiery passion was consuming her lips, whirling her into a vortex of sensations before she could assimilate what was happening. She yielded to the demands of his mouth, her lips parting under the brutal pressure of his, a savage sweetness in the pain he inflicted.

Her flesh pliantly allowed itself to be molded against the intimate contours of his masculine shape. Her hands, wanting to encircle his neck, had to be satisfied with spreading over his chest, fingers slipping inside the lapels of his jacket. Arching her farther backward, he abandoned the responsive delights of her mouth to scorch her face with kisses, then nibbling at her neck until a moaning sigh of pain and passion came from her throat. There was no support from her legs and his arms took her weight. Her hands searched for a way to cling to him, her fingers encountering smooth leather as they curled into the knit of his turtleneck.

He stiffened, then dragged himself away, capturing her hands and holding them against his chest. She could feel his ragged breathing as she swayed unsteadily toward him, not meaning to, but unable to stop. The narrowed screen of his dark lashes concealed the desire she knew had to be burning in his eyes. She guessed her own reflected it and lowered them from the penetrating scrutiny of his gaze. She stared instead at the large hands imprisoning hers.

"I must be out of my mind to get mixed up with you," he breathed savagely.

"I—" Samantha began.

"For God's sake, don't say any more!" he snapped angrily. "It's bad enough already! Come on." He jerked her to the side, his fingers bruising the tender flesh of her arm as he pushed her toward the path, yet keeping her close enough to him that she felt his left shoulder brushing against hers. "We're going back to the house before this gets out of hand."

But it wasn't the harsh command of his voice that stopped Samantha from protesting. It was the fleeting touch of something hard against her shoulder and a series of memories that suddenly joined together like pieces of a puzzle.

The poorly tailored jackets and the fact that she had seen him only once when he wasn't wearing a jacket

of sorts. The way he had abruptly ended both em-
braces when she had started to hold him. The
leather she had touched under his jacket. The hard,
inanimate object that had just brushed her shoulder.

And most of all, the memory of the previous night
when she thought she had seen him slip a gun inside
his windbreaker. She hadn't thought she'd seen
it—she had. What was more, he was wearing a
shoulder holster now.

Why? Why was he wearing it? For protection
against the possibility of intruders? No, Samantha
couldn't accept that; the threat was't that great. *Ask
him*, an inner voice prodded. Laugh and tease him
that he found her so dangerous he carried a gun. But
the cold waves of fear she was experiencing froze her
into silence.

They were nearing the house, its lights growing
brighter. She stumbled and the grip on her arm tightened cruelly to steady her, and she bit her lip to keep
back the cry of pain. Her arm wasn't released until
they were a few steps from the door.

As she entered the house, Samantha tried to keep a
few feet advantage, moving awkwardly into the empty
living room. She stood uncertainly near the massive
stone fireplace, unable to escape any farther. He
stopped just inside the room and she felt the hooded
scrutiny of his look.

Keeping her back to him, she forced her twisting
hands apart and raked her fingers through her hair.
Her heart pounded as loudly as a hammer in the preg-
nant silence. If only he would stop studying her as if

she were a slide under a microscope, she thought desperately. The width of the room separated them, yet she could think no more clearly now than when she had been in his arms.

"I'll have Maggie bring us some coffee," he announced abruptly, irritation making his voice tight and faintly harsh.

"No." Samantha swung around, breathing in sharply as she became impaled by his rapier gaze. Although an unknown terror was racing her pulse, the sudden tremors that quaked through her were caused by his overpowering virility. "I don't care for any coffee," she declared after a second's pause. "I . . . I didn't get much sleep last night. I think I'll make an early night of it."

With the decision made, she started toward the corridor leading to her bedroom. She glimpsed a movement from him and wanted to bolt, but she forced herself, her feet, not to hurry.

"Sam!" his voice commanded slowly.

In the hall opening, she stopped, trying to meet his slate gray eyes without betraying her inner trepidation. As slow, seemingly lazy strides brought him closer, she felt her knees weakening and rested a hand against the wall for support.

Chris halted a foot away, bronzed, rawboned features gazing down at her, lean and hard, rugged and compelling. The line of his mouth had thinned in grimness. His jaw was clenched and taut.

His hand reached out to touch her cheek, his thumb lightly rubbing her smooth skin. Samantha trembled visibly, as his caress flamed through her. Quickly she lowered her gaze, but avoided looking at the bulge on the left side of his blazer. Not even fear could check the desire to be in his arms.

"Please, I'm tired." She tried to speak with bright unconcern.

His thumb slipped under her chin to tilt it upward. "Sam, I . . . ." The urgency of his low voice never had an opportunity to convey its message.

Footsteps approached the living room and his hand fell away as he turned to meet them. Granted a reprieve, Samantha took advantage of it.

"Good night, Chris," she murmured as Tom appeared in the living room. She hurried down the corridor to her bedroom.

Within minutes she was in bed with the lights out. She lay awake for long hours in the dark, thinking. Each time she tried to concentrate on his possible reasons for carrying a gun, her thoughts kept turning to the way he had kissed her and the undiluted passion he had aroused in her.

It didn't make for a restful sleep when she finally did doze. But it was a light sleep that had her rising before eight the next morning.

Chris was already breakfasting when she entered the dining room. His detached greeting was unexpected. Samantha assumed a similar attitude, especially after she noticed the bulge on his left side under the tan bush jacket. Orange juice, coffee and toast were on the table. Her appetite didn't stretch to more than that and she refused Maggie's offer of bacon and eggs when the woman appeared briefly in the room.

"Was there anything you needed from town?" The question was offered negligently as Chris lit a cigarette.

Samantha stared at the slice of half-eaten toast in her hand. After his suspicions yesterday, the inquiry was a surprise. He seemed to be suggesting a shopping expedition. Everything imaginable had been awaiting her arrival here and she couldn't think of a thing that had been overlooked. She wasn't going to admit that, though.

"There are a couple of things," she lied smoothly and let her teeth crunch off a bite of toast.

"Make a list and give it to Maggie. She'll see that you get whatever you need." He shook out the match and tossed it into an ashtray.

Her gaze sliced across the table to his bland expression of aloofness. So she wasn't to be allowed to go into town. But she had to make certain that was really what he meant and it wasn't just her imagination.

"That isn't necessary," she denied, smiling falsely as she added a spoonful of marmalade to her toast. "I'll ride along with her to town. It'll be fun wandering through the shops."

"Maggie isn't going to town." His cryptic reply forced Samantha to meet the hooded charcoal of his gaze. Coiled and alert behind that masked look of ease, he held her attention.

"I don't understand," Samantha laughed self-consciously.

"She's ordering by phone what supplies we need

and a launch will bring them out this afternoon,'' he explained.

"Oh." A small voice of understanding.

There was nothing left to say and she began munching on the marmalade-covered toast. Its sweetness was suddenly cloying.

The morning hours dragged. It was an effort to appear natural and not be consumed by all the suspicions and doubts that had surfaced. And, after last night's tempestuous kisses, Chris's withdrawn behavior was disturbing. He avoided any opportunity to touch her, however innocent the reason, and Samantha's awareness of him was heightened to a fever pitch. The air around her crackled as if an electrical storm was approaching.

Surreptitiously, she glanced at Chris. He was lounging in one of the patio chairs, seemingly unaffected by the undercurrents tormenting her. From where Samantha leaned in a half-sitting position against a protruding rock, his craggy profile was offered for her inspection. Masculine with his sun-bronzed vitality, he appeared relaxed, the tapering length of him stretched out. The even rise and fall of his chest suggested sleep.

They had gone out to the patio after lunch, a meal that Samantha barely tasted, her nerves too overwrought. Her bearing was tuned for the sound of a motorboat, which was the only reason she had agreed to come out on the patio.

Several had passed, catching her interest at the first sound and losing it when they continued by the island. The dull hum of another boat was approaching and she tensed as it droned increasingly louder. Then came the sound she had been waiting to hear. The boat's engine was throttled down.

With another glance at Chris, Samantha straightened warily from the rock, not certain whether he was sleeping or had merely closed his eyes. Striving for nonchalance, she stuffed her fingertips in her denim pockets and strolled quietly toward the path leading to the boathouse where the supply launch would dock.

"Going for a walk?" The lazy voice paralyzed her for an instant.

She turned jerkily toward his chair. "I thought I might." Her smile was tight.

"Headed anywhere in particular?" Behind the idle question she sensed a sharpness.

She hesitated. Should she answer truthfully or lie? No, it had to be the truth. She needed to know exactly what her position was. Her imagination was working overtime. She had to know if what she was thinking was true. Inwardly she was trembling from the decision and its possible consequences.

"I thought I'd walk to the cove," she replied and noted the flicker of grimness around his mouth. While she still had the courage, she plunged forward. "The launch with the supplies is docking now. I heard it a few minutes ago."

"That's hardly an event," he mocked dryly.

"No, but I'm going just the same. Any objections?" She couldn't keep from challenging him even though her heart was in her throat.

"Not really," he answered, but every instinct said that he was lying. He rolled leisurely to his feet. "Do you mind if I make a more stimulating suggestion? Since you want to go to the cove, why not change into your swimsuit first, then we could swim for a couple of hours?"

It seemed a simple suggestion, but Samantha recognized his stalling tactics.

"By the time I changed, the launch would be gone," she pointed out.

"Does it matter?" His hands had slid to his hips, his stance arrogant, the quietness of his voice intimidating.

"Since I was going to the cove to meet the boat, yes, it does matter," she retorted, tipping her head to the side, openly defiant. "But maybe you don't want me to meet the launch? That's why you're trying to think up ways to stop me, isn't it?"

"Now that's foolish." The smile he flashed was cold and without humor.

"Is it?" Samantha taunted. "I don't think so."

"Come on, Sam." He frowned at her words and shook his head. "Why would I want to do a thing like that?"

Pivoting, she stalked toward the path, angered that she had let herself be manipulated that way. He had a streak of cunning as well as ruthlessness. The sound of firm, striding steps on the path behind her chased away the anger.

Looking over her shoulder, Samantha's widened eyes saw him lessening the distance between them.

Since he hadn't been able to stop her through guile, she guessed he wouldn't be above using force.

She bolted from the path into the trees and thick undergrowth and heard Chris call her name, angered and impatient, but this only spurred her on. Branches whipped at her arms and legs as she ran blindly, trying to make a straight line to the cove where the old path had curved. Above her own noise, she could hear the rustle of brush behind her. He was chasing her, but she didn't dare risk a glance back.

There was a small clearing ahead and she ran for it, aware of the noise coming closer. Breaking free of the brush and trees, she tried to dash across the clearing and regain some of the lead she had lost, when a large hand grabbed her arm just below the elbow, pulling her up short and spinning her around.

Her forward impetus deprived her of balance. She couldn't change direction that abruptly and maintain her footing. She tumbled to the ground, dragging him to his knees as she fell. A thick cushion of pine needles broke her fall, pungent and dried by the sun.

Instantly she was kicking and twisting to get to her feet. She nearly made it, but a muscular arm flung her back to the ground. She struck out at him, swinging her fists at any part of him she could hit, attacking him with all the viciousness of a trapped animal. He soon captured her flailing arms and stretched them spread-eagled above her head.

Samantha struggled all the more violently, breathing in panicked sobs. Twisting and writhing, she tried to free herself of the weight pressing into the ground as he half straddled and half lay on top of her. Her head moved from side to side in desperate effort, tangling her brown-silk hair in its pillow of pine needles. He held her easily, letting her struggle uselessly until her energy was spent.

Finally, gasping, Samantha had no more strength left to fight. She glared resentfully into the smoldering steel of his eyes, her heart thudding against her ribs from her exertions. The pine needles were brushing roughly against the bare skin of her arms. She was crushed under his weight, the heat from his body nearly burning the entire length of her.

The hard muscles of his thighs pressed down on her legs. Her breasts were nearly flattened by the granite wall of his chest. Steel-hard fingers gripped the wrists she no longer strained to break free. Mixing with the pine scent was the musky fragrance of his maleness heightened by perspiration to an intoxicating level.

The frustration of defeat gradually gave way to an awareness of the dangerous intimacy of her position. As the knowledge flickered in her rounded brown eyes, she saw it reflected in his. She was afraid to move, afraid if she did, it would be to invite the possession of his kiss.

Tension mounted, her gaze locked by the magnetic force of his. When his charcoal gaze slid to her lips, they softened under its nearly physical caress.

Slowly, taking his time, his mouth descended toward hers, and Samantha exhaled a sighing surrender. Flames were kindled by the languid passion of his kiss, arousing her desire more swiftly than demanding possession would have done. Expertly he explored every corner of her lips and mouth until she quivered boneless in response.

Her arms were released and she wound them around his neck and shoulders. The crushing weight of his body pressing down on her added fuel to the fire raging through her veins, a wild song ringing in her heart. The intimate caress of his hands was an erotic stimulant that brought an urgency to her response. Immediately his kiss hardened in a complete mastery of her senses.

Every nerve end was attuned to him, quivering at his touch. His fingers tugged at the buttons of her blouse, unfastening to gain access to the rounded flesh the material had concealed. As he pushed the strap from her shoulder to release the last confinement, he dragged his mouth away from her lips to plunder the sensitive skin of her throat and shoulders with rough kisses, blazing a fiery trail to the swelling peak of her breast. The sensual touch of his tongue drew a shuddering moan from her throat. His hard male need made her aware of the empty throbbing of her loins and their mindless plea for satisfaction.

His hand remained to cup her breast as he raised his lips toward her mouth, checking his movement tantalizing inches from his goal to read the message in the liquid brown of her eyes.

The gray smoke of his eyes flamed possessively over her face.

An inch from his lips, Samantha knew that this time his kiss would demand an ultimate surrender. She was beyond the point of resisting. She could deny him nothing. The flames of love encircling her heart had vanquished everything else but her wish to be his.

But he stiffened. A sudden alertness entered the dark gray of his eyes as his gaze warily swerved away from her face. Bewildered for a second, Samantha finally heard the sound of someone walking heavily, nearing the spot where they lay entwined on the pine-needle bed.

She breathed in sharply, a combination of alarm, embarrassment and protest. Before she could exhale, Chris's large hand was clamped over her mouth, his piercing gaze warning her into silence.

CHAPTER SIX

IT SEEMED an eternity before the footsteps drew level with their position, receded into the silence of the woods, and the hand was removed from its smothering hold over her mouth. The footsteps had passed within a few feet of them, the thick underbrush screening them from the trail running from the cove to the house.

Soundlessly Chris rolled to his feet and gazed in the direction of the house. Samantha wasn't nearly as quiet as she scrambled to her feet. There had been time to consider the wisdom of her actions and find there was none. She had been ready to give herself to a man who was virtually keeping her a prisoner on this island. She had nearly made his power over her unlimited.

Her fingers fumbled with the buttons of her blouse. They were still shaking too severely from the devastation of his lovemaking to accomplish their task. Her gaze was directed at their ineffectual movements, but she was aware of him moving to stand in front of her. She was incapable of looking at him.

"Sam." The caressive warmth of his voice flowed over her.

When she refused to look at him, his fingers captured her hands and pulled them away from her blouse, permitting it to gape open. He made a thorough inspection of her feminine attributes, his gaze seeming to strip away the lacy bra. Still holding her hands, he twisted them gently behind her back and drew her hips against his muscular thighs. Her bones felt like putty in his hands.

"No!" Desperately Samantha denied the turmoil caused by his nearness.

"No?" His voice was low and mocking, his breath warm against her skin.

"No," she repeated, more decisively this time as she lifted her gaze to his face. The dark glow of his gray eyes nearly destroyed her will to resist. "You wanted me to miss the launch," she accused, "and you've succeeded. Now let me go."

His gaze narrowed to pinpoints of sharp steel. The muscles along his strong jawline worked for convulsive seconds before he released her and stepped away, his expression hard and withdrawn.

Turning her back to him, Samantha quickly fastened the buttons of her blouse with none of the fumbling ineptitude of before. Without another glance in his direction, she started toward the thick undergrowth that separated the little clearing from the trail.

"Where are you going?" His voice rumbled low and ominous in command.

"To the house," she flashed over her shoulder, sarcasm issuing to hide the pain. "Any objections?"

"None," he snapped coldly.

Samantha didn't stop until she had closed her bedroom door. She leaned weakly against its support, her legs trembling. The reflection in the mirror above the dresser revealed her dishevelled appearance, pine needles clinging to her hair and clothes. Pushing herself away from the door, she started walking toward the private bathroom, stripping off the soiled garments as she moved across the room.

Without waiting for the water to adjust to a comfortable temperature, she stepped beneath the freezing shower spray. But the stinging needles couldn't erase the memory of the intimate touch of his hands, nor could the cold water chill the warmth lingering from the fires he had kindled.

Finally, she turned off the taps in defeat, wrapped one towel around her wet hair and with another covered her nakedness. With robotlike movements she returned to the bedroom, pulling clean undergarments from the dresser drawer and walking to the closet. She tossed a pair of light blue bell-bottoms onto the bed and reached for the matching pin-striped blouse.

With it in her hand, she noticed the blue windbreaker she had borrowed from Chris the night she had arrived. She wanted no physical reminders of him. Her fingers gripped the smooth material to violently jerk it from its hanger. It was halfway off the hanger when her arm became paralyzed, unable to complete the movement.

In numbed disbelief, she stared at the inside collar of the jacket. Black lettering spelled out the initials

C.S. That was all, just C.S. Not C.S.A. for Christopher Steven Andrews. Slowly she pulled it from the hanger, examining closely to see if the last letter hadn't somehow become faded. It didn't taken an expert to discern that there never had been another letter following the S.

Crumpling the windbreaker in her hands, she turned to move to the bed. She sagged onto the edge, staring sightlessly at the jacket. One piece of incriminating evidence didn't prove the case. Too many times during the past few days she had been ready to accept the first information as the whole truth. She would not jump to conclusions again, not until she found something more to substantiate her discovery.

Not wanting to risk losing what she had, she stuffed the windbreaker between the mattress and box springs of the bed. The towel around her middle was cast aside as she hurriedly dressed in the clean clothes. Rubbing the worst of the dampness from her hair, she ran a quick comb through it and called it good enough. Entering the hallway, she closed the door on the cyclone mess of dirty clothes and wet towels strewn about the room. Tidying up could wait. Right now there was only one thought in her mind. The living room was empty and she breathed a sigh of relief and satisfaction.

With a cautious glance toward the adjoining rooms, she moved quietly to the study corner, her gaze seeking and finding the briefcase leaning against the side of the desk. She knelt beside it, pushing a clinging strand of hair from her cheek.

Her palms were wet with nervous perspiration, and she wiped them on the material of her slacks before reaching for the briefcase, keeping it upright to examine the area near the handle. The gold initials C.S. looked boldly back at her.

Minutely Samantha examined the leather for any mark or scar that would indicate a third letter had once been there. It never had. She had wanted proof to substantiate the markings on the windbreaker and she had found it. She slid the briefcase back to its former position, her hands settling on her knees to push herself upright.

"What are you doing?" The low, accusing male voice sent shafts of cold fear plunging into her heart.

Samantha turned her head slowly toward Chris standing in the archway to the dining room, his immobility a challenging threat. But he wasn't Chris. Whoever he was, he wasn't Chris Andrews—nor Owen Bradley. Nervously she moistened her lips and straightened. Should she confront him with her discovery? No, she decided, not until she had a chance to think it over.

Her mind raced to find a plausible explanation for why she had been kneeling beside the desk. There wasn't any. Her only hope was to bluff her way out.

"It's none of your business what I was doing." With head held high, she started toward the hallway.

But his long strides caught her before she could reach it. Her wrist was brutally seized and twisted to jerk her toward him. The raging anger of his gaze scorched her face.

"I asked you a question and I want an answer," he growled threateningly.

The pain from his grip was excruciating. The slightest additional pressure would snap the delicate bones in her wrist. Samantha gritted her teeth against the physical agony slicing through her arm, but it helped her remain indifferent to the hard thrust of his thighs that she was forced to arch against.

Frigidly she glared at his harsh features. "Let go of me!" Each word was spoken with icy clarity. "I don't have to answer your question, and if you break my arm, you'll have to take me off the island to have it set."

He compressed his mouth into a taut line of checked violence. Samantha was released with an angry push before he pivoted to stride from the room. Weakly, she stared after him, feeling not at all victorious.

For the rest of the afternoon, she didn't budge from her room. Confusion muddled her thinking. She was obviously a prisoner. It didn't seem to matter whether the island, or her bedroom, formed her walls. The reason she was being held escaped her, no matter how many times she went over it.

If it hadn't been for the fact that she had spoken to her father and knew he was cognizant of her whereabouts, Samantha might have concluded that she had been kidnapped.

But Reuben did know.

The shadows outside had lengthened into evening hours when there was a knock on her door. She tensed, turning from the window to stare at the door.

"Who is it?" she demanded, knowing the answer before it was given.

"Chris," he answered, and opened the door.

"Liar! She wanted to scream at him. *You aren't Chris Andrews! I don't know who you are, but you are not Chris Andrews!* She glared at the bronze mask that so completely concealed any expression. But it wasn't the words on the tip of her tongue that she uttered.

"What do you want?" she asked coldly.

"Dinner's ready."

"Just send some bread and water to my room. That's good enough," she declared with taunting disdain.

The mask hardened. "You will come to the table and eat," he stated, then added, "if I have to drag you there and shovel the food down your throat."

Her gaze challenged the gray shards of his for a few more seconds before she submitted to his edict. The food was tasteless, but she ate some of it. She was aware every second of the speculating glances given her by Maggie and Tom.

Her tight-lipped silence wasn't something they could not notice. The instant dinner was over, she excused herself and retreated to her room, half expecting Chris—or whoever he was—to appear and order her into the living room. He didn't.

The next morning the prospect of spending the day in her bedroom wasn't at all appealing. If she was actually a prisoner, as it seemed she was, then there was no reason for her to be a willing prisoner. Besides, if there was more enlightening information to be obtained, it was unlikely she would learn it in the bedroom.

There was a determined light in her eyes as she emerged from her room. The germ of an idea was taking shape to confront her captor with the knowledge that she knew he was not Chris Andrews. Once he realized that she had seen through his guise, he might unwittingly provide her with some more information. The possibility put a spring to her step.

Rounding the arch into the living room, Samantha instantly spied the man seated at the desk, listening with glowering anger to the telephone at his ear. She stopped, alert to the violent impatience emanating from him. Whatever the person on the other end of the wire was saying, it was displeasing him greatly.

"Dammit, Reuben Gentry!" His voice rumbled across the room, widening Samantha's eyes. "Don't ever say I didn't warn you. You'll be sorry, very sorry." There was a pause, then, "You'll be hearing from me."

On that ominous note, he slammed the receiver and rose from the chair, leashed anger evident in the uncoiling swiftness of his movements. Samantha swallowed, and swallowed again when the lightning fury of his gaze jolted to her. His nostrils flared slightly, as if scenting danger. She couldn't deny overhearing the conversation. The best she could do was pretend she hadn't caught the promise of revenge.

"Was that my father?" she asked, somehow succeeding in hiding the tremors of fear.

"Yes."

Trying to maintain her pose of ignorance, Samantha strolled into the room. Her hands were trembling and she hooked her thumbs in the belt loops of her tight denims.

"When is he coming?" She tried to put just the right note of interest in her voice.

"He's... been delayed for a couple more days."

Samantha hadn't missed the infinitesimal pause in his answer. The penetrating gaze was difficult to meet, so she didn't try and turned instead toward the dining room.

Knowing she had to make some reply to his answer, she sighed ruefully. "I'm going to be back to work before Reuben ever succeeds in getting away." She quickly changed the subject. "Mmm, the coffee smells good this morning."

He allowed the conversation to be diverted, but Samantha wasn't certain she had fooled him. After hearing the telephone conversation, she didn't confront him with the knowledge that she knew he wasn't Chris Andrews.

It was slowly dawning on her that she just might be kidnapped. She had only his word that Reuben knew where she was.

In her mind, Samantha reran the short telephone conversation she had had with her father shortly after she had arrived on the island. First he had asked how she was, received her assurances that she was surviving (Samantha blanched at her choice of words in retrospect), then had tried to apologize for the delay.

But she had interrupted him before he explained the delay.

She had glossed over his apology with the assertion that she knew he was doing everything he could. And there had been his blankness when she had referred to Chris. Finally Reuben had admonished her to do whatever Chris told her. And couldn't her father's preoccupied air have been caused by concern for her safety?

Nausea gripped her stomach at the way the pieces to the puzzle fitted so perfectly. Unwittingly she had probably interrupted a telephone call demanding ransom. By speaking to Reuben, she had proved to him that they were truly holding her captive. If at any time she had betrayed an ignorance of her status or had started to indicate her whereabouts, Chris had been right there, listening to every word, ready to rip the phone away at the slightest provocation.

How easy she had made it for them, Samantha thought dejectedly. The mere mention of her father's name had persuaded her to come away with a perfect stranger. Not once had she questioned his credentials at the newspaper office. Beth had warned her to beware of him, but she hadn't listened. Not Samantha Gentry—she knew it all.

The newspaper office! Another memory staggered her. The letter that had been left for Harry Lindsey had to have been a ransom note. And she had pointed out which office to leave it in. It was all so sickeningly obvious now, even to the new clothes that had been provided for her. She hadn't been allowed to pack her

299

own things because of the risk of being seen with Chris by more people and the delay it would have caused in leaving.

The drive here to Clayton, New York, the fast car that probably could have outdistanced any pursuer, his preoccupation at the restaurant constantly watching everyone coming in and out, the man waiting to take the car when they arrived and the young girl who had joined him at the corner and who would undoubtedly resemble Samantha at a distance, the boat waiting a few minutes out. It all made so much sense now.

If Beth or anyone had happened to see her leave in the car, the man and woman had probably driven it miles away from there before ditching it. And there hadn't been a soul around the dock to see Samantha board the boat. She had even been ordered to wait in the shadows of a building until it had docked, then been sent below once on board. She had been a most cooperative kidnap victim.

The island was an ideal place to hold her. There weren't any nosy neighbors to see her or that she could run to if she discovered what was happening. The river provided the walls to keep her captive. The boat tour of the islands had been to keep her entertained and not become suspicious of what was truly going on. They hadn't stopped anywhere because they didn't want to risk her being recognized. Possibly her picture was in the papers. The same supposition held true for the supply launch. Plus the fact that the island was only a stone's throw from Canada and they could slip across the border to escape once the ransom had been paid. The ransom. The telephone call she had just overheard.

Fear took a stranglehold on her throat. Had Reuben refused to pay the ransom? Oh, God, it was possible, she thought. She had once heard him remark that if no ransoms were paid, there might not be any more kidnappings, declaring it was a crime of barbaric cruelty. Or had he been bluffing to gain time, taking a chance that the authorities, which she knew he would have called in, might find her?

Chris—or whatever his name was—had said "You'll be hearing from me." He could have meant that he would be calling back about the ransom or that he would be sending a message via her dead body. They couldn't very well let her go free, not when she could recognize them.

Her hands trembled and she quickly set the coffee mug on the table before she dropped it. Her gaze slid warily to the man seated across from her, only to drop to the table when she saw his inscrutable charcoal eyes watching her. How much of what she had been thinking had she revealed to him, she wondered in breathless panic.

"Are you all right? You look a bit peaked," he observed smoothly.

"A headache—migraine," Samantha lied glibly. "I'm prone to them the same as Reuben is." She touched shaking fingers to her temple and smiled wanly. "Excuse me, I think I'll go to my room and lie down for a while."

"Can I get you anything?" He didn't seem entirely

convinced, the faint quirk of his brow dryly mocking.

"No, thanks, she replied, quickly making her exit before he could probe further.

Restlessly Samantha paced the room for nearly an hour. She tried to consider the situation rationally and ignore the terror lurking in the corners of her mind. Although the stranger, her abductor—she had stopped thinking of him as Chris, the name didn't really fit him anyway—might be aware she suspected something funny was going on, he might not believe she had realized she was kidnapped. He probably still thought she was convinced he was Chris Andrews.

As his guest, she had to be permitted a certain latitude, though at the same time he was confident that she couldn't escape the island. The question was how could she take advantage of the limited freedom she did have on the island?

There had to be something she could do herself other than simply wait. She couldn't count on being released if the ransom was paid. Escape seemed impossible. Her only hope appeared to be being rescued. But how could she be rescued when no one knew where she was except the kidnappers?

A reporter was supposed to be resourceful, Samantha chided herself. There had to be some way she could get a message out without her abductors' knowledge. The supply launch would probably not come again, so that was out. No passersby ever stopped at the island, which ruled out the possibility of passing a message to them.

Of course, she thought wryly, there was always the

proverbial message stuffed in a bottle and tossed into the water, but the chance of anyone finding it in time would really be slim.

Frowning, she paused beside the window, staring out the panes at the green shadow of trees. What method of communication did that leave? The telephone! The clouds in her troubled brown eyes were dispelled by the light that suddenly brightened them.

Surely there was a way that she could persuade them to let her call her father for some innocent reason? Maybe during the conversation she could give Reuben a clue to where they were holding her. No, her cunning captor would see through the ruse and never permit any veiled message to be delivered.

Yet the telephone might still provide the means if she could use it without anyone listening in. That meant it had to be when no one was around. The middle of the night seemed an obvious choice, but Samantha discounted it. She remembered the night she had taken the midnight walk. No doubt someone was on watch all the time. Any night-time prowling stood a better chance of being discovered.

It had to be during the day when she was more or less free to roam the house and island at will. She would have to choose a time when all three of them were occupied. It was bold and brash, but infinitely more possible of success.

Footsteps sounded in the corridor outside her room. It could only mean someone was coming to check on her. Quickly Samantha flung herself on the bed, stretching out on her stomach and feigning sleep. Her heart was pounding like the roll of a snare drum as the door opened. Even though her eyes were closed, her senses recognized the identity of her intruder.

How many times in the past few days had his presence disturbed her sensually? Too many to count. Those mysteriously dark gray eyes were studying her now lying on the bed and she could feel the vague stirrings within. Samantha tried to breathe evenly, aware of his regard as surely as if he was touching her. Her stranger was dangerous in more ways than one.

When she thought she couldn't keep up the pretense of sleep any longer, she heard the door close. Still she didn't move, not immediately, not until she heard the quiet footsteps moving away from her door. Then she moved cautiously and began contemplating when she might stand the best chance of using the telephone.

At noon, it was Maggie who knocked on the door, coolly inquiring if Samantha would be having lunch. She maintained the excuse of a headache, hoping to lull them into not watching her so closely. When the housekeeper offered to bring her some broth, Samantha accepted, which maintained her pose of illness and provided nourishment for her empty stomach.

The door didn't latch securely behind Maggie. A few minutes after she had left the cup of beef broth, it slowly swung open a few inches, and from the living room, Samantha could hear the stranger's voice.

"I know she suspects something," he stated in a grim, decisive voice. "We couldn't hope to keep her completely in the dark. She's much too clever for that."

"But what are we going to do now?" came Tom's gruff response.

"Keep her on the island until...." The rest of his sentence became indistinct as they evidently moved to another room.

At least, Samantha smiled in macabre humor, there was no immediate plan to dispose of her. It would give her precious time to try to bring about her own rescue.

The opportunity presented itself much sooner than she expected. Almost an hour had passed when she heard the low murmur of voices outside, those of Tom and her stranger. At this time, Samantha knew, Maggie would be in the kitchen clearing away the luncheon dishes. This was her chance, maybe her only chance.

Stealthily, she tiptoed out of her room, down the corridor and into the living room. Listening intently she could hear Maggie in the kitchen and the faint voices outside. Adrenalin pumped through her veins as she picked up the telephone and hurriedly dialed her father's office number.

Her gaze darted apprehensively toward the kitchen as she waited for the telephone to be answered, winding a finger in the coiled cord. Exhilaration flashed through her when a woman's voice came through the receiver.

"Reuben Gentry, please," she requested in a whisper. "This is his daughter calling."

"I'm sorry, but I can barely hear you. Would you please speak up?" the woman insisted.

Samantha gritted her teeth impatiently. "I can't!" she hissed a little louder, silently cursing the wasted seconds. "This is Samantha Gentry, and I *must* talk to my father."

"Did you say it was Mr. Gentry you wanted?" The frowning voice asked for clarification.

"Yes!"

"I'm sorry, he isn't in right now. Can someone else help you?"

"Damn!" she muttered under her breath, rubbing a hand across her forehead. "Put me through to the security...."

The front doorknob was turning. She caught the movement out of the corner of her eye. Her stranger must be coming and she didn't stand a chance of getting out of the living room unseen. The odds were he would see her with the telephone in hand before she could replace it. Her only hope was to leave a message.

Precious time was wasted in making the decision. The door was already opened and the stranger walking in when Samantha turned her concentration to the receiver mouthpiece.

"Tell my father," she began in a loud, clear voice so the woman would have no trouble understanding what she said, "that I'm at—"

A large hand was pressing down the button on the telephone's cradle, breaking the connection before Samantha could complete her message. Frustration and impotent anger glared from her eyes as she looked into the pair of hard gray ones. He pried the receiver from the death-grip of her fingers and replaced it.

"I'm sorry," he said calmly, "I couldn't let you do that."

"You have no right to stop me!" Samantha flashed. "It was a private call. There was something I wanted to talk to Reuben about and I didn't have a chance to speak to him this morning," she defended herself with a lie. "I would have reimbursed you for the long-distance charges."

"I'm sure you would have." He towered beside her, an arm brushing her shoulder.

Inwardly Samantha was quaking, from fear and his disturbing nearness, but she boldly reached again for the telephone receiver. "Then there isn't any reason for you to object if I call him."

His hand clamped over her wrist, not allowing her to lift the receiver. "Sam, I'm not playing games," he warned quietly.

"Aren't you?" Her head jerked toward him, her brown eyes shimmering with defiance and rebellion. Temper threw caution to the winds. "You've been playing games with me ever since you walked into the newspaper office—first letting me believe you were Owen Bradley, then ly—" She bit into her lip, realizing she had virtually admitted that she knew he wasn't Chris Andrews.

The narrowing of his gaze indicated that he had guessed what she had been about to say. Her heart skipped several beats under his piercing look. Samantha had gone too far to turn back. Her only hope was to brave it out without revealing how terrified she really was.

"I don't know who you are, but you aren't Chris Andrews," she declared. "It was all a lie."

"More or less," he acknowledged with remorseless ease.

Spinning away from him in irritation, Samantha muttered, "I don't suppose it would do any good to ask what your real name is?"

He hesitated. "My name is Jonas—"

"Jonas!" Laughing derisively in disbelief, she pivoted back. Her hand sliced the air to cut the rest of his identification off. "Don't bother with the rest. That isn't your name, either."

He slowly looked her up and down in a thoughtful manner then shook his head in unconcern. "Names aren't all that important."

"No," she agreed bitterly. "A man's character or his lack of it remains the same regardless of his name. Jonas is as good a choice as any. It's certainly appropriate. I haven't had anything but bad luck since I met you."

"So you've decided I'm lacking in morals." There was a glitter of harsh mockery in the eyes of the man who now called himself Jonas.

"You've proved that!" she retaliated. "Just how gullible do you think I am? How many times am I supposed to believe your lies? You're keeping me a prisoner on this island. You won't let me off and you won't allow me to see anyone but you, Tom and Maggie. I'm not even permitted to phone my father. What story are you going to come up with to explain all that?''

"None." The rugged bronze features were hardening into glacial ice. "I don't think you would believe anything I tell you."

"You can't expect me to!" Samantha cried. A part of her had been wishing he would weave another believable story. She didn't want him to be a kidnapper. "You've cried wolf so many times that it's impossible! Oh, Chris—Jonas, whatever your name really is," she sighed impatiently, "why can't you let me leave a message for Reuben?"

She didn't know why she asked that. She knew he would never agree to it. The humbling plea had been a gesture of desperation and tears welled in her brown eyes.

His hands settled on her shoulders as he gazed deeply into her eyes, his jaw clenched. "I can't, Sam."

The force of his magnetism and her own attraction to it nearly pulled Samantha into his arms. Instead she wrenched her shoulders away from his grip, hating the way her traitorous heart refused to listen to her mind.

"It's not that you can't! You won't!" she accused in an emotion-choked voice.

"Think what you like," he replied grimly.

"Oh, don't worry, I will," Samantha assured him in a threatening tone.

She stood before him, her hands balled into fists at

her side, tears trembling on the ends of her lashes. This was not the way she had intended to confront him. She had planned to interrogate him mercilessly, convicting him with the facts she already knew.

But somewhere along the way, she had stopped thinking of him as her captor and began looking at him as the man who had kissed her passionately and introduced her to feelings and sensations she hadn't known she possessed.

Beware of the stranger, she thought brokenly, because he can steal your heart.

"I want your word, Sam, that you won't try to use the telephone again."

He regarded her steadily.

"My word?" she mocked. "Why should I give you my word?"

"Because if you don't, I'll be forced to cut the telephone line. I can't take the risk of your phoning anyone and letting them know you're here."

"Wouldn't it be easier just to lock me in my room?" Samantha challenged, her voice taut with misery.

"I hope it won't come to that." But his answer was a warning. "It's up to you."

Her freedom was limited, but she had to keep what little she had if she was going to have any chance at all to help herself.

"Very well, you have it." She had to give in and he had known it.

Pivoting on her heel, she voluntarily went to her room to think of another plan. A glance over her shoulder saw him standing in the same place watching her, his dark features hard and unyielding, and compellingly attractive.

CHAPTER SEVEN

THE WATERS of the St. Lawrence were renowned for their fishing, with black bass and the battling muskie leading the list. Samantha had been watching the small fishing craft moving closer to the island for the past fifteen minutes. Its engine was put-putting in an erratic rhythm that suggested difficulties.

Stretched out on the raft anchored in the cove, she had toyed with the idea of swimming out to the boat. It was easily within her swimming range, but she knew she would not get ten feet before Jonas caught her. Glancing out of the corner of her eye, she saw he was watching the boat as intently as she was.

Since yesterday afternoon they had spoken little, exchanging only necessary remarks. He was her enemy, and Samantha couldn't allow her emotions to come into play.

The bow of the fishing boat swung to point toward the cove. Within seconds the sputtering motor died. His gaze sliced to her, a veiled warning in its narrowed gray depths, before it moved on to the stockily built man standing at the boathouse dock and watching the fishing boat.

"Find out what his trouble is, Tom," Jonas

ordered, his low voice carrying crisply across the dividing waters. "And get him out of here right away."

With a curt nod, Tom acknowledged the order. The fisherman stood up in his boat and waved toward shore. Jonas deliberately ignored the man's hailing. It was Tom who returned it before disappearing into the boathouse. A few minutes later he emerged, manning the oars of a dinghy, and rowed toward the disabled boat.

Propped by an elbow on her side, Samantha watched as Tom reached the boat, talked briefly with the man, then began rowing back. He never glanced toward the raft, but his voice was directed quietly to Jonas when he drew level with it.

"He ran out of gas."

A red gasoline can was in the dinghy when Tom started his second trip to the fishing boat. Frustration curled Samantha's fingernails into her palms. She could see her chance to contact someone from the outside world slipping away. She had to do something to get the fisherman's attention. There might not be another opportunity.

"Don't do anything foolish, Sam," his quiet steel voice warned.

Irritation snapped in her brown eyes at the way he had so perceptively guessed the direction of her thoughts. The wintry gray of his eyes didn't cool her determination. With lightning decision, she pressed her hands onto the raft boards to push herself upright, but she never completed the motion.

His reaction was swifter, rolling sideways from his sitting position to grip her shoulders and pin them to the hard wood decking. He loomed above her, muscular and bronze, a dark cloud of hairs curling virilely on his naked chest. The thumping of her heart had no basis in fear.

"Don't," he ordered. "Just keep quiet."

"You can't expect me to obey you," she hissed. "You know I have to try."

"Your screams won't mean anything. He'll think it's some joke," Jonas argued, a ruthless set to his hard features.

"He won't think it's a joke when I tell him who I am," Samantha retorted, and opened her mouth to scream.

His large hand closed over her jaw, holding it while he smothered her cry with the silencing force of his punishing kiss. The burning possession of his mouth flamed like wildfire through her veins, sweetly savage and torturously mad.

His demand for submission had her reeling lightheadedly.

The full weight of his muscular body spread over her, its heat melting her bones. Although Samantha tried to resist, her toothpick defenses scattered seconds after he had claimed her lips. Pliant and responsive, she acceded to the urgent pressure of his kiss, completely forgetting that she was consorting with the enemy until she heard the reviving chug of the fishing boat's motor.

Samantha twisted free of the male lips in time to

see the fisherman wave to Tom and turn the boat in the opposite direction of the island, gathering speed as it left.

"No!" she moaned brokenly, staring at the boat's wake.

Jonas released her and levered himself away, leaving her flesh chilled where it had felt his warmth. Sickened by the way she had been unable to deny herself the heady pleasure of his kiss, she rested a hand across her eyes, as if shutting out the sight of him would hide the forbidden love she felt growing.

"Did you have to kiss me?" she hurled at him resentfully. "Or is it just a habit with you to maul your prisoners?"

"Believe me, if there'd been a more effective means to shut you up I would have used it." His tone was bitingly sardonic.

The stinging flick of his reply was just what Samantha needed to pull herself out of her misery. Rising to stand upright on trembling legs, she squarely met the wintry glitter of his gaze. Kissing him had been an ordeal for her, too, but one of an entirely different kind.

"In the future, please find another method," she declared, faintly haughty and very proud.

With animal grace he glided to his feet, the coiled alertness of a predator about him, the angry glint in his eye decidedly primitive. His superior height almost made Samantha feel dwarfed as he stood before her nearly naked, muscles rippling toast brown in the sun.

315

"Don't worry, Sam. I'll look for one," Jonas snapped.

"And don't call me Sam," she flashed. "That's reserved for people I like and trust!"

For several charged seconds the tension mounted as they glared at each other. The hard line of his mouth thinned ominously.

"It's time we went back to the house," he said finally.

"I'll bet you're sorry you didn't decide to lock me in my room," Samantha accused bitterly.

"I wouldn't bring it up if I were you. The idea is acquiring more merit every day," he warned.

She clamped her mouth shut. This was not the time to bait him or he might decide to carry out his threat. She had lost one opportunity to obtain help this afternoon. She would be a fool to throw away the chance to have more opportunities simply because she wanted to lash out and hurt him, trying to divert some of her pain to him. Swallowing her spiteful words, she turned and dived into the water. Jonas followed when she surfaced a few yards from the raft.

In the solitude of her room, Samantha relived the scene on the raft. The feeling of wretchedness returned at her failure to resist him and her failure to identify herself in some way to the fisherman. In the midst of her dejection came a glimmer of hope.

Escape from the island had always seemed impossible. The only means of transportation was by boat, and Samantha knew she would never be able to operate the sailboat. It was too large. Swimming to another island or the mainland was out because she had not the strength nor the endurance to cover the distance.

Today, another means of transportation had unknowingly been revealed to her. It was the dinghy that Tom had rowed to the fishing boat. One opportunity had been denied her and another had taken its place. It was up to her to make use of it.

The trick would be to leave without being seen. She not only had to get out of the house, but also make it to the boathouse and row away from the island unobserved. Broad daylight was ruled out. Supposing that she made it to the boat, there was the risk of her being seen on the river in the dinghy, and it would be too easy for Jonas to overtake her in the sailboat. If she was caught, Samantha had no doubt that she would be locked in her room after that.

Any attempt would have to be made in the middle of the night when the darkness could hide her, both on the island and on the water. She had slipped out once unseen, maybe she could succeed again. But this time she wouldn't walk boldly out of the door. Leaving the house would demand furtive action.

She walked to her bedroom window. The trees grew close to the house on this side of the building. There was only a narrow clearing that she would have to cross before reaching the concealing cover of the trees. From there she would have to work her way as quietly as possible to the boathouse path.

It would not be easy with all the thick undergrowth rustling beneath her feet and against her legs. And she would have to be careful not to lose her direction in the dark. A flashlight was out of the question to guide her footsteps.

The glass portion of the window would be raised, but the protective screen was a problem. It was secured from the outside, which meant Samantha would have to pry the wire screen free of its wooden frame. The only tools she had to use, if they could be called tools, were in her manicure set. It was a case of making do with what was at hand as she set to work on a loosened corner of the screen.

By the time she had an opening large enough to crawl through, she had only a few minutes to change out of the swimsuit that had dried on her and into some clothes for dinner. Excitement for her daring plan had built up. Suppressing it was difficult, but she couldn't risk Jonas suspecting her.

During the meal, she said little, letting Tom, Maggie and Jonas carry the conversation. She was aware of the frequency with which the gray eyes regarded her, and she could only hope that he interpreted her silence as being sullen. All the while she kept going over in her mind the route of her escape.

When Maggie began clearing the dishes from the table and Tom had left to look around outside, Samantha wished she could retreat to her room. But it was too soon, so she wandered into the living room.

"You don't have to keep me company," she informed Jonas acidly when he followed her into the living room. "There aren't any fishermen around."

He ignored her comment and lowered his tall frame

318

into a leather chair opposite the one Samantha had chosen. Trying to conceal her irritaion, she picked up a magazine and flipped indifferently through the pages.

"You've been very quiet tonight," he observed.

Samantha closed the magazine abruptly and tossed it on the side table. "Under the circumstances, you can hardly expect me to make scintillating conversation."

The line of his mouth curved, a movement totally lacking humor. "What scheme is running through your mind?"

"Scheme?" Although she tried to sound blank, Samantha realized the color had drained from her face, indicating the accuracy of his perception. She tried to conceal her escape plans in a false candor. "The only thing going through my mind right now is how can I get off this island prison of yours. And failing that, I'm trying to figure out how I can let others know where I am."

He shook a cigarette from his pack and offered it to her. She accepted, bending her head to the match flame in his hand. "Come up with any ideas?" Jonas inquired with the infuriating calm of a man confident that all possibilities had been covered.

Exhaling an impatient cloud of smoke, Samantha seized the first thought that occurred to her. "Yes, one."

"What's that?" A dark brow quirked mockingly in her direction.

"I've been considering burning the house down,"

she announced. "You have to admit that it isn't something that could be ignored. There would be people crawling all over this island within minutes of the first flame licking the roof."

"There would still be plenty of time for Tom and me to get you onto the sailboat and away from the island before the first person arrived," Jonas pointed out. "So it won't do you any good to play with matches."

"I know," sighed Samantha. For an instant, the spur of the moment idea had sounded possible.

"Surely you've had some other ideas," he prompted dryly.

"Well—" for the first time in several days, an impish gleam entered her eye as she remembered one of her more ridiculous thoughts "—I did consider getting a light and flashing a Morse code signal to any ships or boats going by the island."

"What stopped you?"

"I don't know Morse code," she answered ruefully. At his low chuckle, she regretted her lapse. It was hard enough to resist him without putting things on a lighter level. A grim resolve entered her voice when she spoke. "I'll think of something, though."

The cigarette was discarded, half-smoked, in the ashtray. The chair was too comfortable, inviting relaxation. Samantha pushed out of the chair, walking nervously to the fireplace, empty and blackened.

"Sam, I—" Jonas began quietly, a thread of solemnity running through his tone.

"I told you I don't want you to call me that." She

320

kept her back to him, looking sideways from her shoulder yet not allowing his craggy features to enter her vision. "The only thing I want from you is to leave this island."

"It isn't possible for you to leave. Not yet," he added stiffly.

"When?" demanded Samantha, doubting that he would ever let her leave.

He took a long time answering her and she turned slightly to see him. He was studying the smoke curling from the burning tip of his cigarette.

"When?" she repeated.

"I hope not much longer." His veiled look never left the cigarette.

What did he mean? Had arrangements been made by her father to pay the ransom? It seemed to be what his comment meant.

"Have you...have you talked to Reuben?" she asked, holding her breath.

"For a few minutes this afternoon," he admitted.

"What did he say?" she rushed.

His gaze flicked to her briefly, emotionless and aloof. "As I said before, it shouldn't be too much longer before you can leave here," he replied, not answering her question except in the most ambiguous terms.

"How long is not much longer?" Samantha persisted in her search for the time when the ransom was to be paid.

"Let's just leave it that it will be a little while yet," Jonas stated. "Then all this will be all over."

And I'll never see you again. The thought brought a sharp pain to the area of her heart. She turned away from him, knowing his image would haunt her for a long time. The mantel clock ticked in the silence for several minutes.

"I think I'll go to my room," she said finally. There was no point in staying there.

"Good night," Jonas offered when she stepped into the hall.

"Yes." Samantha hesitated. If everything went according to plan she would not see him again. Her gaze slid over him, masculine and vital. "Goodbye" hovered on the tip of her tongue. "Good night," was what she uttered.

There was not nearly the elation she had anticipated when she reached her room. She changed into her night clothes and laid out jeans and a dark blue pullover. Then she climbed into bed to wait for the house to become silent.

She knew there was no risk that she would fall asleep. There were too many things to think about and leaving Jonas was one of them. But that was the way it had to be. She simply couldn't trust him.

The luminous dial of the clock on her bedside table indicated the hour as one. There hadn't been a sound anywhere in the house for the past two hours. Samantha guessed that Tom was somewhere outside on watch since she hadn't heard anything to indicate his return. As she slid silently from beneath the covers, she crossed her fingers that he wasn't near the boathouse.

Dressed in the dark clothing that would help her to blend with the night's shadows, Samantha returned to the bed and stuffed the pillows beneath the covers to form the mock shape of a sleeping figure. The pale moonlight streaming through the window illuminated her handiwork without revealing its falseness.

With a last glance at the bed she tiptoed to the window. It squeaked protestingly as she raised the glass frame higher. She stopped, listening intently as her pulse throbbed in her throat. Deciding no one had heard, she pushed out the corner of the screen she had worked free. At almost the same moment she heard quiet footsteps muffled by the carpet outside in the corridor.

There was only one reason anyone would be moving about at this hour, and it was to check on her. There wasn't time to slip out through the window. The opening was small and she might get caught on the screen wire. And she would never have time to slip under the covers and return the pillows to their proper position before the door opened. She had to hide, and somewhere close.

The cool breeze blowing through the window billowed the drape beside her. Instantly Samantha stepped behind the hanging material, lightly gripping the edges so the breeze wouldn't accidentally reveal her. She had barely slipped behind them when the door opened. The light from the hallway streamed over the bed and she held her breath. She guessed it was Jonas. If he walked to the bed, he would discover

323

her ruse, and she would never be able to escape then.

For long seconds there was no sound, only the patch of light shining into the room to indicate that he had not left. Finally, when she was a quivering mass of nerves, the door closed. Her legs threatened to cllapse with relief, but she didn't move from her hiding place, not for another ten minutes.

With extreme caution, she crawled through the triangular opening in the screen. Every accidental sound she made, no matter how tiny, sent a chill down her spine. Quickly she crossed the narrow clearing into the trees, her nerves leaping at the whisper of leaves against her jeans. She paused there, her breathing shallow as she got her bearings and rechecked to be certain there was no movement from the house. All was silent. No alarm had been raised yet.

She started out slowly toward the path to the boathouse. If her luck held, she wouldn't run into Tom. She crept along through the thick stand of trees, her progress guided more by the sense of feel than sight. The moon was bright overhead, but its light couldn't penetrate the umbrella of leaves.

Danger seemed to lurk in every shadow. The winging of a night bird could send her pulse rocketing. Samantha stumbled onto the path, unaware she was so close until she stepped onto it. She halted, instantly scanning the tunnellike path in both directions. There was no sign of Tom.

Deciding that she could move faster if she stayed on the path, she clung to the shadowed side, moving quickly and quietly toward the boathouse. Twice her overactive imagination made her think someone was following her. Both times she stopped, listening, trying to distinguish any man-made sounds in the night's stirrings. Neither time could she hear anything to cause alarm.

The white glow of moonlight glassed the smooth surface of the cove. A smile of elation curved her mouth at the sight of her goal, but she wiped it away with the sobering reminder that she still had not reached the dinghy. Tom could be there. Using the trunk of a tree as a shield, she studied the boathouse, dock and surrounding rocky land for a sign of him. There was nothing that even resembled his burly shape.

With the aid of the moonlight, Samantha scampered quickly over the last remaining stretch of rocky path, hurrying to the concealing shadows of the boathouse. Leaning against the door, she cast one last glance around before opening the door and slipping inside.

The cavernous blackness enveloped her. She couldn't even see her hand, let alone the dinghy. There was no choice. She would have to turn on the light and risk it being seen. She felt along the wall until she found the light switch and turned it on. The brilliance of the solitary bulb blinded her. For several seconds, she could see only the glaring spots in front of her eyes.

Finally they adjusted to the light. The sleek sailboat dominated the interior of the boathouse, its mast towering toward the roof. But it wasn't the sailboat she was seeking. Then her gaze found the small dinghy, dwarfed by its larger companion.

Success was within her grasp and she started toward it. It was tied near a ladder. Her foot was on the first rung when the door opened. Paralyzed, Samantha stared at Jonas. He returned her horror-stricken look lazily.

"You'll never make it," his low voice said.

Frustration set in. To be stopped when she had come so close was unbearable. Knowing it was foolish and without a hope of succeeding, Samantha started down the ladder. She didn't have a foot in the dinghy when her arm was caught and held by Jonas. She strained with all her weight against his grip, tipping her head back to gaze at him pleadingly.

"Let me go, Jonas," she begged shamelessly. "Please. The others don't have to know you could have stopped me. Please, just let me go!"

His answer was to smile at her grimly and increase the pull on her arm to draw her up the ladder. "It's no use, Sam. Come on."

A second longer she resisted before admitting defeat and let him help her up the ladder. Standing once more on the wood floor, she shoved her hands in her pockets and lowered her chin, seal brown hair falling silkily across her cheeks. Jonas made no attempt to usher her from the boathouse.

"It isn't the end of the world, Sam." There was an undertone of amusement in his low-pitched voice.

"Isn't it?" Samantha flashed in bitter defiance, the husky quality in her voice deepening.

"No, it isn't."

Her lips compressed into a tight line. "How did you know I was here?"

"I followed you."

"You followed me?" Samantha repeated incredulously. True, she had had the sensation a couple of times that someone was behind her, but she had been positive it was her imagination. Her gaze slid to his moccasined feet. "I thought I heard someone, but...."

"I've done a lot of hunting in my time," Jonas replied as if an explanation was really necessary.

"You couldn't have known I was gone," she protested.

"Couldn't I?" he mocked, an eyebrow quirking into his dark hair.

"You came to my room—" she began.

"—and saw the lumpy shape beneath the covers and knew it couldn't possibly be yours." He finished the sentence his own way, glinting charcoal eyes raking her slenderly curved figure with an easy familiarity that warmed her cheeks.

Samantha tried to disguise her reaction with another quick question. "Then why didn't you come to investigate?"

"If I had, I would have found you hiding behind the drapes." The carved lines at the corners of his mouth deepened.

"How did you know I was there?" she breathed in astonishment.

"The breeze was blowing one drape, but the other

was amazingly motionless." Then he added with a knowing gleam, "As if someone was holding it still."

"If you knew I was there, why didn't you just stop me then?" Samantha demanded angrily. "Why did you let me get all this way? Do you enjoy tormenting me?"

Her bitterly accusing tone wiped the vague traces of amusement from his rough features. "I had to know where you were going and what means you were planning to use to leave the island," Jonas replied.

"I could have just been going for a walk," she pointed out airily.

"But you weren't, were you?" he countered. "You were going to try to row across the river in that dinghy, weren't you?"

'So what if I was?" she challenged with a toss of her head.

"Do you realize how small that is?" he asked with a hint of impatience.

"What difference does that make? The river is calm. There aren't any waves that could swamp the boat," she declared, the faint haughtiness still in her tone.

"But there are lake freighters in the ship channel. That little dinghy would be nearly impossible for them to spot, especially without running navigation lights. One of those ships could have run you down without even knowing it," Jonas responded grimly.

"That doesn't frighten me." Denying the shiver that raced over her flesh, she added, "I'd rather risk that than stay here." Her gaze was downcast, but she heard the angry breath he expelled. For a minute, she thought he was going to take her by the shoulders and try to shake some sense in her, but he didn't.

"You don't know what you're saying," Jonas finally ground out with leashed violence.

Samantha acknowledged the warning signal and changed the subject, her gaze sliding to the dinghy. "What are you going to do now?" she asked.

"About you? Nothing. Take you back to the house and put you to bed." He made it sound as if she were a runaway child.

"I meant about the boat," she clarified her question stiffly. "Are you going to chop a hole in it and sink it?" She was suggesting the extreme out of spite for his superior attitude.

"Nothing that drastic," Jonas answered dryly. "But now that I know what you were planning, there'll be a padlock on the boathouse and probably one on the dinghy, too. Combination locks," he qualified, "so there won't be any keys for you to steal."

"And you'll probably be the only one who knows the combination, I suppose." The upward sweep of her lashes revealed the mutinous gliter in her eyes.

"More than likely," he agreed smoothly, a faint glimmer of laughter in the dark silver gaze. "What are you going to do now? Slip into my bedroom some night to see if I talk in my sleep?"

"I doubt that you even sleep," Samantha retorted, irritated by the small tremor that quaked through her at the idea of being alone in a bedroom with him.

"Not very soundly," Jonas admitted, then tilted his head to one side. "What are you going to do?"

"Well, I'm not going to sneak into your bedroom!" she declared vehemently, mostly because it was such a heady thought that she had trouble forgetting it.

"I was referring to any more harebrained schemes you might have running through that mind of yours about leaving the island."

"I'm going to keep trying, if that's what you're asking," Samantha flashed.

CHAPTER EIGHT

THERE WAS an impatient sigh. "Sam, I...." Jonas seemed about to say something, then changed his mind. "You have to stay here."

"Do you expect me to just accept that?" she demanded in disbelief. "Am I supposed to stay here willingly until you say I can leave? *If* you say I can leave?"

"You'll be safe here," he said firmly.

"Safe!" His incredible statement prompted movement. She stepped past him. "How can you say that? How can you expect me to believe that?" Her hands waved the air to punctuate her questions. "How am I safe when I'm being kept on this island against my will? When you and Tom are walking around carrying guns? Maybe even Maggie has one strapped to her thigh, I don't know!" She was so intent on her declarations that she missed the narrowing of his gray eyes. "You expect too much!"

"No one is going to hurt you," Jonas stated quietly.

"Is that right?" Samantha inquired with a disbelieving nod of her head. "Can you speak for the others?"

"Yes, I can."

"You'll simply have to forgive me for not believing you. I've listened to too many of your lies," she declared.

"You have no reason to be afraid."

"So you say." Her mouth twisted with mocking skepticism.

"Samantha, you have to trust me." Jonas didn't try to conceal his impatience.

"Trust you?" The throaty laugh she gave bordered on hysteria, her taut nerves snapping after hours of strain. "How can I trust you? I don't even know who you are!"

This time he did grip her shoulders and give her a hard shake that snapped back her head. "Stop it," he commanded tersely. "You're getting yourself all worked up over nothing."

"Nothing!" The frenzied note in her laughing voice earned her another shake that rattled her teeth and effectively silenced her.

"You're letting the situation seem worse than it is," he barked.

"Am I?" Samantha whispered brokenly, gazing into his compelling face. "I wish you could convince me of that."

His head moved to the side in frustration as he breathed in deeply to control his rising temper. There was an enigmatic hardness in the dark smoke of his gaze when he turned it back to her face. He studied the confused and troubled light in her eyes, a glimmer of apprehension in their brownness that he hadn't been able to abolish. The line of his mouth thinned as he gathered her stiff body in his arms.

"Trust me, Sam," Jonas muttered against her hair. "I swear I won't let anyone harm you."

"I can't trust you," she protested, swallowing back a sob of longing and pushing her hands against the granite wall of his chest.

He held her easily, overcoming her half-hearted struggles as she rigidly resisted his embrace and its offer of comfort. The fine silk of her dark hair was caught in the shadowy stubble on his cheek. The rough caress was unnerving.

"And I can't let you leave the island," he responded thickly.

"I wont' stay," Samantha declared into the smooth material of his windbreaker. "I'll swim if I have to!"

"And probably drown," Jonas concluded sharply. "You're a good swimmer, but both of us know you aren't that good. And I can't believe you'd prefer killing yourself to staying here with me."

She could have told him that under any other circumstances she would have gladly stayed on any island with him. But she simply couldn't forget the fact she was being held prisoner.

"I won't stay," she repeated, straining against the iron circle that held her fast.

"I'll make sure nothing happens to you. You'll have to trust me, darling." The endearment was spoken very casually as if he had called her that hundreds of times.

But it was the catalytic agent that combined with

the firm contact of his muscled length and her undeniable attraction to him that banished her resistance to his embrace. Samantha relaxed against him, letting her curves mold themselves to the hard contours of his body. She felt the moistness of his mouth moving in rough kisses against her hair.

"Jonas," she sighed, then caught it back. "That isn't your real name, is it?"

"No," he admitted indifferently. "But it doesn't matter."

"Yes it does," Samantha protested, because it meant that he didn't trust her. Yet he expected her to trust him when she didn't even know who he was.

His large hands moved up to cup the sides of her neck below her ears, fingers twining into her hair as he tipped her head back to meet the smoldering fire of his gray eyes.

"Nothing matters except this." His mouth brushed over her eyelid, her lashes fluttering against his lips. "And this." He shifted to her cheek and the tiny hollow where her dimple formed. "And this," he murmured against the corner of her lips.

And he kissed her until she was convinced. The masterful pressure of his mouth blocked out all her fears. Her arms wrapped themselves around his neck to cling to him, breathing erratically when he began exploring the sensitive cord along her neck.

"I want to trust you," she whispered achingly.

Jonas lifted his head to gaze into her hungry eyes. "Then trust me," he stated quietly. "You won't be sorry, I promise. I won't let anything happen to you."

There was a barely perceptible movement of her head in acceptance of his words. His mouth closed possessively over hers, burning his ownership deep into her heart. Samantha knew he was wrong. Something had already happened to her. She had fallen in love with him—her stranger, her kidnapper—and there wasn't any way she could reverse the course of her emotions.

His hands slid down her spine to mold her hips against him, the muscular column of his legs scorching her flesh on contact. She melted in his crushing embrace, glorying in the golden tide of surrender sweeping through her, uncaring for the hard thrust of gun metal biting into her shoulder and chest.

The growth of beard scraped at her cheek as he searched out each sensitive area along the curve of her neck and the pulsing hollow of her throat. But the rasp of his beard was exquisite pain, heightening her nerve ends to their full peak of awareness. His large hands moved over every inch of her ribs, waist and hips, arching her more fully against him while they continued to explore the pliant curves of her body.

The musky scent of his maleness filled her senses, sending them spinning with delight. Samantha was no match for his passionate onslaught, so she started a backfire of her own. As she sought the devastating pressure of his mouth, liquid wildfire raced through her veins.

After torturous seconds, he let her lips find his mouth, his kiss hardening as they opened beneath his touch. Locked in each other's arms, they both felt the yearnings for satisfaction in the other.

Finally it was Jonas who ended it, breaking away to bury his face in the silky thickness of her hair above her ear. Her trembling fingers continued a tentative exploration of his strong jawline. The pounding of his heart kept pace with the rapid tempo of hers, his breathing disturbed and ragged.

"I've tried so hard to keep from loving you," Samantha whispered with a frustrated longing for satisfaction.

"You have?" his muffled voice mocked her gently. "What do you think it's been like for me? Every time you're near me, I want to make love to you."

She drew her head away, needing to see his face. "Do you really mean that?" she asked breathlessly.

He smiled, a wondrous smile that softened the firm line of his mouth and made beautiful, crinkling lines at the corners of his gray eyes. His gaze traveled warmly over her upturned face, taking in the soft glow of her eyes and the parted invitation of her lips.

"If you don't stop looking at me like that, you'll find out just how much I mean that," he told her with lazy humor.

Samantha laughed huskily and rested her head against his chest. A sweet pleasure beyond description filled her heart with joy. She closed her eyes to imprint this moment in her mind, wanting to cherish it forever. Right now, it didn't matter that he hadn't said he loved her. He wanted her, with the same fierce ache with which she wanted him.

"Let's go away, Jonas," she murmured. "Let's get in the sailboat and sail away."

There was a sudden tenseness in the arms that held her. Every muscle seemed to become suddenly alert. With deliberate slowness, his hands moved up to grip her shoulders and move her a few inches from him. The smoke screen was back to conceal his thoughts when she lifted her head to gaze at him. She could only guess what was making him wary and she tried to dispel his caution.

"No one ever has to know that you were keeping me on the island," she told him earnestly. "Please, let's go away, the two of us together."

Her hand lifted to caress the powerful line of his cheek. He caught it before it could reach its objective, crushing her fingers in his hand until she gasped at the pain.

"You're hurting me!" she protested sharply in bewilderment.

A muscle leaped in his jaw and a glimpse of turbulent thunderclouds briefly penetrated the smoke screen of his eyes. He released her hand abruptly and turned away. "We are not leaving this island, Sam," he stated coldly.

Her mouth opened, but for a time nothing could come out. How could he continue to hold her prisoner if he really cared for her as he claimed? Did he care for her? Or did just being with an attractive young woman fill him with lust? Or worse, had he...? The paralyzing hold on her throat eased.

"It was all just a trick, wasn't it?" Samantha

squeezed the accusing words through the painful knot in her throat. "You were playing games again, just the way you've been doing from the beginning."

"It wasn't a game," Jonas answered tautly.

"I don't believe you!" she flashed. "You were just using another tactic to persuade me to stay willingly on this island! It would have made it so much easier if you didn't have to guard me every second, wouldn't it? Well, your scheme didn't work!" She resorted to anger to hold back the scalding tears that burned the backs of her eyes and to keep the sobs of pain lodged in her throat.

"Neither did yours," he snarled.

"Mine?" Samantha breathed in hurt confusion. She couldn't have made it more obvious that she had fallen in love with him.

"Save that innocent look in your brown eyes for someone else." His lip curled in a jeer, his gaze raking her length contemptuously. "I don't buy it. There isn't anything you wouldn't resort to in order to get off this island—you proved that very conclusively a few minutes ago. Did you really think you had me so securely wrapped around your finger that all you had to do was pull the string and I'd take you away? Accusing me of using you is like the pot calling the kettle black."

Samantha gasped softly. He believed she had only been pretending to be in love with him so that he would take her away. Her first instinct was to deny it, but pride insisted that she not completely humble herself when he didn't care for her.

"Desperate situations breed desperate solutions," she mouthed the words that would support his accusation.

"It was hardly an original one," Jonas mocked harshly.

"I'll try to do better in the future," she retorted.

"You may not have a chance. I hope not," he muttered beneath his breath as if thinking aloud, then reached for her arm, saying more clearly, "Come on. You're going back to the house."

"What do you mean I may not have another chance?" Samantha demanded, unable to elude the grip of his hand. She was dragged along beside him toward the door. "Are you going to lock me in my room? Or . . . . " She couldn't voice the other thought.

"I don't think I could trust you alone even behind a locked door. If I lock you in, I'll be in there with you." The ominous glitter of his gaze was turned on her, rife with intimate suggestion. "It might even prove to be entertaining."

"You wouldn't dare!" she breathed in alarm, pulling back against his grip to lag behind him.

Jonas paused at the door, an eyebrow lifting in arrogant amusement. "Wouldn't I?" he mocked, and she paled.

The door burst open and Tom's burly figure was silhoutted against the night. "She's slipped away again," he burst out. Jonas's tall frame blocked her from view. "Maggie looked in a few minutes ago and found pillows stuffed under the covers to make it look like she was still in bed. The window screen was pried loose. There's no way of telling how long she's been gone."

"You can stop looking," Jonas said curtly, pulling Samantha forward. "I've found her."

Tom swore beneath his breath in relief. "I thought we'd lost her for sure."

"I'm taking her back to the house now. Get a lock for the dinghy and the boathouse door," Jonas ordered. "Then you'd better see what you can do to patch that screen."

"Right away," Tom nodded.

Samantha was pushed through the door's opening as Tom stepped out of the way. It was a long walk to the house, a walk that was made even longer by the grim silence of her captor. Maggie was waiting in the dining room. She shook her head in relief at the sight of Samantha, but Jonas didn't make any explanation as he marched Samantha through the house to her bedroom and shoved her inside.

She stumbled into the room, regained her balance near the rumpled bed, then turned to face him, frightened yet boldly defiant. He stood at the door, a hand resting on the door knob.

"The screen isn't repaired yet, but I wouldn't try to slip away again," he warned. "I'd find you before you could get off the island."

"Go to hell, whatever-your-name-is!" A rush of bravado strangled her voice.

"Thanks to your father, I probably will," he agreed sardonically and shut the door.

Samantha stood uncertainly where she was, wanting to fly in the face of his warning and sneak through the opening of the screen. But she was convinced he would find her and the consequences might be more disastrous the next time.

A tear spilled down her cheek, then a second. She moved blindly to the bed, stretching out on the covers and burying her head in a pillow. She had no idea how long she lay there in a numbed stupor of pain, her cheeks wet with the slow trickle of tears.

From outside, someone started pounding a hammer where her screen window was. Tom, she guessed. It was only after the pounding stopped and his footsteps carried him away from her bedroom that the tears inreased their flow. For the first time since her childhood years, Samantha cried herself to sleep, silently, muffling her sobs in the pillow.

Her head throbbed dully as the sunlight probed at her eyelids. She pulled the covers more tightly over her shoulders and tried to cling to the forgetfulness of sleep. An awareness crept in, aroused first by the bareness of her skin. She didn't remember undressing and frowned as she realized that she was clad in her undergarments and not her pajamas. She stirred slightly and felt a weight on one corner of the bed.

The painful memories of last night began to surface. She felt raw and bruised mentally as she struggled into consciousness. The back of her neck prickled with the sensation that someone was watching her. The uncomfortable feeling wouldn't go away, and she turned her face from the pillow to glance over her shoulder.

The last dregs of sleep fled at the sight of Jonas slouched in a chair, his long legs propped on the edge of the bed. His elbows rested on the arms of the chair, his hands folded together on the flat of his stomach. Behind the lazily lowered lashes, his gray eyes were watching her, taking in her stunned shock and the trepidation that immediately replaced it.

Samantha quickly pulled the covers up to her throat, remembering his threat to lock himself in the room with her and hotly conscious of her scanty attire beneath the blankets. She had trouble breathing naturally.

"How long have you been there?" Her demand was weakly voiced.

"All night," he answered blandly.

"It wasn't necessary," she protested stiffly.

"I thought it was."

"I didn't try to get away."

"No, and you won't get the chance to try anymore," he stated, uncoiling from the chair and subtly stretching his cramped muscles.

"What do you mean?" Samantha eyed him cautiously. Had he decided to keep her locked in the room?

"I mean—" he paused for effect "—that someone is going to be with you at all times. The only place you'll be alone is in the bathroom, and I suggest you go there now and get dressed so I can turn you over to Maggie and get myself some sleep."

From the glint in his eye, Samantha could tell that he expected her to insist he look the other way while she made her dash to the bathroom. Instead, she pulled the covers from the foot of the bed and wrapped them securely around her as she swung her feet to the floor. Shuffling across the floor in the confining mummy wrap, she took fresh clothes from the closet and dresser drawer, then retreated to the bathroom.

Before the day was over, Samantha learned that Jonas had meant exactly what he said. She was never alone, shadowed constantly by one of them.

During the morning and early afternoon, it was Maggie and Tom because Jonas was sleeping. Maggie was quietly friendly in the time Samantha was forced to spend with her, but it was Tom who seemed the most sympathetic to her plight, his gaze faintly apologetic.

Jonas had monopolized her time so much in the past days that this had been her first opportunity to get to know the others. Yet both Maggie and Tom remained slightly aloof from her. She knew it would be useless to try to enlist their aid in escaping. They were as determined as Jonas that she remain on the island.

At eleven that evening, Jonas announced it was time she went to bed. Samantha wanted to protest, but she knew it was a command he would see obeyed even if he had to use physical force to accomplish it. She couldn't conceal her mistrust of his presence when he followed her into the bedroom.

She hesitated inside, unwilling to change into the revealing shorty pajamas and reluctant to incite a situation she couldn't handle. Besides, how could she even get into bed with him watching her? Her position was so vulnerable, especially because she loved him in spite of everything.

"You might as well change into your night clothes." He accurately guessed the reason for her hesitation. "Otherwise Maggie will have to come in and undress you the same as she did last night." At Samantha's sudden pivot in his diretion, he drew his head back in a considering manner, a wicked, knowing glint in his eyes. "You thought I took your clothes off last night, didn't you?" he chuckled.

Her cheeks crimsoned as she hurriedly looked away. "I had no way of knowing who did."

"Well, you can breathe easier—it wasn't me," he turned with a vague burst of impatience. "So hurry up and get into bed."

Self-consciously, Samantha gathered the yellow shorty pajamas in hand and darted into the bathroom, emerging a few minutes later to see Jonas standing at the window. Before she could slide beneath the covers he turned and saw her.

The pajamas covered more than her bathing suit did, but there was something so decidedly intimate about wearing pajamas in front of a man. She made a project of tucking the covers around her, studiously avoiding the frowning look of concentration being directed at her. Her pulse raced when he moved away from the window. But all he did was switch off the overhead light to throw the room into darkness; then he walked back to the window.

For a long time she was afraid to move. Her muscles became cramped from the restricted position. The covers were drawn so tightly around her that she began to suffocate. Finally, she had to move. She turned, trying to find a more comfortable position, but without much success. The repeated shiftings drew an impatient response.

"I hope you aren't going to sleep as restlessly as you did last night," he said. "I'm not in the mood to keep covering you up all night long."

Just when she had begun to lose some of her embarrassment over the fact that it hadn't been Jonas who had undressed her, it returned with a fury of warmth.

"Thanks a lot," she muttered bitterly. "That's just the kind of comment I needed to induce a restful sleep!" Since it would result in the exact opposite.

"Go to sleep, Sam," he muttered back in a savage undertone.

"I'm trying, but it's not easy with you standing there," she retorted.

"Would you rather I crawled in bed with you?" Jonas snapped.

"No!" The denial was quick and more than a little frightened as her body was first cold, then hot at the thought.

"Forget I asked," he sighed. A task easier said than done. "Good night, Sam. And don't worry, I won't disturb you."

"Good night."

Had it been her imagination or had there been a

slight emphasis on his last word—"you"? Samantha couldn't tell, but she thought it was wise not to ask.

Neither spoke again, although it was well into the morning hours before she finally slept. When she wakened near midday, she found Maggie was in the room with her. The woman explained that Jonas had left for his own room shortly after dawn to get some sleep.

The day's pattern started out as a duplicate of the previous day. The change came in the middle of the afternoon when Jonas appeared to relieve Tom. He and Samantha had been playing a game of gin rummy, but when Jonas sat in his chair, Samantha stood up. His presence dominated the room, making it too confining.

"Can we go outside?" she asked nervously, feeling the disturbance caused by his overpowering masculinity.

"For a while," he agreed, rising to move toward the patio doors, sliding them open, and permitting Samantha to lead the way.

She moved restlessly around the patio, unable to appreciate the view of the gently flowing St. Lawrence River and its cluster of islands. Jonas leaned against a rock, letting her prowl while keeping her in sight. She felt there was an invisible leash stretching from her to him and she wanted to break free of it.

Her steps turned unconsciously toward the path to the boathouse. She hesitated a few yards along the worn trail and glanced over her shoulder. Jonas had moved away from the boulder and was ambling after her, but not attempting to catch up. Evidently he wasn't going to forbid her to go to the cove. Maybe he wanted her to see that the boathouse was padlocked.

Samantha turned her back to the path and continued her aimless meandering pace toward the cove. There wasn't any particular reason to go there. She was only going because there wasn't any particular reason not to go.

On a rocky knoll above the cove, the trees gave way to grass and stone. She paused there, her gaze sweeping the clumps of tree-crowned islands against the backdrop of a milk blue sky. A few elongated puffy clouds were drifting overhead.

As Samantha started down from the knoll, she noticed a motor cruiser growing steadily larger in the distance, but her only interest in it was identifying something that was moving in the quiet afternoon. There wasn't any thought that it could offer her aid. Jonas would see to that.

Strolling down to the water's edge, she gazed at the raft anchored in the cove, but there were too many painful memories attached to it. She dug a toe into the pebbles at her feet, the tips of her fingers tucked in the hip pockets of her slacks. She didn't have to turn around to know that Jonas was nearby; she could feel his gaze on her. The invisible leash hadn't been broken, only the tension had been slackened.

Lifting her head, she stared out across the water again. The large cruiser was coming nearer. It would pass very close to the island, but Samantha didn't take her hands from her pockets to wave at it. To attract the boat's attention would also attract Jonas's, and she would gain nothing in the end except his displeasure and possibly a confinement to the house.

Instead of the cruiser steering a course around the island, she realized with a start that it was heading toward the cove. As it neared the entrance, the powerful engines were throttled down. Her heart leaped at the sight, but her feet were rooted to the spot. At any moment she expected Jonas to come charging down to drag her away before she was recognized.

The cruiser was in the cove now and there was still no sound from Jonas. Biting her lip, Samantha glanced over her shoulder. Jonas was standing in the break of the trees, slightly in their shadow, watching the boat purring toward the dock. His gaze slipped to her.

At this distance, his expression was inscrutable.

Is this another of his tricks, Samantha wondered with bitter pain. The boat must belong to one of his colleagues. Why else was he letting it come in? Maybe he enjoyed tormenting her. Blinking away a brief welling of tears, she looked back to the cruiser.

The engines were stopped and a dark-suited man was making the boat fast to the dock. When it was secure, two more figures emerged from the cabin. Samantha stared at one of them, not believing her eyes.

He was a few inches taller than she was, his physique just beginning to show a losing battle against weight, dark brown hair salted liberally with gray. When he turned toward land and she saw his handsome square face and clear, discerning brown eyes, she knew she wasn't mistaken.

Joy rose at the sight of Reuben Gentry, her father, only to be checked by the realization of what this meant. She was being rescued, which meant that Jonas would be caught. Her gaze swung to the path's knoll and Jonas. The trees were still concealing him from the view of the boat's party. Their eyes met, hers begging him to run, to get away while he had the chance.

"Sam!" Reuben was calling to her, a strong voice, vital and powerful like the man.

Samantha ripped her gaze from Jonas, forcing a smile, only half-glad to see her father. She freed her feet from their roots and made them carry her toward her father, slowly gaining speed until she was nearly running into his opened arms. Tears blinded her vision as she stopped before him.

"Reuben," she murmured in a chocked whisper.

He tipped his head to one side, his hands settling on her shoulders. "Are you all right, Sam?"

The comforting touch of his hands slid her arms around his waist, muffling her silent sobs in the expensive material of his jacket.

"Yes, I'm all right," she managed to say huskily, but she wasn't. Her arms tightened around him. Very, very softly, she cried, "Daddy!"

He held her for a few more seconds, then began to gently untwine her arms from around his middle. His brown eyes were warm with deep affection as he wiped the tears from her cheeks.

"I haven't had a welcome like that since you were six years old," he teased. Samantha tried to laugh, but it was brittle and harsh. Reuben looked beyond her in the direction of the trail. "Where are the others?"

She glanced at the two dark-suited men, standing quietly, stern-faced, on each side of her father. She saw the bulge of their jackets and paled. Quickly she looked over her shoulder. There was no sign of Jonas. It was wrong to hope he had escaped.

"At...." She didn't want to tell, but she had to. "At the house, I think. There's a path through those trees."

The two men started forward, and Samantha moved to one side as her father started to follow. He stopped and looked at her, an understanding light in his brown eyes.

"Are you coming?" he asked gently.

"No." She couldn't. "I'll wait here—on the boat."

The two men were waiting for him. Reuben Gentry nodded in acknowledgment, then moved to join them. Samantha turned away, wiping the tears from her cheek and determined she wouldn't cry anymore.

CHAPTER NINE

SAMANTHA STARED into the coffee mug, wishing she could lose herself in the seemingly fathomless void of the dark liquid. A man, probably part of the crew, had brought it to her shortly after she had come aboard the cruiser.

Half of it was gone and the rest had cooled to an unpalatable stage. Still she clung to the mug, needing to hold on to something to keep her sanity while she waited in the cabin.

It had been almost twenty minutes since her father had left for the house. There hadn't been a sound, not a gunshot, nothing, only the lapping of the water against the cruiser's hull. Her nerves were virtually raw and bleeding, not knowing what was happening and not wanting to know, yet imagining.

She had drawn the curtains in the cabin. She didn't want to accidentally see them bringing Jonas in. She caught back the sob of agonizing pain that rose in her throat.

There were footsteps on the dock, hollow and ominous, echoing over the boards. Samantha tensed, following them in her mind as they boarded the boat and approached the cabin door. Refusing to turn around as it opened, she closed her eyes and tried to get a grip on her senses. She didn't want Reuben to see her torment, not right now. She breathed in deeply and blinked at the ceiling.

"Did they...give themselves up?" she inquired tautly.

The door closed. "Not exactly."

At the agonizingly familiar sound of that voice, Samantha swung around. Her fingers lost their grip on the coffee mug and it shattered on the floor, scattering pieces of pottery and spattering brown liquid. Her horror-widened eyes stared at Jonas.

"What have you done with Reuben?" she demanded in alarm.

"He's at the house." His features betrayed only a firm determination. The gray eyes were unreadable. "Would you like to join him?"

"Would I like to join him?" Samantha laughed bitterly. "Have you taken him captive, too? Oh, Jonas, you won't get away with it," she declared with taut pain. "Not Reuben Gentry!"

"My name is Cade Scott."

"Cade Scott?" she repeated in bewilderment. The name was familiar, but she was too emotionally trapped to concentrate on why it was known to her.

"I work for Reuben," he stated blandly. "I handle all the security for him."

"Security?" Samantha felt like a weak echo. It was difficult to assimilate his sudden influx of new information. She took her head. "Then...."

"I know you must have jumped to the conclusion

you were kidnapped, but there wasn't anything I could do about it," the man now identified as Cade Scott continued. "I was following Reuben's instructions. My hands were tied."

"Reuben's?" Then she realized she was doing it again. "But why? Why should my father want me held prisoner on this island? It doesn't make sense!"

"It was for your own protection. It—"

"For my own protection?" Samantha interrupted. "Why should I need protection?"

"Over the last few months, your father has received a series of threatening letters and phone calls. He didn't take them seriously until someone took a shot at him a couple of weeks ago." At Samantha's gasp of fear, he added, "The man missed, but he convinced Reuben, as I had been unable to do, that he wasn't making idle threats."

"What does this have to do with me if he was after Reuben?" she frowned.

"The day I came to the newspaper office, your father had received a phone call from the man that morning. He said he had decided Reuben should live, killing him would be too easy. He would get his revenge on Reuben through you. He knew what town you were in, where you were working and what name you were using," Cade Scott explained. "With that much information, we had to believe he would harm you. I had to move faster than him to get you out of there before he could make good his threat."

"And that's why you brought me here." She felt a shiver of fear dance down her spine.

"The island is isolated, easier to guard. Intruders would be spotted immediately. We decided it was the ideal place to hide you," he stated in the same impersonal tone he had used since he entered the cabin.

Samantha raked her fingers through her hair, flipping it back.

"Why didn't you tell me all this in the beginning? Why was it such a deep dark secret?"

"I told you—it was Reuben's orders. He didn't want to alarm you. Which is why I wasn't able to tell you my real name. Reuben was certain you would make the connection to his security section and become suspicious." He snapped a lighter flame to a cigarette. "I don't think he realized you weren't a little girl anymore and had long ago stopped being afraid of the dark."

"So you went through that whole charade of being Owen Bradley, then Chris Andrews and the mysterious Jonas!" Samantha exclaimed impatiently. "Didn't you think the constant parade of names would make me suspicious? That's not even mentioning your refusal to let me leave the island or speak to anyone else. Which raises another question. Why wouldn't you let me call Reuben?"

"Because we didn't know how the man was getting his information. It was conceivable that it was being relayed to him by someone in your father's organization. I couldn't let you leave a message where you were in case it got in the wrong hands," he returned smoothly.

Her anger was rising. "You could have explained,

somehow," she accused, "instead of letting me think I was a prisoner. That you and Tom and Maggie were holding me—" She broke off to ask sharply, "I presume that Tom and Maggie work in the security department, too?"

"That's right."

"When you realized that I thought I was kidnapped, you should have told me," Samantha protested bitterly.

"I couldn't. You—"

"I know, Reuben had given orders," she flashed. "But you could have explained to him. I was positively terrified, and for nothing!"

"I did try to convince him, but he's like a bulldog. Once he gets his teeth into something, he won't let go. He insisted on sticking with the original plan for you to know nothing of the threats." Cade regarded her steadily. "I believe you overheard the last part of the conversation I had with him about it and misinterpreted it."

Samantha vividly remembered the one he was referring to and Cade's anger when he warned Reuben he would be sorry. "Yes," she nodded crisply. "I thought Reuben was refusing to pay the ransom."

"The original plan should have been scrapped when Reuben discovered he couldn't join us," Cade commented absently, glancing at the wispy trail of smoke rising from the end of his cigarette.

"Was he planning to?" Samantha inquired with vague skepticism.

"Yes, we thought it was best if he was here with

you in case the man changed his mind and made another attempt on his life, but the authorities persuaded him to stay in New York where the man could contact him again."

"In that case, why is he here now?" she demanded.

"The man was arrested in the night. The danger is over." Cade stubbed the cigarette out in the ashtray, the bronze mask firmly in place.

Yet something in his tone made her ask, "How long have you known?"

"Since around five this morning."

Approximately the same time that Maggie had indicated he had relinquished his guard over Samantha and gone to bed. But that wasn't what made her temper ignite.

"And you let practically another day go by letting me believe I was kidnapped. You could have explained all of this to me before Reuben arrived," she accused angrily.

"Yes, I could have," he agreed with the utmost calm, blandly meeting the snapping fire of her gaze. "But I didn't think you would believe me. As you pointed out before, you listened to too many of my lies to listen to anything I said. I knew Reuben was on his way, so I waited for him to support my story. I'm telling you the truth, Sam."

Samantha turned away, pain bursting in her heart at the sound of her name on his lips. She believed him. Everything fitted, all the evidence that she had misinterpreted. Even the initials C.S. turned out to be right.

C.S. for Cade Scott.

She had known who Cade Scott was. She had heard Reuben praising loud and long the man who headed the security division of his various companies. By some quirk of fate she had never met him until he had brought her to this island paradise that her imagination had turned into an island hell. But the initials alone hadn't been sufficient to jog her memory of a man she hadn't met.

"If only I'd known!" she groaned softly.

"I wanted to tell you," Cade said quietly. "I nearly did a couple of times."

"I wish you had," Samantha sighed, remembering the pain she had experienced when she discovered she was falling in love with a stranger who had kidnapped her. The love had tormented her. At least now she didn't have to feel so guilty about loving him. "I wish you had, regardless of what Reuben wanted," she repeated.

"I take orders from your father. He's the boss," Cade reminded her.

The words were a death knell. Cade Scott worked for her father and she was the boss's daughter, an excellent prize for an ambitious man. And the relentless quality about him assured Samantha that he was an ambitious man. He would get where he wanted regardless of whom he used along the way.

"I'll assure him of the thorough job you did protecting me," she declared with a brittle smile. "You did your very best to keep me entertained, even resorting to some drastic methods, but they worked.

And it's only been in the last couple of days that I decided—wrongly—that I'd been kidnapped. You weren't to blame for that. I'm sure Reuben will be very proud of you."

His gaze narrowed, slicing over her face. "Not everything I did was to entertain you, Sam." There was underlining emphasis on the word "everything."

"Of course not." She laughed huskily to hide the quivering of her chin. "It was good fun for both of us."

A brow flicked upward, arrogant and withdrawn. "That's all it was."

Yet she sensed there was a question behind his statement and it hurt. "Yes, that's all it was," she said, but the poignant catch in her voice wasn't convincing.

Cade took a step toward her and Samantha pivoted to face him, on guard against the explosive attraction his presence made her feel. Like quicksilver, his gaze glided over her face, the vulnerable light in her brown eyes, then stopped on her moist lips. Her pulse accelerated.

"You're lying, Sam. It wasn't just fun for either of us," he said, starting forward again.

She retreated, a fragment of the broken coffee mug crunching beneath her foot. "Please, Jonas...." With a broken laugh, Samantha corrected herself. "It's Cade, isn't it? You see, I don't even know what to call you. Please, I need time to think. It's all so confusing. Leave me alone, Cade, please?"

He hesitated, then grimly conceded. "Okay, we'll

do it your way this time." He turned on his heel and walked to the cabin door. "I'll tell Reuben you've decided to wait for him at the boat."

Cade was gone before Samantha could acknowledge his last statement. For several minutes she listened to the sound of his footsteps as he left the boat. Finally she bent to pick up the pieces of the broken mug until tears blinded her vision and she could no longer see them.

By the time Reuben Gentry returned to the boat, Samantha had washed away any trace of tears. She had even managed to find some humor in her escapade, however bitter, when they discussed it. Luckily her father had no intention of remaining on the island, even overnight.

Samantha gladly accompanied him, needing to get away from Cade before she committed herself to something she would regret.

At twenty-two, she had learned not to give in to impulse. She already had too many scars where people couldn't see them. Cade didn't return with them. Reuben claimed Cade had a few ends to tie up and would follow the next day.

Samantha wondered if he was giving her that chance to think.

Reuben didn't seem to expect her to go directly back to the newspaper. Samantha needed a few days to lick her wounds in private and come to some decision about Cade. There was no question that she loved him. The question was what would she do with that love?

Four days after her return, the telephone rang. Samantha stared at it. She didn't want to answer it. It was Cade—she knew it as surely as if he was standing in the room. Cowardly, she let it ring, wanting to avoid the inevitable. But it was inevitable and it was better not to postpone it. On the fourteenth ring she answered it, hardly aware she had been counting.

"Sam, this is Cade." His low voice moved through her like a golden flame.

"Hello, Cade, how are you?" She congratulated herself on the calmness of her reply. It wasn't indicative of her racing heart.

"Fine," was the automatic response, but he didn't return the inquiry. "Since Reuben's out of town, I wondered if you were free for dinner this evening."

Samantha breathed in sharply as he stole her excuse. Cade worked for her father and being in charge of security made him cognizant of Reuben's whereabouts.

"Actually—" She was stalling, trying to think of a plausible lie.

"Sam," Cade interrupted in a quietly firm voice, "I want to see you."

Her legs didn't want to support her as her heart skipped several beats. She clutched at the table, fighting the waves of longing. If the sound of his voice could do this to her, what would happen if she saw him again? To be forewarned was to be forearmed—wasn't that what they said? Wouldn't it be better to see him now than to wait for some time when she might be unprepared, hence vulnerable?

"Actually," Samantha continued, "I don't have anything planned for this evening."

"I'll pick you up at seven," he concluded.

"Yes."

After an exchange of goodbyes, Samantha hung up the telephone, her hands shaking, a giddiness in the pit of her stomach. She closed her eyes tightly. She had to get control of herself before tonight.

The thin organdy blouse of apricot and the long cream-colored skirt gave her a sophisticated appearance, but the luminous brown eyes gazing at her reflection were troubled and apprehensive. Her features were strained with the expression of poise.

The doorbell rang and Samantha jumped. This would never do, she scolded herself, and hurried into the living room. Carl, Reuben's houseman, answered the door as she entered the room. Cade's glance slid past the houseman to Samantha. Her steps faltered under the appraising sweep of his gaze, lazy and warmly charcoal gray.

"Ready?" he asked quietly.

His rough features were more rugged and compelling than she remembered, the dark brown of his hair growing thickly away from the slanted forehead, the heavy curve of his nearly black eyebrows, the steady regard of dark smoke eyes above the angular planes of his cheeks, the slight broken bend of his nose, the strong, well-shaped mouth, and that casual air that hid the steel. Samantha felt light-headed.

"Yes, I am." The breathless catch in her voice revealed the way he disturbed her. Normally, she would have invited her date in for a drink, but not this time. "Shall we go?" Her voice was closer to normal.

"I have a cab waiting," Cade agreed.

Samantha walked to the door, glancing at Carl, who held it open for her and smiling into his gentle face. "I have my key," she told him.

His mouth curved slightly, taking her hint. "I won't wait up for you, then. Have a nice evening, Samantha."

As he closed the door, she felt Cade's questioning gaze. "Carl has been with Reuben for years. When I first started dating, he was the one who usually waited up until I was safely home, and always when Reuben was out of town. He's a dear. I don't know what Reuben would do without him." She was willing to discuss anything as long as it didn't directly relate to her and what she was really thinking and feeling at this moment.

"It's good Reuben has Carl, then," he commented as they walked toward the elevators at the end of the hall. "You won't have to worry about who's taking care of Reuben when you aren't here."

"You mean when I spread my wings and leave the nest for good to embark on my career as a journalist," she added with forced brightness.

"Or marry. Or both." His sideways look held her gaze for pulsing seconds.

Before Samantha could recover, the elevator doors were opening and his large hand was applying pressure on the back of her waist to guide her inside. An involuntary thrill of pleasure ran through her at his touch, unnerving her and taking away her ability to speak. Cade didn't seem to expect a reply as he pushed the ground floor button and turned calmly back to her.

Samantha had the sensation of falling. She couldn't tell whether it was caused by the soundless descent of the elevator or the enigmatic look in his eyes as it ran over her face. Either way the pulse in her throat was throbbing madly.

"I haven't told you how beautiful you look to-night." The seductive pitch of his voice was almost too much.

"Thank you," she returned, striving for lightness to keep from sinking completely under his spell. "You're looking very attractive, too." She forced her gaze to break away from the hold of his and let it rush over the dark evening suit he wore. "It's a definite improvement not to have the bulge of a shoulder holster under your jacket."

"When did you guess?" Cade asked thoughtfully. "The night you sneaked back into the house after your walk and we mistook you for an intruder?"

"Yes," Samantha admitted. "I saw you slip the gun inside your windbreaker. After that, I put two and two together and realized it wasn't poor tailoring that made your jackets so bulky."

"That was the beginning, wasn't it? When you started to mistrust me?"

The elevator had stopped at the ground floor, the doors gliding open. Samantha managed a brief "more or less" agreement as they stepped out. Conversation was pushed aside by the sight of the doorman walking quickly forward to open the door for them and the taxi driver standing impatiently on the sidewalk near his car.

No further reference was made by either of them to her enforced stay on the island while they dined at one of the more popular cabaret clubs in New York City. Afterward, the entertainment offered precluded the need for conversation. Yet the undercurrent of awareness flowed constantly between them.

The slightest contact of his hand or any part of him vibrated through Samantha. Each time his gaze slid to her lips, she seemed to stop breathing. Basically, though, Cade kept his distance, not trying to penetrate her defenses except by a subtle look or touch. It was as if he knew he could destroy them any time he wanted to.

Dancing followed the entertainment. Samantha knew that she could not risk the feel of his arms around her and suggested Cade take her home. He didn't object. In the taxi home, he made no attempt to sit close to her as they exchanged polite comments about the entertainment they had seen.

At the apartment building, Cade didn't ask the taxi to wait. When the taxi drove off into the night, Samantha knew the hour of reckoning had arrived and hoped she was up to it. She nodded stiffly to the doorman as Cade escorted her into the building and toward the elevators.

Neither spoke during the ride up to the floor of her father's apartment. The silence added to the tension that had been mounting inside Samantha since Cade's phone call that afternoon.

At the apartment door, she made a weak attempt to dismiss him. "I had a lovely evening, Cade. Thank you."

His mouth quirked mockingly. "You're inviting me in," he stated, and took the key from her hand.

"I . . . I really am tired," she protested nervously.

The key turned in the lock and Cade pushed the door open. Then his hand was between her shoulder blades to gently push her into the mock foyer entrance of the living room.

"You know we have to talk, Sam," he said quietly, and walked past her, moving familiarly toward the bar in the far corner of the living room. She guessed he had been here before with her father.

Since she couldn't afford to relax, Samantha avoided the comfortable chairs and sofa, walking to the far window that overlooked the bustling city, aglitter with lights. Too soon, Cade was beside her, offering a glass of gin and tonic. She accepted it, staring at the cubes of ice rather than meeting his gaze.

"I'm not sure I know exactly what it is we have to talk about," she said defensively.

"About us, of course." Cade lifted his glass to his mouth, blandly meeting her involuntary glance over the rim of his glass. Her heart jumped to her throat as she looked wildly away from the disturbing light of his gray eyes.

CHAPTER TEN

"WHY OF COURSE?" Samantha questioned with a brittle laugh of fake bewilderment. She took a quick, retreating step away from him, masking it under the pretense of turning from the window's view.

"Before tonight, I had some doubts myself," Cade stated, following her with his eyes.

"Doubts?" she breathed, trying not to sound as interested as she really was.

"Not about the way I felt," he expanded on his statement, "but about you."

"What do you mean?" Her attempt at a bright, unconcerned smile was tremulous, wavering visibly under his inspection of her mouth.

"I wasn't sure if the way you responded to my kisses on the island was because of me or because you were trying to enlist my help in getting off the island."

"And now?" She held her breath, clutching her drink in both hands.

Cade set his glass down. Samantha couldn't make herself move when he walked to her. His hand lifted the luxurious silk of her seal brown hair away from the side of her neck, the roughness of his thumb stroking the throbbing vein that was exposed. He still hadn't answered the question. It didn't matter because his touch made her forget what she had asked.

"Are you afraid of me, Sam?" he inquired.

"Yes." Her breathing was shallow, nearly nonexistent.

"Because of the way I make you feel?" Cade persisted gently.

As if hypnotized into telling the truth by the rhythmic, seductive caress of his hand, Samantha answered yes. Her gaze was riveted on the glass in her hands.

Her eyes still followed the glass when Cade removed it and set it aside. But she seemed incapable of looking higher than the lapel of his jacket, the dark material contrasting the white of his shirt.

"I thought you were attractive the first time I saw you at the newspaper office, so open and unassuming. I admired you immediately." His voice caressed her, quickening the drumbeat of her pulse beneath his thumb. "One of the first rules a man learns when he's supposed to protect someone is to pay attention to what's going on around him. On the island, I found myself watching you. That amounts to a cardinal sin in my profession, Sam."

"Does it?" she murmured, since he seemed to expect her to say something.

"Looking at you wasn't enough. Every time I got close to you I wanted to kiss you." Samantha noticed the muscles tightening in his neck. "Hell," he muttered, "I wanted to make love to you. I thought it was what you wanted, too, until that night in the boathouse. I decided then that you were using my attraction for you to persuade me to help you escape. But you weren't, were you? You really meant it that night when you said you wanted us to go away together. It wasn't a trick, was it?"

"Cade, please!" She couldn't admit that. Her head moved to the side in protest.

"I realized it wasn't when your father's boat docked. You didn't run to him, not immediately, Sam. No, you looked at me, wanting me to run, to escape before I was caught, even though you believed I'd kidnapped you. You were hoping I'd get away, weren't you?" Cade demanded relentlessly.

"I don't know what I wanted or what I hoped," Samantha denied in a tortured whisper.

"You stubborn little minx! You love me but you won't admit it," he sighed with wry amusement.

"I can't." And by saying that, she admitted she loved him.

His hand slipped around her waist while his fingers curled tighter around her neck. He bent his head closer to hers, and their breaths mingled, warm, moist and intoxicating.

"It's easy, darling. Just repeat after me—I love you." Even word was carefully enunciated and her brown eyes watched the tantalizing nearness of his mouth as it formed the words. "Say it," Cade commanded lowly.

"I—" her lips moved fractionally closer to his "—love—" he moved to meet her halfway "—you."

The possessive fire of his kiss burned the last of her defenses and her lips parted willingly. Samantha wanted only to give herself up to the abandon he was arousing. Desire flamed white-hot, born no longer of just sexual attraction, but now fueled by a deep, abiding love.

She obeyed the molding power of his hands and strained against him, glorying in the exploratory caress of his hands. There was no thought of restraint as he found the secret places to give her pleasure.

His voice, husky and low with passion, murmured near her ear, "It's easy to love you, darling."

Instead of thrilling her, his words had the effect of a cold shower. He spoke the truth, a truth that Samantha had forgotten when she was swept away by her love. It was easy for a man to love Reuben Gentry's daughter. Look at the dowry she would bring with her!

Slowly she began withdrawing her responses from his touch. Cade objected for only a few seconds, then seemed to blame her innocence for the sudden reticence to turn the embrace into something more. He held her loosely in his arms, rubbing his chin against the side of her forehead.

"I left you alone and gave you time to think. Now, Samantha, my love, will you marry me?" It amounted to a command.

"I can't," she replied with hesitation.

His chin moved away from her head in surprise, and she immediately took the opportunity to move out of his arms. Gathering her resolve, she lifted her gaze to meet the piercing gray of his eyes, confused and searching.

"What do you mean—you can't?" Cade frowned. "Haven't I made it clear to you—"

"You've made it very clear," she interrupted briskly. "But I won't—I can't marry you."

"Why? Surely I'm entitled to know," he demanded, trying to control the hardness that was trying to take over his voice.

"Ask me to be your mistress or your lover." She was trembling with the pain breaking her up inside, but she kept her voice steady. "But don't ask me to be your wife, Cade."

"What the hell are you talking about?" Cade exploded. "If I wanted you for my mistress, I would never have asked you to marry me!"

"Then I'm sorry, but the answer is no," Samantha said firmly.

"My god, Sam, you love me!" he argued savagely. "Why won't you marry me?"

She turned away, widening her eyes to hold back the tears. "Don't be deliberately obtuse, Cade," she replied tightly. "I haven't forgotten who I am. I'm Reuben Gentry's daughter. You work for him, he's your boss."

His fingers dug into her elbow, roughly spinning her around. The wintry blast of his gray eyes chilled her to the bone. His hard features were frozen in rigid anger.

"And I'm not good enough for you to marry, is that it?" he snarled. "The boss's daughter can't stoop to marry a lowly employee." She closed her eyes against the contempt, keeping her face expressionless. "Forgive me, Samantha Gentry—" his voice was thick with sarcasm "—for insulting you with my proposal."

The bruising grip on her elbow was removed. A few seconds later, the apartment door slammed and Samantha was alone. What was worse, she had never felt so alone.

REUBEN GENTRY pulled a dinner roll apart and began buttering one of the halves. "Carl tells me you were out with Cade one evening while I was gone." His brown gaze slid to Samantha for confirmation.

"Yes, that's right." It was a struggle to keep her voice calm and indifferent. The mention of his name had the power to crush her, and she carefully avoided glancing up from her plate.

"He's a good man, Sam. They don't come any better," he commented. "I trust him implicitly, but I guess I proved that, didn't I?" He chuckled. "I not only would trust him with *my* life, I trusted him with yours."

"Yes, I guess you did," she agreed tautly, then pushed her plate away, her appetite gone.

"Was there something else you would like, Samantha?" Carl looked pointedly at the food left on her plate, silently chiding her, as he had done in the past few days, for eating so little.

"Some coffee later," Samantha answered.

"I imagine you got to know Cade fairly well while you were on his island," her father commented, not dropping the subjct as Samantha had hoped.

371

"Fairly well." Then the rest of Reuben's words clicked in her mind. "His island?"

"Yes, it's been in his family for years. His grandfather lost all of the family fortune in the Crash, like a lot of other people. About the only thing he salvaged was the island. I guess it was his grandfather's way of clinging to the dream of what the Scott family once was," Reuben explained in a musing way. "The original house was destroyed by fire twenty years ago. Cade built the present house himself, literally."

"I didn't know," she murmured.

"Of course, working for me, Cade doesn't get to spend as much time there as he'd like." He shrugged. "What did you think of it, Sam?"

"It was beautiful." Nearly paradise, she could have added. For a short while, it nearly had been. She discovered it was going to be painful imagining Cade returning to that island. She didn't want to think about him against that backdrop where there were so many memories.

"Will you be seeing Cade again?"

Unwillingly, Samantha met the sharp probe of her father's eyes and quickly let her gaze fall to the white tablecloth. "No," she answered flatly. She could sense another question rising and added quickly. "Do you mind if we don't discuss this, Reuben?" It was a clipped request, virtually impossible to ignore.

"If you say so, Sam," Reuben conceded. There were several minutes of silence before he spoke again. "Harry Lindsey called me today. He wondered when you were planning to come back to the paper."

"I don't know." She gave a shake of her head in irritation.

"Do you want to go back?" he asked quietly with that shrewd perception that was one of his biggest assets in the business world.

Samantha tensed, then sighed. "No." Work, and involvement in something besides her own heartache, would probably be the best medicine, but she didn't want to go back to the small-town newspaper. Her planned career didn't seem very important right now without the man she loved to share it with. Later she might find solace in it, but it seemed a poor second best.

"Sam." Again her father's voice came, quiet and probing. "Are you in love with Cade?"

Her hands closed tightly over the edge of the table and she violently pushed her chair away, rising swiftly. "I told you I didn't want to discuss him," she protested angrily and stalked out of the dining room, hot tears welling in her eyes.

Her teeth were biting into her lip as she stopped in the center of the living room. She widened her eyes, blinking wildly to hold back the tears. A pair of hands settled gently on her shoulders to turn her around.

"Leave me alone!" she demanded tautly.

"All we've got is each other, Sam. And Carl, of course." Reuben smiled. Miniature duplicates of his daughter's dimples appeared near his mouth, coaxing and endearing. "If you can't use my shoulder, whose will you use?"

"I'm a big girl now," she stated flatly.

"Even big girls get hurt. Sometimes I think the pain grows bigger as a person grows up," he said with a touch of wisdom. "Obviously you've fallen in love with Cade Scott."

There was a painful knot in her throat. Samantha swallowed it and nodded. "For all the good it does me."

"You mean he doesn't love you?" Her father bent his head slightly to peer at her face.

Samantha couldn't tell him the truth. How could she possibly explain that she had refused Cade's proposal of marriage because she knew it had been offered as an easy step to a higher rung on the ladder of success? Cade hadn't asked *her* to marry him; he had asked Reuben Gentry's daughter. As much as she loved him, she couldn't marry him under those conditions.

"It's no use, Reuben." She shook her head sadly and chose a way that wouldn't hurt her father. "He despises me." Which was true. His parting words had been filled with contempt.

"Despises you?" Reuben frowned. "I find that hard to believe."

"That's because I'm your daughter and you're prejudiced." She managed a wan smile.

"Well, if he despises you so much, why did he take you out?" he demanded, unconvinced by her statement.

"Because I asked him," Samantha lied.

"I see." He considered the information thoughtfully.

"I'll get over it," she assured him, but not really believing it herself.

"Yes." He gathered her into his arms and held her close, his cheek resting against her head. "You got over your broken engagement four years ago, didn't you?" he reasoned gently. "But you didn't love him, did you?"

Samantha shuddered against her father's chest, balling a fist against her mouth. "No," she whispered tightly. In another second, she knew she would be crying if she stayed where she was. Tears only seemed to make her misery worse. She breathed in deeply and pushed herself out of her father's arms. "You haven't finished your dinner."

"You sound like Carl now," he smiled down, understanding lighting his eyes. "Have coffee with me while I finish?"

Samantha nodded, returning his smile stiffly, and slid a hand under his arm as they returned to the dining room together.

A WEEK SLIPPED BY, then two. An undemanding pattern began to form. Not rising until nearly noon, Samantha would fill the afternoon hours taking long walks to tire her out and allow her to fall into exhausted sleep after spending the evenings with her father when he was in town. Which was nearly every night, as if he knew how vital it was for her not to spend the long night hours alone.

Three times Reuben had entertained business guests at dinner and Samantha had acted as his hostess. Only two people knew her well enough to see the agony she hid so convincingly. They were Reuben and their houseman, Carl Gilbert, and they kept her secret.

A hand lightly touched her shoulder and Samantha rolled onto her back, drawing the bedcovers with her, bleary-eyed from heavy sleep. She managed to focus on the image of her father.

"What is it?" she questioned in a sleep-drugged voice.

"I wondered if you could get up early enough to have lunch with me today," he said in a chiding tone. "You're beginning to act like a pampered little rich girl, sleeping until noon every day."

"I know." But there was forgetfulness in sleep and that was a rare occurrence in her waking hours. There wasn't any need to explain to Reuben. "I'd like to have lunch with you," Samantha agreed with a tired nod.

"Sam," he said, his expression suddenly serious, "would you like me to talk to Cade?"

Instantly she was awake. "No! Reuben, please, don't do that," she begged in alarm.

One corner of his mouth lifted to form a rueful line. "I'm afraid I already have."

"No!" It was a low protest and she pressed her head deeper into the pillow, shutting her eyes. "What happened?" She wasn't sure if she wanted to know.

"I tried to lead up to the subject of you gradually, Sam," he admitted. "I didn't seem like a meddling father, so I called him into my office to discuss something else that's been on the planning board for nearly a year. Before I'd even got that out, Cade was telling me what I could do with my plans and my daughter."

"What plans, Reuben?" Samantha breathed warily.

"Our security operations have grown so large over the past few years that I'd decided it should be a separate enterprise. I wanted Cade to head it and offered him an option to buy stock in it," he explained.

"Oh, no!" Samantha moaned, guessing exactly what construction Cade had placed on that.

"His reaction was much more vocal than that," Reuben declared ruefully. "He seemed to think I was trying to buy you a husband by giving him a position of respectability and importance. He said something else, too." He studied her thoughtfully.

"What's that?" She breathed warily.

"Some nonsense about if he wasn't good enough for you to marry before I made him the figurehead of some company, he certainly wouldn't be afterward."

Samantha blanched. "What did you say?"

"I told him that being a snob wasn't among your faults and that the one thing I would never do would be to buy you a husband," Reuben concluded.

"Did he say anything to that?" she asked weakly.

"He gave me a cold look and walked out of the office." He pushed back the sleeve of his jacket to glance at his gold wristwatch. "I have to get to the office. We'll talk about it at lunch. Twelve-thirty?"

"Fine," Samantha nodded.

When Reuben left, Samantha knew she would never go back to sleep and lethargically dragged herself out of bed to dress. Over and over in her mind the hope kept running that maybe she had misjudged Cade. He had refused the advancement in his status outright. But supposing she had, would it ultimately change anything?

Obviously Reuben hadn't convinced him that she wasn't a snob and didn't believe herself too good for him. And after the things she had said, how could she convince him to the contrary?

She wandered restlessly through the apartment. The irony of the situation was beginning to grip her. She had been so afraid some man would marry her because of her father that she had turned away the only man who might really have loved her. It was a bitter fact to accept.

The doorbell rang and Samantha let Carl answer it, presuming it was the dry cleaners with a delivery. It was a shock when she turned from the living-room window and saw Cade walking out of the foyer entrance into the living room. Joy leaped into her heart at the sight of him, tall and vital and, in her eyes, incredibly handsome.

"Cade!" she breathed in recognition, and would have run into his arms if his voice hadn't stopped her.

"Reuben made me a proposition yesterday." The clipped voice was low and harsh. "He nearly convinced me that you weren't connected with it. It doesn't matter because I'm accepting it and you as part of the bargain."

Samantha stared at him, her joy fleeing. The offer of a company of his own had become too much to resist, she realized with a pang.

"I'm afraid you're too late." She lifted her head proudly. "The offer has been withdrawn."

"We'll see about that," Cade responded with ominous calm.

His long strides carried him across the room to Samantha. At the last minute she tried to escape, but she had left it too late. With unbelievable ease, he picked her up and tossed her headfirst over his shoulder. An arm was clamped around her legs to hold her there.

"Put me down!" she raged as he began carrying her from the room. Carl stood by the opened front door, eyebrows raised, amusement edging the corners of his mouth. "Carl, do something!" she beseeched.

"What would you suggest?" the houseman shrugged.

"Call my father!" she shouted as Cade entered the hall and walked toward the elevator. Doubling her fists, she pounded on his back. "Put me down this minute!" The elevator doors opened and he carried her in, not acknowledging her order. "I don't want to marry you!" she snapped.

"That's too bad, because you're going to marry me," Cade snapped back.

The elevator stopped at the third floor and a middle-aged woman walked in. The silence was deafening. Samantha reddened, embarrassed beyond words.

"Put me down!" she hissed. "You just wait until my father hears about this!" she threatened.

Cade's head turned toward the woman eyeing them with wary curiosity. "Wives," he mocked, "they run to daddy at the first sign of trouble."

The doors opened on the ground floor and Cade walked out with Samantha over his shoulder before she had a chance to explain to the woman that she wasn't his wife.

"How dare you let that woman think we were married!" Her voice was choked by the impotency of her anger.

"It's only a matter of time." He nodded to the doorman as he swept out of the building to a waiting taxi. He more or less tossed Samantha into the back and slid in after her before she could get herself turned around. "The J.F.K. airport," he told the driver.

"No!" Samantha cried angrily, leaning forward to the driver. "This man is kidnapping me. I demand you take me to the nearest police station."

"Sure, lady, sure," the driver nodded, then glanced at Cade and winked.

Samantha turned to Cade, her anger dissolving into tears. "How can you do this?" she demanded.

"We'll be married in Las Vegas, fly back and honeymoon for a couple of days on the island, then come back here," he stated grimly.

"I won't marry you," she denied vehemently.

"You made the conditions, Sam." Flint gray eyes sparked fire.

"I didn't make any conditions," Samantha protested in despair.

"Look." Cade grabbed her arm and pulled her back from the edge of the seat, roughly drawing her to his side. "I'm accepting the charity of your father's proposition. And you're going to fulfill your part of the bargain by marrying me."

"It's not charity." Her brown eyes widened. "Reuben knows the last thing I would want is for him to buy me a husband."

"Really?" he taunted.

"Yes, really. Besides, he doesn't even know you proposed to me before. I let him think you despised me. Reuben was asking you to head the new security organization because he thought you were the man for the job. It had nothing to do with me," she breathed, suddenly hopeful at Cade's frown. "Cade, why do you want to marry me?"

"Answer me this," he commanded arrogantly, ignoring her question. "Why did you refuse to marry me?"

Samantha hesitated, then swallowed her pride. "Everyone who ever mattered has been interested in me because of my father. I knew you were attracted to me, but I thought you were only offering me marriage because I was the boss's daughter. I thought I'd grown used to people using me to get to Reuben until I met you. I love you, Cade," she sighed, "but I couldn't marry you thinking you were just using me to get ahead. Are you, Cade? Are you marrying me now so you can have that advancement?"

"Are you serious?" He shook his head in disbelief, the flint hardness leaving his eyes to change them into a warm gray. "I thought it was the only way I could have you. At first I was angry because your father tried to buy me the respectability that had kept you from saying yes. Then I realized that I loved you too much to care. I wanted you for my wife any way I could get you. And I decided you had to love me, too, in order to go begging to your father."

"I love you the way you are," Samantha whispered.

"And I love you." He pulled her close to his mouth. "I don't give a damn who your father is."

He kissed her long and hard, crushing her in his arms until the power of his love left her boneless. The firm caress of his hands drew her onto his lap as he searched out the sensitive areas of her throat and neck that he had discovered before.

Long, tempestuous minutes passed before Samantha remembered they were in the back of a taxi riding down a busy New York street. The driver's mirror gave him a front-row seat. She resisted the exploring caress of Cade's hands.

He read her mind and laughed softly against her trembling lips. "Darling, there isn't anything that a New York City taxi driver hasn't seen taking place in his cab." But he did bridle some of his desire, although he still held her on his lap. "A few more hours and we'll be in Vegas. I've waited this long. I can wait until then."